THE PRIEST'S MADONNA

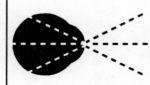

This Large Print Book carries the
Seal of Approval of N.A.V.H.

THE PRIEST'S MADONNA

AMY HASSINGER

THORNDIKE PRESS

An imprint of Thomson Gale, a part of The Thomson Corporation

Detroit • New York • San Francisco • New Haven, Conn. • Waterville, Maine • London • Munich

Thorndike Press® Large Print Clean Reads.

The text of this Large Print edition is unabridged.

Other aspects of the book may vary from the original edition.

Set in 16 pt. Plantin.

LIBRARY OF CONGRESS CATALOGING-IN-PUBLICATION DATA

Hassinger, Amy, 1972–
    The priest's madonna / by Amy Hassinger.
      p. cm. — (Thorndike Press large print clean reads)
    ISBN 0-7862-8828-0 (lg. print : alk. paper)
    1. Saunière, Bérenger, 1852–1917 — Fiction. 2. Mary Magdalene, Saint — Cult — Fiction. 3. Rennes-le-Château (France) — Fiction. 4. Housekeepers — Fiction. 5. Occultists — Fiction. 6. Catholics — Fiction. 7. Clergy — Fiction. 8. Grail — Fiction. I. Title. II. Series.
    PS3608.A86P75 2006
    813'.6—dc22
                                          2006014989

Published in 2006 by arrangement with G. P. Putnam's Sons, a division of Penguin Group (USA) Inc.

Printed in the United States of America on permanent paper
10 9 8 7 6 5 4 3 2 1

For Adam

But Christ loved her more than all the disciples, and used to kiss her often on the mouth. The rest of the disciples were offended by it and expressed disapproval. They said to him, "Why do you love her more than all of us?" The Savior answered and said to them, "Why do I not love you like [I love her]?"
— "The Gospel of Philip," in the
Nag Hammadi Library

The body is the garden of the spirit.
— Tony Kushner

PROLOGUE

Bérenger and I first met at Sainte Baume on the eve of Sainte Marie Madeleine's feast day, July 21, 1877. He was twenty-five, I was nine. We were only two of the many pilgrims who had come from all corners of the country: Bourgogne, Limousin, Bretagne, even some from Paris. My mother was pregnant with poor Christophe, though it was early enough that I did not yet know.

We rode by train to the coast, where we caught a ferry to Marseilles. The boat was full — it was difficult to find seats, as we arrived late — and I saw faces of all sorts: the ruddy, wind-scoured cheeks of old farmers; gentlemen of my father's age, sharply dressed in vests and bow ties; young children, brows smudged with dirt; older girls in fresh pinafores, hair prettily braided; and some young men who gathered in groups to play cards and smoke. But mainly I saw women of my mother's age, and though they all wore their differences plainly on their faces and in their clothing — some wore fancy hats, shawls, and lace-up boots, others wore *sabots* and covered their hair with plain silk scarves — they bore themselves with a similar anticipatory air.

Though the train ride was thrilling, it had been unbearably hot. We had been sitting across from an unpleasant woman and her two equally unpleasant sons who entertained themselves by insulting my five-year-old brother Claude, and so I was glad to finally board the ferry and feel the wind off the Mediterranean. My mother allowed us to roam the decks. We explored all three levels, then stationed ourselves on the top deck to watch the sea boil in our wake. Gulls flew overhead, crying in their mournful way, and we fed them a crust of bread.

It was then that I noticed Bérenger. Young and dapper in a trim black suit and collar, with striking dark brows, he stood chatting with my mother, who had joined us on the top deck. I assumed he was a stranger passing the time.

We arrived at Marseilles as evening was coming on. Mother took us to a café for a bit of bread and cheese before our hike up the mountain. We sat and chatted with a young family while we ate. By the time we set out, the day had cooled, which we were thankful for, because it was a steep climb and we were tired.

The small cave was already full when we arrived. We found a place toward the back. It was damp and cool, despite the press of bodies. I sat on a stone and Claude rested his head in my lap. Stroking his hair, I watched the sky darken and the stars appear as we waited for the Mass to begin.

"What do you see, *maman?*" I asked my mother, who stood beside me.

"Nothing yet. It's dark."

I must have dozed. The next thing I remember is my mother rousing me excitedly. I opened my eyes to see candlelight trembling against the walls of the cave. Claude was now sleeping at Mother's feet, his head resting on her coat, which she had bundled into a pillow. I stood, straining to see over the heads of the crowd. In a whisper, I asked my mother what was happening, but she shushed me.

Then the young man in front of me turned around and I saw that it was the same man who had been speaking with my mother on the ferry. "Do you want to see?" he asked.

I nodded, embarrassed.

To my amazement, he squatted in the dirt in front of me and bowed his head. "Climb on my back," he said.

I looked to my mother for approval, but she was immersed in the service. The young man was smiling broadly at me, amused by my shock at being invited to clamber onto the back of a strange man. "You've come all this way," he said. "You shouldn't miss it."

Glancing at my mother once more, I decided to do as he bid. I lifted my skirt slightly, then grabbed hold of his shoulders and wrapped my legs around his back. As he stood, grasping the undersides of my knees to steady me, my mother turned, startled by the sudden movement. I had never seen her look more horrified. "Marie!" she said loudly, waking Claude and turning heads. My face burned, and I pushed against the young man's back, wanting him to drop me. But he addressed her by name and told her it was all right. "I urged her to do it, Madame," he said. "It would be a shame to have come all this way and not to see the Madeleine herself."

To my surprise, my mother's face softened, and she assented.

From my new position, I saw that the lit grotto was more spectacular than I had imagined. It extended before us a few dozen yards. Votive candles had been placed in niches in the rock as well as given to the

people at the front of the congregation, so that the cave brightened as it deepened. The priest was surrounded by light as bright as day, and when he held up his hands to consecrate the bread and the wine, his palms shone like polished marble. Candle-light illuminated the gathered congregation, some of whom I recognized from the ferry. In the daylight, their faces had been mundane, but here they glowed.

As the priest bent to sip the wine, I noticed the reliquary behind him: a golden head, borne on a miniature palanquin. Inside that reliquary was the skull of Marie Madeleine herself, the woman whom Christ had loved so dearly as to appear to her first after his resurrection and exhort her to spread the word among his disciples. I knew her then as the repentant sinner, the converted prostitute, fallible, faithful, devoted. I had read in my *Lives of the Saints* that she had come to France from Palestine in an oarless boat, put to sea by heathens who intended for her to drown, that she helped spread Christianity in Gaul, and that she spent her last thirty years in this very cave, praying to the Lord she so loved in life. Here I was, in her hermitage, enclosed by the walls she had gazed upon for so long. Feeling light-headed, I tightened my grasp

11

around my young man's neck.

When it came time for communion, he set me down so that he could join the line. As he did not return to his original spot, I saw no more of him, nor did I see more of the service that night. But I was not disappointed; I had seen enough to ignite my imagination, and when the Mass was finished, I filed along behind my mother and the other pilgrims as we descended the hill, feeling as though I had taken part in something distinctly separate from the time and space in which I was accustomed to living.

How simple faith was then! How sincere my religious feeling, my reverence! I am past mourning that loss now — though I did, for years, the loss of that childhood gift of untarnished wonder. I wonder still. I stand in awe now and then. But those moments, though brilliant, are ephemeral, quickly eclipsed by the shade of the mundane. Can we ever return to that primary faith, that easy worship? What does it take? We become so burdened by our innumerable failed loves, our injuries, inflicted and endured. We forget. We grow old.

I am in search of absolution, even if it must be from a God I love too shallowly, too selfishly, a God I battle like a willful child. What do I know of God? My understanding is a bramble, an unpruned olive tree strangled with vine, not helped by the years I've spent praying, reading, pondering, asking for some small clarification, some minute glimpse of the infinite. Despite my blindness, despite my stubborn heart, I petition him daily, I ask him to forgive me my trespasses, to grant me peace. I repent. I gave away Bérenger's presents years ago: the dresses of Parisian design, the string of pink pearls, the gold bracelet encrusted with diamonds, the lace gloves that buttoned primly at the elbow. I burned all the papers he left that would have given me access to his bank accounts in Limoux, Paris, Carcassonne, Angers, and Budapest. I have never once slept in the Villa Bethania, the villa he built for me. I have not been to Mass in years, nor will I return, not after the way they treated him, hounding him to his death. But I follow the forms, and not only out of habit, for they do give me comfort. I say my novenas daily and pray often to my little *santon*. Every morning, after I change the holy water, I kneel before the altar and make my humble devotions. I ask for God's forgiveness.

God, this famous God, Bérenger's God, and always mine, too, though I resist and abuse him, God asks too much of us. We must reject our very natures, become only a whisper, a breath of ourselves. We must dwindle and squeeze into the one crevice of our hearts that is humble and kind, chaste and patient, diligent and liberal with love. It is too much! We must, as the prophet says, do justice, love kindness, and walk humbly — but one slip, one misstep along the path, and we initiate an avalanche, and though we grasp at saplings and boulders, we cannot stop our somersaulting descent.

CHAPTER ONE

In those years we lived in Espéraza, a small city straddling the banks of the bending Aude. We had a cozy apartment above my father's hat shop, a place redolent of steamed felt, shellac, rabbit fur, and wool, and peopled with hat forms standing on workbenches like sculpted busts. Though we were not wealthy, Father made a good living and enjoyed his work. He employed five men and treated them like family — they ate their midday dinners with us, and slept on the workroom floor when they were fighting with their wives or sleeping off a binge. Father entertained them with political diatribes and songs as they worked. He often said that if he had his life to live over again, he would be a cabaret singer. "Enough of this decent living, this persnickety business of fulling wool and counting money," he'd roar. "Give me the stage, give me Paris!" Mother would roll her eyes while he belted out the first phrases of "Coupo Santo" in his rich baritone, his handlebar mustache vibrating.

Our apartment was modest but comfortable: one bedroom, a kitchen, and a dining room. When the weather was poor or the river was threatening to flood, Claude and I — and our foster sister, Michelle, after she came — would sometimes wander down to the warm shop to watch the men work and listen to their stories. This was where I learned of the wild woman who lived with the bears in the mountains, and of Autanette, the daughter of the wind, whose father saved her from unwanted suitors by turning her into stone. This was also where I learned about my father's passionate distaste for the Catholic Church and his strong socialist views. He was outspoken and loved an argument, and he would often provoke the workers who were royalists, baiting them and then trouncing them soundly with his own republican manifesto. More than one worker stormed out of the shop in a fury on these occasions. Usually they returned the next day, when their tempers had cooled.

Michelle, I should explain, was my dear friend and sister from my tenth year onward. She came just after the death of my infant brother, Christophe, several months after our pilgrimage to Sainte Baume. After he died, Mother wore a blank stare and stopped scolding Claude and me when we were naughty. Father worried. He began bringing home tins of *grisettes* and tortes sent by the sister of one of his workers, a Mme Lèvre. Claude and I enjoyed the treats, of course, and Mother wrote a note of thanks. I suppose M. Lèvre had his request in mind all along.

It so happened that the Lèvre family had a cousin, M. Baron, who had just lost his wife to consumption. M. Baron was done in by grief; he refused to leave his smithy's shop, and spent his days and nights at the forge, hammering incessantly, his face blackened with soot. He seemed to hardly recognize his daughter, who was my age and in need of good meals, schooling, and company. Father told us this story one night at dinner, and I remember being angry with him for telling such a story in Mother's presence — one that could only make her feel worse. But the next day, when Michelle arrived bearing a battered suitcase and a bunch of half-wilted lavender, I understood why he'd spoken.

My father must have thought that it would cheer my mother to have another child around the house. Or maybe M. Lèvre was a remarkable salesman. Whatever the reason, Father, impulsive as ever, had agreed to take Michelle in without consulting my mother. She was furious; she wept and raved. She wanted nothing to do with another child, especially a practically grown girl. What she wanted was a baby — her baby, Christophe — back again. Didn't Father know the difference between an infant and a prepubescent girl? But my father's word was his word, and he had given it to M. Lèvre. The matter was closed. I pitied Michelle, for my mother would barely look her in the eye, and the rivalry that might have easily grown between us did not so much as germinate. She had raven-black hair that she wore in plaits, and small, intelligent eyes. She must have understood my mother's grief for Christophe, for she left her alone and did not hover or cling. It was skillfully done; Mother could observe Michelle from a distance and could see how quickly the rest of us took to her. Before long, it was as if she had always been a part of our family. We dreaded the day that her father would call to claim her again. As it turned out, M. Baron died a few months after his wife, and Michelle and all her quiet, sad wisdom was ours to keep.

■ ■ ■ ■

In the fall of 1884, when Michelle and I were about sixteen, my father hired a vagabond. Gaunt and shoeless, he'd come from a tiny mountain village west of us, close to the Spanish border. We didn't know much about him, and he didn't speak our patois — his was broader, his pronunciation closer to Spanish — but my father hired him anyway. He clearly needed the work. My mother fed him and let him sleep in front of the hearth, and the next morning my father set him to work boiling the carded wool into felt. I don't know what his real name was, but the men called him *le bandit.* He slept on the workroom floor.

One afternoon, my father got into an especially heated argument with one of the men about the hypocrisy of the Church. That night our bedroom filled with smoke. I woke first, coughing, and ran barefoot to the window, scorching the soles of my feet on the floor. Father jumped first, then caught Claude, Michelle, and me. Mother appeared at the window, weeping, her arms full of lace and linen. "Jump, Isabelle!" my father yelled. He broke her fall, collapsing beneath her weight. The church bells began to clang then — someone had raised the alarm — and men came quickly, carting buckets of river water. They doused the fire, but not before both our house and the workshop were destroyed. And *le bandit* was gone.

We walked through the charred ruins that next dawn, searching for anything salvageable. The walls of the workshop still stood, but they were streaked with soot; the tables were blackened and crumbling, the carding machine half melted. "The devil's gone walking," I heard one of the old women say, and this was how I imagined it ever afterward: that the devil had stepped on our house and left an inferno as his footprint.

So, we moved — to the nearby hilltop village of Rennes-le-Château. My father bought the house sight unseen, swayed by the low price and the reputed beauty of the village. ("Magnificent views of the mountains," he repeated to us, "and an ancient castle, just down the road!") But, as my mother had suspected, the purchase price proved too good to be true, for the house, like most others in the village, had been neglected for centuries. The incessant wind whistled through the cracks in the mortar, chilling us to the teeth. My mother forbade us from walking near the edge of the cliff beyond the church because she worried that the wind might send us over.

They say that the wind is the breath of phantoms. If this is true, then Rennes-le-Château was a village full of spirits, for the *tramontane* blew all the time. It seemed the wind even brought word of our arrival and the circumstances surrounding it, for the villagers appeared to know all about us: where we'd come from, what we'd lost. They did not welcome us sympathetically. When we climbed the hill, accompanied by a mule carrying the few things we'd managed to save — the lace tablecloth, the bed linens, several pewter dishes, a few books, their pages fragrant still with smoke — no one greeted us. They treated us from the first as if they knew that we felt coming to Rennes-le-Château was a debasement. And though neither of my parents ever said as much, I saw that there was truth in this assumption.

Father took what he insisted was a temporary job at the new hat factory in Espéraza, a place he had long decried for the inferiority of their products. There his expertise was largely disregarded. He was expected to do the same menial labor as any other worker: operate the levers, remove the forms from one machine and place them in another. He grew bitter and perpetually tired, for the walk to Espéraza from Rennes took an hour each way. He — and Claude, once he turned thirteen — left at dawn and returned well after dark, leaving Mother, Michelle, and me alone in our unfriendly village.

The first morning we arrived, Mother and I went together to collect our water from the pump, which sat at the far end of the château square. Several women stood in the center of the square. Silence fell as we approached, and though my mother greeted each woman, she received no more than a nod in return. Mother turned the iron wheel that powered the pump and we filled our buckets and then made our way back, past the staring group of women. I concentrated on spilling as little water as possible. The silence felt like a scolding, especially as their voices began to hum once again as we reached the crest of the hill.

There were exceptions; not everyone was so unkind. The grocer welcomed me when I stopped in for flour. The mayor came — in time for our midday dinner — to introduce himself. And Mme Gautier, the butcher's wife, brought us a lamb pie. But she did not stay long and spoke in a whisper, even when we'd closed the door behind her, as if she was afraid of being overheard. How I longed for our first Sunday! I had the idea that the village would transform itself for Mass — that somehow the shared ritual of communion, of kneeling together to pray, would initiate us into the community, and that we would finally be welcomed as neighbors.

Mother, Claude, Michelle, and I walked the short distance uphill to the church that first Sunday. (Father only accompanied us on Easter or Christmas, when Mother insisted.) I noticed again, as I had already on several occasions, how the dome appeared lopsided, as if it had been gradually sliding earthward since the eleventh century, when, we'd been told, it had been built. Moss grew between the limestone bricks, and pigeons nested beneath the porch roof. The interior was in even greater disrepair: the walls were of varying thickness and almost seemed to ripple. Most of the windows had been blown out by a storm some years back, and the wind whistled through the nave. The main altar was nothing more than a stone slab supported by two stone pillars. On the slab stood a wooden tabernacle from which the gilt had begun to peel. A secondary altar set against the wall consisted of another stone pillar, this one cracked down the length of one side, topped with a statue of the Holy Virgin and decorated with a plaque that bore the devotion of the Miraculous Medal: "O Mary, conceived without sin, pray for us who have recourse to thee." The only object of beauty in the church was set in a niche behind the main altar: a gilded Christ figure, haloed and robed in blue, two fingers extended in blessing.

The nave was tiny, with seats for maybe seventy people. Most of the congregants were women and children. As at the fountain, talk ceased when we entered, and heads turned. The first pew had been left empty, and I guessed this was a test to see if we would have the audacity to sit there. My mother wisely chose the last pew instead, and we slipped in beside her and knelt, bowing our heads. I sensed that even our prayer — customary before the service in our home church at Espéraza — was interpreted as an unctuous rebuke, for it was not the custom at Rennes-le-Château. I felt as if I'd swallowed a stone.

The priest at that time was a man who seemed as old as the church itself. He doddered up the aisle, swinging the censer, his hands shaking so that I feared he might drop it. His sermon was impossible to follow. He spoke so slowly that by the time he reached the end of a sentence, I'd forgotten where he'd begun. People slept or chatted. He didn't seem to notice — he carried on as if we weren't there, as if the Mass was solely a personal communication between him and God.

When he died later that year, his requiem was a somber festival. Soon afterward, hopeful rumors spread through the village about the young priest who was to be appointed in his place. He was coming from Clat, we heard, where he'd served for three years. My mother showed some interest in this news — she must have known Bérenger's whereabouts at the time and guessed it was he.

The day he arrived was warm and clear. I was outside sweeping the front stoop when I saw him coming up the path. The hem of his cassock was white with dust, and sweat had darkened the cloth below his arms. He carried a small yellow valise, dusty as well. Heads peeked around half-open shutters. He smiled at a few faces, but received barely a nod in return.

As he approached our house, his face brightened and he greeted me by name, which surprised me. I did not recognize him — it had been eight years since we'd met — but, wanting to appear more welcoming than my neighbors, I bowed my head and returned his greeting. He set down his valise and, placing his hands at his waist, stretched backward, causing his back to pop like pine in a fire.

"You don't remember me," he said, smiling devilishly. Having the upper hand in this way seemed to amuse him, but as he spoke, I *did* remember him: he wore the same expression of roguish delight when he hoisted me on his back at the grotto.

"Yes, I do remember you. We met at Sainte Baume."

"A-ha! And you're all grown up now. A young woman."

My mother appeared at the door and exclaimed, "It *is* you!" before rushing to greet Bérenger with a kiss on each cheek. "I knew you had been at Clat," she continued. "What a coincidence!"

"A lucky one," he said.

"How is your dear mother?"

They exchanged pleasantries — Bérenger asked after Father and Claude and expressed his regret at the change in our circumstances. "Mother told me of the fire," he said, shaking his head. "Such a loss."

"It can't be helped," my mother said, dismissing the subject, which was her way with unpleasant topics. Michelle emerged, her hands still black with soil from the garden, and curtsied as Mother introduced her. "I'll be glad to show you the presbytery," Mother said, "though I'm afraid you will find it disappointing. It hasn't been lived in since God knows when. The last priest stayed with his sister in Rennes-les-Bains." She instructed us to set another place for our midday dinner, and then escorted Bérenger up the hill.

Michelle and I prepared the *estofinado* and the tomato salad, chatting excitedly all the while about Bérenger. The fact that Mother knew his family gave us a feeling of privilege. And though we would never say it out loud, we were thrilled by his looks — the dark, commanding brows, the thick black hair, the mischievous grin, and the athletic build that was not entirely hidden by his cassock. When my mother returned with Bérenger, Michelle served him dinner, demurely spooning the cod onto his plate and giving him an ample amount of sauce and potatoes. I poured the wine.

While we ate, Mother continued to inquire after Bérenger's family. His father, it appeared, had been mayor of Montazels at one time and now served as the steward of the old castle. His brother David was a Jesuit who taught school in Narbonne. He had several other siblings, one or two of whom had children. When Mother asked again after his mother, he sighed heavily, but said only that she was "the same as ever." Mother nodded sympathetically, then changed the topic.

"You'll stay with us, I hope," she said. "Until we can get the presbytery into a livable state again."

Bérenger raised his eyebrows and looked at me, which made me blush. "That's very kind of you," he said. "But I couldn't impose."

"Nonsense," said my mother, and she brooked no further protests.

So Bérenger became our boarder. He slept on the floor by the hearth, his feet to the fire, his head beneath the table, and until my father found him a cot, he smelled of food: garlic, sheep's blood, goat cheese. The primitive accommodations embarrassed me, but Bérenger seemed not to mind. He was always cheerful, despite his habit of rising early and staying up well past midnight reading scripture. He ate with us at dawn, and when Father and Claude left for the factory, he went to church to conduct morning Mass. After Mass, he worked in his office: a table and chair in a cleared corner of the presbytery kitchen. There he updated the parish accounts, which the previous priest had neglected. When he did not have church affairs to tend to or his own devotions to practice, he busied himself with making small repairs and constructing serviceable furniture for his own use (I know this because Michelle and I made it our habit to stop by the presbytery often, under some pretense or another). My mother, who had offered her services as his housekeeper at a modest rate, tackled the formidable job of cleaning up the presbytery and maintaining the church. This doubled her work, of course, so Michelle and I took on more responsibility at home.

But together we were efficient, and managed to finish our chores by early afternoon most days. It was my mother's belief that if we were well educated, we might have a better chance of marrying genteel husbands, and, in Espéraza, we'd had a small library of books that we'd taken great pleasure in, reading aloud to each other from Balzac and Hugo as well as the *Lives of the Saints* (which Mother insisted we read daily). But we had managed to salvage only a few volumes from the fire — a history of the French Revolution, the letters of Abélard and Héloïse, one or two Balzacs — so in Rennes our studies slowed. Rather than bore ourselves with the same old stories, we would stray to the open pastures where the hill began to slope toward the valley. From there we could see the red rooftops of Es-péraza and the towers of the new factories, puffing smoke from their mouths like fat industrial dragons. We would chew on sprigs of wild rosemary and thyme and look out over the *garrigues,* talking of Bérenger and what we imagined he thought of his new home.

MIRYAM OF MAGDALA

Miryam rose at dawn from a restless sleep. The house was quiet, her sisters and parents still asleep. She pulled on her cloak, wound a sash at her waist, tucked a leather purse beneath it, and left the house, sandals in hand. Outside, she slipped them on and walked to the shore to watch the fishermen haul in their nightly catch. Torches bobbed on the lake, marking the location of boats that were still out. As they approached, the men extinguished their lights and prepared to unload their seines full of small silver *musht,* some still quivering with life.

Miryam had lately heard tales of a teacher traveling through the Galil, healing the sick. Great throngs of people had gathered near

Kfar Nahum to hear him speak and watch him perform his miracles. It was rumored that he and his followers had now camped just outside of Magdala, and that they would be passing by the city that very day. This was why she slipped early from her bed: she intended to seek out this itinerant prophet.

"These are the stages of the people of Yisrael, when they went forth out of the land of Egypt," she whispered as she watched the fishermen spread their nets on the shore to dry. A few began to build a fire several feet from the shore, close to where she stood. Some of them looked in her direction, then looked away. They knew she was well beyond the customary age of betrothal and yet unmarried, a woman incoherent in her speech, wild in her actions, possessed, it was said, by seven devils.

A wind blew off the lake, chilling her. But though the sun had not yet warmed the air, the men were stripped to the waist. Sweat dripped from their hairlines and snaked down their backs as they squatted by the flames, cleaning some of the fish with bright blades. They ate the roasted *musht* for breakfast, picking the thin bones from their tongues.

CHAPTER TWO

At the time of Bérenger's arrival, I knew little about the political tenor of the country. My father had taught me simply that the republicans stood for the common person, the true Frenchman, while the monarchists wanted to maintain the rule of the wealthy elite. Times were changing, according to him, and it was the republicans who would usher in modernity.

But Bérenger, I learned, was as passionate as my father about politics — and he was a monarchist. He arrived in Rennes just as Jules Ferry and the fledgling republic were excising the tumor of religion from society. Divorce was legalized; Sunday was no longer an obligatory day of rest. Public education was declared free, mandatory, and lay-taught, causing Bérenger's brother David to lose his teaching post. Bérenger deeply resented the republic's antireligious militancy.

These changes barely affected my family, though my father and mother argued when divorce was legalized. Mother did not have political views, on the whole, but she supported the Church in all things. Religion, in my father's mind, was a tower of lies constructed to contain and dominate the populace. Normally, my parents avoided the subject, but the divorce ruling set my mother's blood boiling. The day she heard of it, she raged at my father from the moment he set foot in the door, as if he had cast the deciding vote. She took it personally: if his Republic had legalized divorce, then he must support the notion, and therefore must be planning to divorce her. She wouldn't allow it, she told him. "Let no man put asunder!" she shouted, clanging the ladle against the soup tureen until M. Paul, who lived next door, knocked to see if all was well.

Imagine, then, my father's unease at Bérenger's presence in our house. Under our own roof, a cleric *and* a monarchist! The first night Bérenger arrived, Father eyed him suspiciously over our meal. When we had cleared our places and they were sharing a smoke, he broached the topic. "We've an election coming. Three months."

Michelle and I were sitting by the door,

trying to make use of the last light leaving the summer sky. She was sewing the eyes on one of her dolls — she was quite good at making dolls from scraps of fabric, pretty pebbles, pinecones, and dried berries, anything she could find. I was knitting, but I laid my work in my lap when I heard my father's comment.

"Indeed," Bérenger said.

"Will you vote?"

"I always vote."

"Mm-hmmm," said my father. Then, impatiently, "For whom?"

Claude was bouncing a ball in the dust outside; I motioned to him to stop. Bérenger shifted in his chair. "I know your position, monsieur," Bérenger began, "and I respect it. I am, however, of a different mind. The Republic has done innumerable injuries to the Church, and to society, in my opinion. I can't, in good conscience, vote to support such a government. As a priest."

"Ha! How about all the injury the Church has done to the Republic? To France, better yet! Where should we begin?"

"Maybe we'd better not."

"Is your cause that insupportable? Not even worth an argument?" A silence. "Your Church —" my father prompted, in a threatening tone.

"Mine, too, Edouard," interrupted my mother. "Your children's, too. Don't forget."

"Hush," snapped my father. "Your Church," he began again, but faltered. He was bursting to release the floodgates of his political opinion — how the Church peddled lies in exchange for money and power — but he knew how proud my mother was to have Bérenger in our home, and how much Michelle and I admired Bérenger. If he embarked on one of his diatribes, he might succeed in out-arguing Bérenger, but he would lose our esteem. "Let's just say," he said, after a long moment, "that we have our quarrels."

"A good quarrel aids the digestion, Edouard. It's how we stay so trim, isn't that right?" Bérenger clapped his hand against his belly.

My father lit another cigarette. "Is that it?" he said, finally. "I thought Isabelle had put me on a diet."

My mother laughed nervously. Michelle and I exchanged an astonished look. We waited for more discussion, but none came, so Michelle picked up her doll, and Claude began once again to bounce his ball. The men smoked in silence until dark, when we retired to bed and Bérenger to his candlelit reading. They did not speak of politics again until the election.

On Bérenger's first Sunday in church, the sanctuary was full. Almost the entire village came to Mass that morning — people who hadn't attended for thirty years were there, pressed against the walls and standing in the entryway. Even my father came. Women forwent their customary cotton shifts and headscarves for linen dresses and straw hats. Men wore jackets and clean white shirts. Shaved and scrubbed faces arrayed the pews and the back aisle of the tiny church, newly swept and dusted. The sight of so much effort, so much hope and sincerity, made me shy. I met no one's eyes. We waited amid shifting feet and coughs for Mass to begin.

Finally, the cantor — M. Lébadou, who was enthusiastic but always off-key — began the introit and Bérenger, dressed in a gold chasuble and bearing the censer, processed up the nave, accompanied by the Baux brothers. He beamed at the crowd, his cheeks flushed with excitement. As he approached the altar, his eyes momentarily lit on me, and I smiled despite my impulses toward discretion — he looked so joyful, so earnest, so handsome. My mother had been lamenting since his arrival how poorly attended Mass was, probably as a way of tempering his hopes. He must have known that people were there mainly to satisfy their curiosity. Still, he preached effusively that day; his voice, a rich baritone like my father's, rang out with authority and passion. He promised his best efforts as curé for us; he dedicated himself to Rennes-le-Château as shepherd — promised to counsel us, to tend to us when we were sick in body or spirit, to lead us in the virtuous path toward God, and he charged us, for our part, to follow him as a good flock.

Afterward, people seemed buoyant, chatting happily and watching the children. The Baux boys, wild once again, relieved of their ecclesiastic duties, chased after one of the dogs. Women gossiped. Men lingered and joked, standing near their families.

Bérenger was ebullient. He knew he'd touched people. Perhaps he believed that he'd come to a faithful village, a place where the Church still held sway over the hearts of the villagers, where his word as God's mediator would be respected and obeyed. He undertook his primary task — to transform lives into journeys, deaths into homecomings through the administration of the sacraments — with admirable zeal.

As soon as he arrived in Rennes, he began making pastoral visits. My mother told him which families might be particularly needful — the wives who had lost husbands, the jobless men, the mourning families or those who had newly welcomed a child — and he knocked on their doors right away, without waiting for a request or an invitation. After thirty years of neglect from the previous curé, most people were surprised by Bérenger's genuine concern for their well-being. When Mme Fauré, a thin and timid woman with nostrils that flared like a horse's, gave birth to a baby boy, Bérenger went with my mother and me when we brought the egg, bread, and salt and spoke the traditional blessing, "Be good like the bread, full like the egg, and wise like the salt." A few days later, at the boy's baptism, Bérenger presented him to the congregation with such jubilation that we broke into applause. When old M. Baudot fell from his roof while trying to repair it and broke his hip, Bérenger sat with him and told him jokes, including a few that involved foolish old men who acted younger than their age. He even visited Mlle Martinez, a Spanish Gypsy who had a shack in the woods several kilometers from the village and lived off the squirrels and porcupines that wandered into her traps, as well as the grapes she stole from the neighboring vineyards. Everyone said she was crazy and not to be trusted, but Bérenger insisted that she was part of the parish and a child of God.

People were flattered by his visits. They took an interest in Bérenger as they had never done with the previous priest, bringing him small gifts — freshly baked bread, snared partridge, truffles discovered in the woods. One of the Baux boys brought him an asp skin, spread and tacked on a board. Little Marguerite Mouisse, who lived with her shepherd father in a hut near Le Bézu, presented Bérenger with a bound bunch of dried asphodel stems. "Matches for your cigarettes," she said in her thin voice, giving a tiny curtsy. The children especially liked him, for he led a rollicking catechism class and often rewarded those who recited the text correctly with sugared almonds or candied chestnuts. (I had the honor of helping to lead the class, so I witnessed his generosity firsthand.)

Bérenger loved the gifts, of course, and the attention, but he cherished even more the increased assembly at church. Remarkably, several of the men who had rarely set foot in the church began to appear regularly on Sundays and even occasionally on weekday mornings. Mass became a happy, even festive occasion, and the church — though the roof still leaked onto the altar when it rained — transformed from a dungeon into something resembling a haven, mainly through the force of Bérenger's personality. Even the old woodworm-infested confessional saw an increase in traffic. But while Mass drew newcomers of both sexes and all ages, the newly eager penitents at confession consisted almost entirely of the married women of the village, women of my mother's age, women who desired Bérenger's attention.

One day, before seven o'clock Mass, I entered the church to change the holy water and was startled to see three women — Mme Montaucon, Mme Baptiste, and Mme Fauré — kneeling in the pews, evidently waiting their turn. An actual queue! For confession! The sight ruffled me; I had to quell an urge to send them all away. My mother snorted her disapprobation when she heard of it. But my father found it funny, and from that day on, asked Bérenger nightly how many confessions he'd heard that day. "Madame Baptiste come again today?" he'd ask. Mme Baptiste was a homely but flirtatious woman whose husband had lost his arm at the hat factory and could no longer work. He spent his days at the tavern. "One of these days she'll offer to take *your* confession, now, won't she, Monsieur *le curé?*"

Bérenger laughed; he enjoyed my father and his expansive ways, despite their differences of opinion.

The fact was that my father was jealous of Bérenger and the amount of time he spent with my mother throughout the day: the midday dinners we shared, the assistance Mother gave him before and after the Mass, the myriad little housekeeping tasks she completed for him in the church. Confession particularly bothered him — he could not stand the fact that my mother met privately with Bérenger and voluntarily told him her most intimate thoughts. "What do they *tell* you, anyway?" he would ask Bérenger.

"Edouard," my mother would scold, "he can't repeat it. It's confidential."

Bérenger, for his part, seemed not to mind my father's prurience and even encouraged it by dropping a few tantalizing details — nothing to implicate anyone, but enough to pique my father's interest. "I hear all kinds of things," he'd say. "You'd be surprised, monsieur. Let us just say that some of these women have led full lives."

My father would throw up his hands. "I should have been a priest."

"God forbid," said my mother.

Though my father may have been jealous, he must have known that Bérenger posed no true threat. They respected each other, Bérenger and my mother. She was not like the *mesdames* who called themselves friends of Bérenger's but were none. She never debased herself as they did, bringing him cake, uttering low-toned gossip in his presence in order to "apprise him of the goings-on in the parish." Those women sought Bérenger out to sanctify their days; they baptized themselves in his attention and called their desire devotion. He scolded them only when they became too demanding. He turned Mme Baptiste away from the confessional once, when she'd come too many days in a row. "You've nothing to tell me, Germaine," he said. "Go home."

But my mother was not like that. She truly cared for Bérenger. She was sensitive to his moods, joyful in his company. She respected his privacy and never pestered him when he was put out about something. Their friendship was based on mutual regard and affection. One had the sense that, had circumstances been different — had my mother been fifteen years younger, say, and not happily married to my father, and had Bérenger been a draftsman or a builder — they might

42

have courted each other, might even have married. But it was a subtle affection they shared, expressed always in smiles and silent acquiescences. There was no frustrated passion, nothing like the damning blushes and freighted stares I tried so hard to disguise. It was the way my mother was with many men: easy with them, never flirtatious, but always genuine and affable.

I admired this quality of my mother's and wished I had been blessed with it. I tried to emulate her but Bérenger flustered me. Whenever he addressed me, I became uncharacteristically tongue-tied and studied my feet. When he was home, I barely spoke. My mother remarked on my silence on more than one occasion: "What's the matter with you, then?" she'd say. "Did you sell your tongue to the butcher?" But I didn't want to speak. I wanted only to watch Bérenger's movements around the house: the cozy way he leaned against the doorjamb to chat with my mother as she cooked, how he knelt with Claude on the dusty floor to help him with his inventions.

At seventeen, I was too old to fuss over homemade grape pickers made from cast-off wheel spokes and twine, but Bérenger did not let me remain completely aloof. He would draw me out at the dinner table, asking my opinion, calling me his *petite érudite,* his little scholar. Occasionally he would call me over and read to me from one of his books. "Marinette," he would say, "Marinette. Come listen." *The Imitation of Christ* was a favorite of his at the time, as were the sermons of Père Bourdaloue — reading that proclaimed the vanity of worldly pursuits and the peace obtained from spiritual ones. I would stand at his shoulder or sit on the edge of the nearby chair and watch his face as he read, observing the way he lifted his eyebrows when his glasses slipped down his nose, as if it would help to right them. He read quietly, compelling me to move close. I reveled in the fondness his nicknames implied, but also felt slighted by their diminutive effect. I did not want to be his "little" anything: I wanted to be his obsession, as he was mine.

What confusion I endured! What a morass of conflicted feeling! I felt drawn to him as strongly as if we were bound by an invisible sash. I wanted always to be near him, to inhale his peppery scent, to watch him as he worked, the way he held his breath when he concentrated and then released it all at once, in a forceful explosion of air. I wanted only to please him. I was prepared to do whatever it took to maintain and increase his regard for me, and I expended the full force of my reason and imagination striving to understand how I could best delight him. If I attended Mass regularly, if I listened attentively to his impromptu evening lessons, if I performed my duties as his assistant in catechism class, if I treated my family members with kindness, if, in short, I behaved like a perfectly devout and selfless young woman, expressing none of my own desires and living to fulfill the needs of others — his needs — then it seemed he would continue to bestow his generous affection on me. I strove to accomplish this, then, as best I could. But my piety was impure: it was desire that motivated me, desire for him, my priest.

One day, about a month after Bérenger had come, I was walking by the presbytery when I heard his voice floating through an open window. He had been away visiting his family, and so I was surprised to hear him, having been unaware of his return.

"She calls it upon herself," he insisted. "She provokes him."

"He has no cause to react that way, provocation or no," my mother responded.

"No. But she knows what a volcano he is, and still she taunts him."

"Was she hurt?" Mother asked.

"A dislocated shoulder. Some bruises."

"Poor woman."

Bérenger sighed.

Hearing a shuffling near the door, I ran off toward the grassy hill, where I would be out of sight. He had been talking of his mother, I was sure, and her suffering in the face of his father's violent rages. What pain! And how brave Bérenger was, to have to endure such a father, such a family. He became suddenly twice as enigmatic, and thereby twice as attractive. I told Michelle what I'd heard, and she nodded wisely, as if she might have guessed it herself. "It must be why he doesn't sleep much," she said. "He probably has bad dreams."

I spent my free moments over the next few days lingering about the presbytery, hoping to overhear more snatches of conversation. I longed to learn as much I could about Bérenger. Where did he go on his daily walks, for example, when he sometimes disappeared for hours at a time? What had he thought of Carcassonne, where he'd been at seminary? What was it like growing up under the supervision of such a brutal man? But I heard nothing more. Bérenger came upon me unexpectedly one day as I loitered beneath his window, and though he greeted me warmly and indicated no sign of suspicion or irritation, I was mortified. The last thing I wanted was to annoy him. I had to find other occupations.

Michelle and I had recently become interested in Mme Laporte, the mayor's wife, who lived in the château. She was as tall and slim as a cypress, and carried herself with an unusually aristocratic air. She wore high-necked blouses decorated with an amber butterfly brooch, and her shoes were fine leather rather than wooden *sabots.* Yet even though she held herself apart from the other women, they respected her. They addressed her in the marketplace, nodded to her at the grocer's, and generally seemed to accept her as one of their own.

Of course, the fact that her husband was the mayor helped. He was a portly, well-liked, jovial man who spent evenings chatting with the men outside the *tabac,* and had been known to offer his help during the grape harvest, in exchange for one or two bottles of the vintage. I had never met a more incongruous couple. The mayor went out of his way to earn the affection of his citizens; Mme Laporte was indifferent to public opinion. The mayor spoke in a broad, boisterous voice, peppering his speech with guffaws and expansive gestures; Mme

Laporte spoke softly, barely above a whisper, and I had never seen her smile.

One morning I happened to wake early and, meaning to get a head start on the day's work, I dressed and set out for the water pump. A fog had overtaken the village, obscuring my vision of all but my immediate surroundings. The whole village seemed to be asleep still: light shone through the slats of one or two shutters, but most were dark. I felt powerful, waking so early, and I imagined myself to be a kind of benevolent guardian fairy, walking the streets at dawn to ensure that all was secure. The square was empty, the château nothing but a white shroud. All I could see was the low stone wall. Just above it hovered what appeared to be a human form — a back and shoulders and a head. This was a true fairy, I feared, or worse, a ghost. I froze.

As the filmy shape did not move, I began to wonder if the fog had not deceived me. I stepped forward, the fog thinned, and the misty figure developed more definite proportions: white-clothed bony shoulders and arms; coarse, unbound hair. It was not hovering above the wall, but sitting on it, straight-backed. I halted once more, aware now that it was no fairy at all, but only Mme Laporte, dressed in her nightclothes, staring into the fog. She must have sensed my presence, for she turned to face me. Her expression betrayed no emotion, only calm interest. We regarded each other for what seemed an unbearably long moment, but before I could think of what to say, she stood down, bowed her head solemnly, and then walked into the mist toward the château.

Michelle regarded this as further evidence of Mme Laporte's exotic character. What had she been doing out there so early, alone and undressed? Praying? She had appeared to be in a contemplative state, but we had never seen her in church, which made us wonder if perhaps she was a Protestant, or, even more tantalizing, a Jew. The mayor was at church every Sunday, and though it didn't seem to matter to him that he was unaccompanied, it struck us as strange, even scandalous. Also, Mme Laporte was childless. Without children, and with a maid and a cook responsible for the housework, what did she find to do all day long?

"I'll thank you not to waste your time dwelling on the misfortunes of others," my mother snapped when we asked her why she thought the Laporte family had no children. The word *misfortune* only tantalized us further. Mme Laporte grew into a tragic figure, a woman tortured by grief for the lives of the children she would never bear. Michelle began to speak about her with a knowing tone, as if she alone, having lost both of her parents, understood the woman's sorrow. At first I deferred, but I soon tired of my sister's claims on Mme Laporte and her pain, and resolved to speak directly with her to find out more for myself.

We took to lingering in the square, hoping to catch Mme Laporte coming out of her house. We had practiced ways to initiate conversation: *It's such an impressive castle, could you give us a tour?* and *We know of a Mademoiselle Laporte in Espéraza — is she a relation of yours?* (We knew no such person, but were prepared to present her address, a description of her appearance, and her father's occupation, if pressed.) She disappointed us. If anyone emerged from the château, it was the cook or the maid. Neither Michelle nor I had enough temerity to knock on the castle door, so our hopes of conversing with her quickly withered.

We turned our attention instead to the château itself. The only impressive thing about it was the extent to which it had eroded. Half of the roof had fallen in, and the clay tiles that remained were chipped and dirty. Vines crawled over the window-sills and clung to the ruined stone walls like matted locks of hair. The grounds were modest and consisted mainly of overgrown grasses and brush, sloping precipitously downward on the east side. There was a small garden against the south wall. Several of the doors were gone, so we could sneak in and wander through the abandoned half, where the still intact arches of the interior gave onto empty cavities of ancient rooms and floors dusty with limestone silt.

We had heard legends of a secret network of caves in our area that refugees had used as a passageway long ago. Supposedly, one could gain access to the caves on the castle grounds and follow the tunnels to their end, which was said to be Blanchefort, a nearby hill where the ruins of another ancient castle stood. The stories of those underground tunnels captivated me. I dreamt of them snaking beneath the village like a trapped myth. Largely through my instigation, Michelle and I grew bolder in our explorations in and around the ruins of the castle, looking for these subterranean corridors. We tapped on doors, moved aside rusting plows, and even went so far as to begin digging a hole where the earth seemed loose and perhaps more recently disturbed.

I don't know why we should have been so surprised when Mme Laporte finally came upon us one afternoon. We were trespassing, after all, and openly at that. But when she did find us, we were so frightened and ashamed that we cringed like schoolchildren.

"Have you found anything yet?" she said kindly. She sat on a half-crumbled wall near us and removed her hat — straw, with a torn crown. Her coarse hair was streaked with gray and swept into a messy twist. "I never could," she continued, "though it hasn't been for lack of trying. I'm beginning to think it's just a legend." She sighed.

This was too much for me; I found my voice. "What legend?"

"Why, the underground passage. The escape route of the Visigoths and the Cathars. The buried treasure. Isn't that what you've been looking for?"

"Yes," I admitted. "But we didn't know about any treasure. Or the Visigoths or anyone else."

"We're sorry for trespassing," Michelle said. "We were wrong, and we won't do it again." She recited this apology as if it were a spell to fend off whatever terrible punishment Mme Laporte might have in store. Madame had by this time risen to the status of sorceress in Michelle's imagination.

"It may have been walled up," Madame

continued, "though whoever filled it in did a very thorough job. There's not a trace of it left. I *have* found a pair of ancient graves and a flint spear tip."

"Where?" I was amazed.

She gestured vaguely. "Nothing as exciting as buried treasure. Though I must admit, I tend to be skeptical of such things."

"Who were the Cathars?" I asked.

"Oh, but don't you know of them? I had thought all the children in the village learned about them in school."

I shook my head, embarrassed.

"The Albigensians? They're also called by that name."

"Oh, them," I said hastily. "They were heretics."

Mme Laporte's face registered no surprise or scorn at my provinciality, only that gentle regard.

"Yes, according to the Church. They were Manicheans, dualists. Purists, in many ways. Peaceful people. They lived here, all over this region. This hilltop is supposed to have been one of their strongholds. The story goes that they fled the crusaders through the underground passageway, escaping over the Pyrenees to Spain." When she spoke, she looked toward the middle distance, forming her sentences as if she were read-

53

ing aloud. "They were said to have been the keepers of a great treasure, housed at Montségur — a ruined castle not far from here. But when the crusaders vanquished the castle, they found nothing. Only, I imagine, the heaps of bodies of those who had starved or died of dysentery during the siege."

Michelle shuddered. She kept looking at me, trying, I suppose, to communicate that she wanted to leave, but I ignored her.

"Just before the castle surrendered and those hundreds of *perfecti* were burned, a few believers escaped down the sheer slope of the mountain, which was unguarded. Where they ended up is anyone's guess. They could have come here, treasure in tow. It would have been only a day's journey by horse. Though why a people whose belief system spurned the corruption of the Church would put so much stock in a material treasure, I've never been able to figure out."

"Where — How do you know all that?" I asked stupidly.

She smiled — an absent, melancholy smile — and stood, shaking her skirt to free any clinging dust. "Follow me."

Michelle prodded me in the ribs and when I turned, she whispered loudly, "We should go," but I widened my eyes at her reproachfully. This was what we had been hoping for: a chance to talk with the mysterious Mme Laporte. And how fascinating she was proving to be! I was not about to give up now. Michelle, bless her, would not leave me alone with such a strange and potentially dangerous woman.

Madame led us back outside, around the perimeter of the castle, and then through a side door that opened into the kitchen. She nodded at Mme Siau, the cook, who narrowed her eyes at us as we entered (she had also undoubtedly observed us sneaking around the grounds). We passed through the kitchen — which was not so very different from our own, only bigger and better stocked — and then through the dining room, which boasted a long mahogany table, empty except for a three-pronged candelabra that held the dribbling stumps of unlit tapers, four dining chairs, and a plain mahogany sideboard. I was surprised at the modest décor. I had expected the windows to be draped sumptuously in velvet, the floors carpeted in Oriental rugs, the shelves adorned with silver urns and blown-glass vases. But the rooms, though high-ceilinged, were drab and dark, the air chilly, even though it was midsummer and the temperature outside was hot and dry. There were very few objets d'art, and those that were displayed on the mantel above the cold hearth appeared to be of sentimental value only: a pewter cat, settled on its haunches; a framed embroidery of two figures holding hands and the lettering "Simone and Philippe Laporte, 1869."

Mme Laporte led us up a broad staircase and down a hall into her library. And oh, the books! I had never seen so many. Five or six floor-to-ceiling bookshelves spanned the walls, each of them filled to their limit. Stacks of books grew up from the floor as well, like boxy stalagmites in a dry, commodious cave. A fire crackled in this hearth, and there was a real cat — gray, not the black we might have expected — curled up on the seat of a tattered rose fauteuil. Mme Laporte gestured for us to sit down, but as the fauteuil was already occupied and the other choice was a chair whose caning appeared untrustworthy, we remained standing. Madame had pulled the only other chair in the room — a sturdy plank chair that had been sitting behind the desk — up to one of the shelves and, standing on it, began passing her fingers over titles. Her willowy frame and her height appeared even more marked as she stood several feet off the floor.

"The best place to start, I always think, is with the original documents themselves. Of course, you could begin with *La Chanson de la Croisade contre les Albigeois,* which is probably the most well-known tale of the crusade, but it's really a romance rather than history. Mind you, the documents themselves aren't perfect either, since they were written mainly by the crusaders and the church authorities, so their argumentation and observations are hardly objective. Still, they're useful, if you can keep in mind the point of view." She spoke quickly, almost to herself, and I struggled to follow.

Finally, her fingers lit upon the title she was looking for, and she slipped it out from its place and flipped through it, pausing to smooth some of the pages. Satisfied, she turned to us, smiling apologetically. "History often resembles nothing more than a collection of other people's prejudices and opinions. But, so it is."

Grasping the arm of the chair, she stepped to the floor, then came around the desk to hand us the book. Michelle stepped backward; I took it.

"Come back when you're finished with

that one. I've several you might find interesting."

"Thank you, madame," said Michelle, and
curtsied.

On the way home, Michelle insisted that
we shouldn't return. She would have nothing to do with the book. I hid it beneath the
tinderbox and took it out when no one else
was around.

It made difficult reading, and I struggled
through it, skipping long passages and skimming the rest, for the language was anti-
quated and formal, and I could not focus
my attention on it for very long. It consisted
of a collection of writings by twelfth- and
thirteenth-century clerics, all criticizing the
group of people that Mme Laporte had
called the Cathars, and who, in the book,
were more often referred to as heretics and
blasphemers, liars, sodomites, savage beasts,
loathsome reptiles, and angels of Satan's
light. What had prompted these vicious
epithets, I could not tell.

I knew, though, as I tried to extract some
meaning from the words, that I was right to
hide the book, for it was obvious that
neither my mother nor M. *le curé* would
have allowed me to read it. It sent a frisson
through me each time I opened it, and I
half-expected the pages to writhe with

snakes. At first I wondered if Michelle was right, if Mme Laporte was a witch, but I couldn't reconcile the idea with her kindness and her gentle demeanor.

That book and my decision to read it marked a divergence in the path that, until that summer, Michelle and I had been walking together. I had not yet considered that Michelle and I would lead different lives. We had always talked of our futures as if they were one and the same: *we* was the pronoun we used, rarely *I*. In our afternoons on the hillside, we talked of traveling — to Paris, perhaps, as I had suggested one day, fresh from some small disagreement with my mother. "We'll work as chambermaids," I said. "Lots of girls do. You can make good money. Enough to be able to buy what we need and to go to the cabarets at night."

"Cabarets!" She laughed.

Other days, we spoke of moving back to Espéraza together, finding two brothers to marry. "They'll be handsome and rich. And we'll all live together in the same house," I planned.

"And have babies at the same time."

"We'll push their prams through the marketplace, side by side."

Michelle laced her arm around my waist, leaned her head on my shoulder. "We'll be together, always."

That same summer, Gérard Verdié began to take an interest in Michelle. Gérard was very handsome — tall and muscular, dark curls, ruddy cheeks, and an extravagant smile. He lived in the village and worked in his father's vineyard just outside of town. He began to walk by our door on his way home from the fields. If we happened to be outside, he would stop to chat, and though he never had very much to say — he would inevitably remark on the weather, or on how well the eggplants seemed to be growing — Michelle smiled warmly and returned his remarks with statements that made it seem as though he'd made the most astute of observations.

Michelle began to insist on feeding the chickens and gathering the eggs at just the time when Gérard was due to pass by on his way home. Her trips to the chicken coop grew longer and longer, until on one occasion she had not returned for half an hour. This time, Mother noticed, and asked me to go find her, as the table needed to be laid.

Michelle was not at the chicken coop, nor in the garden. I called her name softly, not wanting to draw attention to her absence, but got no response. The chickens clucked and bunched at my feet; they had not been fed. I saw to that, then ducked into the coop, gathering the eggs in my skirt, all the while wondering where Michelle was and what I was going to tell Mother. As I turned toward the house, I noticed the cellar door was ajar. I nudged it open with my foot. "Michelle?" I ventured, then descended the dark staircase.

There was a sudden animal motion and a very male grunt. As my eyes adjusted to the darkness, I saw a horrified Michelle, her hands pressed to her bare breasts, her hair slipping from its pins. Behind her, Gérard struggled to extricate his torso from the potato bin. I clapped my hands (which had been holding the edges of my skirt) to my mouth, causing the eggs to break in dull wet sounds against the dirt floor. Then I fled up the stairs, my heart pounding, blood rushing to my face, and, without thinking, ran into the house, shutting the door behind me. Mother stood at the kitchen threshold, a dripping spoon in her hand.

"What happened?" she said.

I stared at her, unable to think what to say. "Michelle —" I began. "Michelle."

"What, Marie? Is she all right? What is it?"

I felt the door pressing against my back

and moved aside to let Michelle in. She appeared normal — her hair back in place, her blouse buttoned and straightened. Her face, however, was blanched and her eyes were fierce. She looked at me, trying to discern what I'd said, if anything, to Mother, and then turned to Mother and apologized with all the grace she could muster: "Forgive me, *maman*. I was distracted by a rainbow, and I walked to the hill to see it better. I know I've neglected my chores. Forgive me." And she bent her head, as if in penance — a touch I thought a bit excessive.

"And where are the eggs?" asked Mother.

Michelle glanced at me, and then responded quickly. "I dropped them. I'm sorry."

Mother became incensed. No eggs to put in the soup? She had been counting on them. And what would M. *le curé* think of an eggless *aigo bouido?* She made Michelle apologize to him at dinner.

Michelle and I did not talk about the scene in the cellar that night, nor the next. Embarrassed, we avoided each other: we went directly to sleep rather than whispering, as we normally did, and we did not sit together on the hill. She disappeared shortly after we had finished our chores and, finding myself alone, I slid my forbidden book from beneath the tinderbox and read at the table.

A few days later, when I went to collect the eggs, I was surprised to find Michelle sitting against the cellar door, weeping. I knelt beside her.

"What's wrong?" I asked.

"Oh, Marie," she said, and then began to weep again, as if I'd reminded her of whatever was giving her pain. I knelt beside her for some time, scratching a design in the dirt while I waited for her sobbing to subside. Michelle had lately acquired a taste for drama, so I was not too concerned at her profusion of tears.

"It's too awful," Michelle said, and then began a whole new round of weeping.

"Just give me a hint. Is it about Gérard?"

"Sort of," she said.

"Did you have a fight?"

She shook her head. "You won't guess," she said.

"Did he — withdraw his affection?"

She looked at me and burst out laughing.

"What?" I asked, offended. "What's so funny?"

"You sound so prim," she said.

"Well, I don't know what to say. You won't tell me what the problem is." I stood up and brushed the dirt from my skirt.

"Wait," she said.

"I have to get the eggs."

"I'll tell you. Just sit down."

I squatted: a compromise.

"Monsieur Marcel came today to talk to Mother. Did you see him?"

"Yes," I said.

"Do you know what he was here for?"

"No, Michelle! Why must you have me guessing all the time?"

"He was here to ask for my hand. In marriage."

I stood up so quickly that I stumbled and almost fell face forward into the grass. "Marriage? But you hardly know him!"

"We've spoken several times. At market. He's very kind." She had recovered from her weeping fit remarkably well, and was now speaking with almost complete equilibrium.

"How old is he?"

"Not that old," she said. "Twenty-eight."

I was too baffled to speak. Marriage? We had always assumed we would both marry, but I had only considered it from afar, as I did the mountains on a clear day.

"Well, what did Mother say?"

"She said it's a good offer. Monsieur Marcel is a lawyer, you know. He makes a good living — or will, anyway."

"And what about Gérard? Didn't you — weren't you planning to marry him?"

"No, no. Gérard would make a poor husband. He's already got too many girl-friends. I'd be lonesome. And besides, who wants to be a farmer's wife? The work's too hard."

"But you don't want to marry Monsieur Marcel, do you?"

"Well," she hesitated. "There's no one else in town, anyway, who earns such a good living. Except for Doctor Castanier." She burst out laughing once again at this, and I might have joined in had I not been so shocked — the idea of marrying Dr. Castanier, whose nostrils sprouted hairs, was indeed laughable. But I was quiet. All of this was beyond my understanding.

"The thing is," she began again, "he plans to move. To Carcassonne. He has an offer there for a position that will earn a higher salary. And what will I do then, so far away from you and Claude and *maman* and *papa*?" She began to cry again, and this time, I put my arm around her shoulders and held her, for I knew her grief was sincere, and I saw that it would be mine as well.

M. Marcel came that night and spoke to

Father while the rest of us — excepting Bérenger, who was out — waited outside. Claude whittled while Mother, Michelle, and I sat in anxious silence on the bench by the front door. When Father came to call us back in, he laughed. "You look like you're in line for the guillotine! This is a happy occasion!" he bellowed. "Let's have some smiles, some joy!"

Inside, M. Marcel sat at the dining table looking as nervous as we were. His hat was off, revealing the thinning hair at his crown. His face was kind and pleasant, though his chin was small and receded too quickly into his neck. When we entered, he stood and bowed his head solemnly, then made his way around the table to pull out Michelle's chair. He made quite a show of it, and had we been in a different state of mind, we would surely have teased him, for he appeared so painfully earnest. But we simply took our seats. Then my father formally announced that M. Marcel had offered to take Michelle's hand in marriage, and that he approved of the match. "You don't know each other well yet, this is true. But this is what an engagement is for. You find out you don't like each other, you call it off. It's practical."

M. Marcel nodded seriously, his brow

creased in strenuous agreement.

"*Maman* and I had only met once when I proposed. And look at us — how happy we've been. Eh, my piglet?" (This was my father's pet name for my mother, whose nose turned up just slightly.) They clasped hands across the table and regarded each other so amorously that I had to look away.

He turned to Michelle, his eyes wet with affection, and, leaning forward, said, "*Chérie,* it is for you to decide."

I thought Michelle would surely burst into tears at this, for she had always been sentimental when it came to my father, whom she regarded as her savior. But she kept her wits and, turning to M. Marcel, she bowed her head and said, "I accept."

A few minutes later, Bérenger returned, and as he removed his hat, Claude shouted out, "Michelle's getting married!"

Bérenger took in the scene — all of us at the table, Michelle smiling demurely, M. Marcel sitting anxiously upright — and strode over to kiss both of them on the cheeks. "Congratulations!" he roared. "What wonderful news! Let's drink to your health, shall we?"

Mother got the wine and Father poured us each a full glass. Standing, he held his aloft. We all followed suit. "To Michelle and

Joseph. May they live long and bear me many grandchildren."

"Papa!" Michelle scolded. Father laughed. M. Marcel sipped from his glass, his cheeks already rosy, his eyes shiny with glee.

"Marie will be next!" Claude teased.

"Yes, *ma chérie,*" Father added. "Who will come calling for you?"

I stared into my wine, avoiding Bérenger's eyes.

"Gérard, I'll bet," said Claude. "He lost one sister, why not try the next?"

"Shut up," I said.

"Leave the poor girl alone," my mother said. "You're not too far behind anyway, Claude," she added. "A working man, you are."

"I'll never get married. Who needs a wife? She'll only take my money."

"Oh, now," my mother said.

As they bantered, I stole a glance at Bérenger. To my surprise, I found him watching me with a startling intensity, as if he were trying to discern my thoughts. I flushed; he looked away.

From that point on, Gérard stopped coming and instead, every evening after supper, M. Marcel would knock gently on the door. Michelle would sit with him at the table while Mother and I cleaned up after dinner, taking care not to make too much noise so we could listen. They did not talk of anything interesting. M. Marcel told Michelle of his work, peppering his conversation with apologies for its tedium — the bulk of his job was devoted to writing up contracts between business partners. Michelle told him of her pleasures — sitting on the hillside with me in the afternoons, making dolls. She had gotten quite good at it and had been thinking about trying to sell some at market. M. Marcel encouraged her and suggested that when they moved to Carcassonne, she could even set up a shop, if she liked, to sell dolls to children. Whatever she liked, he said. He repeated this often.

Claude's tactlessness aside, it was natural that both my mother and I would begin to wonder about my own prospects for marriage, now that Michelle was accounted for. Mother was discreet — she never pressured me, and I was grateful for it. Though I was not as striking as Michelle, I was passably pretty — I owned a full figure and plump lips, though I was cursed with Father's thicket of a brow. We both expected that I would eventually find a husband, though I knew no one, save Bérenger, with whom I could envision a future. I spoke occasionally of finding someone as nice and gentle as M.

Marcel (whom we now called Joseph), but with perhaps more of a chin. Mother nodded, humoring me. We both knew I had little desire to find anyone at the time, though only I knew why.

SEVEN DEVILS

The first rose in her as bubbles in a broth, exploding into hilarity in the midst of prayer or the nightly blessings of the bread and wine. The second devil poured itself into her heart as an inattentive vintner pours wine into a wineskin, filling it until it stretches thin. Possessed by this devil, the sight of a child with its mother or a suckling calf made her feel as if she had been filled to bursting; she ached, became dizzy, wept inconsolably. The third came on her as a fit, causing her limbs to thrash and her head to roll. Under the sway of this devil, she had once swept her arms across a jeweler's table, scattering amulets of lapis lazuli, beaded anklets, pendants of hammered gold under the feet of the crowd. The fourth leapt from her lips as fiery language, rough words that scandalized her mother and sisters. This devil possessed her as she strolled by the booths displaying spices, fragrances and incense, dates, wine, oil, calves and lambs.

She tried to clamp her lips tight, but she couldn't keep the forbidden language from spilling out. "Leper! Leper! May God plague you with pustules!" The village had declared her a menace and forbade her from attending the market.

The fifth devil sat by her bedside after dark, humming insistently and whispering unintelligible syllables in her ear, robbing her of sleep. The sixth took hold of her hands when she was alone and passed them through her loosening hair and over her breasts and her thighs, making the blood rise in her face and her breath come quickly in her throat. And the seventh — the seventh was the worst of all, for the seventh was always with her. It cowered in her heart and while she moved about her house weaving, baking, studying the Law with her father, dining, bathing — constantly whispering Torah to herself, verse after verse — it threatened her; at any moment it could rise and stretch and occupy her whole being, causing her blood to chill and her body to slow until all she could do was curl herself into a fist, immobilized by fear. She whispered God's word to keep the devils at bay.

These were the seven reasons why Miryam, at the age of nineteen, was still unmarried and why she sought the healer

71

from Natzaret. It was dawn: she walked alone along the shore, avoiding the roads where she could easily be stopped by Herod's soldiers. Gulls flew over the lake, diving for fish. Her sisters would be waking now, running to tell their mother about her empty bed, and she wondered whether her mother might secretly welcome her disappearance. But she kept on, stopping from time to time to shake a pebble from her sandal. Soon she came to a place where the sloping bank began to level out. She climbed a small rise and leaned against a cypress tree to rest. Fields of whitening wheat extended before her, rippling in the wind that came off the water. A few workers were scattered across the fields, their head coverings bobbing above the plants. She believed that the man and his followers would be camping somewhere here, on the Plain of Gennesaret — it was flat and there were many grassy clearings that would offer excellent ground for camping — but she did not see them as she surveyed the expanse before her.

The heat of the day was beginning to rise, and she removed the shawl that covered her head and shoulders and laid it on the ground, letting the air cool her face and neck. She could feel the devil within her stirring — she did not want it to wake, and she thought that if she closed her eyes and tried to make herself peaceful, it might doze again. She sat in the shade of the tree and tucked her feet beneath her. Leaning back, she closed her eyes and tried to will the sleep that had eluded her the previous night to overtake her now. But the devil was not so easily dissuaded. Before long, it had stretched itself to standing within her and was now looking out through her eyes and re-creating the view she had previously seen as benign: now the wheat plants that had been rippling so gently in the breeze appeared to her as thousands of spears piercing the breast of the great sighing beast that was the land; now the white heads of the workers as they dipped amid the plants were the pale bellies of gigantic spiders, coming toward her on long lascivious legs; now the sheltering tree she leaned against had become the body of a serpent, rigid and poised to strike. She scuttled away from it and rolled into a ball like a mealworm, covering her head with her arms. "So the people of Yisrael," she whispered, "set out from Rameses, and encamped at Succoth. And they set out from Succoth and encamped at Etham, which is on the edge of the wilderness."

Time passed. She felt a light touch on her spine and when she lifted her head, he was there, kneeling beside her. He was very thin — his cheeks hung from the bones beneath his eyes, and his mouth seemed too large for his fragile face. "Miryam," he said gently. She got quickly to her feet and pulled the cloth back over her head. He remained where he was, looking up at her like a child gazing at his mother. "Here you are," he whispered, as if it was he who had been seeking her.

CHAPTER THREE

One afternoon, after the heat of the summer had passed, I happened to be upstairs fluffing the featherbed when I heard the front door open and the swish of Bérenger's cassock as he entered the house. "Isabelle?" he called out. I held my breath, then answered.

"She's gone to the butcher's, Monsieur *le curé*," I said as I descended the ladder to the lower room. "She'll be back shortly."

"Oh, Marinette," he said. He laughed, as if surprised to see me, then waved an envelope in the air. "The most wonderful thing. I've just received a letter from —" He stopped to laugh once more, in disbelief. "You won't believe me."

"Who?" I asked, intrigued.

"The Archduke of Austria." He enunciated the title emphatically, with evident pleasure. "He's written to inquire about our church."

"What for?" I asked.

"It's incredible, really. He wants to send us some money for its restoration. It appears his sister is the Reverend Mother Josephine, abbess at the convent in Prouilles. I'd no idea she was a Hapsburg," he added. "In any case, he says she's often spoken to him about our beautiful village and our poor dilapidated church, and he has grown fond of it through her stories. He asked if we're still in need of funds."

"Really?" I said. "What luck."

"A blessing, Marie. A gift from God. Praise his holy name."

"Amen," I added. We stood in awkward silence, aware of the faintly illicit flavor of the moment: he had taken me into his confidence. He looked around once more, as if he expected my mother to appear from behind the sideboard. Anxious to maintain his attention, I asked, "And how will you respond, Monsieur *le curé?*"

"Why, I'll let him know that we would be indebted to him for his generosity, that we are undertaking the necessary steps to perform a renovation . . ." He looked pointedly at me. "In fact, Marie, do you have a moment? I would like to answer him immediately, and your handwriting is so well proportioned."

We walked over to the presbytery, where he shouldered open the door. The interior air, though still reeking of mildew, had improved since he'd set up his rudimentary office. He had swept the stone floor clean and pushed all the debris — the rotting chairs and boards, the loose bricks — into the next room, leaving a salvaged chair and a trestle table, his desk. The afternoon sun cast an elongated grid of light on the dusty floor.

I sat at the desk. He leaned over me to lift several sheets of stationery from a corner pile, then handed me a pen from his breast pocket. It warmed my palm.

"Rennes-le-Château, the eighteenth of September, 1885," he began. I wrote, struggling to form my best letters. It was a highly formal message, the language invariably deferential to the status of his addressee. Bérenger invoked the humble position of our village and church, and our great fortune at having captured the archduke's attention. He dictated in a labored fashion, often stopping and asking me to read back what he'd said, so that by the time we had finished, the stationery was littered with irregular lines and blacked out phrases. I read out the final version.

"What do you think, Marie?" he asked

when I'd finished. "Does it sound well to you?"

"Fit for a prince," I declared. "I'll recopy it."

Bérenger nodded, though his expression was distracted and anxious. "Listen, Marie. I've been thinking — I'd like you to keep the news of this letter to yourself for the time being."

I hesitated only briefly before answering, "Certainly, monsieur." But I wondered why he wanted to keep the archduke's offer a secret. It appeared as though he had just lit upon a thought that made him wary, though what it might have been I couldn't have guessed.

He bowed his head. "Thank you, Marinette. And thank you for your help." He leaned over me to see the letter once again, his shoulders shading my hands.

I took a clean sheet from the pile and began to recopy.

He hovered only a moment more and then began to pace about the room like a restless mule in a stall. Though I kept my eyes on the page in front of me, I could feel him watching me as I wrote, and I could not help but wonder what he saw. I finally met his gaze with my own.

"Tell me, Marinette," he said. "Why is it

that I haven't yet seen you at confession? Are you that free of sin? As much an angel as you seem?"

The question surprised me. I blushed to the roots of my hair and studied the page once more.

"I'm teasing you," he added, as a sort of apology. But I could not help but feel chided.

When I had finished the closing line of the letter — which Bérenger had dictated as "Your servant in Christ"— and he had signed the letter with his own perfectly measured hand, he set out immediately for Couiza where he might find the postmaster. That evening, as Mother and I prepared the supper, I wished I had asked Bérenger whether I might at least share the news with her, as it appeared he had intended for her to hear it first. But I kept silent.

Bérenger was right, of course: I had been avoiding confession. I feared the intimacy of it, feared it would be too provocative, that my feelings for him would be evident in my voice and my demeanor. Though, to be sure, I was not yet exactly certain what my feelings for him were. I knew they involved want: I wanted his attention, his affection, his presence. I could not admit,

79

even to myself, that I wanted his touch — it was too awful, too sinful a thought. But I felt it when I stood by him, when I leaned over him to serve him his plate — the need came over me like a sudden hunger, so powerful that it stole the strength from my muscles and made me fear I might collapse at his feet. His physicality overwhelmed me — his robust figure, his dark complexion, his impetuous grin. But it was his gaze that captivated me. I could not turn away from it. It seemed to simultaneously ask and tell me who I was. No other man in Rennes-le-Château shared that intensity, that seriousness of purpose. No one looked at me as he did.

To please him, I felt I should confess. I reflected on what I had done that I might be able to reveal to him — what sin I could admit to that would convince him I was making a sincere act of contrition. I could disclose my envy for Michelle and her upcoming wedding, divulge the fact of my laziness, tell him of angry words I had spoken to my brother. All of these I could confess sincerely, for I was sorry for them, and absolution would help ease my mind. But they were evasions, I knew. There was one item — other than my unmentionable lust, of course — that was potentially more serious, more dire as far as the state of my soul was concerned. And that was the education I'd been receiving in secret from Mme Laporte.

Madame was the most abstemious person I had yet met. Certainly she was much more so than Bérenger, who savored his food, wine, and smoke. She seemed to exist almost completely in her mind. Her large head virtually teetered on her neck like an overripe fruit, while her body was waif-like, insubstantial. She never sounded a footfall when she walked; rather she seemed — as she had that strange misty morning — to hover just above the ground, floating her way up the stairs and across the hall to her library. The cook, Mme Siau, had taken to bringing treats — almond cake or orange biscuits — when I came, but Mme Laporte never ate them. Occasionally, she sipped coffee, which she took black, but I never saw a morsel of food pass her lips. It seemed that she was nourished, instead, by her own imagination.

It was this imagination of hers, her ability to speak of the distant past as if she'd witnessed it, that I relished. I listened eagerly to her tales of the Cathars, who lived six centuries before I was born and practiced their heretical religion on our little hilltop just as they did throughout the region.

The Cathars ate no meat, eggs, or cheese — no food that came from flesh, for they believed that flesh had been created by the devil, whom they knew as *Rex Mundi,* the king of the world. It was *Rex Mundi* who had moved upon the face of the waters and sculpted an Adam from dust. The true God reigned solely in the heavens, having nothing to do with the earthly creation. "Have you ever wondered, Marie," Madame asked me one afternoon, "how a good God could have created the guillotine?" The Cathar God, she said, was pure perfection, and as such, could not have made our world. Only the souls of men housed a spark of divinity. These souls traveled from body to body, life to life, over time, until they attained perfection and could finally join with God in the heavens. This was accomplished by renouncing the material world through the sacrament of the *consolamentum,* a spiritual baptism that had to be received before death in order to achieve salvation.

"So many of the peasants of that time," she recounted, "ate only two meals a day of porridge and weak ale and wore their tunics until they became rags on their backs. They spent their days threshing the grain on fields they didn't own, weaving endless skeins of flax and wool into cloth. Of this meager income, the Church demanded ten percent. And for what? To pay for the ermine-trimmed albs, the satin miters, and the golden staffs of the bishops, to fund their feasts of wild boar, goose, and hare, their debauched nights with well-kept concubines. The *perfecti*"— these were Cathar monks who traveled through the countryside, fasting and preaching like Jesus' own apostles —"simply appeared holier than the so-called holy men of the Catholic Church. You can imagine the appeal."

That the God of Genesis, the God who had created man, should be thought of as the devil was a great heresy in the eyes of the Catholic Church. But an even greater heresy was the Cathar disdain for the cross. For they believed that Christ did not die on the cross. They believed, in fact, that he didn't die — because he had not truly lived. Being perfect as his Father, Christ could not have taken on the imperfections of human flesh. His appearance on earth in human form was a semblance, a divine optical illusion. Cathar theology rendered the Church's central symbol — ritually kissed by the priest at the beginning of each Mass, piously traced by congregants over their own hearts — meaningless.

During the twelfth and thirteenth centuries, this region, our region — from the Pyrenees, along the Mediterranean all the way to the Rhône, and as far west as Toulouse — graciously hosted this burgeoning religion. Nobles protected its practitioners; many nobles practiced the religion themselves. As it gained power, it threatened the Church, which responded by launching the brutal Albigensian crusade.

In her accounts of the crusade, Mme Laporte dwelt on the grisliest details, describing the butchering of torsos, the mass incinerations of bodies — hundreds at a time. She told of the massacre of seven thousand at Béziers, Cathars and Catholics alike, spurred on by the Abbot of Cîteaux, who commanded the balking soldiers to "kill them all. God will know his own." She described the flight of hundreds of Cathars to seek refuge in mountaintop fortresses like Montségur or Peyrepertuse. There they faced sieges that, if they didn't bring immediate death by a blow to the head from a catapulted stone or an arrow lodged in the heart, threatened a more protracted one by dysentery, starvation, or dehydration. "Death by dehydration can occur within just three days," she told me with her usual impassive expression. "You go mad, you know. Raving mad."

I would walk home, my head filled with images of charred skin, gutted corpses, wild-eyed children spinning in a final fury before they fell, desiccated, to the ground. I began to have nightmares: visions of mobs approaching with buckets of steaming tar ready to slather on my naked skin; the sensation of rope looping at my ankles and wrists and the ominous tugging of restless horses at the other end. And yet I read the books Madame gave me and returned week after week, to eat cakes and hear her tales. They quickened my pulse, filled me with a sumptuous fear.

At first I did not question why she knew so much about the Cathars and their barbarous end. Her affinity for their philosophy seemed consistent with what I knew of her: her temperance, her apparent indifference to her own possessions (except, perhaps, her books). She embodied the virtue of renunciation that Bérenger so extolled. Yet she was not a Catholic and so was unaffected by Catholic doctrine. It surprised me that someone so apparently irreligious could be so virtuous.

"How is it that you know so much about all this?" I finally asked her one afternoon after she'd told me of the bloody siege of Carcassonne.

She appeared startled at the question and did not answer me right away. I sipped my coffee, worrying that I had somehow offended her. Finally, she replied, "It interests me. The history of the area. I suppose I like to have a sense of where it is I live."

I let the subject drop, though her answer seemed incomplete.

I suppose confessing my secretive relationship with Madame — particularly the pleasure I took in her gruesome tales — would have been enough to satisfy Bérenger. But what I could never confess to was the seedling of doubt, planted by my father and now pushing its way toward the surface of my mind. I had always assumed, as my mother had told me, that my father was like the prodigal son who would someday return home to the Church. "And when he does," she said, "God will welcome him with open arms." But as I came to know Mme Laporte, my opinion changed. I began to wonder if perhaps my father was right. The Church, it turned out, was fallible; more than that, it was capable of corruption, hypocrisy, and great evil. This institution that called itself God's own bride, that claimed to be the only true messenger of his holy word, that promised salvation and won the trust and faith of so many — this institution was guilty of terrible crimes.

It sickened me, this new apprehension. How could the Church that commanded us not to kill be capable of massacring thousands in the name of God?

I raised my questions with Mme Laporte, but she could not answer them. "I'm not a proper counselor for you on matters of religion, Marie," was all she would say. It was clear that she held the Church in contempt, though she never said so outright. I did not want to talk to my father about it — his reaction was too predictable. Neither could I talk to my mother; it would hurt her to learn of my doubts. Michelle had lately become oblivious to anything but Joseph and her upcoming wedding. And Claude was too young to be of any help. I was left, then, with Bérenger.

I did not know him well enough yet to be able to predict his response, and this made me both curious and wary. Would he scold me for expressing my horror at what the Church claimed — albeit hundreds of years ago — was a righteous war? Or would he acknowledge the Church's fallibility? Would he punish me for my doubt? Tell my mother? Or, worse, forbid me from seeing Mme

Laporte again? I feared this last the most, not only because I was loath to give up my visits with Madame, but also because if he assigned me such a penance, I would be compelled to obey, and as a result might resent him, a thing I could not stand. Instead, I carried my unspoken questions within me like an ulcer until they began to cause me psychic pain.

When the smell of stale incense and melted wax — smells that had once comforted me — began to fill me with dread, I resolved to speak with Bérenger. My motives were genuine, I believed: I hoped he might tell me something that would reconcile the Church's past foibles — even sins — with what I believed was its present beneficence.

Bérenger, I knew, was in the habit of taking a midday walk just before dinner, and I hoped to intercept him on his way. I chose an afternoon when my mother had gone to Espéraza for the day to visit a friend who was ill. Michelle and I were normally responsible for preparing the midday dinner, which would have prevented my leaving the house just before noon, but I started the meal early. I worked quickly and nervously at the rest of my chores that morning, hastily milking Geneviève, our goat, and beating the dust from the carpet in a fury. I told Michelle nothing — we shared little with each other now. She knew and disapproved of my visits to Madame and I could not bear to hear her fretting over her lack of a trousseau or repeating word for word Joseph's latest declaration of love. After hanging the wash, I stole down the path that led to the château, then passed the château by and continued downhill toward the road that Bérenger would be traveling.

It was a late summer day, hot and dry, and the red dust settled in my mouth and nostrils, tasting of iron. I thought of a legend we'd heard from Mme Paul: that the devil had buried a treasure in these mountains, and one morning, when he had nothing else to do, had spread the millions of pieces of gold over the earth. "Gold's all around here," she insisted, when my mother raised her eyebrows skeptically. "Monsieur Flèche found a piece once when he was a boy. Ask him yourself." We later did, and though he denied finding any himself, he told us a story about a shepherd who, while looking for a lost ram, had fallen into a cave somewhere on the hillside and emerged hours later with both the ram and a kettle full of gold coins.

As I walked, I kicked at pebbles in my

path, idly searching for a glint of yellow. When I approached the slope descending from the graveyard, I saw Bérenger. He was stepping carefully to avoid the rocks and brambles that interrupted the narrow trail. He wore his cassock, which set off his face, square and tawny above his clean white collar, his cheeks dark with the shadow that clung to them. "Good morning, Monsieur *le curé*," I said, affecting a tone of mild surprise.

"Marie!" He lifted his walking stick toward me in a salute, then studied the path again until he reached a level.

"I was just going for a walk," I said.

"Well, then, we're of the same mind, you and I. May I join you?"

As we descended, the panorama opened before us. There were the fields, planted with wheat, barley, maize, and grapevines, bursting with green and the first tinges of autumnal brown. Bordered by wild growth — large bushes of broom, dwarf and umbrella pine, Kermes oak and cypress — the fields appeared, from a distance, to be patches on a great quilt, laid over the swells and dips of a recumbent body. Above the valley rose the mountains, increasing in height as they increased in distance. They stretched on, one after the next, the larger ones hovering ancestrally over their smaller companions. The ruined ramparts of Coustaussa and Blanchefort hulked over the valley, as natural as if they'd grown out of the rock, wild castle-plants. Limestone broke the surface of the hills now and then, like the bones of an ancient buried skeleton gradually becoming unearthed. The soil, as I've said, was red, but there were places where the red blended to brown or beige, as if the color had bled in the rain.

This vista was what we gazed upon as we walked, Bérenger and I. It relieved us of some pressure, for there could be no such thing as awkward silence in the presence of such beauty — silence was the only way to approve of such a sight. So we walked a ways without speaking, listening to the pebbles crunching beneath our feet, the clucking of hens and the occasional call of a rooster from the village above.

He spoke first. "I had a view of this hill from my bedroom window when I was a boy. I used to scan the hillside, looking for caves."

"Did you ever find any?"

"Oh, yes. Not from my window, of course. But when I searched on foot, that's when I got lucky. I noticed a draft coming from within some vines, and when I parted them, sure enough, there was my cave. I was so thrilled, I just squatted there, feeling the cold, smelling the earth. I thought I'd found my own special place, assigned to me by God." He laughed a little and shook his head. "Foolish. I crawled in. It was deep — it extended straight back for a hundred feet or so and then dipped suddenly into pitch darkness. I had no light with me, so I couldn't continue."

"Did you find anything?"

"Nothing. Only a ring of stones and some charred wood, which disappointed me, since it meant that someone had been there before. I vowed to return with a light, and I did try, several times, to find the place again. But I never could. I found other caves, but none of them were as deep or as intriguing as that first one."

"There's supposed to be a secret underground passageway through the caves here," I offered timidly. "That people used to use as an escape route."

"Oh, there are all kinds of stories. Secret passageways, tunnels, hideouts. Hidden treasure. The kind of thing boys love."

"Not just boys."

He stopped his striding for a moment to regard me, an amused expression on his face. "Don't tell me you've been searching,

Marie?" My abashed silence gave him his answer, and he guffawed, as if at a clever joke. "Wonderful!" he exclaimed. "And have you found anything?"

"No," I admitted. Then, encouraged by his evident pleasure at my interest, I continued, "I've become very interested in the legends, though. I've been interested to hear, especially, about the Cathars — how they might have used an underground passageway to escape the crusaders." I faltered, losing courage.

Bérenger chuckled, "Yes, well. They're intriguing, all those tales. Unreliable as anything."

Forcing myself to continue, I said, "I've been meaning to ask you about that, Monsieur *le curé*. About the Cathars and the Albigensian crusade. All the thousands of people who were slaughtered, burnt at the stake — by the Church. I've been, well, thinking about it . . ." I trailed off. He had stopped walking and had raised his head, casting his eyes to the distant hills.

"By the Church's army," he said.

"Yes." I hesitated a moment longer. "I hope you'll pardon me, Monsieur *le curé*, but I've been troubled by it. I can't understand how the Pope could have ordered those men to kill all those people like he did."

Bérenger smiled sadly at the ground. "What have you been reading?" he asked.

"Oh, history books. Father bought them for me in town." I might have told him of my meetings with Mme Laporte, but his sudden change in demeanor unnerved me.

"I didn't know you were interested in history, Marie."

He squatted to examine a thistle, his thick fingers probing the spiny bulb beneath the washed-out purple flower. "The Marian thistle." He picked it and handed it to me. "They're supposed to protect one's faith."

"Thank you," I said.

He began walking once more. "It's not an easy thing, the question you've asked, Marie," he said.

"I know."

"The crusades were hundreds of years ago, of course. Things have changed." His walking stick scraped against the stony path. "The Albigensian heresy was a great danger to the people. It was leading hundreds astray. You've read, I suppose, about their beliefs, what they claimed to be true?"

I nodded.

"It was heresy, pure and simple." He sighed again. "You know the story of Elijah and the prophets of Baal, Marie." And when I didn't respond, he began to narrate the story, enunciating the words emphatically, as he did in his sermons. "In Israel under King Ahab, there were hundreds of false prophets, men who worshipped Baal. One day, Elijah called all these prophets to the top of the mountain. There he proposed a test to prove to them who was the one true God. They would prepare two bulls for burnt offerings — one to be sacrificed to Baal, the other to the Lord. Then they would each call upon their God to light the fires. The God that sent down fire to burn the offering would have proven himself as the true God.

"So they prepared the offerings and set them on two pyres, one next to the other. And the prophets of Baal called on their god to come and light their pyre. All morning and all afternoon they called. But Baal didn't answer. Then Elijah stepped up to his pyre and commanded it to be drenched with water. And the people poured vessel after vessel of water on the offering until the bull and the wood were drenched, and the pyre stood in a pool of water. Then Elijah called on the Lord. And immediately God answered him with a searing flame that leapt from the sky and consumed the bull, the pyre, the stones it stood upon, even the pool of water beneath it. And the people, when they saw this miracle, lay down and declared glory to the Lord God, the one true God of Israel and of all the world."

The story was familiar — I had heard it before — but in Bérenger's telling, the characters suddenly took on more majestic proportions. Even God himself, whom I had remembered as being helpful, sending the fire down in order to save Elijah from his predicament, became ireful and destructive. Then Bérenger added the final, damning conclusion to the tale, one I had not remembered.

"And then, Marie, Elijah gathered up the prophets of Baal, those false prophets who had led the people of Israel away from their one true God, and he slaughtered them. According to the Law of God, false prophets are condemned to die. Deuteronomy 18:20."

This ending dropped like a rock into the pleasant morning and the tenuous webbing of my faith.

"The Cathars were false prophets, Marie." He spoke more gently now, aware that he'd shocked me. "Pope Innocent the Third was obliged to kill them. He was kinder, even, than Elijah. He tried other methods first:

discussion, debate, appealing to the nobles to stamp out all signs of the heresy among them. But none worked. And so he finally followed God's Law." He studied my face. "The heretics were always given the chance to renounce their beliefs and return to the true Church. Those who chose to return were accepted with joy. Those who didn't, well . . ." He paused. "Sometimes war is necessary in the name of God."

"Because the Church's power was threatened," I said.

"Because people's souls were threatened! Because the heretics were leading people straight into hell!" He struck his walking stick against the ground, then glared at me.

His anger startled but did not scare me — my father had acquainted me with bluster. I waited a moment, studying my flower, then said in a measured tone, "But the Cathars believed their faith was true. How could they be forced to believe something different? And if someone pretended to believe something to avoid being killed, it would be a lie, which is also a sin. And wouldn't God know he was lying?"

We had reached a fork in the path. One way led farther down the hill, into a thickening forest of oak and pine. The other veered left and stayed open, rising again. Bérenger stood at the fork, glaring downhill, ominously silent.

"I've angered you," I said heatedly. "I should not have brought it up." I realized with chagrin that my fervent curiosity had gotten the better of me. I feared I had lost his approval.

He turned to face me, his hands folded as if to control them. "You are very intelligent, Marie," he said. "But the problem with human intelligence is that it strives to understand what it cannot understand, and in doing so, destroys the beauty and the mystery of the ineffable. We proclaim the *mystery* of faith, Marie. It is a mystery and must remain so." He gazed at me for a long moment, until I felt I had to break the gaze or be swallowed. I looked back in the direction from which we'd come: from our position, I could see only the dusty trail we'd taken down the hill, which rose steeply, obscuring the view of the village.

"I suppose I should start back toward home now," I said. "I have dinner to prepare."

He nodded. "Leave a plate for me. I'll be walking a while longer."

When I had reached the crest of the hill once more, he called to me, "Marie! Come to confession!"

She went with them over the objections of Kefa, who thought such a woman would discredit their cause. She was the only woman yet to join them, though there would be others later. Yeshua walked beside her. At one point, Kefa fell back and tried to coax Yeshua away. "We have things to discuss," he said. "Things that don't concern a woman." But Yeshua would not leave her, and so Kefa walked with them, fuming.

Yeshua was shy with her. With others he could be genial and talkative, but with her he fell silent, and seemed instead to be listening intently, even if she wasn't speaking — as if he were listening for the hush of her blood as it maneuvered the particular turns of her veins.

It was thirty years since the death of Herod the Great, thirty years since rebels had risen up against the empire, thirty years since Varus's legions had swarmed the countryside, raping, razing, battering, smashing. Everywhere, the synagogues spoke of destruction: columns rose in the open air, supporting nothing; stairways led into emptiness. Old women's eyes were still glazed with grief for their murdered children, and there were few old men, for so many of them had been dragged into slavery in far-off corners of the empire. They were a people in need of healing. Yeshua spoke to them in what remained of the synagogues, declaring the end of oppression and death. "The hour is fulfilled!" he shouted. "The Kingdom of God is near! Repent and believe in the good news!" Some believed and were joyful; some quietly hoped and yet doubted; some were pained by what they heard as arrogant nonsense; and some demanded proof, a sign from God.

And so Yeshua healed. He placed his rough palms over the eyes of a blind man, and when he removed them, the man fell prostrate before him, crying, "Light! Light!" He stood before the thrashing body of a boy and commanded the demon to depart; it left with an ungodly roar like the crash of a great wave against a ship's hull. They brought him their blind and lame, their hemorrhaging and leprous, their maniacal and possessed, and he healed them, one by one. But even these signs were not enough for some, for there had been other healers before Yeshua, and weren't they all still here, yoked to the Roman plow?

Miryam, though, was hopeful. She whispered the words of the prophet Yeshayah to herself as she walked, "For a child has been born for us, a son is given to us; authority rests upon his shoulders, and he is named Wonderful Counselor, Mighty God, Everlasting Father, Prince of Peace."

Her father was a *chazzan,* the leader at the synagogue, and he honored the scriptures above all else. No woman in all of the Galil was as well schooled as Miryam. Her father did not believe, as some did in her village, that women were unfit for study. From the age of four, when her father had first read to her the story of the creation of the earth, Miryam had memorized Torah. Even then, before she manifested any outward signs of her possession, she felt the devils gripping her mind. Only her father's voice, singing the scripture, had the ability to loosen the grip, to ease her building agony. She asked him to read the words again and again, and then she repeated them. "The Spirit of God was moving over the face of the waters," she recited, and she saw a vast stretch of sea, the Galilee at night, dark and churning in a wind. "Let there be light," she recited, and the sea glowed from its depths and fingers of yellow light fractured the darkness. "Let the earth bring forth living creatures according to their kinds," she recited, and they appeared: ibexes kicking up mountain stones, wild boars snuffling through the cedar, asps uncoiling and spreading their hoods. In this way, she managed to keep her devils at bay.

But as Miryam grew older, it grew more difficult to pacify the demons. They seized her when she paused to take a breath; her whispering grew faster, louder, and more frenzied. It became clear that no man would have her as his wife. Her mother, feeling Miryam's agony as her own, encouraged her to devote herself entirely to learning scripture. "Is there not here another prophet of the Lord of whom we may inquire?" Miryam whispered and, "Heman the singer the son of Jo'el, son of Samuel, son of Elka'nah, son of Jero'ham, son of Eli'el, son of To'ah," on and on. Her affliction had earned her fame in her village, but her devotion made her famous in towns throughout the Galil, even as far as Kafr Nahum. Visitors to her village might hear her whispering and kneel before her, asking for a blessing, but the village mothers pulled their children close when she passed. Some threw stones.

Yeshua, though, was not afraid. "What a gift Abba has given you, Miryam!" he said. "To have his word always on your tongue! What a blessing!"

But Miryam felt cursed. The pronunciation of sounds did not equal knowledge. She wanted release from her incessant whispering; she wanted peace, she wanted discernment, she wanted understanding. Yeshua, she hoped, could teach her these.

He walked among them and spoke with them, but seemed simultaneously to be walking in seclusion. He appeared to be listening, enraptured — it was as if God himself was speaking in his ear. This, after some time, was what Miryam grew to believe: that Yeshua's Abba spoke to him as her own father spoke to her.

Chapter Four

Bérenger's insistence on defending the Church rather than soothing my heartache wounded me. I punished him with silence for a time, and he avoided me, sensing my anger. Still, I longed to be near him.

Thankfully, our battle of wills did not last long. One afternoon, he plunked himself in the chair beside mine as I sat shelling peas for winter storage. When I didn't look up, he began whistling the tune to "Marinette, Marinette, la Petite Coquette."

"Please stop whistling that song," I said, in as dignified a voice as I could muster.

"Ah, she speaks. I had begun to wonder whether you'd lost your voice."

I kept my eyes trained on the pods between my fingers. "Why should I speak when I have nothing to say?"

"Oh, but that's not true, Marie. You do have something to say. You're angry with me."

I raised my eyebrows.

"I don't blame you," he said earnestly. "I did not give you a very good answer to your question."

I graced him with a look. "No, you didn't."

"I responded reflexively," he said. "I didn't think."

"Do you really feel that way? That the Church was in the right? To murder all those people?"

Bérenger sighed heavily. "What I think, what anyone thinks, doesn't change what happened. Yes, undoubtedly, the Church has made mistakes. But that does not change the fact of its singularity, that, through the grace of God and his son Jesus Christ, the Church grants us salvation."

"I suppose so," I said cautiously.

"You are right to wonder about these things, Marie. You are right to think about justice. Christ was a lamb for justice, for peace. But I don't want to see your questions undermine your faith. That's why I spoke roughly to you."

"I understand," I said, my eyes still on the peas.

He leaned toward me, positioning his face in my line of vision so I could not help but look at him. In a whisper, he said, "But I should not have spoken so roughly. Marie, please. The last thing I want is for you to be angry with me."

"All right," I said, raising my head and finally meeting his eyes. "I forgive you."

He leaned back in his chair, his face momentarily stricken with relief, as if he'd just barely evaded some great calamity. Then, abruptly, he stood and, smiling his mischievous smile, gave a charming little mock-bow.

I was glad to be free to enjoy his company once again, and for that reason did not press the point. But the question remained: Did he truly believe that the Church had been justified in its massacre of all those thousands? In the absence of any definitive answer from him, I made up my own. I assumed he'd been carried away by his desire to defend the Church, and so had spoken insincerely. In this way, I was able to resume my former fantasies, in which we were free to love one another, though they were complicated by this new insight, this small window into his bewildering intransigence.

Then came the election. In the weeks leading up to election day, my father spent his nights in the tavern with other men of his political persuasion. I imagine they raised glass upon glass to Robespierre, Gambetta,

Clemenceau, and the Republic. We could always tell when Father was about to come home on those nights, because we could hear him and his companions in a rowdy rendition of "La Marseillaise," sung all the way home. Once in the house, Father would stumble wordlessly past Bérenger, who was usually reading by the hearth, and climb into bed with Mother, muttering about his great misfortune at having to share his home with a priest.

This was a change. Since the time my father had decided to spare Bérenger his usual political harangue, the two had gotten along well. They always shared a smoke after dinner. Bérenger had taken to helping Father with small repairs around the house — patching the roof, rehanging the door when it fell off its hinges — and in return, Father had begun taking an interest in Bérenger's own building projects. Bérenger had drafted a renovation plan for the church, which included a reconstructed roof, stabilized walls, a new altar with a new set of steps leading up to it, a new confessional, and a new floor for the nave. He and Father pored over the plans together, discussing the merits and risks of various materials: tile, stone, plaster, glass. Bérenger had not yet heard back from the Austrian and spoke heatedly about the immediate necessity of renovation. Father happily denounced the episcopate, the mayor, and the village council — with whom he'd had disagreements in the past — for their refusal to put forward any money for the project. He told bad jokes, which Bérenger laughed at heartily. They avoided discussing politics or religion.

But as the elections neared, those subjects became more difficult to avoid. It happened that a local boy, Jean-Baptiste Durier from Couiza, was up for a seat in the Chamber. He was a republican, and while many of the men in the village would have voted rightist — or, more commonly, would not have bothered to vote at all — because Durier was a *terradorenc* they had become republican, if only for the purposes of this election. My father would forgo his customary after-dinner smoke with Bérenger and head for the tavern. Bérenger began leaving copies of his Catholic weekly, *La Semaine Réligieuse de Carcassonne,* on the table for my father to see, especially when the headlines were particularly antirepublican: "Enemies of Religion Converge on City Center," or "Bishop Calls Laicization of Schools the Work of the Devil." My father would drop the paper in the dust outside the front door, letting its pages scatter.

One night, after I had been sleeping for some time, I woke to the sound of my father and Bérenger arguing.

"Your Church is doomed," Father said to Bérenger, his voice smug with liquor.

"What makes you think that, Edouard?" asked Bérenger calmly.

"The Republic will prevail. When Church and State are finally separated, the Church will sink fast."

"And why is that?" asked Bérenger

"Who's going to dole out money voluntarily to an organization that gives them nothing in return?"

I heard my mother rummaging for her slippers and nightcap.

"Nothing?" Bérenger said.

"Empty promises. The worst kind of lies. A fluffy cushion in heaven after you die! Convenient! An IOU, payable only upon death!"

Claude was stirring and Michelle was awake. She leaned over and asked in a whisper, "What's going on?"

"Shhh," I said.

Mother descended the stairs, a candle in her hand. "Edouard! Come upstairs this instant!"

But he ignored her. "Tell me, Monsieur *le*

109

curé," he continued. "Do you believe in God?"

Bérenger's voice was soft but sure. "Of course."

"You believe you're going to be frolicking in the clouds, playing the lute? You're an educated man, for God's sake!"

"I believe in eternal life, yes, if that's what you're asking me."

"Eternal life. What does that mean? Describe it to me!"

"In heaven, we meet God," Bérenger said with conviction. "As Paul tells us, 'For now we see through a mirror dimly, but then face to face.' If I knew what God looked like, Edouard, I would describe him to you with joy. But I don't yet."

"How do you know it's not just darkness, dirt in our nostrils?"

"Because I know the sustaining strength of God's love. 'For God so loved the world that he gave his only son, that whoever believes in him should not perish but have eternal life.' "

"For Christ's sake," my father roared, "stop quoting someone else's words and think for yourself for once!"

"Edouard!" shouted my mother.

"Answer me this, Monsieur *le curé:* What kind of a father would crucify his own son?"

"That's enough, Edouard!" said my mother, and this time the ominous tone of her voice must have caught his attention, for a moment later I heard my father's heavy footsteps on the stairs. I lay down and turned my back toward the door, as did Michelle and Claude, and we were motionless as my father undressed and climbed into bed. Within moments, he was snoring. Downstairs, my mother apologized tearfully to Bérenger. "It tortures him, it does," she said. "He wants to come back to the Church, he wants to believe, but he won't let himself. It's the men at the tavern. If they ever knew he was going to church, he'd never hear the end of it."

"They're the same as he is, Isabelle. They're just the same. Too scared to face the truth."

"I'll pray for him, for all of them."

They went on like this for some time. I stopped listening after a while. My father's question rang in my ears. What kind of a father indeed? I lifted my pillow and took out the Marian thistle Bérenger had given me on our walk weeks earlier, now half-dried and crushed flat. It smelled faintly of decay. I lay back, holding it, but I could not sleep, even after my mother returned to bed and all was quiet. When I finally drifted off, in the early hours of the morning, I dreamt of vast empty spaces, scorched ground stretching into eternity.

On the day of the election — a Sunday, as was customary — people gathered early in front of the church and stood in factions, whispering, exchanging glares and jibes. An election offered some sport, and the village loved it almost as much as the occasional running of the bulls in Espéraza: the suspense, the antagonism, the anticipation of a sweet and bloody victory. Everyone wanted to hear the Church's word on the subject; it was another element in the drama. Even Mme Laporte came that morning, her hand on the mayor's arm. She wore a round hat fixed with a swatch of tulle that dipped over her eyes; her graying hair, usually straying from an unkempt twist, was well brushed and neatly arranged in a chignon at the nape of her neck. I gaped at her; she smiled discreetly and nodded her head in greeting.

No one knew for sure what Bérenger would say that morning. Normally, he followed the missal scrupulously and did not often preach about politics or public affairs. Nevertheless, we all knew his political position: he wanted the monarchy to be restored and Catholic power to be reinstated as the

State's intimate ally.

Dread overcame me when he stepped up to the pulpit, for his expression was rigid, his jaw set, his eyes as hard and evasive as they had been the day he recited the story of Baal and the prophets. It seemed as though he was afraid to look at anyone for fear they might try to change his mind.

"Today is a moment of truth for our nation," he began, "our *département,* our village. Today we will see whether religion and divine law will be upheld in France, or whether God himself will be tossed aside like a rotten vine.

"Since the fall of Sedan, the republican parliament has steadily looted its own spiritual inheritance and the inheritance of its children. We have seen the secularization of our schools and the Lord's Day profaned. We have seen the legalization of divorce, a practice condemned by Our Savior Jesus Christ. These laws and practices, handed down to us over the centuries, inscribed in our Holy Scripture, have been cast aside by Jules Ferry and this provisional Republic, which, may I remind you, was created as a temporary solution. The majority of Frenchmen do not want a parliamentary government. They have been living with it until the proper monarch is ready to step forward.

113

The majority of Frenchmen want the reinstitution of stability and righteous governance: they want a new king.

"We need leaders in this country, true, honorable leaders! Our world is changing. It is evident to us even here, in our remote village. The factories are taking men away from the fields, women away from their homes, children away from their schools and games. True, they provide a welcome income, but they threaten the souls of our children. Our young ones leave home too early, before daybreak, and spend their days in dank, dusty interiors, under improper supervision.

"And it is not only in the factories, my faithful ones. No, this corruption is happening here in Rennes-le-Château itself. The most innocent among us, those whom we are counseled by Christ to emulate in the purity of their faith, these very children are losing their faith."

At these words, my heart quickened, for I knew he was speaking of me.

"What kind of a world are we living in when our cherished innocents are questioning the Word of God? When even our youth can conceive of a world without the Creator, a world governed only by humans and the ruthless forces of Nature? Are we intent on raising nihilists? Only the Church can save our children from the desolation of faithlessness. Do not slander the Church in your homes"— this directed toward my Father —"do not allow the blessed bride of Christ to be spoken of as a whore in your kitchens or in the tavern or the streets. If you harbor such thoughts yourself, repent, for you do not know the day of your death. If you have tainted the name of the Lord, if you have sown doubt among his people, I beg you, repent, or you will spend the rest of eternity in the devil's house, paying for your sins with your own flesh and blood."

The church was silent, stunned. The chilly air of the sanctuary seemed to vibrate with the strength of his words. He began again, this time in a softer, more compassionate voice, "But for those who open their hearts and accept the love that our God has offered us in the gift of his only Son, a heaven awaits, more blessed than anything we can conceive of with our meager imaginations. Yes, my friends, believe it — you will see God in heaven.

"Our country faces a moment of adversity. Its citizens are turning away from God, replacing devout leaders with secular ones, repealing laws that have long been in place to ensure the proper education of our children. So the ballot poll today is a solemn moment indeed. We will either triumph in support of our Church and our God or descend another step on the ladder of secularization toward the devil's house. We must vote in support of the Union of the Right, my friends, in support of the restoration of the monarchy and the restoration of the Church to its rightful partnership in the governance of the people. Repent and pray, pray to the Holy Virgin, that we may yet see our countrymen and our brothers in Christ once again walking the path of righteousness."

We sang the Creed, then took communion in a shocked silence. After Mass, people filed out of the church and went immediately home. The village was quiet that day, but the polls were well attended. Bérenger's sermon had a strange effect, for though it infuriated many, including my father, who did not speak to Bérenger for the rest of the week and who blamed him for Durier's loss and the gains the rightists made across the country, it impressed people. It may even have changed several minds. Everyone liked a powerful sermon, everyone liked a priest who spoke his mind and really *said* something. People respected passion; it meant you had a heart, a soul. Bérenger had already won the hearts of most of the women through his magnetism and his pastoral visits, but his sermon won him the esteem of the men as well, both monarchists and republicans, once they got over their anger. They seemed to defer more to him after that Sunday.

For my part, I was deeply disturbed. I hated his threats of damnation, his condemnation of those who might have disagreed. I was furious at him for using my private doubts as material for his sermon, and not only using them, but misrepresenting them: he had implicitly and unfairly accused me of atheism. I had never questioned the existence of God — not in his presence, nor even privately. It was only the actions of the Church I had objected to. But these things — the doctrine of the Church and the presence of God — were so linked in Bérenger's mind, so dependent upon each other, that to question one meant to question — and, by extension, deny — the other.

Once again he had betrayed me, revealing himself to be someone other than the man I thought he was, a man I could not love. I resolved to put him out of my mind, to cultivate another obsession. I asked Michelle who she thought might make me a good husband, and she joyfully listed the names of several boys in our village.

"Martin is dull," I replied.

"But he's reliable. And sweet."

"And how could you think that I would ever love Arnaud? He probably has pimples on his tongue."

"Marie. That's unkind. And anyway, they'll go away in a few years. He's sort of handsome, underneath all that."

We did not speak of the sermon at home. Bérenger deferred to my father's rage, and behaved humbly. He made an effort to uphold civility, greeting everyone politely, speaking with my mother as if all was well. Suppers together were silent. I refused to meet his eyes.

One night, my mother declared that she couldn't sit through another evening of my father's black mood, and if he was so determined to sulk, then he should go do it somewhere else. My father, evidently hurt, set down his fork and stood. "Mother," Claude coaxed, but my mother glared him into silence.

"Politics has no place at our table," she insisted.

I, in turn, glared at Bérenger, who was responsible for this disruption. He sat next to me. The color had risen in his face, and despite myself, I felt my own cheeks warming in sympathy. He looked mortified. As my father donned his jacket, Bérenger stood, gripping his napkin. "Edouard. Please consider my point of view. I have an obligation to express the views of the Church. Grant me that, anyway."

My father pulled his cap on his head, and left, the door slamming behind him.

"Edouard!" Bérenger called after him.

"Let him sulk. He'll get over it soon enough," said my mother.

"But what if the Church is wrong?" I blurted out.

"Don't you start, Marie," my mother said.

"I don't believe the Church to be wrong in this case," Bérenger said.

"When do you ever believe the Church to be wrong?" I asked. Claude was staring at me gleefully, entertained by my audacity. Michelle looked anxious.

"In the past. Certainly. On occasion."

"Such as?"

"Marie, don't be impudent," said my mother.

"I can't think of anything at the moment," Bérenger said, stabbing his fork into a piece of meat, as if to change the topic.

"I can," I said. "Anyway, I don't think you really believe that. That the Church has made mistakes. I think you believe it's infallible."

"It is, isn't it?" Michelle offered, in an effort to lighten the tone of the conversation, to make it an intellectual exercise. But argument was not her forte. "The Pope is anyway," she added, unconvincingly.

"How would you know if the Church made a mistake?" I continued. "You seem so intent on defending it, how would you be able to tell if it overstepped its bounds, if it did something indefensible?"

"Marie," my mother warned. "You will not speak that way to Monsieur *le curé.*"

"You sound like Father," said Claude, giggling.

"And what's wrong with that?" I snapped.

"I understand your point, Marie," Bérenger continued. "One can't trust an institution run by men to be infallible. But the Church is not just a creation of man." He turned toward me, his knee touching the edge of my seat. "It was established by Christ and is run according to the word of God. It is his Kingdom on earth, in the world but not of it. It is as holy a thing as we have." He gripped my arm. I dropped my knife. "I hold tight to it, Marie, because it is from Christ. It is God's unfolding revelation, and for that reason I will always,

always defend it."

We stared at each other as his words rang out in the silent room. His grip just above my wrist relaxed as the moment lengthened. I was aware of the others, but I dared not move, for I didn't want him to drop my arm. I held his gaze until he released me. He looked at his plate, evidently flustered.

"Bravo, Monsieur *le curé*," said my mother. Her eyes were wet. I feared she might applaud.

Fortunately, the preparations for Michelle's wedding soon distracted all of us. To pay for the trousseau — a surprise for Michelle — my father spent his free hours fashioning several fancy hats to sell to old customers, and so was too busy to bear a grudge. Our house became civil once more. Joseph dined with us more regularly, which helped alleviate any persisting tension. In church, Bérenger resumed a milder tone in his sermons.

It was a hopeful time in the village. The harvest had been good, grain and grapes both. Bérenger declared it a blessing from God, and it did seem that way. The year's plenty allayed ancient resentments: old foes shook hands, gossip became less malicious. The harvest festival was raucous that year.

All the village turned out. The Verdiés opened the new wine and most of us drank until we were giddy or sick. Mme Ditandy, mistress of one of the larger houses in the village, made a gorgeous harvest bouquet — a cross of dried maize, lilies, and grass — and M. Ditandy hung it above the entrance to the square for all to see. M. Malet played his accordion, Messieurs Baudot and Fauré joined him on guitar, my father and M. Lébadou sang, and we danced into the early-morning hours.

Our family, as a kind of surrogate family for Bérenger, finally began to gain acceptance that fall. Mme Paul came out to chat with Mother as she was hanging the laundry; Mme Gautier, the butcher's wife, became her good friend. And, most memorable of all, Michelle and Joseph married in a wedding that entranced the whole village. Michelle swept her beautiful black hair into a sophisticated twist and circled it with a garland of anemones. She wore a silk dress that Joseph had bought for her with a bodice of lace that lay like sea foam at her throat. Mother and I helped her dress, and I kissed her before the ceremony and whispered encouragements in her ear.

Then Toussaint came, and with it, the beginning of winter. The oaks, figs, and laurels were bare, the thistles flowerless. It rained for days at a time. The red soil absorbed the rain thirstily but still blew in the wind, dirtying the stucco houses.

One morning, as I was in the midst of preparing the midday dinner, M. Deramon, the postmaster, arrived with a letter for Bérenger. He refused to give it to me until I wiped my hands on a towel, and even then, he warned me to handle it carefully. "Can't you see who it's from?" he admonished, his arthritic finger poking the return address: Monseigneur Calvet, Carcassonne. "Monsieur *le curé* is not at his desk, otherwise I would have brought it to him directly."

"Don't worry, monsieur, I'm not going to add it to the stew." I set it on the chair by the door. M. Deramon eyed me suspiciously before he left. He disapproved of young women.

I handed the letter to Bérenger after I served him dinner. He received it with raised eyebrows and opened it immediately. Mother and I ate as he read.

He gave a short laugh. "I've been suspended," he said. He set the letter on the table beside his bowl.

"What?" said my mother. "What do you mean?"

"The Minister of Religion has suppressed

my salary. I must leave immediately for Narbonne. The bishop has a teaching post at the seminary for me." He slurped his stew as if the news were no more than a minor alteration in plans.

"What?" said my mother, her voice quiet with horror. "How can that be?"

"It is what it is. A priest does not make his own fate." He did not look at either of us. I could tell from his brusque speech that he was wounded.

"But why would they suspend you?" I asked.

"Because I counseled my congregation on how to vote. Because I guided my flock in the appropriate direction for the faithful." He slurped forcefully.

"But they can't do that!" my mother said. She stood. "How can they do that?"

Bérenger shrugged. "The world is changing, Isabelle." He finished his stew and set his spoon beside his plate, then looked at me pointedly, as if he had something important to tell me. I felt my pulse race. I could not tell what was in his mind, but his gaze was full of passion, and I began to hope — against all reason — that he might take me in his arms.

Finally, he set his napkin on the table. "Very good stew, Marie," he said. Then he stood and declared that he would pack his bag.

That night, Mother and Father argued at supper. "This is just what you've wanted since he arrived!" said my mother.

"It is not what I've wanted," my father said. "You know me better than that."

"How do I know you weren't the one who told on him in the first place?"

"Now, Isabelle," said Bérenger. "Edouard would never have done such a thing."

"Shut up!" my mother screamed at Bérenger, shockingly. Claude laughed with surprise. Mother burst into tears and ran upstairs, where she muted her sobs with a pillow.

"You'll have someone else to continue your catechism, Claude," said Bérenger. Claude nodded solemnly.

"We'll miss you, Bérenger," said my father.

"I'll miss all of you," said Bérenger, looking at me. "Very much."

NATZARET

They reached Natzaret on the day before Shabbat, climbing the hill into town. Some of the townspeople welcomed them joyfully, but Yeshua's mother — also called Miryam — ushered him into the house, her face tight with anxiety. "There are people here who want to kill you," she said. "They have heard what you have been saying." She pleaded with him to stay home that night, not to come to the synagogue at sundown, for she feared for his life. But he scolded her.

"So they're not happy with me." He shrugged. "Should this keep me from worshipping my Father?"

But Miryam was frightened. She watched anxiously as Yeshua and his brother Yakov donned their prayer shawls and phylacteries. Miryam held the fringe of Yeshua's shawl as he prepared to go to the synagogue, and when he shook her off and left with his family, she opened her throat and howled as loudly as a cow bearing her calf. Kefa struck her and she fell to the floor. He closed the door and barred the exit from the outside. "Do not open your mouth while we are gone," he said, "or I will cut out your tongue myself."

The fear came then, overtaking her like the quiet night. The air was cooling quickly as the light left the sky. She strained to hear voices, song, anything from the synagogue, but she could not. Only the crickets offered a respite from the unanswerable silence. But soon their chirping became louder and louder, swelling into a unison scream. She raced from corner to corner, knocking over stools and baskets like a trapped beast. She fought the urge to throw herself against the mud walls. She could not stay inside.

There was a small ladder leaning against the wall. This she perched on a bench, allowing her to reach the underside of the roof — a covering of mud-caked branches spread across several planks of wood. She scratched at the mud with her fingernails. The ladder tipped beneath her, causing her to fall twice. Once she caught her jaw on the edge of the bench and bit into her tongue, tasting blood. Eventually, a few branches came loose and fell to the floor. She tore at the roof then, pulling more branches onto herself and tossing them aside, until she had opened a hole large enough to climb through. Then she grabbed the edge of one of the planks and, exerting all her effort, pulled herself up through the hole. Yeshua's family would be angry with her for destroying the roof — they would probably forbid her from entering the house again, but she did not care, so frightened she was by the night and his absence and by the unknown fate that awaited him.

She could see the synagogue from here: the door was closed, but a flickering light leaked from beneath it. She jumped to the ground and ran there, her skirts in her hand. The door opened with a creak, releasing the scent of the mint that had been sprinkled on the floor before the service. She hesitated at the entrance, afraid she might be discovered. But no one came, so she continued in, circling the inner room to find the stairs that led to the balcony, where the women sat. A ring of children played knucklebones at the door; she crept behind them and slid against the wall, trying to keep out of sight. Yakov's wife sat with her daughter on her lap and Yeshua's mother sat next to them, stroking her granddaughter's hand.

One of the boys in the ring — the son of Yakov — ran to whisper something in his mother's ear. She turned and then nudged Yeshua's mother, who also turned. They studied Miryam curiously. Earlier that day, Yakov's wife had asked Yeshua's mother who "that woman" was. "Yeshua sits by her and walks with her," she had said, her voice full of implication. "Has he found his new wife?" Yeshua's mother had shaken her head and sighed; she did not know, she said, but she hoped not. She had seen Miryam twitching and whispering to herself.

Miryam could not see well through the screen, but she could hear. It was Yeshua chanting now. She knew his voice better than her own. It sang out with solemn passion the verse from Yeshayah, "The Spirit of the Lord is upon me. He has sent me to bind up the brokenhearted, to proclaim liberty to the captives. To proclaim the year of the Lord's favor." Then there was a pause, and she felt her heart rise into her throat.

"Today," he said, "this scripture is fulfilled."

There was a tense silence and then an explosion of sibilant whispers. The children stopped their game and looked toward the screen.

Yeshua continued, "I speak to you in the Spirit of the Lord God of Yisrael. His day has come. The lame walk! The blind see! Demons flee from him! Rejoice in his name!"

"You are out of order," said the *chazzan,* standing next to him on the bima. "Please."

"I have come to tell you that the Kingdom of God is here. You've all been waiting — you need wait no longer!"

"Who are you to say that you speak in the Spirit of the Lord?" thundered a broad-shouldered man.

"Why do you question me?" Yeshua responded.

"You expect us to swallow what you're saying? You, the son of Yosef the carpenter?"

"You think I am a charlatan because you have not seen my miracles for yourselves."

Another voice spoke, low and gruff, "That's right. We have people in need of healing here, among us, in your home country."

Another voice: "Why did you not heal your father, if God gave you such a gift? Why not your wife?"

Several voices spoke at once now, some shouting. One finally emerged, the loudest: "Even if he can do such things, how do we know it's God who has given him this power?"

Then there came a great crash. Miryam rushed forward with the other women and children, and pressed her nose against the screen. Yeshua had thrown the chair from the bima, and it had splintered on the ground below him. The men closest to the platform were covering their heads; one had fallen to the ground and was being helped up by another.

"I should have known this would happen here!" Yeshua roared. "I should have predicted you — the people of my own village — would receive me with hatred and loathing! But listen to me, Natzaret! In the days of Eliyahu, when the heavens gave no water for three and a half years, how many in Yisrael were made widows? How many starved? And yet God sent Eliyahu only to Zarephath in Sidon. In Sidon! And in the days of Elisha, when so many were lepers, how many were cleansed in Yisrael? Only one! Naaman the Syrian!"

"What are you saying, Yeshua?" someone shouted. "That God has no love for his own people?"

"When his people scorn his words, spoken to them in love, when they spit on his offering to them, how can he love them?"

The men's voices then erupted in rage, a roar so loud it seemed to shake the foundations of the synagogue, even the bedrock of the mountain. Women grabbed their children and ran downstairs, fleeing the chaos. Only Miryam and Yeshua's mother remained. They watched the men rush toward the bima in one movement, like water filling a hole. Five of them scrambled up the steps to the pulpit and surrounded Yeshua, yelling and pushing. One of the men — broad-shouldered and the tallest of the five — wrapped his arms around Yeshua's chest and pulled him toward the stairs while the others followed, still shouting. They were met at the base of the stairs by several of

Yeshua's followers. Andreas grabbed the legs of the broad-shouldered man in an effort to topple him, but another man pulled him off. Kefa fought with another man and Yakov and Yochanan tussled with three others. More men leapt into the center of the struggle until the whole grappling body of men resembled a great beast, thrashing in pain.

The *chazzan,* still standing on the bima, shouted, "Stop! Stop! You are desecrating God's holy day! You are desecrating Shabbat!" over and over, his voice breaking.

Miryam began to wail and the noise raised several heads. But the broad-shouldered man was dragging Yeshua toward the door, helped by two others who held his feet and legs. Several followed, though most were still engaged in the fighting. Miryam and Yeshua's mother rushed downstairs.

The men dragged Yeshua to the escarpment just beyond the synagogue. Hundreds of feet below, past jagged, jutting rocks, a thin stream wound.

"Noah! Let go of him!" screamed Yeshua's mother.

"Go home, Miryam," one of them said. "You've been a good mother. Go home now." He approached her, his arm extended, but she moved away. She was trembling.

"He's done nothing to deserve this death," she called out again. "He is a son of this town, a son of his father, a son of God, like any of you! Let him go!"

Yeshua struggled, but the broad-shouldered man called Noah held him too tightly.

"He speaks of God's love as if he alone knew what it was to be loved by God," Noah said. "He is a blasphemer and should be killed!" He heaved Yeshua toward the cliff.

"Don't do it, Noah!" shouted a voice from behind Miryam. It was Yakov, Yeshua's brother. "Do you want the mark of Cain on your forehead for the rest of your days? Yeshua is your brother, just as he is mine."

Noah hesitated just long enough for Miryam to rush forward headfirst and butt him in the gut like a goat. Startled, he stumbled and released his grip on Yeshua. "Are you God's arbiter," Miryam screamed, "that you may presume to know his will, to know to whom he grants his favor? How can you call him a blasphemer, he who has put an end to the suffering of so many? What can you do but inflict suffering?" She spat at his feet and then ground the spittle into the dirt with her heel. "May you die one thousand deaths, each more painful than the last!"

"Hark, the demoniac speaks!" said a man standing next to Noah. The others laughed.

"Get gone, woman," said Noah, pushing her aside. "You risk your life meddling in the affairs of men."

Meanwhile, Levi, one of the twelve who had just come running from the synagogue, clasped Yeshua to his chest and led him away from Noah and the cliff. Andreas, Shimon, and Yochanan came to stand beside Levi and Yeshua.

Then the *chazzan* approached. He walked slowly, his head bowed, his fingers tangled in his beard. They waited. The group's anger seemed to dissipate in the night air, making room for the deeper, graver sensation of shame.

"You have behaved like children," the *chazzan* said, his voice trembling with rage. "You have profaned God's holy day, defiled our meeting place. Is this what he asks of you? I am ashamed, I am disgusted, I am heartbroken."

Noah stepped forward, addressing the *chazzan*. "Rabbi," he began, "is it not Law that a blasphemer should be put to death?"

"What is the blasphemy, please, Noah, that Yeshua has committed?"

"You said yourself — desecrating Shabbat."

The *chazzan* sighed. "The destruction of property is not a true desecration of Shabbat, according to the Law. Nothing to deserve death. Though it does go against the spirit of the day, the spirit of peace." He looked at Yeshua sternly, then turned back to Noah. "Your violence, Noah, also was out of place."

Noah breathed deeply, as if to control his anger. He raised his eyes toward the sky, where a single star shone against the black.

The *chazzan* continued. "You must learn not to resort to force. Debate and disagreement is all well in God's sight, for it is a way to come to know him better. But violence is an abomination. Make your offering, Noah, and pray for God's forgiveness. And the rest of you." The *chazzan* then turned to Yeshua. "Yeshua."

"Yes, Rabbi," said Yeshua. He stepped forward.

"You are a gifted teacher and healer, Yeshua. God has blessed you with many gifts. But how can you say that God does not love his people? I don't wonder that Noah became so angry. You must respect the eternal love of God for Yisrael. You, too, should pray for forgiveness."

135

Yeshua bent his head. "Yes, Rabbi," he said.

"We have enough trouble from Rome," said the *chazzan*. "Why do we make more among our own kind?" All were silent.

Then Noah spoke once more. "Rabbi. I have a proposition. You say that Yeshua is a gifted healer. I don't doubt it. But why won't he perform a healing for us? Demonstrate his skill? Why doesn't he simply heal this poor demoniac woman he travels with?"

All eyes turned toward Miryam, who was standing close to Noah. She looked from man to man and then turned her head sharply to Yeshua. He stood in the center of the group. He looked weary and sallow, as if he needed a good meal and a good rest. She could see he wanted to make the attempt, if only to show them what he could do, but she also saw that he would fail. He was too tired. From behind him, she saw Yakov's wife running toward them — and she thought of the ravaged roof, the fallen ladder and upended bench, the branches and mud flaked on the floor.

"Yeshua," said the *chazzan,* "Noah makes an honest request."

Miryam watched as Yeshua turned to her and lifted his hands weakly toward the sky — but she could not stay to see him fail, nor could she face the rage of Yakov's wife. She ran, following the edge of the cliff until she found a narrow goat path leading down the steep escarpment. She scrabbled down this path, grabbing at rocks and thorny brush to steady herself. She heard Yeshua's voice calling her, and knew that he and the others would catch her if she did not hurry.

She noticed a small opening in the rock, just behind a stubborn sapling growing out of the mountainside. She slithered into it. It opened into a spacious cave with enough room to stand in. It was cool and damp. She wrapped her cloak more tightly around her shoulders.

"He who touches the earth and it melts," she whispered, then listened to her voice resound.

She climbed onto a flat stone close to the wall and curled her knees into her chest. She would not sleep. When the dawn light penetrated the darkness in the cave, she would crawl out into the open air again and hike down the mountain to meet Yeshua and the twelve on their way out of Natzaret.

CHAPTER FIVE

I mourned the *loss* of Bérenger. I had grown accustomed to the delicious anticipation I felt before each meal, knowing I would be near him, and now the days stretched on joylessly, one more tedious than the next. The future seemed to promise only monotony, an infinitude of chores: chopping vegetables, plucking chickens, gathering eggs, cleaning out the chicken coop, scrubbing surfaces and chasing interminably after dust, folding and hanging clothing and linens, milking Geneviève day and night, gathering wood for the hearth. The unending work! It took so much labor simply to exist! And without Bérenger, existence seemed thin and beside the point.

I was not alone. The whole village missed him — his affability, his broad smile, his generosity. We were cruel to each of the visiting priests who were sent to us. Parents kept their children from catechism class;

people boycotted Mass. The fall that had seemed so blessed, so full of promise, became a dismal winter. Fed by the village's new obsession — the identity of the tattler who had gotten Bérenger suspended — gossip flared like a forest fire, demolishing every reputation in its path.

Mother still would not absolve Father of guilt. She was sullen in his presence. When he tried to make a joke, she glared, and when he touched her hip affectionately, she swatted him. Finally, after a few weeks of this behavior, my father could take no more. "Here, Isabelle," he said, thrusting a paper in her face. "Maybe this will convince you of my innocence." It was a petition protesting Bérenger's suspension. His was the first signature. "Bring this around the village," he said. "Get as many people as you can. We'll show it to the mayor."

"What can the mayor do?" retorted my mother. But she picked it up and weighed it in her hands, as if it were an attractive fruit she was considering at market.

The next day, Mother began circulating the petition. She brought it first to Mesdames Gautier and Paul, who agreed to help her collect signatures. A week later, armed with more than a hundred names, they presented the petition to Mayor Laporte.

The mayor, duly impressed, stamped it with his seal and sent it to the bishop, accompanied by a letter of his own.

It was a lonely time for me. Michelle and Joseph had moved to Carcassonne a few weeks after their wedding. I began to visit Mme Laporte more frequently. If she was busy, she let me into the library, where I happily ensconced myself among her books. Bijou, her cat, kept me company. With a hunger born of isolation and small-minded provincialism, I read Zola, Voltaire, Hugo, Flaubert, and Stendhal, wondering at the expanse of knowledge, the breadth of life — both imaginary and real — beyond our little village. I read Darwin's *Origin of Species,* and was shocked and bewildered by the implications of his assertions. I read Renan's *Life of Jesus* in one afternoon, thrilled by his illicit ideas about the humanity of Christ. To his lights, Christ was not the messiah, not God, but a radical visionary, a man who believed in the possibility of achieving the ideal. And he was fallible; he had preached about the imminent end of the world, and time had proven him wrong. Renan's courage became my new standard. I vowed to imitate his daring, to honor my own thirst for truth over doctrine, and in doing so, grew more disdainful, more distant from the Church. It was just as well that Bérenger had gone, I told myself. He was too old-fashioned, too doctrinaire. How could I ever have imagined we could love one another?

As my reading and my knowledge deepened, I found it hard to leave Madame's library and return to our small, crumbling house, where the wind blew through the widening cracks in the walls with greater and greater force. As I worked, my mind journeyed — to Paris, where women carried poodles like purses. To Brazil, where men penetrated the wild Amazon in slow-moving barges, scouring the overhanging branches for a new species of monkey. To the American West, where land stretched on — plain, river, mountain, enormous sky — where herds of buffalo thundered across open spaces. My old longings to explore and see the world returned full force as my life in Rennes — my loneliness, my ceaseless chores — began to seem unbearable.

My visits with Mme Laporte were no longer secret — my mother knew. I had told her on a whim one afternoon when she asked me where I was going, and to my surprise, she did not object. She simply asked me why, and when I told her that Madame knew a great deal about history and I liked reading her books, she nodded gravely. She approved of study. As long as I completed my chores, she said, I could spend my free time how I liked. I was almost eighteen, after all. But the gossips minded. "Why do you spend your time shut up inside that castle, a pretty girl like you?" Mme Baptiste once asked me from her window as I walked by.

I shrugged. "What else is there to do?"

Others were of the same opinion as Mme Baptiste. They had long ago learned to tolerate Mme Laporte's eccentricities, but were reluctant to accept a developing eccentric in one of their own children.

Then a strange thing happened. Gérard, who had disappeared so suddenly from Michelle's life, reappeared in mine. He stopped me one afternoon as I was walking to the château. I greeted him, intent on moving on — I was still embarrassed by the scene I'd witnessed the summer before.

"Where are you off to, then?" he asked.

"To see Mme Laporte."

"Why?" he asked. "Don't you know she's a Jew?"

This startled me, for two reasons. Michelle and I had entertained the thought that Madame might be Jewish when we first became fascinated with her, but I had not

142

thought of it since then, and had not imagined our idle fantasies to be true. Secondly, Gérard pronounced the word *Jew* with alarming distaste. I'd grown protective of Madame. She was an anomaly, a learned woman with a formidable intellect, and therefore precious. I knew her mind threatened people; it did me, on occasion. But her intelligence and her gentleness seemed to me to be qualities more deserving of emulation than derision. Whenever people so much as wondered about her in my presence, I defended her snappishly.

"Jesus was a Jew," I countered. And I continued on my way.

That was a new idea for me, gleaned from Renan. I had never before thought of Jesus as Jewish, nor had the Church given me any reason to think he was. As the Church presented him, Jesus was the anti-Jew, born Jewish but in his life transcending, even rejecting, his birth. The implication was always that to be Jewish was shameful, wrong. When Jesus rebuked the Pharisees, he was not merely rebuking their hypocrisy, their slavish attendance to the letter rather than the spirit of the law, he was rebuking their identity — or so it seemed, according to what I had been taught. The title *Jew,* in my mind, and in the minds of most of my fellow Catholics, equaled *Pharisee,* which, through the language of the New Testament and the story of Christ's passion, translated as *traitor* or *enemy.*

But I understood the Pharisees to be different from the Israelites, the ancient Hebrews that we read about in the Old Testament. The Israelites were recognized as our ancestors, a people to revere and cherish, the founders of our faith. It was a contradictory position, for while the Jews before the time of Christ were depicted as honorable, after his arrival they transformed into evildoers, godkillers — in the worst language I heard from the pulpit — or, at best, ignorant, misguided fools who knew not what they did. I wish I could say I objected to this attitude from the beginning, but I did not. I knew no better.

But: Gérard. After that day he first spoke to me, he appeared more frequently — passing me on the street or walking by our house when I happened to be outside, as he had with Michelle. Each day he greeted me and then stood in place, waiting for me to say something. I was not as skilled as Michelle at conversation, nor did I have the advantage of liking Gérard, so our interactions were always strange and uncomfortable. I could not figure out what he wanted from me. He couldn't be courting me — he was far too handsome and had long had his pick of the girls in the village, from whom, as Michelle had told me, he had sampled widely. What's more, it was clear that a more unlikely pair could not be found. It was not that I was ugly — my skin was smooth and my figure appealing. Inspired by an engraving I'd found in one of Madame's books, I had taken to wearing my thick hair swept back in a loose topknot, which caused it to puff about my face. My mother thought it excessive, and it undoubtedly served to cement the notions people were forming about my eccentricity, but I thought it flattered me.

Gérard evidently thought so, too, for he complimented me on it. "It brings out your pretty eyes," he said. I did not thank him; I thought he was teasing me. But he went on complimenting me day after day — on my dress, my hair, my face, and even, backhandedly, my intelligence. "You read too much," he said. "Girls shouldn't be as smart as you." Soon it became clear that despite the obvious foolishness of the match, Gérard was indeed courting me. Claude gloated.

I am sure our relationship would not have evolved much beyond those initial conversations had my mother not noticed his interest and encouraged it. She sent me on errands to his family's farm to buy bottles of their wine just at dinnertime, so they would be obliged to invite me to eat with them. And whenever Gérard walked by, she rushed out to greet him and invited him in. He was not what she'd hoped for as a husband for me — Joseph, Michelle's husband, came closest to the ideal: a kind and responsible man with a steady, generous income. But Joseph had also taken Michelle away from us. Gérard, she knew, was unlikely to leave Rennes-le-Château.

My mother's enthusiasm was more than evident to Gérard, even if mine wasn't. I was awkward and strange with him. The fact was that he bored me to the point of disgust. His good looks had made him proud; he bragged about the number of girls who were in love with him, as if to notify me of how grateful I should be that he chose to spend his time with me. He talked of his family's vineyard and goats, narrating each day's progress in excruciating detail. Worst of all, he couldn't read. When I unwisely spoke to him about Renan, he rolled his eyes. "Here she goes again," he said, "talking nonsense." His mind and spirit were wholly provincial. Everything I had come to hate about Rennes seemed embodied in Gérard.

I took refuge in the weekly letters we

received from Bérenger. His kind inquiries after each of us and his accounts of his days in Narbonne softened my memory of his doctrinal militancy. He had been appointed as a teacher at the *petit séminaire,* where boys prepared for the priesthood, and his letters poked gentle fun at the innocence of his students. One was perpetually falling asleep in class; another popped chestnuts in his mouth every time Bérenger's back was turned. Sometimes he wrote about his brother David, who also taught at the seminary. (I gathered David was a heavy drinker, for he was frequently getting into midnight scrapes and having to be rescued from cabarets and other questionable places.) Occasionally, Bérenger alluded to invitations he had received from influential new acquaintances — a count, a duchess, a highly decorated soldier, a prize-winning actress. It appeared that he had become something of a minor hero among his fellow monarchists. He always included a line personally for me, asking whether I'd been reading or how the garden was faring. And he sent gifts: a model ship for Claude, a pretty coral necklace and an embroidered handkerchief for me. I wore both proudly.

"Once I get enough money, I'll buy you a

gold necklace," Gérard said. "With diamonds."

Gérard courted me all that spring. When the lilacs began to bloom, he brought me bunches of them, telling me that I should wear them in my hair. I left them scattered on the table. He would bring baskets of food just at midday and ask my mother if he could take me for a picnic, knowing, of course, that she'd order me to go. I went and nibbled sullenly on the bread and cheese. He filled my glass with wine and then scolded me for not drinking enough. "What's wrong with it? My mother bottled this especially for you." And when I finished the glass just to keep him quiet, he filled it again to the top.

"I'll get drunk," I protested.

"Drunk girls are more fun," he said.

I will admit to being moved by his good looks. His lips were red and full, like a woman's, and they stood out appealingly against the flat planes of his tanned cheeks. He wore his hair longer than the other boys in town, letting his loose curls dance at his ears and neck. He was strong and well-proportioned — more lithe and lanky than Bérenger. He always looked as if he'd just come from a party, smiling rakishly and ready to frolic. There were times on our picnics when, tipsy from the wine he'd urged on me, I could look at his face, framed by the wind-bent grasses and the sharp blue sky, and think it might not be so bad to marry him. There were times when I allowed him to kiss me, when I gave myself over to the sensual pleasure of his lips on my face and neck, his broad hands against my back, pressing me to him. But then, inevitably, he would speak and I would remember how dull he was.

He was persistent — almost admirably so, considering how poorly I treated him. He thought I was testing him. He'd say, "How am I doing so far, Marie? Give me some idea," as if I were keeping score. He laughed off my rejections, which became more and more biting. I once told him that if he were a sheep dog, the sheep would herd him. "What do you mean?" he asked.

Then, one day that spring, a month or so after Gérard had begun courting me, we received news that Bérenger would be returning. The mayor proudly waved the bishop's letter, declaring that it was our petition that had brought him back. Whether it was or it was simply that Bérenger had completed the term of his suspension, we couldn't tell, but the fact of his imminent return rekindled hope in the village. My mother finally forgave my father, who sent Claude and me downstairs to sleep by the hearth that night.

Spirits grew buoyant. Many sentences began with the words, "When Monsieur *le curé* returns . . ." and the gist of what followed was that all would once again be well. Rumors of the tattler were still bruited about — Madame's name was mentioned, just one more amid the others — but their pace decreased and their savagery diminished. To my mother's delight, my father rounded up a group of men, including M. Baptiste, M. Paul, and old M. Baudot, and set to refurbishing the presbytery. They swept the floor of debris, hauled out the rotting bedposts and chairs, patched and whitewashed the walls, and replaced the cracked roof tiles until the place was livable. They blissfully hammered, hefted, sawed, and caulked, walking around with pliers and putty knives hanging from their belts like swords and daggers. When they were through, my mother and I cleaned the place thoroughly and arranged an assortment of donated furniture.

I was overjoyed. I let myself imagine that Bérenger was returning for the love of me, that he had been tortured by his absence from me, and had gone to the bishop begging to be reinstated at Rennes. I felt I no longer had to endure Gérard's advances, no longer had to entertain the notion of marrying him, now that my true love was returning. Even if I had to live the rest of my life as I had lived it until this point — cleaning, cooking, mending, tending — I felt that if I could do it in Bérenger's presence, I would be happy. He would be my freedom.

I began to ignore Gérard. My mother scolded me fiercely. "You don't have to marry him, Marie. But you may not treat him like your dog. Have some pity for the poor boy."

As summer neared and the date of Bérenger's return approached, I grew anxious. I worried that he might have forgotten me. I dreamt of embracing him. Gérard's kisses — as disgusted as they made me after the fact — had aroused a new awareness in me. What would a caress be like from someone I truly loved? I longed for it, dreamt of it, ached for it, while simultaneously punishing myself for even considering such a thing. A kiss from Bérenger, however sweet, however passionate, however yearned for, would be an unforgivable transgression. Even if I had rejected the Church, even if I became a diehard anti-cleric like my father, it would still be a mortal sin to tempt a priest.

I was in this Abélardian frame of mind when Gérard caught me by the arm in front of the château one afternoon. He said he had something he wanted to speak to me about, in private. I answered him roughly. "What do you want?"

"Come here, Marie," he said angrily. "Can't you slow down for a minute?" He led me across the square to the water pump and then down the stairs to the grassy hill that supported the ruined wall of the castle. I backed into the branch of a flowering tree, which caught in my hair like fingers.

He looked at me fiercely. "I want to ask you if you'll marry me," he said.

I laughed. "What?"

He looked away, at the fields beyond the road, greening with wheat and barley. "You heard what I said."

"Why are you asking me that, Gérard?" I said, in disbelief. "Honestly. Why?"

"What do you mean?" He was stung.

"We're completely unsuited. Why don't you ask one of the ten other girlfriends you have?"

He gritted his jaw. "I'm asking you."

"Look, Gérard. It's not a good idea, our getting married. We'd kill each other on our wedding night."

"That's not what I'd be doing," he said and wrapped his hand around my neck to pull me toward him.

I knocked it away. "No. More likely, I'd kill myself."

He stared, finally hearing me. "You don't want to marry me?" he said.

"No, Gérard! How can I tell you more plainly? I think you're boring and dull and I don't want to marry you. The end!"

"You're a whore, is what you are." His words came like a hand against my face. "You're just waiting for that no-good priest to come back so you can open your legs for him, aren't you? Can't you see I'm trying to save you from becoming a priest's whore?"

I was shocked, not only at the violence of his words but also that he'd guessed my feelings for Bérenger. I turned away and tried to walk back to the stairs, but he grabbed my elbow and pulled me to him, then pinned me against the castle wall with his hips and began kissing me with an open, biting mouth. I screamed, but his mouth muffled the sound. He grabbed at my breasts with one hand and with the other lifted my skirt, and fumbled with my waistband. He would have torn off my underclothes had Mme Laporte not appeared at his side, a small silver pistol in her hand.

"Why don't you go home now, Gérard," she said calmly.

He released me; I moved away. He stepped slowly down the grassy slope. When he reached the path, he sprinted to the top of the hill, where it joined with the main road that led through town. Safe there, he turned and shouted, "The whore and the traitor — a perfect match! Marie, did you ever think about who betrayed your darling priest? Don't you know never to trust a Jew?" Then he disappeared around the corner, in the direction of the village.

I tried to straighten my dress, but Gérard had torn the blouse. The best I could do was hold the fabric closed so as not to expose my camisole. Hair fell about my ears and in my eyes. I spat on the ground, then wiped my mouth with the back of my hand.

Madame sighed — one of the few displays of distress I had seen her make. She replaced the safety on the pistol and slipped it into her skirt pocket, then regarded me tenderly. I fought to keep tears from rushing forth. "Come inside, Marie," she said. "Let me lend you a frock." She offered her arm and I took it, more for psychological support than any physical need. We entered the château through the kitchen. Mme Siau raised her eyebrows when we came in, but did not say a word.

Upstairs, Madame selected a dress for me and let me change in her bedroom, shutting the door behind her. I stepped out of my own ruined shift and pulled Madame's linen frock over my head. The bodice was tight; I could not cough without feeling as though I might pop all the buttons off the front. Madame's kindness, her defense of me — armed, even — was the more remarkable thing. The pistol was shocking, but I was so grateful for her intervention that it did not occur to me to wonder why she owned it. Overwhelmed, I shed a few tears.

The bedroom seemed to be hers alone. There was a single bed in the room and a vanity table, as well as a bookshelf and a night table, on which perched a few leather-bound books and a lantern. On the vanity was a brush, a comb, and a mirror, all silver, laid out as if for a guest. I sat at the chair in front of the mirror, and examined myself. My topknot had slipped sideways. My cheeks were blotchy. I looked to be ill, drunk, or an idiot. I unclasped the hairpins and, using Madame's brush, repinned my hair.

Madame's window looked onto the church and the cemetery, just adjacent. I wondered if she really was a Jew, and if so, whether it offended her to have her bedroom look onto a church. I figured Gérard must have been making up lies. From what I knew of Jews, they kept to themselves and did not intermarry with Catholics, which Mayor Laporte most certainly was. It puzzled me again, the fact of their marriage — especially after seeing this room, which was so clearly the room of a woman who spent her nights alone.

I returned the brush to its place on the table and left the room to meet Madame in the library, just down the hall. There she poured me a small glass of brandy. I sipped it, welcoming its searing path down my throat.

"The dress suits you," said Madame.

"Thank you," I said, pulling self-consciously at the bodice.

"Sit down, Marie." She gestured toward a chair.

"Thank you, Madame, for your kindness. I'm in your debt."

"I am glad I was here."

"How did you know we were there? Could you hear us?"

"I saw you from my window. When Gérard led you away by the wrist it made me wary. I don't like to see my friends in danger." It was the first time she had called me a friend. I felt a rush of affection and with it a sudden desire for intimacy.

"Gérard is a pig," I said, my voice trembling. "He did the same thing to Michelle last summer. I walked in on them." The thought had not occurred to me until I'd spoken it that Michelle might not have welcomed his advances. My rage grew, fueled in part by remorse for having possibly misjudged my sister. "And the things he said about you! He should be in prison."

"The things he said about me are true, Marie," she said. She was standing by the fireplace, which emanated warmth from its bed of white ash. In her hand was a small china cat, which she stroked with her thumb. "I am a Jew. And I did write to the Minister of Religion last fall after the sermon Monsieur *le curé* gave before the October elections. Though I do not consider myself a traitor. That's Gérard's interpretation."

I felt winded, as if I'd received a blow to the stomach. I pressed my lips to the outside of my glass and held them there. When I lifted them away, they left a foggy print.

"I hope I haven't betrayed your trust," Madame continued. She set the cat on the mantelpiece above the fireplace and walked toward her desk. "I was not aware that *l'abbé* was a special friend of yours. Though, to be sure, I will not take Gérard's word as to the truth of that." Opening the top drawer of her desk, she removed the pistol from her pocket and replaced it in the drawer. Then she sat behind the desk on the edge of her chair and folded her hands on the ink blotter.

"Well, no, he's not. I mean, not in the way Gérard says." My cheeks burned. I sipped the brandy once more. "He's family, really," I muttered.

Madame nodded and looked at her hands. "I am sorry if I have caused you pain."

I took a deep breath. "Why did you do that? Write to the Minister of Religion?"

She sighed again. "I did not agree with the opinion that *l'abbé* expressed in his sermon. I felt his ideas were dangerous. I still do."

"Why?" I asked accusingly. I agreed with her of course, but was not in the mood to say so.

She smiled sadly. "I should have thought you would understand why."

"Because you're Jewish?" I said meanly.

"It has nothing to do with my origins. Religion must have no role in just governance."

"But you didn't even know him," I protested. I felt the pulse of anger spread through my fabric-constricted chest as I spoke. "You never went to church except for that one day."

"I only needed a day to hear what I heard."

"You wanted to get rid of him."

"Marie, I do not consider it wise for us to discuss this now. You are distraught and you must rest. Please come back tomorrow if you like." She stood and walked to the door. I understood the cue and followed.

I did not return the next day, nor the next. Instead, I busied myself with helping my mother prepare the presbytery for Bérenger's return. I told no one about Gérard. Mother did not ask why he stopped visiting; I suppose she figured he had finally come to his senses. Gérard, for his part, did his best to spread gossip about me, telling people he'd lost interest in me because I was frigid and mean. I endured dirty looks and cruel jokes from his friends. I missed Madame's library, missed my afternoons of reading by the hearth in her rose fauteuil with Bijou purring on my lap, missed Mme Siau's coffee and cakes, missed Mme Laporte herself and her gentle erudition. But I could not forgive her, regardless of how much I might have agreed with her as-

sessment of the sermon. She had sent
Bérenger away from me, and that fact
overtook all reason.

I looked, instead, to Bérenger's return.

He arrived on a July afternoon, almost
exactly a year after he'd come the first time.
The clouds were high, the air dry and warm.
We all gathered at the door of the presbytery, where the mayor made a speech and
my father and the other proud renovators
stood aside, grinning. Bérenger shouted for
joy when he saw the cleaned and furnished
presbytery and clapped each man on the
back. He hugged my father hard. "This was
your idea, Edouard, was it not? Now I'll be
out of your hair."

My father laughed. "I won't deny it," he
replied, returning the hug.

M. Flèche, the baker, served an orange-
chocolate cake with buttercream icing, and
we all sat at the outdoor tables in front of
the *tabac,* eating cake, drinking coffee and
wine, and listening to Bérenger talk about
Narbonne.

"I spent entirely too much time with
adolescent boys! And the whole city smells
of rotting fish. I prayed every day to be sent
back here, to this beautiful village."

"Come now," my father prompted.

"You're misleading this group. What about all those wealthy new friends of yours? You planning to keep that a secret?"

Bérenger laughed. "I should have known you wouldn't let me get away with it."

"Did you really get to meet Imogène Lille?" asked Mme Fauré, her baby on her hip. Mme Lille was an actress whose fame extended even as far as our remote village.

"I went to several salons at her house."

Mme Fauré gasped.

"She's a very gracious lady. Very concerned with political affairs."

M. Lébadou, evidently annoyed, said, "Why'd you come back here, then, if you were such a personage there?"

"Do you have to ask?" Bérenger replied, his eyes twinkling. "How could I stay away from all of you?"

"And tell us, Monsieur *le curé*," began M. Baudot in his slow, husky old man's voice. "Have you been forgiven? Has the State pardoned you?"

There was a tense silence as we waited for Bérenger's answer. We were unsure whether he might take offense. But he smiled and said pleasantly, "Since when does the State have the power to forgive?"

We luxuriated in the warm afternoon as it extended into evening, drinking, snacking

161

on the sausages and bread brought out by M. Ditandy, who owned the tavern, and reveling in the festive mood. Eventually, most of the women left to tend to children and supper. Darkness fell and a chill entered the air. Mother had gone, as had Claude, who was bored, but I stayed on, having assured Mother I would make sure Father didn't drink too much. When it had gotten quite late, Bérenger, a bit tipsy himself, made an announcement. "I had planned to save this until Sunday, but I can't keep it to myself any longer. We have the good fortune of being graced with a generous gift from a donor who has taken an interest in our village. The gift will provide us with enough money to replace the roof of the church and to begin to renovate the interior. Please, all of you, say a special prayer of thanksgiving tonight for the grace of God and the generosity of strangers."

A murmur rippled through the gathered group. My father spoke up: "Who's the money from?"

"The donor wishes to remain anonymous."

Another murmur.

"We'll have a true temple now," Bérenger continued. "A fitting house of worship. Praise be to God."

There was an awkward silence and then someone offered a "Hallelujah," and a few people echoed him, joining in with applause, which swelled until the whole group was clapping. Bérenger beamed.

I tried to find a private moment with him in the next few days, not only because I wanted to ask whether the anonymous donor was the Austrian archduke, but also to provoke some kind of personal recognition from him, a special greeting for me alone. But it was impossible, for Mother had a thousand chores for me to do at home while she helped him get settled in the presbytery. And Bérenger himself appeared preoccupied, his thoughts almost wholly bent on the execution of his great project: the renovation of the church.

First, he hired a contractor and a team of workers from Limoux to repair the roof. The men hauled a cartload of tiles up the hill and spent sweltering September days laying the tiles beneath the hot sun. Old M. Baudot grumbled about how Bérenger had spent his money on Limoux workers instead of hiring some of the able-bodied young men in Rennes. "He's the one who doesn't like the young ones working in the factories." But on the whole, the town was pleased to see that the church was being cared for.

My hope for a particular acknowledgment from Bérenger was not to be fulfilled. But I didn't mind; his presence was thrilling enough. I performed my duties with a renewed dedication, knowing that now I was doing them, at least in part, for him. I julienned carrots and diced shallots with precision and, when it was my turn to cook, planned elaborate dishes: barbecued pheasant rubbed with rosemary and lavender, a *cousinat* from chestnuts I'd collected myself, rabbit served with cream sauce and juniper berries. On days when I tended to the church — Mother and I had taken to alternating our duties, to alleviate some of the monotony — I ironed the linens reverently, lingering over the stoles and chasubles. I swept and dusted, removing the layer of white silt that sifted into the nave as the men worked on the roof. I washed and dried the cruets, polished the chalice and paten and the candlesticks and trimmed the candles. I replaced the water in the font, which Bérenger blessed every morning before he said Mass. When the deliveries of the Host arrived from Narbonne, I opened them, handling the canisters as if they were baby birds.

I still half-believed in the transubstantiation of the wine and the Host into the blood and body of Christ, even though my anxious questioning had by that time undermined the edifice of my faith. It made no sense. I could argue against it easily, but I could not argue it away. I wanted it to be true, even as I knew it could not be, in much the same way that, as a child, I'd longed for Père Noël to be real even after I knew he wasn't. Such a miracle, and yet so mundane! A daily incarnation. It was the final relic of my faith, and I held it in reserve, tucked deep in the tissues of my heart. Once Bérenger returned, I again went faithfully to Mass, huddling in the chilly nave most mornings at seven, along with my mother and a handful of other women. I scrutinized the dance of his hands over the Host and the wine as he recited the blessings and raised the paten and the chalice skyward, searching for a sign of disturbance, some evidence of the wafer and wine becoming flesh and blood: a drop splashing on the altar, a falling crumb.

Bérenger was pleased with my frequent attendance at Mass. "You've been gathering thistles, Marie," he said, winking. I did not contradict him.

I plotted various methods of catching Bérenger alone, just to talk with him (as I told myself), or perhaps to tell him something about what I'd been reading. I reveled in his presence when he stood close to me, breathing him in, rebelling against my desire to touch his arm, to take his hand. Had he given me any indication that such a touch would be welcome, I might have dared — I was that besotted. Thankfully, he was too consumed by the construction projects. After the work on the church roof was completed, another team of workers, also from Limoux (more grumbles from Baudot), set to work supporting the sanctuary vault, which was threatening to collapse. They bolstered the outer walls by building four new arches in the church interior. Bérenger rarely left the sanctuary all winter.

Despite our best efforts, the church interior was a mess. White dust coated every surface. Walking across the floor was like stepping in an enormous floured cake pan. The pews were sloppily rearranged to accommodate the steel structures that supported the half-built arches. These extended into the center aisle of the nave and blocked the view of the people who sat behind them during Mass. People began to complain, first to Mother and me, and then to Bérenger. We counseled patience. "Would you rather the roof fall in?" Bérenger ca-

166

joled. "Would you rather worship under the open sky, in the wind and the rain?"

It was at this time, in this dusty disarray, that I made our first discovery.

EXORCISM

The night he finally healed her was moonless. He had spent the day preaching under the ruthless sun. She had gone to a nearby well seventeen times for water for him, and each time she had returned with an empty pail, for members of the crowd had stopped her and helped themselves. The last time, she had fallen on the ground in frustration and begun to weep. She could not bear the crowd, how ragged, how incessant it was. So many people, lame, disfigured, diseased. Children with distended bellies and kindling for legs. And everywhere, eyes, enormous eyes, beseeching, like the eyes of goats just before the sacrifice. How could all these needs ever be met? Miryam wept until her tears became shrill laughter and she rolled and thrashed about on the ground.

When her fit subsided, she saw that a small crowd of people had gathered around her.

"Isn't she with him?" one man said.

"She's his wife," responded an old woman.

"Don't be a fool," said another. "How could a devil like that be his wife?"

"If she was his wife, don't you think he'd have healed her by now?"

Miryam scrambled to her feet and ran across the field, away from the stares and condemning voices. She came to a boulder and tucked herself into its shadow, hidden from the crowd. There she stayed until dark fell and the crowd had dispersed.

She could see that the group had lit a fire and gathered around it, but she did not want to join them, for she knew that they were ashamed of her. She wanted Yeshua. She wanted him to heal her, but she was frightened. She had lived with her demons all her life. Who would she be without them?

Still, she wanted to be with him, to care for him. To put her own hands on his sallow, sunken cheeks and stroke her thumbs across his flaking lips, to rest her forehead against his and drink his breath like a tonic. She wanted to feel his rough palms against her skin, to feel them spread across her shoulders and back like wings, to feel them press her belly, cup her hips, to feel them hold her, keep her together, keep her whole, for she felt now that without his hands on her, she might separate from herself, her soul beading like oil in water, beading and then sinking into the dry earth.

"Yeshua!" she shouted. "Yeshua!" Again and again she screamed his name until she heard footsteps thumping toward her. She held out her arms for the embrace she hoped would come — but it was Kefa.

"He's not here," he said. "Can't you be silent?"

"Where is he?" she asked.

"Gone off to pray." Kefa carried a torch and held it close to Miryam's face. She flinched and backed away. "Why don't you bathe? You're filthy."

She hissed at him like a viper. After he left, she fell asleep.

Some hours later, she awoke. It seemed that something had changed near her, as if the wind had suddenly ceased to blow. She sat up and put her hand against the rock, which was still warm from the day's sun. Her fingers brushed something hard and smooth — leather — and she scooted backward, afraid.

"It's me, Miryam," he said. He was sitting on top of the rock, his sandaled feet hanging where her hand had been. He jumped to the ground. "I didn't want to wake you."

She stood. "No," she said. "I mean, thank you."

"Why were you calling me?" he asked.

"You heard me?" she said.

"I wasn't far away."

She didn't know how to respond. He stood before her, the cavity at his throat gently swelling and caving with his breath. The span of his shoulders seemed vast, and she imagined herself encircled in his sinuous arms, his callused, dry palms warming her back. She wanted him to tell her she was special, to say out loud that he loved her more than all the rest. But how could she ask him to make such a statement? His eyes — large, dark, heavy-lidded — made her think of the enervating eyes of the crowd, and she saw that her desire for him was no less desperate and despicable than the desire of the multitudes. She was just another hen pecking at his feet. She turned and ran into the dark.

"Miryam!" he called, and followed her. She ran faster, feeling the strap of her sandals digging into her heels.

"Don't run, Miryam!" he shouted. "You're always running!" She felt a breeze at her elbow from his hand as he tried to catch her, but she pulled her arm out of reach and kept on. The well was up ahead — she'd made the trip often enough that day that she could find it even in the dark. It would be a long fall and the water would be cold, but it would be no darker than the night.

She reached the well and gripped the stone, then threw one leg over the side. A cold wind rose from the hole, and she balanced for a moment, feeling the contrast in temperature between the warm night and the frigid depth of the well. In that moment, he grabbed her around the waist and dragged her off the edge, scraping the inside of her thigh against the stone. He threw her to the ground and stood over her, panting.

She curled into a ball.

"Stand up," he said. When she did not move, he shouted it: "Stand up, Miryam!" He grabbed her wrist and pulled her to her feet, but she fell again to her knees, her face in the dirt, and covered her head with her arms. He could beat her if he chose; she would not look him in the eye again.

"Miryam!" he shouted again, a lament. Then she felt him kneel before her, felt his hands cover her own. He whispered, still out of breath, "Don't you know, Miryam? Don't you know how I need you?"

She began to weep, her tears falling on the dusty ground. He took her by the elbows and gently lifted her until she was facing him. He smoothed her hair, brushed the dust from her face, cupped her chin in his hand, and then kissed her lightly on the mouth. His lips were dry. She kept her eyes closed, wanting only to feel, not to see. His breath warmed her face. Then it was gone. She opened her eyes. He knelt in the dust facing her, his hands open, palms upturned, as if waiting for her to place a gift into them.

"Let me heal you, Miryam," he said. "I need you with me. Let me heal you."

"Oh, Rabbi," she said. She bowed her head and folded her hands at her chest, as she'd seen others do.

And as the seven devils left her, one after the next, keening like petulant gulls, racking her body with convulsions, he held her, and when the last one was gone — its wailing becoming thunderous, and then dissipating into the night until there was no sound but the clicking and whirring of the insects and the sure beat of his heart, so close, as if inside her head — he lifted her in his arms and carried her through the field, back to the fire, where he laid her on a bed of grass, pulled his cloak over her, and sat with her, his hand on her head, warming her scalp, until she fell asleep.

Chapter Six

It happened early one spring morning, before Mass. I was sweeping the sanctuary floor when M. Lébadou cleared his throat behind me. "Excuse me, Marie, but I want to show you something."

I followed him to the base of the bell tower stairs. He pointed to the old oak baluster that usually stood in the corner of the hall. It was lying on its side as if it had been kicked over. Chunks of plaster littered the floor beside it. "I was just coming in to ring the bell," said M. Lébadou, "when I saw this." His lips quivered with rage. "That baluster is hundreds of years old. It's been here since the church was built. There's no cause for these fellows from Limoux to tear the place up so. The Lord's house isn't some wood shop."

I bent near the baluster to lift it, and noticed a strange glint inside the capital. A section of it had been cut away, leaving a hollow shaft. On the floor was the missing piece. When the baluster fell, the piece had been knocked from its slot, revealing this narrow hiding place, where something glinted.

I righted the baluster, then stood in front of it, blocking M. Lébadou's view. "Yes, monsieur, you're right. I'll have a word with Monsieur *le curé*."

"The whole job's a disaster," he muttered as he plodded up the spiral staircase to the bell tower.

When he was out of sight, I reached inside the slot and pulled out a small silver flask, corked with a handcut plug and engraved with the initials *A.B.* I brought the flask to my nose, expecting the scent of liquor, but I smelled only dust. When I tried to remove the cork, it turned to powder in my fingers.

The bell clanged brilliantly, deafeningly, four, five, six times. With one of my hairpins, I scraped away about a third of the cork still lodged in the neck of the flask; most of the rest of it fell into the bottle. Inside I saw a tiny rolled piece of paper.

By this time, I heard M. Lébadou making his slow way down again, so I quickly slipped the flask into my pocket and then fitted the dislodged piece of the capital back into place. As he came into view, I was sweeping up the plaster debris. He stopped on the final step and leaned against the railing, catching his breath. He was spry, but the climb up and down the stairs had winded him. "Pardon me, Marie," he said, "but I wonder if you know what else Monsieur *le curé* intends to restore around here." His voice was accusatory, as if the whole renovation project were my idea.

"No," I said. "He doesn't share his plans with me."

M. Lébadou raised his eyebrows. "He acts as if all that's old is rotten. But there's virtue in age, too, Marie. You can tell him." Taking the final step down to the floor, he ambled proudly outside.

Quickly, I sat on the bottom step and tried to shake the paper into my hand. A stubborn piece of cork blocked it, so I pierced the corner of the paper with my hairpin and extracted it. It was brittle; I unrolled it gingerly. At the top of the page was a small sketch of what appeared to be the interior of our sanctuary. The artist had paid the most attention to the secondary altar — the small one, recessed into the north wall, dedicated to the Virgin — and the area surrounding it, outlining the stones in a darker tone. Beneath the sketch were a few lines of text, apparently Latin, composed in small and shaky lettering.

I walked back to the nave. Mme Flèche, the baker's wife, had arrived and was kneeling in her pew, her head bent over her rosary. I rolled the paper tightly and held it against the flat of my palm, then went to examine the Virgin's altar. I counted the number of stones before it, noticing the largest stone directly in front. It seemed abnormally large, in fact — larger than any other stone on the floor. Then I left, glancing once again at Mme Flèche. Her eyes were closed, her lips silently enunciating the words of the prayer.

Outside, I saw no one about, and so I unrolled the paper once more. The drawing was a near-perfect replication of the altar, down to the dimensions of each of the stones on the floor. I noticed a new mark: a faint dot in the right-hand corner of the largest stone.

I felt vulnerable standing in the daylight, holding the crumbling piece of paper. Already one of the corners had flaked into my palm. I could not carry it around with me, even in my pocket, without inflicting further damage, nor did I know of a proper hiding place. I decided to bring it to Bérenger, as he would be able to translate the Latin, and would certainly be able to keep it for me.

He opened the presbytery door at my knock, a piece of bread in hand. "Come in, Marie, come in," he said, pulling out a chair at the small kitchen table. He offered me the seat, then halted when he saw my face, which must have appeared disturbed. "Is something wrong?"

Nervously, I presented him with the paper and flask and described to him where I had found them. I pointed out the details I had noticed, including the faint dot on the largest stone before the altar. Bérenger peered at the paper with interest.

"What does it say? The Latin."

He paused a moment before answering. "It's a fragment from scripture. Job. 'Have the gates of death been revealed to you? Have you seen the gates of deep darkness?' "

"Strange," I said.

He examined the paper again for some time. Then, popping his last morsel of bread in his mouth, he said, "Show me where you found this, Marie."

At the base of the bell tower stairs, I showed him the wooden baluster and slid the section of the capital away to reveal the hollow compartment. He knelt before it as I had and peered into the slot, then slipped

177

his hand in and felt around. When he found nothing more, he fitted the piece of the capital into the slot, then removed it and slid it in once again. "Remarkable," he whispered.

"Whoever hid it went to a lot of trouble," I said.

"Yes."

"What do you think it means?" I asked.

"I really couldn't say," he said, thoughtfully rubbing the flask with his thumb.

"Do you think something's been hidden? That dot seems intentional."

"Such as what?" He turned to me from his squat.

"I don't know. Something valuable."

"A treasure, you mean?" His eyes flashed, as if he'd uttered something scandalous.

I shrugged self-consciously. "Maybe."

"Could be," he said. "Or it could be the dot is just a drop of ink that fell on the page."

We had no time to discuss the paper further. Bérenger had to prepare for Mass, and I had my chores to attend to. But I spent the hours away from him thinking of nothing but the little flask, the parchment, and its possible meaning. It had to have been a priest who composed the message. Even now, most of the adults in our village could neither read nor write — they got their news at the tavern or the market, memorized scripture at Mass, and learned fairy stories and folktales from their grand-parents. Ours was one of the few literate families in town. It might have been pos-sible that the writer had copied the text from a Latin Vulgate Bible, which he or she would have gotten from the priest. But even so, to have carved the slot so carefully from the baluster — it would have taken time, and could only have been done by someone with regular access to the church.

So, likely it was a priest who had written the message and hidden the flask. But what would he have hidden beneath the stone? And why had he included the grim passage from Job?

The conversation at dinner that afternoon was strained and fueled almost entirely by my mother. Bérenger and I were too dis-tracted to talk. I kept glancing in his direc-tion, only to meet his impenetrable stare, at which point I'd look away. Moments later, we'd play the game again. I could not understand his gaze; I thought he might be angry with me, though I could not figure out why. Exasperated, my mother finally set her spoon down and scolded me. "Stop playing the coquette, Marie! You're driving us both batty!"

When the meal was finished, I declared I had to do some dusting in the presbytery, and I followed Bérenger, practically tripping on his heels. Closing the front door behind us, I said in a triumphant voice, "He was a priest!"

But he was not interested in my hypothesis. "Listen, Marie. You haven't told anyone about that letter I received last year, have you?"

"No," I replied, surprised by the question.

"Not Michelle? Not even your mother?"

"No, no," I assured him. "I haven't told a soul, monsieur. Just as you requested."

He breathed an audible sigh of relief. "Thank the Lord."

"Why?" I asked.

He studied me. "You must have guessed the identity of our generous donor, Marie," he said finally.

"I had a suspicion, yes," I said.

"It was he who got me reinstated here. I owe him a great debt of gratitude." And he proceeded to tell me the following story.

Late one night, a man had arrived on Bérenger's doorstep in Narbonne, carrying an envelope with a letter from the archduke. The letter instructed him to open an account at a certain bank in Perpignan. The archduke would then transfer three thousand francs to Bérenger's account within a week. It also informed him that he would be hearing from the bishop about his reinstatement in Rennes-le-Château. The only caveat was that Bérenger would be expected to report to the Austrian from time to time on the progress of the restoration and to inform him if he found anything out of the ordinary.

Bérenger took the train to Perpignan the following morning, opened the account, and then returned to Narbonne to await further news. As promised, a few days later he received a letter from Carcassonne informing him that his services were once again needed here, in Rennes-le-Château.

"Evidently, the man wields a great influence with the Church, Marie. He must be powerful indeed."

"Yes," I agreed, amazed. "So the flask, the message — do you think he knows of it?"

"I'm not sure. But I have promised to tell him what I find."

"Yes," I said, gloomily. I was reluctant to relinquish the discovery just then, to hand it over to a strange man in a foreign land who, for all I knew, might send another messenger to take the flask, lift the stone, and remove whatever was underneath it.

Bérenger, perhaps sensing my reluctance, added, "I would be grateful, Marie, if you would help me draft the letter."

And so we spent the next hour together in his new office on the second floor, which consisted of a handsome rolltop desk, a kerosene lamp, and two chairs. A gnarled oak branch stood in the corner of the room — something he'd picked up on one of his walks — and on the wall across from the desk was a terra-cotta crucifix supporting the body of Christ. Bérenger dictated the first few sentences, but once he began to tell the story of finding the flask, he faltered. "How exactly did it happen, Marie?"

I began to narrate the story aloud once more, but he interrupted me.

"Why not simply write it down. You were there."

He watched my hand as it traveled over the page and stopped now and then to dip the pen in the ink. I wrote the account from Bérenger's point of view, referring to myself as "my housekeeper."

"How well you write, Marie," he said, startlingly close. I looked up in surprise. He was gazing at me with such affection I felt myself redden, brow to ear, and I had to look back down at the letter.

"Where did you learn to write so well?"

he asked. "My seminary students didn't write half as well as you."

"Books, I suppose," I said, staring at the letter. "I am fond of them."

He nodded approvingly, and I continued my account, more haltingly this time, impaired now by my self-consciousness.

When I had finished, he took the paper from me and read it over.

"Wonderful," he said. "And let's add a line . . . 'I will await your instruction, dear sir. Yours in the service of Christ, Bérenger Saunière.' "

I complied, then slid the paper to him for his signature. "I wonder what he'll do," I said as he signed. "Do you think he'll tell us to lift the stone?"

"I've no idea," Bérenger said. He had little patience for musing. "We'll have to wait for his response."

And so we waited, interminably. I visited the small altar daily, lingering before the stone, imagining what might be hidden beneath it. A silver chalice, encrusted with jewels? Ancient holy writings? A rusted, chipped chest brimming with gold? I thought of the long-ago priest, prying the edge of the stone loose, hefting it open, digging away the dirt and rocks, the accumulation of centuries of dust. Removing a cloth-wrapped package from a satchel, and covering it with shovelfuls of red dirt. I imagined he must have grieved over the loss of something so precious.

Weeks passed, and then a month, and still we heard nothing. I itched to lift the stone. Time after time, I pressed Bérenger, insisting that there would be no sin in looking, that the Austrian had not forbidden him from pursuing any clues he might find. "Maybe that's what he intended. After all, he set you on this course, didn't he? Maybe he hoped you would stumble across the flask and then lift the stone yourself."

But Bérenger steadfastly refused, insisting that we had to wait to hear from the archduke before taking any further action. He even put off my requests to examine the parchment again, and would not entertain hypotheses as to what might be hidden beneath the stone or what the cryptic text might mean. "Maybe it's a code of some kind," I suggested.

"It's no use guessing. It could be anything."

"What do you think it is?"

"I really can't imagine, Marie."

As a way to distract myself — and perhaps to punish Bérenger for his obstinacy — I decided to visit Mme Laporte. I realized, with some shock, that I had not visited her since the day of the terrible episode with Gérard. I had, of course, returned the frock she'd loaned me, and though I'd seen her in the village now and then, always exchanging a few civil words with her, I had not been to the castle for more than a year.

I appeared at her door the next afternoon, a plate of cookies in my hand. The anger I once had felt toward her had dissolved, and in its place there was only shame at my long absence, especially after she had been so kind to me. When she greeted me as usual with that calm, welcoming expression, I was greatly relieved. She ushered me in and called to Mme Siau to bring coffee to the library, as if no time at all had passed.

I was different with Madame than I was with Bérenger. With him I could be brazen. It had become my way of courting him. Since I'd failed to behave perfectly piously — I had criticized the Church in his presence — I had taken to displaying the whole of myself as a kind of challenge, a glove thrown down: Take me or leave me, this is who I am. But with Madame, I was gentler, influenced as I was by her quiet, contemplative nature. Her presence never failed to soothe me. Her meditative step, her catholic interest in the world, the quiet of her household were all a stillness I entered into, an expanse in which I was made to confront not only myself, but the sloughed-off skin of history.

After we made small talk for several minutes about the weather and the progress of the church renovations, Madame asked if I'd come to hear her explanation for why she had reported Bérenger's sermon to the government.

"Oh, no," I protested. "It's all right." The incident, long past now, embarrassed me.

"I would like to share it with you, Marie. I think you may find it illuminating."

"All right, then. If you like."

"I was not born here in Rennes," she began. "I moved here as a teenager, from Lyon, where I spent my childhood.

"We had a good life there, my family. My father was a professor of history. My mother was educated and she educated me, bringing me to museums, teaching me English, Latin, and Hebrew. I was an only child. We danced together in the evenings after supper. My mother would play minuets and waltzes on the piano and my father swung me about the room as if I were a grand lady in the king's court." The memory seemed to transport her, and she remained quiet a

186

moment, savoring it.

"My father was very principled. An idealist. He believed that humanity's God-given destiny was to progress toward the divine, but that in order to progress it was necessary to know where one had been. So he studied history. He was a republican, though not a revolutionist. He hated war. And he loved his country. He wrote for the newspaper occasionally, praising France for making the Jews full citizens. He believed France was the blade of progress, that we would eventually lead Europe toward our ideals. Liberty, equality, fraternity. Those words were like scripture to him."

She looked down at her hands, which were folded in her lap. Purposefully, she unfolded them and laid them flat across her thighs. "He was killed by a mob of anti-Semites just before Easter. They dragged him from our home and beat him to death with clubs and the butts of their rifles. They stuffed his mouth with crumpled newspaper pages and set fire to them.

"We did not have much money saved, and so my mother had to send me to live with my father's cousins here in Rennes-le-Château. The Laportes. She had no family alive in France."

"So Mayor Laporte is your cousin?" I

asked, immediately embarrassed by the hasty tone of my question. Her confession flustered me; I did not know the appropriate way to respond.

"Second cousin, yes."

"But he's not Jewish."

"No. My grandfather — my father's father — converted to Judaism to marry my grandmother. They were unconventional people. When my mother wrote to Mme Laporte, Philippe's mother, it was the first time our families had spoken in thirty years. The Laportes took me in under the condition that I come alone, without my mother."

I imagined a younger Mme Laporte, trudging up the dusty hill from Couiza, dragging an overstuffed bag behind her in the dirt. "What did she do?"

"She moved to Paris. She couldn't stay in Lyon."

"I'm sorry about your father," I said.

She shook her head impatiently. "I've told you this, Marie, not to inspire your pity, but because I want you to understand why I reported l'abbé to the government. Religion is a potent force — both for good and for evil. As a man-made creation, it is imperfect; as an institution, an organized body of people, it can be dangerous. The men who killed my father believed they were acting faithfully, according to what their Church had taught them — they were avenging the death of their God, whom they believed had been killed by my father's ancestors. They used Christian ideas to justify a brutal, evil act — a sin, if ever there was one."

I nodded, thinking of her pistol. Had she ever feared for her own life?

"This is why," she continued, "religion must never partner with government. It is powerful enough as its own independent entity; it influences the moral worlds of every member of its body. But when it partners with government, it becomes a source for great evil." Though her face remained calm, the fierceness of her gaze and the intensity of her voice betrayed — for once — her emotion.

"I hope I haven't said too much." She leaned back in her chair and looked kindly on me. "I know you are a faithful Catholic, Marie. I imagine you find strength and hope and joy in the practice of your religion. I begrudge you none of that."

"Yes, of course. I know," I said. It was not the right time to share my own disillusionment with her. It seemed trivial, weightless next to what she'd told me.

"It remains a puzzle to me — how some people can be so uplifted, so transformed

189

by their religion and others can fall so low, descending into darkness even as they live."

"I guess it's the devil going walking," I offered.

She laughed, a surprised, delighted laugh. "Yes. That's right, Marie. The devil going walking."

Summer arrived, and still we had not heard from the Austrian. I grew perturbed with Bérenger, who continued to behave as if he were indifferent to the mystery of the flask and its message. I had even started to entertain the notion of creeping into the church by night and lifting the stone myself, when he took me aside one day and announced that the new altar was due to arrive the next week. It was, he explained, to be a gift from Mme de Guiraud, a native of Rennes-le-Château. Her family had owned the old sawmill and had moved to Narbonne when the mill closed, before our family had come to town. Bérenger had called on her several times during his stay in Narbonne, and she had been charmed by his manners and his feeling for her home village. When he learned he would be returning to Rennes-le-Château, Mme de Guiraud offered him the gift of a new altar, designed to his specifications. An artist in Toulouse had been building it, and Bérenger had just received word that it was finished.

"To install it, the workers will have to remove some of the flagstones in the floor. I'll ask them to remove the stone that's marked on the drawing, and we'll be able to see whether there's anything to your theory then."

I was, needless to say, elated. I awaited the altar's arrival with fidgety anticipation.

It came, hauled uphill by a faltering mule, who lay down to roll in the dust once relieved of its burden. Behind the cart were a few laborers from the fields who'd followed it uphill, curious about what lay beneath the dustcover. People came out of their houses to watch as Bérenger helped the driver and his assistant lift the altar from the cart and stagger with it into the church. Inside, one of the men removed the cloth. Several people gasped at what was revealed: a gilded tabernacle, crowned with a golden cross on a pedestal, and the table itself topped with Italian marble.

"You must have spent all your money on this, Monsieur *le curé*," said M. Verdié.

Bérenger seemed not to have heard him. He was studying the altar's surfaces, fingering the gild.

"The boss said you'd paint that yourself,"

one of the men said to Bérenger, when he bent to examine the face of the altar, which was strangely bare: an unpainted plaster bas-relief that swelled here and there in the shape of a head, a draping robe, a cross.

Bérenger nodded. He got to his feet, rubbing his fingers against his cassock. "Very nice," he said, and then ordered the men to remove the old altar and install the new one in its place.

I lingered in the church that day, sweeping the floor several times, dusting in invisible niches. It took the men some time to remove the old altar, massive and ponderous as it was. Though I had chores to tend to at home, I would run back to the church whenever I could and stand outside the door, listening for the sounds inside, the scraping of iron against stone. I heard it finally, just after the midday dinner — grunts and groans crescendoing into a great roar — and I rushed in to see two men hefting the stone upright, dust billowing into the air, and Bérenger dropping to his knees to examine what lay beneath.

I ran to stand beside him. He lifted a dusty and cracked leather valise from the dirt. Its contents chimed dully. I could see that he wanted to open it but did not trust the workmen. So he simply touched the bag, fingering its cracks, as if the leather itself were a thing to be admired. Still in the dirt lay a small leather-bound book.

The men dragged the stone away from the shallow hole and were about to lay it back down, when I stopped them. The underside of the stone was contoured. Stepping closer, I could see that the contours were patterned, intentional, carved. Bérenger noticed the same thing and instructed the men to turn the stone over and lay it down, face up. As they did, he tucked the leather-bound book into his cassock.

The four of us knelt before the stone, each on one side. I took a cleaning rag from my belt and wiped the surface thoroughly. As the layers of dust came off, the contours grew more distinguishable, though years — centuries — of shifting soil had ground them down, blurring the shapes. There were four panels on the stone, set off from each other by patterned arches. On the bottom left, a figure stood by a horse, which drank at a trough. Above the arch that circumscribed that panel, two animals were pictured, one fleeing the other. To the right of that, another panel showed the two animals facing each other, on either side of a tree trunk, their teeth bared. And below that panel, beneath another patterned arch, a knight rode his horse, a spear in one arm, an indistinguishable object in the other — an urn, a figurine or maybe even a child.

"You've got something here, Monsieur *le curé,*" said one of the workmen. "Something old."

The other sat back on his heels. "What's in the case?"

A look of desperation passed over Bérenger's face. I could see the impulse to hide the bag, get rid of the workers — it was the same impulse I'd had when I found the flask in the baluster. Instead, he bravely worked the sticky latch open.

The case released a metallic scent, like blood. Inside was a scattering of items: a silver chalice and bowl, a tiny copper bell ornamented with a red cross, a frayed silk stole, a golden censer and chain. There were a few porcelain statuettes — Saint Roch, Sainte Germaine, the Virgin Mother — and a large golden cross, like the one that crowned the new altar. A small framed painting of a grieving Sainte Marie Madeleine, her hair long and loose, lay at the bottom of the case, and scattered across the face of this painting were dozens of coins.

The worker who'd asked about the case reached for one of the coins, but Bérenger quickly moved the case away.

"Treasure!" exclaimed the other worker, half in jest.

Bérenger snorted. "They're nothing but old church things. Left here by an earlier priest. Not worth much."

"What about those coins?" asked the other worker suspiciously.

"Just old brass medals from Lourdes."

"They look gold to me," said the worker. "Louis d'or pieces. My father had a few when I was a kid."

Bérenger picked one up. "They're light as air," he said, before biting it. "See? Brass. If it were gold, your teeth would sink right in."

"Let's see." The worker held out a hand.

Bérenger tossed the coin in the case and snapped it shut.

"Please replace the stone, facedown. When you've finished that, you may go."

"Wait!" I protested. "Why?" I wanted to examine the stone. If nothing else, I thought it should be replaced with the relief work exposed, so that others could see what an extraordinary thing we'd found.

He fixed me with a stern gaze. "Marie. I'm sorry, but this is not your business. Do as I say, please," he instructed the workmen once more, and when they had completed the task, he followed them out of the sanctuary, the case in one hand and the old book in his pocket.

I followed, alive with anger. "How dare you say it's not my business?!" I shouted. "I found the flask! I brought it to you!" The crew of workmen were all around the grounds of the church — on the roof, near the bell tower, gathered in a group by the outer wall just near us. They all watched, intrigued by the spectacle of a girl chastising a priest.

Bérenger strode toward the presbytery, his back rigid. I followed, ready to enter with him, but he shut the door behind him. I pounded on it. "Bérenger!" I yelled. "Let me in!"

Some of the workmen burst into laughter. I walked home in fury and despair, ignoring their voices, pitched high like mine, and mocking, "Bérenger! Oh, *mon cher curé!* Oh, Bérenger!"

THE SINNER

She was unfamiliar with herself. A new quiet dwelt in her — her thoughts came in a hush, her movements were slow and gentle, a steady forward motion. She felt strangely light, spacious, her mind an empty sunlit room. Her vision, too, was affected: the men she'd seen before through the lenses of judgment and fear, who had appeared rough and brutal, uncaring and ambitious, now she saw as simply hungry for the love of God. They were children, all of them, as temperamental and as easily soothed. The demons were gone: the curses that leapt from her lips, the thrashing, the inopportune laughter, the heartache, the wakefulness, the lust. Most of all, the fear. The fear was gone, and with it went its handmaidens: anxiety, anger, hatred, worry, self-obsession. How cluttered, how obscure her world had been! She could not believe she had lived with such obstructions to her perception, in such a profound darkness. Life, she saw now, was light, it was light.

It was the morning, its delicate breath of dawn over the mountains. The way it gilded the dew-misted grasses as she collected cedar branches for the fire and the brown conies and green lizards scurried into leafy darkness. It was the heat of the flames on her face and hands, the iridescent scales on her fingers after she skewered the fish. The crescendo of the dawn's tender yellow into riotous pinks and oranges and then full, prismatic daylight! How daring it was, how joyous! Even the darkness existed in relation to the light, as its absence. Even the night had the hopeful light of the moon and stars, a dim reflection of the coming joy of morning.

The crowds were changed, too. Their eyes, which had enervated her to the point of madness, were now shining moons reflecting the resplendence of God. They were just as desperate, just as needy, but they no longer threatened her, for now her mind was peaceful. Her consciousness was a single flame burning. It was this peace she now offered the people who bunched and clamored and shouted and wept. *Shh,* she wanted to tell them all. *Shh,* stroking their hair and cheeks. *We are temporary residents here. Look around you at the beauty. Taste what is good. Be kind to one another. Know joy. You will be traveling soon.*

More women had joined their group. Yochanah, who had left Herod's royal court to travel with them, Shoshannah, and Shlomit, among others. They began to seek her out, shyly, drawn to her newfound peace. Though she was young and did not have the status of a married woman, she had followed Yeshua the longest, and this gave her an authority that seemed now to suit her. The women all worked together, buying food and necessities, preparing the meals, washing the clothes, drying them on rocks in the sun, serving and pouring and clearing and cleaning — but they deferred now, in their gestures, the cants of their heads, the volume of their voices, to Miryam of Magdala. She beamed among them like a beacon.

The crowd that followed them was growing. Yeshua seemed both invigorated and agitated by the force of the multitudes. He could no longer reach everyone with his voice unless he stood on slopes, stone walls, roofs — even on the decks of fishing boats in order to be seen and to avoid the swarming pressure of the crowds. Miryam and the other women ministered to the people, bringing fish and bread, dripping water onto the parched lips of the sick, listening to Yeshua when they could. Miryam hummed while she moved through the crowds.

While they were in Naïn, Shimon the Parush scholar — a wealthy man who enjoyed entertainment and had heard of the crowds that came to see Yeshua — invited Yeshua to dine at his table, along with several other men, all prominent members of the city. Levi, who knew Shimon and did not like him, urged Yeshua not to go. "He wants to humiliate you. Pardon me, Rabbi, but he considers himself of a higher order than you — and he wants you to know it." But Yeshua ignored him. He accepted all invitations — from publican or Parush, leper or executioner. And he wanted Miryam to come, too.

"They'll turn me away," she protested. "A woman not your wife?"

"I want you there," was all he would say. She assented nervously. She feared that they were entering a trap of some kind; she had known people like Shimon in Magdala — people who cared only for status.

Miryam dined with the women and children in a separate room, though they could hear the men's voices easily. They bent their heads as Shimon blessed the food in the next room, and when the men were finished with the wine of the benediction, the servant brought the dregs of the cup in to them. They feasted on pickled roe, sheep's tail, cucumbers and olives dressed with honey and cream, lentils boiled with leeks and coriander, and breads flavored with cumin and cinnamon. For dessert the servants brought platters of dates, figs, pomegranates, almonds, and cashews. The wine was spiced. The children ate quickly and left the table to play; the women spoke of their families in hushed voices, so as not to interrupt the conversation of the men. They asked after Miryam's family, assuming she was Yeshua's wife. "Where are your children?" they said. "Do they not travel with you?"

Miryam had only half heard the question; she had been listening for Yeshua's voice in the next room. "My children?" she asked. "I have no children." She knew the proper thing would be to clarify that she was not married to Yeshua or anyone else, but she could not bring herself to admit it.

The woman who had asked her apologized, then turned away and did not address her again, nor did any of the others. This suited Miryam. She was too preoccupied with the well-being of Yeshua.

Suddenly, the men's conversation ceased. The women hushed immediately. There was a long pause. Finally Shimon spoke. "A true prophet would know who it was that was touching him like that," he said, his voice replete with scorn. "And wouldn't allow it."

Yeshua spoke. "Shimon," he said.

"Yes, Rabbi," Shimon said sarcastically. Another man laughed.

"I have a question for you."

"Ask it, then," said Shimon.

"There was a creditor who had two debtors. One owed five hundred denarii and the other owed fifty. Neither could pay. So the creditor forgave both debts."

"A foolish creditor," said Shimon; laughter followed.

"Here is my question. Which of his debtors will love him more?" asked Yeshua.

"The one who borrowed more, of course. He was forgiven a larger amount."

"Look at this woman," Yeshua said. The women exchanged surprised glances. Who could he be talking about? All the women were in their room. Miryam stood and, stepping between the dishes of food, made her way to the door. From there she could see the men. They ate in the Roman fashion: reclining on divans, their heads near the table, their legs stretched toward the wall. A young woman, her head uncovered and decorated with a jeweled silver strand, her shoulders and feet bare, knelt by Yeshua. She held one of his feet in her hands and kissed it again and again, as if she were sipping from a goblet. Blood rushed to Miryam's face and neck.

"I am looking at her. It's hard not to," said Shimon. Then, abruptly, he commanded his servant, "Get her out of here. She's embarrassing our guests and defiling the meal." The servant moved toward the woman, but Yeshua sat up and lifted her to his side. The servant stood over them, hesitating.

"When I came tonight, Shimon, you did not wash my feet, kiss my cheek, or anoint me with oil, as is proper with guests. This woman, who does not know me nor has the responsibilities of a host, this woman has washed my feet with her own tears and dried them with her hair. She has anointed them with ointment and kissed them as if they were the faces of her own children." The woman broke into sobs and laid her face in Yeshua's lap.

"She's a whore, Yeshua," said one of the men. "She's a professional at making men feel good."

"I don't care what she is," Yeshua continued while the woman sobbed into his thigh. "She is full of love, and her sins, numerous though they may be, are forgiven."

"Who are you to forgive sins?" said Shimon angrily. "Take her away, I tell you," he said to his servant, who approached the woman once again and lifted her roughly from Yeshua's lap.

"Your faith is great," Yeshua said to her. "It will keep you."

The servant led the woman to the door where Miryam was standing, and she stood aside as they passed, noticing the woman's crooked nose and missing teeth. Yeshua and the other men watched her leave; then their eyes fell on Miryam. She knew she should hide herself; it was not right for a woman to interrupt a gathering of men, but her face and chest tingled with anger and humiliation.

"Who is she, Yeshua?" she asked.

"The women are bold tonight," said Shimon.

Yeshua met Miryam's eye, but his expression told her nothing. Then he turned back to his dinner.

"If you think I have invited you to my house in order to humiliate you, you are wrong," she heard Shimon say, but she did not stay to hear the rest. The servant who had escorted the woman outside was coming back in; Miryam left by that door.

The night was cool, the moon full and high in the sky, shining brightly on the road. The servant had thrown the barefoot woman to the ground. She wept there, her forehead pressed into the dust. Miryam stood against the warm stone wall of the house. The woman lifted her head and regarded Miryam with kohl-smudged eyes.

"You're his wife," she said.

"No," said Miryam. "His wife is dead. He has no wife."

The woman got to her feet and brushed the dust from her clothes and hair. "You're one of those women, then, who follow him around?"

Miryam looked away. She hadn't known that anyone had thought of her in that way, as "one of those women."

"I'd like to go with you. I wish I could. But I have children. You're lucky," the woman said. "Shalom." She began to walk away.

"Why did you do that in there?" Miryam asked, her voice raised. The woman turned. "Why did you touch him like that?"

"Don't be jealous," she said. She shook her head. "You're with him all the time. I only had this one chance. I took it."

"You didn't know him, then?"

"No. Don't worry. He's never come to see me."

"Weren't you afraid you'd be thrown out?"

The woman laughed. "I'm not afraid of Shimon. We're acquainted." She raised her hand. "Shalom," she said again. "God be with you." And she walked down the road toward the center of the city, her shoulders like sanded marble in the moonlight.

Miryam watched the woman go, then walked in the opposite direction, down the hill in search of water. She wanted to bathe her feet, to sink her toes in mud. She missed her family. She missed the smell of her bedclothes — lake water and rosemary, from where they were hung to dry. She missed her father's voice, his gentle attention. She missed the cascading laughter of her sisters. And her mother! How she missed her mother, her quiet concentration, her patience, her anger even, for it was an anger Miryam understood. She did not understand Yeshua — his anger or his love for her.

Nor did she understand her desire. It had not completely left her. It was no longer a thirst of the skin, but a gentler spreading warmth, like sunlight heating her from within. When he came to her at night and rested his head in her lap, weeping sometimes with exhaustion —"A man's life is anguish, Miryam! It is a long journey of agony and anguish!"— she laced her fingers through his thick hair and massaged his scalp, all the while feeling herself softening. At times, she wept with him — but while he wept for humanity, she wept for herself, for her loneliness. It shamed her.

CHAPTER SEVEN

I was furious with Bérenger for treating me so dismissively. I had thought we were partners — I had brought him the flask, after all, and he had confided the Austrian's secret request in me. But he had disregarded my wish to examine the stone, and was hoarding the case and the book, a discovery we'd made together. I felt excluded, not only from the secrets we'd been sharing, but also from his affection. I punished him once again with a broody silence. I hoped he might come to me with an apology, a joke, a modest display of remorse. He did no such thing. He spent most of his time in the church, painting the bas-relief on the face of the new main altar. If I entered the nave to sweep or dust, he did not look up. If I addressed him, he answered politely, but briefly.

He was not much of an artist, and it puzzled me why he'd chosen to paint the picture himself. But as I watched, as the colors brought definition to the shapes and exposed the scene — Marie Madeleine in her grotto, kneeling before a thin cross of green wood, a book open at her elbow and a skull at her knees — I understood. I saw how worshipfully he touched the brush to her skin, her golden dress, her long curls and heavy eyebrows, how he lingered over her face, mixing and remixing his colors to achieve the perfect shade of rose for her cheeks.

One afternoon, bitten by envy, I accused him: "You're in love with her, aren't you?"

He turned, startled. "Marie. I didn't know you were there."

"The way you paint her. The way you linger over her body with the brush. It's almost . . . immoral." I blushed as I spoke, for I hadn't found the right word. It wasn't immoral at all: it was endearing and seductive.

He snorted. "There's nothing immoral about loving a saint. On the contrary. Adoring a saint softens the heart, makes us more willing to receive the grace of God."

"Why her, though? Why not Mother Mary? Or Saint Francis? Or Jesus himself, for that matter?"

He looked at the painting. "It's her ardor,"

he said. "The tears of the Madeleine make God bend toward all of us, make him willing to forgive us. If it weren't for her, we'd all be damned from birth."

"Aren't we already?" I pressed.

"There's our baptism, Marie. Baptism remits the stain and punishment of original sin. You know that."

"But it doesn't save us."

"Not by itself, no. We sin and we sin again. Only the grace of God and a willing heart can do that." He began to paint once more.

His piety both chastened and enraged me. "What have you done with the things you found under the stone?" I demanded, unable to contain the question any longer.

"I've put them away for the time being. I've written again to the Austrian, and I will wait upon his word." He spoke with studied calm and continued to paint, his eyes remaining on the bas-relief.

I felt this news as further insult, for he hadn't requested my help with the letter. Wounded, I left him alone with his saint.

His aloofness filled me with melancholy. I felt lonelier than during his exile in Narbonne, for at least then I had the comfort of hope: that he'd return, that he'd be near, that we'd grow to love each other. But the future had arrived. He had returned, he was here, working at his desk or beside me in the church, physically present and yet inaccessible. I concluded that he felt no love for me.

I could not wallow in my self-pity for long, though, for I had to remind myself of the rectitude of his behavior — he was, after all, a priest. How could he love me? It was I who was in the wrong for trying to win his favor. I chastised myself repeatedly, and having suffered well, resolved to extend my martyrdom into the infinite future: I would obey Bérenger's implied request and stay away. I would perform my duties in the church and the presbytery when expected, but invite no further friendship.

This resolution was all very well in the abstract, as a form of atonement, but the enactment of it proved a challenge. There were two confounding elements: first, the nature of my own personality, which was not, alas, inclined toward silent suffering; and second, there was the matter of the knight's stone (as I had come to think of it) and the items we'd uncovered beneath it, items I was determined to investigate further.

As Bérenger clearly did not intend to share any more information with me, I resolved to pursue the matter on my own.

Using my father's pen and the clean side of a scrap of butcher's paper, I sketched the carved surface as I remembered it. My sketch looked something like this:

I thought it was a decent reproduction, though the scale was imperfect, and I could not remember the particular ornamentation of the arches. The figures told an undecipherable story. What was the knight carrying? Was it a child? And what did the animals — bears, perhaps — indicate? Were those scenes — the fight and then the flight — supposed to tell some larger story, something happening beyond the more intimate scenes with the man and the horse?

Was it a hunting scene of some kind? They were unanswerable questions based on the little I knew.

After some agonizing, I decided to bring my sketch to Mme Laporte. Bérenger would have forbidden it, and had he given me any welcoming cues — a smile, a soft look — I might have brought it to him instead so we could mull over the questions together. But he hadn't.

"Michelle sent this drawing to me," I told Madame. "She saw the carving in a church in Carcassonne."

"It must be a very old carving," she said, peering at the paper.

"How old?"

"Well, it's difficult to tell from the sketch, of course. But these animals — very ancient stone cuttings often make use of animal patterns like this one."

"What did they mean?"

"Oh, it depends, of course. Depends on the animal." She stared at the drawing. "These look like bears."

"That's what I thought."

"Bears held something of a sacred status during Merovingian times. Fifth and sixth centuries," she added. "I'm not sure why, exactly. Something to do with the power of the animal, probably — its strength, its ability to hibernate and yet maintain that strength."

"You think this is that old?"

"Possibly."

A quotation came back to me, and I spoke it aloud, on an impulse. " 'Bow thy head humbly, revere what thou hast burned and burn what thou hast revered.' " They were Saint Rémy's words, words I had been made to memorize many years earlier in school. I had last recited them in front of my class in the frigid schoolroom, my hands trembling from nerves and the wintry cold. Saint Rémy had spoken those words at the baptism of Clovis, the most famous of the Merovingian kings. Clovis was a convert to Christianity. We had learned to recognize him as a hero, the new Constantine, the king who had brought the light of Christ to the people of France in the Dark Ages.

"Yes," Madame said, lifting her head. "Clovis is the Merovingian king most people know about. The dynasty was named for Mérovée, his grandfather. They were said to have magical powers, to be able to heal the sick with the touch of a hand."

In the fifth century, France was called Gaul and Rennes-le-Château was a Visigothic city known as Rhédae. The land still spoke of this ancient city: Roman roads still scarred the surface of the hills, and from time to time, the red soil spat out shards of amphorae and brick, thinned Latinate coins, arrowheads, and bones. "You can still find ancient Visigothic skeletons around here," Madame said. "There are many tombs in these hills."

"La Capello," I said, realizing.

"Yes — that's the largest. You know it?"

I nodded. Gérard had told me of the place: an abandoned chapel on his uncle's land. Nothing was left of the building except for some large, roughly cut stones, tumbled in disarray on the ground. Years ago, his uncle's father had dug up one of those stones — large and flat, half buried — in the process of building a wall. Beneath the stone, rising out of the soil, were smooth white bones: skulls, femurs, knobby vertebrae. The bones were piled thick and deep, enclosed by four buried stone walls. His uncle's father, horrified, had replaced the stone and forbidden his children to set foot on that part of the property. He left the wall unfinished. Gérard had taken me to see the spot: it was overgrown now, tufts of broom straddling the tombstone — similar in size and shape, I now realized, to the stone we'd unearthed in the church.

"The Merovingian kingdoms were to the

north and west of Rhédae," she continued. "The kings themselves actually had very little to do with this region, until Dagobert II."

Madame, it must be said, loved legend as much as history. Two forces battled within her: the impulse toward accuracy and the guilty desire to augment the facts with magic, gore, and acts of heroism. Her language grew voluptuous and her expression animated when she told a tale, though she was always careful to qualify it as such.

When Dagobert was only five, she said, his father, King of Austrasia — the northeastern region of Gaul, an area that included present-day Cologne and Metz — died, leaving Dagobert in the care of the nefarious Grimoald, the mayor of the palace. Grimoald sent Dagobert to Ireland, spread the word that the prince was dead, and hastily enthroned his own son, Childebert. Within days, angry subjects had deposed Childebert and taken him and his father to be killed. Kingless, Austrasia fell into thirty years of chaos, with seigneurs battling each other for power, until Dagobert II, now a monk, returned from Ireland in 674.

Here Madame paused and leaned forward, her eyes bright with delight at what she was about to reveal. "Before going to Austrasia, though, Dagobert may have come here, to this hilltop, to Rhédae."

Dagobert, it was said, married a Visigothic princess whose father was the Count of Rhédae. They were married in Rhédae — perhaps even on the site of our present-day church, where another church likely stood. They dwelt here together while Dagobert waited until the proper moment to reclaim his northern kingdom. When he finally was reinstated as king, he amassed a good amount of gold, which he is said to have kept in Rhédae.

What a thrill! To think that an ancient king had been here, on this very hill, had known this place, its red soil, its winds, its breath-taking views of distant mountains. And to imagine what he might have brought with him! Great chests of ancient treasure could be sequestered beneath the church: gold, jewels, ancient tapestries and mosaics, all of which might have belonged to Dagobert II himself. It took all my will to hold my tongue; I so longed to tell Madame every-thing. I had not been so far off, then, to think of treasure! And treasure so ancient — how much more exhilarating would that be!

I drummed my fingers against the arm of the chair while Madame finished her story.

Dagobert II did not rule for long. One afternoon while he was resting beneath a tree, his own mayor drove a lance through his eye. The same man then went on to murder Dagobert's family. His wife and her children, including the heir, Sigebert IV, were supposed to have been killed in the raid. But some believed that Sigebert IV survived and lived to father a whole line of unacknowledged kings.

She stopped abruptly. "Forgive me, Marie. I've gone on far too long. And I still haven't told you anything of value that concerns your stone."

"No," I said. "No, it's been very helpful."

She examined my sketch one more time. "I wish I knew more about the history of Carcassonne. It may be a local story depicted here." She rubbed the top of the drawing with her thumb, as if the ink and paper offered the same texture as the engraved stone. "It's interesting that the horse and rider stand beneath the animals and trees. It's as if they are riding beneath the ground." Then she looked at me sharply, and I felt sure she had penetrated my lie. "Where exactly was the church, Marie, where Michelle found this?"

I shrugged, unwilling now to reveal anything more. "Oh, I don't know. She didn't tell me."

She stared at me a moment longer, then turned again to the sketch. "I'll tell you. If Michelle had found this stone here in Rennes-le-Château, there would be more to say."

At home that evening, my mind buzzed. *She knows,* I thought, *she knows. Bérenger won't trust me again.* Our dinner was interminable. I couldn't look at Bérenger for fear my eyes would reveal my treachery. It was only when I was lying in my cot that night, listening to my father's ragged snoring, that I realized I was worrying over nothing. Madame would tell no one. As long as I'd known her, she had been utterly discreet.

The important question was what more she had to say.

I wondered, after hearing the story of Dagobert II's presence in Rhédae, whether the knight's stone covered Dagobert's tomb. Dagobert might have been buried beneath the floor of that ancient church. The stone, remarkable as it was, could have been saved to pave the floor of our own church, hundreds of years after his death.

As I lay awake, I re-created his murder in my mind, down to the crunch of his skull as it splintered beneath the lance, and then imagined his loyal mourning subjects transporting his corpse on a rickety cart over the rocky hills and valleys that spanned the distance between the Ardennes, where he was killed, and Rennes-le-Château. Growing more and more convinced that his corpse was there, buried deep beneath the surface dirt, I even considered sneaking into the church with my father's crowbar and shovel. The only thing that stopped me was that I would not be able to lift the stone alone.

It was impossible to sleep, so I crept downstairs with a book on the Merovingians that Madame had lent me. I read by candlelight and found, to my disappointment, that the whereabouts of Dagobert's remains were well documented. He had been buried in Stenay, the capital city of his kingdom. Two centuries after his death, the Church canonized him — the book did not explain why — and his corpse was transferred, but only to a different church in the same city. Almost a thousand years later, during the Revolution, Stenay was taken, the church destroyed, and Dagobert's relics dispersed across France. His skull was thought to be at a convent in Mons.

Reading further, though, I was heartened to learn of the discovery of a Merovingian tomb during the restoration of a church in Tournai, Belgium. The mason who'd made the discovery found a startling array of treasure, including, strangely enough, a purple silk cloak embroidered with three hundred gold and garnet bees. Also in the tomb were a leather purse full of gold coins; four weapons — a sword, a saber, a lance, and a throwing hatchet, all ornamented in gold and cloisonné; a golden bull's head, also in gold and garnet; and a gold seal ring, emblazoned with the name *Childerici Regis*. King Childeric, the father — as I learned from the book — of Clovis.

This was promising news: a tomb found during the restoration of a church. *And* it had contained a collection of coins, perhaps like the ones we had found in the valise. Good omens, I felt. I was certain now that my knight's stone was a gravestone, and while it might not be the tomb of Dagobert or Childeric, it might very well contain some other ancient king's corpse, along with his own catalogue of jewel-encrusted weaponry and artifacts. Perhaps the priest who hid the flask had been the first to discover this tomb, and because he didn't want its wealth to be plundered by revolutionaries, he turned the stone over, burying its engraved face in the dirt. Maybe he hid the flask in the capital of the baluster for a trusted friend, someone who might be able to smuggle the tomb's treasure into more peaceful territory, to reserve its wealth for the Church or for France — or for himself.

Though I had answered some questions by reading, there was still the matter of what more I might learn from Mme Laporte. It was my choice: I could continue to pretend that Michelle had found the stone or I could trust in Madame's discretion.

I returned to Madame's early the next morning. No one answered my knock, which surprised me because I knew Madame to be an early riser. I wandered around the castle grounds, heading toward the wall that abutted the church cemetery, where I knew I might get a glimpse of her window. I did not intend to spy; I had only the vague notion of looking for a light in the room, some evidence of whether or not she was awake. I was in a strange state of mind, having spent a sleepless night squinting at the small print of the Merovingian history by candlelight.

Leaning over the château wall, I looked out over the *garrigues.* Sunlight flashed from the bits of mica in the stone wall. The sky trumpeted its brilliance. I wondered at the crisp teeth of a Kermes oak leaf, watched a butterfly alight on a cyclamen and marveled at the perfect fluting of its wing. Dagobert II himself might have marveled at the same sight. How near the past was! A thousand years was a breath, the turn of a head.

A footfall broke my reverie. M. Laporte, his cap pulled low over his forehead, was peering quizzically at me.

I stood at once, brushing dust from the breast of my frock. "Pardon me, monsieur. I came to visit Madame. When do you expect her to be at home?"

"Mme Laporte is away, Marie," the mayor replied uneasily. He must have wondered why I had come to see his wife at such an odd hour of the day. "I've just left her at the train station."

"Where's she gone?" I asked, stunned.

"To Paris."

"Paris? Why? When will she be back?"

"Not for some time. Her aunt has just passed, Marie. She's gone to see to her affairs."

"Oh," I said, dumbfounded. She had mentioned nothing of a sick aunt. Why hadn't she told me she would be leaving? Or had she only just found out, yesterday afternoon after our visit — received a telegram, perhaps, and decided to take the first train out this morning?

"Excuse me, please, Marie," the mayor said, when I failed to say anything further. "I haven't yet eaten my breakfast."

"Yes, of course, monsieur," I responded, then walked slowly home.

By the end of that summer, renovation came to a halt. The roof was repaired, the new altar installed, the windows in the nave replaced by a glazier from Bordeaux. There was more to be done — the structure of the church needed buttressing and we had not yet begun to refurnish the interior — but Bérenger had run out of money. He had still not heard from the Austrian, despite a second letter informing the archduke of the knight's stone and the items we'd found beneath it.

Bérenger took to traveling. He told us that he was visiting his mother in Montazels or his brother in Narbonne, and, carrying his satchel, he would set off before dawn to make the hike down the hill. He would leave for one day or occasionally as many as six. He continued to avoid me. Despite my resolution, I could not leave him alone. I brooded when he was gone and confronted him when he returned, asking where he'd been, what he'd been doing. I tried to keep my questions lighthearted and polite, but I am afraid I could not fully disguise the undertone of need. I longed for him to confide in me. But he would tell me nothing, only that he had had family business to attend to.

When he was home, Bérenger spent a good deal of time in his office with the door closed. His correspondence increased substantially. It seemed each morning he had a few new letters to post, and he began to receive numerous letters daily, from all corners of France: Alençon, Montpellier, Amiens, Bayonne, as well as many from Narbonne. Some envelopes boasted an array of colorful stamps and were marked with such exotic addresses as Perugia, Barcelona, Prague, and Budapest. M. Déramon grumbled about the increase in volume. "I'm not a pack mule, you know," he would say, dropping the letters on the kitchen table.

One afternoon as I was going to change the linen in Bérenger's bedroom, I noticed him in his office, sitting before a pile of letters, perturbedly slicing open each one. I stood at the threshold.

"When did you get to be so famous?" I asked.

To my relief, he smiled, then lifted the stack of letters, demonstrating the weight of the load. "All of this, just today."

"Who are they from?"

He shook his head. "It's my own fault. I posted a few advertisements in the weeklies for Mass requests, thinking it might help our financial situation. Now I can hardly keep up with the receipts."

I nodded sympathetically, pleased that he was sharing this information. In the past, he had received occasional requests for Mass intentions — Masses said for a particular person or institution. Enclosed with each request would be a small honorarium of one or two francs. It was a common practice among country priests, whose meager salaries required some sort of augmentation. "Maybe I can help," I suggested. "At least with the receipts."

"Oh, Marie," he said, and his voice sounded genuinely appreciative. "You're a godsend."

As I entered the requests in Bérenger's notebook of Masses — noting the number of intentions requested, the name of the correspondent, and the amount of the honorarium, and leaving a column open where Bérenger could mark the date on which he had fulfilled the request — I was startled to see that he had received hundreds of requests for Mass intentions in the past few months alone. The accumulated honoraria amounted, then, to several hundreds of francs. And as the Church prohibited priests from fulfilling more than three requests a day, Bérenger had begun to fall behind.

Once the list of unfulfilled requests had swelled to fill five pages (each of which took about two weeks to get through), I brought the notebook to Bérenger, suggesting that it might be wise to send some of the intentions, honoraria included, to his brother David or the curé in Rennes-les-Bains. "Otherwise, I can't see how you'll be able to fulfill all of these," I said.

His face darkened momentarily. "I'd rather not just yet," he said. "They'll taper off eventually, and then I'll be able to catch up."

Though Bérenger had granted me his attention once more, he had grown more studied in his propriety, not as freely affectionate as he once had been. Rather than sit beside me and marvel at my writing or my bookkeeping skills, he left me alone in the office. He did not seek me out for company, only if he had a task he wanted me to complete. His eyes no longer lingered on my face over dinner. In fact, he had begun to request more frequently that he take his dinner alone in the presbytery. He always treated me with civility and even kindness — holding doors for me, praising my work on occasion — but he no longer singled me out. I began to wonder if I had misunderstood, if perhaps I had taken the smiles, the affectionate comments, the looks to be specific to me, when they were only his way with all women.

It occurred to me in my more compassionate moments that Bérenger's aloofness might have stemmed from his efforts to resist temptation. Still, I longed for him. All the pores of my skin seemed to open when he stood near me. My vision seemed to sharpen in his presence: colors intensified, edges grew more defined. With him, I was alert, engaged; without him, my senses dulled. The lust was physical, yes, but it went deeper than the skin — it lived within me like chronic pain.

I invoked an old fantasy: Bérenger and I, living side by side in a chaste marriage, sure of our mutual affection. What would the harm be in that? It was customary for a priest's housekeeper to live in the presbytery. And how could the Church keep us from loving each other? The law prohibited only fornication, and I felt sure we could avoid that.

I grew merciless. Knowing Bérenger to be

a creature of his appetites, I decided I would court him with cuisine. He had told me once that he preferred my cooking to my mother's. "Your mother's dishes are very good," he said, "but yours are temptations." So I tempted him: I made cassoulet with ample meat — bacon rind, pork loin, and sausage — and prepared the goose confit myself. I insisted that M. Gautier, the butcher, sell me only the freshest cuts he had. At home, I chose only the most perfect vegetables for Bérenger's meals. He liked to hunt and would sometimes bring home a pheasant or a hare for us to prepare. I would roast it long and slow in a stew of wine, blood, and rosemary. I stuffed sheep's tripe for him with ham, eggs, thyme, and garlic, and sliced it thin as paper. I splurged on bottles of Côtes du Roussillon and Blanquette de Limoux instead of buying the cheaper carafes from the Verdiés' vineyard.

My mother scolded me for being wasteful. "Monsieur *le curé* does not pay us enough for all this," she said, "and your father's pockets are not lined with gold." But as long as Bérenger enjoyed my meals, I kept on. Claude and my father were pleased. Claude even suggested I go to work as a chef for one of the bistros in Espéraza. "The owner is my friend's father," he said proudly. "He'll get you a job." My parents seemed to like the idea — perhaps they thought it might be an opportunity for me to meet a prospective husband, someone who wasn't already discouraged by my reputation for eccentricity. But Claude did not pursue it, and it was soon forgotten, to my relief.

Bérenger noticed my efforts. "You've outdone yourself, Marie," he said on more than one occasion, and even though he did not grace me with his roguish grin, he spoke with genuine warmth. My attention — selfishly motivated as it was — seemed to touch him.

One evening, as I entered the presbytery to deliver his supper, I found an unopened envelope on the kitchen table. The paper was creamy and fragrant with lavender water, the handwriting unmistakably feminine. The return address displayed no name, only the city of origin: Narbonne. I gave it to Bérenger at supper. He sliced it open, then read hungrily.

"Who is it from?" I asked, affecting a thoroughly unconvincing nonchalance.

He acted as if he hadn't heard and read the letter through once more, shaking his head in amused disbelief, then scoffed and tossed it into the fire.

But the next morning, as I was sweeping the hearth, I noticed the same creamy paper tucked into a protected ledge behind the andirons. Its bottom edge had been burned, obliterating the final lines of the letter. I hastily plucked it up and began to read.

Monsieur l'abbé,

The person who writes you must hide her name. To tell it would be to compromise it and to give you an unfavorable opinion of her. Yet do not judge her badly, do not think her intentions wicked, oh indeed, she has never had the slightest desire to damage the respect due a priest, a minister of God. She loves you with a deep and ardent but pure and disinterested affection. This devoted one, to sacrifice herself for you — it would be the realization of her dream, the end of all her anguish. You have captured her heart, if I may say so, despite herself, because she has long battled this irresistible attraction. She fought, she prayed, but neither battles nor prayers could extinguish this pure and noble flame that will burn in her soul as long as her body has a breath of life. You will never understand all she has suffered because of you, all she still suffers, her life is a martyrdom, an exile more cruel than death. She knows quite well how much this letter will shock you, you will find it unseemly; she finds it so herself, but does not the heart have its weaknesses, its folly? Oh, pity her, I entreat you . . .

I took the letter upstairs to Bérenger's bedroom, where he was dressing for Mass. I knocked once, then opened the door. He stood at his wardrobe in his undershirt. A hollow the size of a thumbprint nestled between his collarbones.

"So this is your secret," I snarled, tossing the letter at his bare feet. He glanced at it, but did not yet pick it up. "How pathetic."

He pulled on his cassock and buttoned it, neck to feet, as if I weren't there. He did this to inform me of the inappropriateness of my behavior — his raised chin and haughty eyes told me as much — but I was unapologetic.

"This is who you visit when you go to see your 'family,' then. This pitiful woman."

He bent down to pick the letter up and inspected it. "Fire is not what it used to be," he quipped.

How I longed to swat him! If I'd been a man, I would have swung him a punch without hesitation. But I knew how ludicrous it would be, my puny fists falling on his chest, like the paws of a cat. Instead, I funneled my anger into a beastly roar that filled the room and the presbytery, and undoubtedly penetrated the exterior walls.

"Marie!" he said sharply. "Enough." He stepped past me, walking through my fury as if it did not crackle in the air around me, and continued downstairs. I could only follow him, my rage making me cling to him as if I had been soldered there, a bracket of iron fixed to his indomitable back. I stood behind him as he sat at the table. When he asked for his tea and bread, I did not move. He laughed, to my further consternation. "You're jealous, Marie?"

I had an urge to fling the kettle at his head. "You'd better leave," I said. "Before I hurt you."

This made him throw his head back and guffaw. "Oh, Marie," he said, turning toward me. "How wonderful you are."

I found this disarming to say the least, and rather than face his open affection, I turned to the fire, where the kettle was beginning to steam. I poured his coffee and served it to him with his bread. He thanked me, beaming as if I'd blessed him. "You haven't answered my question," I said.

"I have nothing to do with this woman. Is

it my fault that she's written to me?"

"It might be," I said. "You might have encouraged it."

"Why do you think I threw it in the fire?" he asked. "If I were attached to her, whoever she is, do you think I would have burned her letter?"

"Don't pretend you don't know who she is."

"I don't really," he insisted, his mouth full now with peach jam and bread. "Well, I've wagered a guess, but I can't be sure." He chuckled. "It's as you say, Marie. She's a lonely woman, certainly to be pitied, and unfortunately has attached her affection to a priest. It's not an uncommon occurrence." He twinkled his eyes at me.

"What do you mean?" I said, my anger rising once more. "Are you implying that I — ?"

"No, no, Marie," he said. "I was only teasing."

"Don't you dare put me in the same category as her."

He took a sip of his coffee, then set the cup on the table. "I would never do such a thing." The tone of his voice was sober now, genuine. "Really, Marie. Marinette. You are in no other category but your own."

And despite my anger, I welcomed the

sound of my nickname on his lips again.

It was the first time we had alluded to our mutual affection. Somehow, our reference to it — couched in innuendo as it was — freed us both. It alleviated my anxiety, for I saw that not only was Bérenger aware of my feelings, he did not discourage them. He had given me a kind of permission, then, permission to love him. And thereafter, he seemed able to let down his guard in my presence once again. He was also more sensitive to my anxiety. Now, before leaving, he would take my hand and hold it for a long moment while he said good-bye. "I'll return in three days, Marinette. Take care of things while I'm gone." Despite the seeming neutrality of his words, I heard these gentle farewells as declarations of love.

I am not sure why my oblique admission of love effected this change in him, for I was still a menace to his integrity as a priest. I had made no promise of stamping out my desire. Perhaps he saw how helpless I was in the face of my love for him and pitied me for it. Perhaps he simply decided he was tired of struggling against me. Whatever the reason, he grew tender with me once more — but his tenderness took on a new character. It could no longer be mistaken for brotherly teasing. I was older; we were both wiser. It was an intentional tenderness, expressed in all the subtle language of adult communication: gazes, courtesies in speech and gesture, words carefully chosen, and very occasional and fleeting well-placed touches — the elbow, the shoulder, the small of the back.

The perception of having won him made me glad, of course. I grew less desperate, less lonely, less fearful. But it was a mixed joy, for I regretted the difficulty he faced in loving me. I lay awake nights, punishing myself for tempting him, vowing to renounce his affection in the morning for his own good, all the while knowing I would do no such thing. It was the worst sort of hypocrisy, for while I felt his agony in temptation, I was not willing to relieve him of it. Yet I felt I could keep my private vow that we would remain proper, that our love, while unchaste in spirit, would never cause him to literally transgress.

Our interactions were changing, the way we spoke and moved informed still by the effort of restraint, but underpinned with a new trust in the strength of our mutual feeling. We remained chaste in every way, even more so than we had been, for we barely spoke. I cooked and cleaned; Bérenger worked and ate. It was as if we were at either end of a high wire and the faltering step of one would send the other tumbling into blackness. We exchanged only the necessary words, which were mainly his: the instructions on which linens to set out for Mass, which vase to dust, which pieces of mail to post. And though I knew he relished what I prepared for him, he rarely mentioned food — or hunger.

We knew now what we were entering into. It was what I had hoped for, though the reality proved both more thrilling and more mundane than what I had imagined in the soft light of my imagination. There would be no banns, no ceremony, no declaration — not even a private one — but it was to be a marriage. A silent marriage, relatively chaste, but one that would surge forward, nonetheless, the way marriages do: in dailiness, in the shared tasks that form a life. Above all, in shared meals, our sacrament.

Our meals went this way: Bérenger sat at table and spread his napkin on his lap. I poured his wine. He sipped, nodded. I set the food before him — a soup or stew, a hunk of bread, a meat, a salad, a cheese — and then sat across the table from him, listening as I ate for Bérenger's soft, involuntary groans of satisfaction and the scrape of his spoon against the bowl.

When Miryam arrived at the camp after leaving Shimon's house, most of the men and women were asleep, the men in the open air, the women in their tent — woolen cloths draped over branches and tied to stakes in the ground. The fire still burned. Yehudah squatted by it, poking at the embers with a long stick. Miryam nodded to him and moved toward the tent, ducking to enter.

He called to her, "Where is Yeshua?" He was standing, the stick hanging from his hand.

Miryam walked closer to him so as not to wake the women. "At Shimon's. I left early."

He nodded, his eyes on her. It was unusual to leave a dinner early, but it had been unusual for her to go in the first place. They had all long ago given up notions of what was usual.

"Come," he said instead. "Stand by the fire."

She did not trust him. She trusted none of the men, except for Yeshua. Many of them were young and unmarried and inclined to look on the women lustfully. She had heard one of them joking one night, "They cook and clean for us, do everything a wife does. Why not do a wife's duty in bed, too?" There had been scattered laughter.

One night, before Yeshua had healed her, before any of the other women joined their group, a man had come to her, his face covered by a cloth. He had feverishly touched her, as if she were a whore. "Keep quiet," he said, "I won't hurt you."

She had been sleeping deeply — a rare occurrence — and so woke only partly at first. She believed herself to be dreaming still, and allowed him to touch her, allowed herself to feel his hands against her body.

As the stranger began to undress her, she awoke fully. *This should not be happening,* she thought. Keeping her eyes on his neck, she moved forward as if to kiss him and instead bit the flesh at his collarbone, as if she were biting into a leg of lamb. All the while she thought, *This must not happen.*

The man screamed a curse and recoiled, his hand to his neck. She had broken the skin; blood-metal was on her tongue. He struck her across the face. She fell back and when she looked up again, he had gone. There were noises from the others then, voices, a flint struck against a stone. Footsteps approached her.

Levi spoke, "Miryam?"

"Yes," she responded, her heart beating.

"Are you all right? We heard a sound."

"Yes. I'm fine," she said. "I heard it, too. It frightened me."

"It's all right," he said. "We're keeping watch now. You can go back to sleep."

She looked now at Yehudah and wondered if he might have been the man. His fingers were long and slim, as the man's had been. Yehudah's whole body was slim. He stood and stepped like a heron, carefully lifting his long legs, as if afraid he might step in goat dung.

"What is it?" she asked.

"Come closer," he said. "I don't want to yell."

She did, warily. She stood opposite him, the fire between them. His face was streaked, as if he'd been crying.

"I'm worried, Miryam," he said. He looked into the fire. In his eyes, the flames pitched and soared.

She didn't respond. She was not prepared or willing to accept the stumblings toward intimacy that the other men occasionally made with her. They saw her closeness with Yeshua — unorthodox, improper — and thought she should be their intimate as well, should listen to them, hold them. But she would not be passed from man to man as if she were a loaf of bread.

"I'm worried," he continued. "People are noticing now. They're gathering in great crowds. They're ready to drop everything and follow us."

"Pardon me," Miryam responded. "But isn't that good news?"

"Yes, of course," he said impatiently. "But Yeshua needs to *lead* them, not just talk to them. They'll only grow, these crowds, the closer we get to Yerushalayim. He has to steer them in the right direction, otherwise they'll overpower him and we'll lose everything, all the progress we've made."

Miryam watched the fire. Yehudah's voice was loud, too loud for the night. "How should he steer them? Isn't healing them, teaching them, enough?"

"You've seen how the soldiers stand at the edges of the crowd, keeping watch. If Yeshua doesn't take control, they will."

"What are you suggesting, Yehudah?"

"I'm suggesting rising up, Miryam," he said, raising the stick toward the sky. "It's time to move forward, take action. Or at least start putting the idea in people's minds. Otherwise we'll never get anywhere."

"You want him to lead the people into rebellion?"

"Yes!" he shouted at the sky. "Rebellion!

Revolution! Pry the dirty Roman fingers from our land!"

"Shhh," she said.

"We're wasting time, all this puttering around with miracles and teaching. We need to organize, to march — we need to unite against our common enemy!"

"You don't want people to be healed?"

"No, no. Of course I do. It's not that. But that healing — that has nothing to do with our message. It's just a way to get people to listen."

Miryam continued to watch the fire.

"Listen, Miryam," he said. He stepped around the fire and took her arm roughly. "Yeshua's changed. Can't you see it? He's losing focus. He gets distracted too easily. He used to talk like he had the voice of God thundering in his ear. But he's grown quieter now, sadder. Sometimes I wonder whether God has left him."

She wrenched her arm from his grasp. It had been him, she knew it now. She recognized the feel of his hand. "And if he has, you're prepared to leave him, too?" she said. Her voice was indignant, as if she herself had never doubted. But Yehudah's doubt was so ugly, so self-concerned, she found her own dwindling.

Yehudah smiled ironically and shook his

head. "I forgot who I was talking to," he said. He pursed his mouth with disgust. "Why do you let him come to you, Miryam? A well-bred woman like you? A *chazzan*'s daughter?"

She fixed him with a stern glare. "It's none of your business what I choose to do."

"Aren't the sins of all Yisrael our business? That's what we're about here, is it not? Saving Yisrael from her sins? We're all accountable to each other."

"You are in no position to judge my sins, Yehudah. Pull the log from your own eye."

"Ah, she quotes him, even. A true disciple." He tossed a twig into the fire; they watched it flare in a thin line. "He won't marry you, you know. He told me himself. A wife would get in the way of his ministry, he said."

"I'm not looking for a husband. I have no need of a husband. I have a Rabbi." She grieved a little, speaking these words. She would die unmarried, childless, alone. It was not what she had planned.

"A woman is either a wife or a whore, Miryam. I see you've made your choice." He walked away, toward the trees on the edge of the clearing.

Miryam watched him go, still feeling the grip of his hand on her arm. There was so much ugliness. She squatted in front of the fire, resting her chin on her knees. The mind was unfailingly ugly — the contortions it made in order to conform to the desires, the rationales it erected. Yehudah was jealous. It was a scent, like the wine on his breath. He was jealous of Yeshua's gifts, of his growing fame. Of her. She could not condemn him — she was just the same. Shame washed over her at the thought of the woman who'd kissed Yeshua's feet. Ugliness, hatred, were too much in the way.

Yehudah, she knew, loved Yeshua, perhaps more than the others. When he listened to Yeshua speak, his eyes grew ardent with admiration and belief. When Yeshua was gone, it was Yehudah who wanted to dwell on his words, to mince each sentence like a leek and taste the sounds on his own tongue. Yet while he loved Yeshua's ideas, he despised his humanity. He had no room in his heart for the imperfections that make up a person, for the weaknesses, the pain, for the stumbling, the falls, the dead ends that accompany a great trek. He required Yeshua to be perfect and humble; he demanded he love them as fully as God, but could not abide his need to be loved in return.

The fire popped as a log broke and fell into the ash. Miryam brushed a cinder from her robe. The problem with Yehudah was that since he did not tolerate weakness, he could not love any man on earth. He could only love God. But God had made man, in full knowledge of his shortcomings, and he had pronounced him good. To call man evil was to contradict God's own judgment, to denounce his creation. To hate a man, any man, was to hate God.

Miryam stood, overcome with a sudden longing for Yeshua. She wanted to thank him, to tell him how she loved him. She lifted her arms to the sky, beheld the brilliant moon and the stars scattered like seeds, and sang softly,

"O my dove, in the clefts of the rock, in the covert of the cliff, let me see your face.
Let me hear your voice, for your voice is sweet, and your face is comely.
Catch us the little foxes, the little foxes that spoil the vineyards, for our vineyards are in blossom!"

CHAPTER EIGHT

We were discreet. We had nothing to hide, really; we had committed no sin, at least not literally. But we knew the way gossip flared in our village, and we were not anxious to be the subjects of the next conflagration. Bérenger still acted as though he was a member of the family, taking many of his meals with us — though I served him in the presbytery just as often. I was careful not to speak too familiarly with him in front of anyone outside of the family. If anything, our behavior became more awkward, for we were both so aware of the joy we felt in each other's company that we had to concentrate in order to disguise it. Even so, we performed the most mundane actions — passing a plate, greeting each other — with a new buoyancy that was impossible to hide.

My parents recognized it. It was a minor relief for my father, I believe, for he no longer had to worry that Bérenger might tempt my mother in his absence. Having made no personal investment in the incorruptibility of priests, he saw our arrangement as I did — as an irregular marriage — and even approved of it, as if it were a political statement, as if I'd wooed Bérenger in order to weaken the Church. My mother had a more difficult time. My closeness with Bérenger brought about their alienation; it lost her a friend. It was a gradual process, the transference of Bérenger's allegiance, and perhaps necessary, for it would have been awkward if both my mother and I were his confidantes. She retreated gradually, allowing me to step forward and assume the role of Bérenger's primary companion. She may have acted out of respect for my father's unspoken jealousy, but I believe she wanted, in her own way, to encourage our companionship, for my sake. It was not easy for her. She still hoped I would marry, and even suggested young men from time to time, though she always withdrew her suggestion when she saw the distaste on my face.

On my twentieth birthday, Bérenger gave me an amulet of polished amber on a gold chain. My father whistled low, admiring the stone. Tears stood in my eyes; I touched Bérenger's wrist in gratitude. My mother looked away.

She came to me the next afternoon, solemn-faced, and asked me if what people were saying were true.

"I haven't heard the gossip, *maman*," I said, searching for how to respond. When I saw that she would not elaborate — she had set her jaw in a position that indicated it would not soon open — I continued gently, "So I can't speak to its truth. But I can tell you that I have a deep affection for Monsieur *le curé,* and I believe it is one that he shares for me." I blushed as I spoke, even imagining she might share my pride, as I'd finally won the heart of a respectable man.

"Understand me, Marie," she whispered, her voice like a razor. "I will tolerate your friendship as long as it remains only that. But if you ever tempt him to break his vow, I will no longer call you my daughter."

"We haven't sinned, *maman*," I insisted, desperately. "He's broken no vow." She held up her hand, signaling the end of the conversation, and left the room. But I did not doubt her word. I knew the strength of her will.

Nor did I resent the boundary she'd drawn. I believed our love could remain pure, that it could rise above the morbidity of the flesh. I told myself that after the unfortunate episode with Gérard, I wanted nothing to do with physical love. Ours would be a marriage of minds, I felt sure, even as I basked in the sensation of arousal.

Our chastity became a source of titillation. My body temperature rose in Bérenger's presence. If he stood with me as I cooked, I grew clumsy: spoons, onion husks, whole sausages landed on the floor. I made foolish spelling errors when I took his dictation, distracted by the proximity of his hand to my shoulder. When he spoke, I gazed at his mouth, his eyes, the hair curling at his ear. The days passed quickly this way, as I lolled in the warmth of his attentions.

But my fantasies of our intellectual intimacy were far more glorious than the reality of our conversations, which were often arguments, even confrontations. Bérenger had a way of making me bold. I demanded to know his mind, his *real* thoughts, not parroted doctrine. I couldn't help myself: I challenged him. I asked for substantiation; I pressed him to expand his statements; I needled him, prodded him, pushed him. Knowing beforehand what he would say of Renan, I brought him up anyway, then listened scornfully as Bérenger rejected him. Darwin, as I had expected, produced a similar reaction: Bérenger declared Darwin's vision of existence to be an earthly hell, a place of clamoring selfishness, purposeless suffering, a world devoid of God's loving order, his compassionate and just administration.

"How can you, as a devout Catholic, tolerate such ideas, Marie?" he would ask, incredulous. "You allow your mind too much sway over your heart."

"God gave me a mind and a heart," I retorted.

"God gave you a mind, yes, and with it the ability to choose. But he also gave you the sole righteous choice: the path, through his Son, that leads to him, to the accomplishment of his will."

"But how can you know his will with such conviction?" I asked.

"The doctrines of the true Church express his will. That's all I need."

"But the Church is created and led by men."

"Marie! Your incessant questions will end up extinguishing your faith!"

Virtually any religious discussion we embarked on ended in this manner, with a peremptory declaration from Bérenger. He clung to doctrine as a small child does to its mother. His closed-mindedness infuriated me.

But despite our differences, our affection for each other only grew. I believe it was even fed by our impassioned arguments. And the moments of reconciliation were sweet. Bérenger might bring my hand to his face and press it against his cheek, resting the weight of his skull in my palm. *"Mon petit ange,"* he would call me. My little angel.

"Mon ours fou," I would respond, touching his lips with a fleeting finger. My crazy bear.

As my mother had noted, the village had discerned our intimacy despite our discretion. Exactly how they divined the nature of our relationship I do not know. Maybe it was the wind. Whatever the source, word spread quickly and, as is common with rumor, inaccurately.

Rural people are practical. A priest is useful for blessing the planting of crops in the spring and the harvest in the fall. Crossing oneself before sowing seed or slicing bread is good luck. Ringing the church bell or tossing pieces of priest's dung — pebbles affixed with wax crosses — keeps away a bad storm. Religion, too, is practical. If you are ill, you pray to the proper saint: Saint Eutropius for dropsy; Saint Cloud for boils; Saint Dietrine for herpes; Saint Aignan for ringworm. If you want a husband, you go to the grotto at Saint Salvaire and throw a stone against a rock. Celibacy is impractical, even suspect. A priest who takes a lover can therefore be accepted, even embraced — by some. Such a priest can no longer hold himself above his parishioners as purer and less stained by sin than they: he becomes one of them, and thereby earns their respect. Such a priest can enter the inner rooms; he can sit with the rest of the family by the bed as a woman labors to give birth; he can mourn the dead by their deathbeds openly and without formality. He can weave himself more tightly into the fabric of his parish.

There were some like my mother, generally the more faithful parishioners, who wanted their priest stainless. Mme Flèche, who prayed in the church every morning before Mass, began to eye me with contempt, as did M. Lébadou and his wife. Mme Montaucon affected a disdain for me — she turned down a different path if she saw me coming, or averted her eyes when passing me was inevitable — but I knew her haughtiness was born of jealousy rather than offense. Given the opportunity, she would have stood proudly in my place. On the whole, people recognized our relationship for what it was — or what it would become — and generally acted as if they had ex-

251

pected it all along.

Of course, Bérenger's reputation was hard to tarnish, after he had made such commendable progress in the church. The roof was finished, the red of the new tiles almost indecent next to their weather-worn neighbors. The sanctuary vault no longer threatened to collapse. A beautiful chestnut confessional had been installed in the sanctuary as well as several new pews, which had seemed a questionable decision at the time but proved to be wise, as the number of attendees on a Sunday began to increase. People were pleased. They enjoyed the magnificence of the gilded marble altar and tabernacle and the sky-blue wall of the apse behind it. The face of the altar was now filled in with Bérenger's Marie Madeleine scene, which had come out quite well. And a set of new marble steps led from the nave to the choir, which was set off by a low balustrade. The rest of the interior was still plainly decorated — the floor the original cold stone, the walls unadorned, the nave as yet empty of art — but most of us liked it that way. We were proud of our church — no one more than Bérenger himself, who went so far as to invite the bishop to admire it. On the day the monseigneur blessed the church, the village swelled with pride and forgot, temporarily, to wonder aloud where Bérenger had gotten the money to accomplish such an impressive restoration.

The topic was not buried, though. Everyone remembered the difficulty Bérenger had originally faced in funding his projects, and that when he returned from Narbonne, an unspecified donor had solved his financial problems, at least temporarily. The question resurfaced in the tavern and at the market: Who had given M. *le curé* that kind of money? Why? Who would care about our little church? Added to this mystery, there was now the matter of the "treasure" Bérenger had found. For word had gotten out; the workers who had helped lift the stone had not kept silent. The story of M. *le curé*'s treasure hummed through the village and traveled as far as Limoux, where I heard it from the tailor one day when I went to have a new set of trousers made for Father. He asked me if it was true — if Bérenger had found riches beneath the church, and if he was keeping it all for himself. I assured him it was not, that he had only found some worthless old paraphernalia, buried there by a former priest.

It had been more than a year since Madame had gone to Paris, more than a year since I'd brought her my sketch of the knight's stone and she'd left me with the cryptic statement that had it been found in Rennes-le-Château, there would be more to say. I had written her a letter soon after she'd gone, sending my condolences at the passing of her aunt. At the end of my letter, I had alluded to the comment she had made about the knight's stone. Her response, some weeks later, revealed nothing. It thanked me for my wishes of condolence and assured me that all was well. She explained her long absence by saying that her aunt had left some discrepancies in her affairs that had to be straightened out. She said nothing regarding the stone and its mysteries, only that she would be returning to Rennes-le-Château in the future, and that we would continue our discussion upon her return.

I began to wonder again about the items we'd found beneath the stone: the painting, the heavy golden cross, the silver chalice and bowl, the tiny bell, the censer, the porcelain *santons,* and the moldy silk stole. Also the coins, which Bérenger had claimed were brass medals. I had seen no sign of any of them since the day we'd found them. Where exactly had he put them? I thought again of his frequent trips and the satchel he always brought with him.

When I brought the subject up that evening, Bérenger stiffened. "I thought you'd forgotten all about that."

"No," I said, disturbed by his obvious agitation.

"Well, I'd appreciate it if you'd put it out of your head, Marie. Really. There's no reason to concern yourself with it."

"Excuse me, but there is. I was very interested in that stone. And the message the priest left. The gates of death and all that."

"Yes, well. He was probably in trouble at the time. Priests were hunted in those days, you know. Maybe he feared for his life."

"Maybe. Still, I think there's more to it than that, don't you?"

He shrugged. His nonchalance was unconvincing.

"Where did you put that old case, anyway? And everything inside of it?"

He looked at me pointedly, as if deciding whether or not to trust me. "If you must know, I sold it."

"Why? To whom?"

"Oh, there are antiques dealers who go in for that sort of thing."

"And the coins?"

"Those I deposited in the bank. Turns out they were louis d'or pieces after all." He avoided my eyes.

"But I thought you wanted to wait to hear from the Austrian."

"Well, I waited long enough. It's been almost two years, and we haven't heard a thing. I've needed every penny I can find to make this renovation happen."

I thought of the incessant Mass requests, the accumulated honoraria. "Well, why didn't you tell me at least?"

"Because I knew you would protest. Forgive me, *ma chérie,* but I am responsible for the church and its finances: these are my decisions to make."

"What about that book?"

"That's just an old register. Church records."

"You didn't sell that, I hope."

"Oh, no," he said. "No, that is truly worthless. It's around here somewhere."

Though he had answered my questions straightforwardly, I couldn't help but feel he was keeping something from me.

It was soon after that discussion that the Austrian finally paid us a visit. He arrived on a wet March morning, conspicuous in his finery: foreign tweeds, alligator-skin shoes, and a brushed felt hat capping his sleek hair. He wore a trimmed beard, walked jauntily, and spoke impeccable French with a clipped, imperious accent. I answered his knock, my hair covered by a handkerchief, my hands raw from scrubbing soda. He asked graciously for "Monsieur *le curé,*" but his expression betrayed how quickly the sight of me had moved him to judgment: woman, servant, poor, ignorant. My hand flew to my handkerchief, as if I might be able to change his mind by rearranging my hair.

I led him to the church porch, where Bérenger was sketching plans in a notebook. Seeing us, he set down his notebook and pen and greeted the stranger cordially. When the man introduced himself, Bérenger appeared momentarily horrified. "So glad to finally make your acquaintance, monsieur," he said, recovering and offering his hand. "What an honor."

"The honor is mine, Monsieur *le curé.*"

"I hope our humble village has not disappointed you."

The Austrian laughed. "The walk uphill has already offered me more beauty than I could have imagined. What a glorious place."

"I thank you," Bérenger responded. A silence ensued. Bérenger looked like one of his hunted hares, eyes unblinking, caught off-guard at the moment of his death.

"Perhaps the gentleman would enjoy a tour, Monsieur *le curé*," I offered.

"A fine idea."

"Yes, yes," Bérenger hurried. "Just the thing. Though it's a shame your arrival could not have coincided with a sunny day, when the views are more splendid."

"We might start with the church," said the man as he walked toward the door, eyeing the exterior.

"Of course. We've been very busy with our efforts at restoring the building, as you can see." Bérenger followed the man inside.

I longed to go with them, but it would have appeared strange, so I set to work preparing a suitable meal for their return, congratulating myself for having dusted thoroughly that morning. They remained in the church more than an hour — longer than even the most detailed tour warranted. I was making an errand home when they emerged, and I noticed that Bérenger's expression had grown dark and guarded. Deep in discussion, they continued past the presbytery to the fields beyond, where they might catch a glimpse of the red roofs and smokestacks of Espéraza beneath the cloud cover.

When they returned, another hour later, the top leaves of the salad had already wilted. I picked them off, setting them aside to feed to the rabbits, and laid out the bowls for the stew. Bérenger gave me a grateful grimace.

"You must understand my position," the Austrian was saying. "Certainly, I don't require you to agree with it. I have nothing against priests. Far from it, in fact. The priests I knew in Vienna have been some of the most outspoken voices, the most daring minds I've known. Though there were a few whose souls belonged not to God but to the emperor. In any case, my question is this: Why the inconsistency? How can both Saint Paul and the gospel accounts be true? It seems to me that either Christ rose to heaven, body intact, and that explains the disappearance of his corpse from the tomb, or he didn't — his rising was purely spiritual and his body remained here, below, as Saint Paul has it."

Bérenger answered immediately, his face charged with the passion of his argument. "Saint Paul says, as do the gospels, that Jesus died for our sins, was buried, and rose again on the third day in accordance with the scriptures. And that he appeared to Peter, the apostles, and then to more than five hundred brethren at one time."

"But what does 'rose' mean? Or 'appeared'? We speak of them as if they mean 'in the flesh,' that he appeared in the flesh to the apostles and the crowd of five hundred."

"And so he did. 'See my hands and feet,' " Bérenger quoted. " 'A spirit has not flesh and bones as you see that I have.' "

"Exactly my point," exclaimed the Austrian. "We read that passage in Luke. But Paul says, in no uncertain terms, 'Flesh and blood cannot inherit the kingdom of God, nor does the perishable inherit the imperishable.' Flesh does not rise, then, in Paul. It's impossible there, but possible, even imperative, in Luke. It's contradictory, my dear *curé.* You can't deny that."

"I can and will. Paul preached the resurrection. It was the essence of his message. 'If the dead are not raised, then Christ has not been raised; if Christ has not been raised then your faith is futile.' "

"But raised *how?* Paul says, 'We shall all be changed.' From the perishable to the imperishable. From the flesh to the spirit. As Christ was. His *spirit* is what ascended. Is that not right?"

"*Noli me tangere,* Christ said to the Madeleine. 'Do not hold me back, for I have not yet ascended to the Father.' How could she hold back a spirit?"

The Austrian leaned back in his chair. "Never get into a quoting match with a priest," he laughed. "I still haven't learned that lesson."

Bérenger's eyes flashed, his fingers kneaded the table. "Christ ascended to the Father bodily, and was changed from flesh to spirit after his ascension."

"A-ha," the Austrian said, sitting upright once again. "So the magic happened then in heaven?"

"Yes," said Bérenger, though his eyes were wary. "Most likely."

"Most likely?"

"You concern yourself too entirely with the literal. These are matters for God, not man."

"Agreed. Man is concerned primarily with the flesh. And does not flesh imply sin?"

"As it is commonly used, I suppose," Bérenger conceded.

"Jesus, then, being born into the flesh — could he have been fully free of sin?"

"What a question."

"Pardon me, Monsieur *le curé* — I don't mean to cause you offense. It is a question that has fascinated me for years now, and I can't help but ask it of one who is better schooled in theology than I. Having lived as many years as I have and seen much of the world, I have the notion that one of the characteristics that defines humanity is sin. We cannot escape it, it seems."

"You're wrong," Bérenger replied. "It may be rare, but it is possible. Think of our saints. Bernadette, Germaine —"

"Yes," the man interrupted. He rubbed his forehead vigorously. "Is it not possible, though, that Jesus was born into the flesh as a man, lived a man's life, complete with sin and repentance, and then rose above it, as a saint does — perhaps even higher in his devotion and communion with God until he ultimately achieved union with the divine?"

"Jesus, as you know, was not born through sin, nor was his mother, the blessed Virgin. They were, therefore, not subject to the same tendency toward sin as the human race is, who are conceived in sin. It's difficult for most people to apprehend the mysterious union of mortal and immortal that characterized our Savior — that he could be fully man and fully God at once. Too commonly I have seen people try to reduce Christ, to make him into something smaller than he was, because their minds are small themselves, too small to contain the enormity of Jesus. You are trying to make him common. You should look to the

Madeleine, if that's the kind of holiness you desire, the rising above sin. She's the very model of a penitent sinner."

"A wise comment. Yes, perhaps." He sipped his wine and nodded again. The argument seemed to be finished, and I was about to step forward to clear the plates when the Austrian spoke again. "Forgive me once more, Monsieur *le curé*. For argument's sake, grant me an assumption. If Saint Paul's declaration, that the flesh cannot inherit the kingdom of God, is in fact the truer statement —"

"One is not truer —" Bérenger protested.

"Please." He smiled hostilely. "Allow me to finish my thought. If we assume that in fact Christ did not rise from the dead in his own flesh, but rather in spirit, then the question remains: Where did his body go?"

"I can't argue according to false assumptions."

The Austrian pressed further. "Wouldn't you admit that it's possible the body might have been stolen — by those closest to him, perhaps, who wanted to give it a proper burial?"

"No. I would not admit that. Then the message the apostles preached throughout Palestine for the rest of their lives would amount to pure lies. I will never admit such a thing."

"No, I suppose not." He smiled again, smugly this time, and I felt a keen dislike for him and his aggressive grinning. "Others do, though, or did. The Knights Templar, for example, may have held fast to just such an idea."

"Then they were blasphemers, and earned their fate."

The Austrian paused, letting the viciousness of Bérenger's statement penetrate the moment. The Templars, a medieval monastic order who had acted as a kind of police force in Jerusalem during the Crusades, had been arrested *en masse* in France, tortured, and many killed. Then he leaned forward and said gently, "Forgive me, Father. I see I've angered you."

"Not at all," Bérenger insisted, through clenched jaws.

"I have a reputation for incorrigibility, as you can see."

"His body was raised to heaven," Bérenger said in his sermon voice. "You need trouble yourself no longer with the question. Get rid of such crazy notions. That old priest — he had obviously lost his faith to suggest such a thing. It happens sometimes, sadly. Such people are deserving of pity and care, but not respect. Put him out of your head."

He gave a sinister smile. "I will do my best to follow your advice," he said. He slipped his hand beneath his coat pocket and removed a silver cigarette case. He offered the open case, fragrant with tobacco, to Bérenger, who refused. Striking a match on a flint the size of his thumbnail, the Austrian said, "I am a man of the world, Monsieur *le curé*. I do not go in for holiness, as you have undoubtedly already observed. Things that pertain to this world interest me. I remain interested in your lovely little church. Despite our differences, I do hope you will continue to keep your eyes open for me. There are five thousand francs available for your projects if you agree." He bowed his head in a feigned sort of deference as he made the offer.

This astounded me, and I could not help but gasp — audibly enough that it startled Bérenger from his prideful fury. He turned abruptly to where I stood by the hearth. "Marie! Leave us at once," he said.

Humiliated, I followed his order. I saw the Austrian only once more, from my kitchen window some hours later, when a dusty pink had begun to color the low-lying clouds. He carried his jacket over his shoulder and whistled as he walked.

I found Bérenger in his office as soon as the man had gone. "Did you take it?" I asked. "Did you accept his offer?" I had chosen — rather graciously, I thought — to ignore his abrupt dismissal, as it evidently stemmed from his tamped-down rage at the archduke.

"You should have removed yourself, Marie," Bérenger replied angrily. "It wasn't appropriate for you to be there."

"Why?" I asked.

"I shouldn't have to tell you every time I need privacy."

"How was I to know he was going to offer you money?" I retorted.

Bérenger glared at me. "It has nothing to do with money. Our conversation was not for your ears."

"Don't be ridiculous. We've had conversations like that ourselves."

He remained silent.

"All right. I'm sorry. I didn't mean to trespass on your privacy."

Bérenger grunted an acknowledgment of the apology. He was busying himself with his papers, avoiding my eyes. I waited in vain for him to offer more information.

"Pardon me, *mon cher,*" I ventured again when he remained silent, "but you must allow me my curiosity. Did he speak of the letters we sent? Did he say why he hadn't responded?"

"He was away at war."

"Oh. A soldier."

"A blasphemer," Bérenger muttered.

"He's ruffled you."

"He's no friend to the Church, Marie."

"Was he angry you'd sold the old church things we found beneath the stone?"

"No. He seemed uninterested in them. He was far more taken with slandering Christ's holy name."

"Did you show him the stone?"

"Yes," he said. "In fact, we lifted it together. He wanted to make sure there was nothing else beneath it." He sighed. "The man gives me a headache."

"But why is he so interested in our church?"

"He's been entirely brainwashed by rubbish fed to him by the Freemasons. It's a terrible pity, really. All the rest of the Hapsburgs are faithful Catholics. He's a lost sheep. Sometimes this happens to royalty, sadly. They do have a tendency to fragility in their blood. Occasionally, a child is born a bit off." He shook his head. I waited for the story I could sense was coming.

"It turns out," Bérenger began, "that he first heard of our village not from his sister

267

the abbess, but from an old French priest he had met as a young man. This priest used to sit by the fountain in the central plaza in Vienna, blessing everyone who passed, forever smiling. They called him *l'abbé des sourires.* He slept beneath the church eaves. Most people paid him no attention, but our young prince befriended him. *L'abbé des sourires* had fled France after the Revolution. There was only one thing he had left undone, a task he had promised to complete for a friend of his but couldn't, so quickly had the violence erupted in his village.

"This friend, a priest *l'abbé* had known in seminary, had written to him often of a particular parishioner of his — the lady of the village, and a great patroness of the church — who had grown sadly deranged. She insisted on her own divinity, insisted that she and her family had descended from Jesus, who she believed, God forgive me, had sired a child with Marie Madeleine."

"A child?"

"I told you the man was off." Bérenger spoke heatedly.

"Evidently," I said. I would have to proceed carefully if I wanted to hear the whole story.

Bérenger sighed scornfully, then continued. "The village dismissed the woman as

268

mad, and the priest was inclined to agree, except for the fact of the woman's repeated visions. The woman had episodes, it seems, moments when her face was transformed. This was what convinced the priest apparently, after he witnessed one of her episodes — the appearance of her face. Normally wrinkled and troubled, it grew still and gentle, like a child's, and a smile of such grace and blessedness grew on it that she appeared to be welcoming our Lord himself." Bérenger himself appeared momentarily transported, and I thought I glimpsed the light of curiosity in his eyes. But he collected himself and added, "Those were the words the archduke used."

"Of course," I said.

"The woman described her visions to this priest as they visited her, one by one, and as he heard them it seemed to him that she was receiving a new gospel, told to her directly by Marie Madeleine. The priest took to writing each vision down, showing them to no one. They terrified him. When she died, he was greatly relieved, and he buried the book of the transcribed visions with her. But the visions haunted him day and night until he was compelled to dig up the grave. He planned to burn the book. But when he exhumed the grave — a few years after the lady's death — he found that the woman's body was uncorrupted. The book of her visions — which the priest had tucked beneath her, lay open on her belly as if she had been reading it." He stopped. He appeared shaken.

Gently, I prompted, "What did the priest do?"

"He removed the book and reinterred the body. Soon enough, the Revolution came, and he fled the country."

"He must have been terrified," I said.

Bérenger was quiet.

"But what was his friend — *l'abbé des sourires* — supposed to do for him?" I asked. "What was the task?"

"Just before he left, the priest wrote *l'abbé* a note, telling him to come as soon as possible. Apparently he feared the church would be looted, and he had hidden something he wanted *l'abbé* to protect."

"The book," I said.

"Probably."

"But did *l'abbé des sourires* have any idea where to look? Was he supposed to find the flask?"

"One can assume. The archduke didn't say specifically." Bérenger was scowling. I wanted to comfort him — I rarely saw him so agitated — but I knew I would not be able to keep the excitement from my voice. We sat in silence for a long moment.

"What a story," I offered weakly.

"Ridiculous," he huffed.

Then, cautiously, "What about that book you found beneath the stone? The old church register?"

"That's merely a list of baptisms, weddings, funerals, and burials. Church business."

"Are you sure? Have you read the entire thing?"

"Yes, as a matter of fact. Cover to cover. There's nothing in there about any visions."

"Can I see it?"

"Why? You don't believe me?"

"It's not that. I just — I just want to see it. It's interesting, Bérenger." I was losing patience.

He shrugged unconvincingly.

"I'm surprised the Austrian didn't ask to see it himself."

"Why should he? He didn't know it exists."

"Didn't you write him about it? When you found all the other things?"

"I didn't list every item we'd found. I merely mentioned that we'd found a stash of old church paraphernalia. Nothing very interesting, or even all that unusual for that matter."

"But surely he asked you about those things on his visit."

"Yes. He did. He asked if I had found a book matching his description. I said no."

"You didn't even mention the register?"

"No. Why should I? It's not relevant."

"It simply seems like you were keeping it from him for some reason."

"I didn't trust him. He spoke too freely about sacred ideas. The man is a Freemason, Marie. He's been seduced by the Templar Knights. He thinks they harbored some secret knowledge that they learned during their residence in Jerusalem and passed down through the centuries, knowledge about the whereabouts of Jesus' bones. God help the poor man."

I hummed sympathetically.

"Apparently, one of the ancestors of the madwoman was a Templar himself," he added. "Bertrand de Blanchefort."

"Blanchefort. The castle ruins just east of us."

"Yes. That was the Blanchefort family home centuries ago."

"But what does the Austrian think the Templars have to do with the madwoman's visions?" I asked.

"He thinks the woman might have known something. He thinks she may have revealed some of the Templars' secret knowledge in her 'visions.' "

"I see."

"The whole thing is completely absurd. The man is a maniac." He rubbed his face with both hands.

"So you turned down his offer, I assume." Bérenger was silent.

"The money he offered you," I said. "You accepted it?"

"Don't speak that way to me. It was a gift."

"In exchange for a service."

"Nothing more than to keep my eyes open."

"And to report to him what you found."

"I was not prepared to have such a man rooting around our church."

"You should have refused his money, then," I insisted.

"Our church is in need, Marie."

"But you lied. You promised him something in exchange for his money with plans never to deliver it."

Bérenger lunged forward and swiped the surface of his desk. A glass paperweight flew against the wall, shattering. Papers sprayed into a momentary storm before settling haphazardly at our feet. He stood before me, glowering with rage. "And how do you make your living, I ask you? Preying on a man's weakness! Wriggling your way into his home and his heart through your constant, unrelenting temptations! Don't pretend to such purity, my dear Marie. You're wiser than that."

I exhaled sharply, feeling his words as a blade in the gut. I reached behind me for support and found the back of a chair. "I hadn't thought my presence to be so reprehensible to you," I said quietly.

He turned toward the hearth, his shoulders a stone wall.

"I'll leave, then," I said. And I did, shutting the door firmly behind me. I did not begin to weep until I reached the crest of the hill, where the path continued downward through the broom and brush toward Espéraza. I walked for a long time, until my tears had dried, and my hands had stopped trembling.

Bérenger apologized later that day. He brought me a small bouquet of early anemone and woodrush. "I spoke rashly, Marie," he said. "I took my anger at the Austrian out on you, unfairly. Please forgive me."

I accepted the apology and the bouquet. But his fury left me shaken, and I found it difficult to return to my former unfettered joy in his company, not only because of the violence — the shattered paperweight, his accusation — but because I feared he was right. I had been selfish. All this time I had been so focused on my own desire to be with him that I had been blind to his anguish, how I wore him down. I was ashamed and saddened, and profoundly confused. Hadn't we entered into things together? Hadn't he wanted my company? His words had cudgeled the story of our companionship, knocked its features askew.

I avoided him for the next several days, asking my mother to bring his supper. When I had to address him, I did it with a new reserve in my voice and my demeanor.

Bérenger noticed. He became overly jovial, trying to lighten my mood with jokes and little kindnesses. He brought flowers often —"to brighten the house," he said, smiling sorrowfully at me — and requested my company when he went for his daily walk. He had embarked on a project to collect a hundred round stones for a grotto he intended to build in the church garden, and said that he needed my help. I refused, declaring I had too much to do at home.

Finally, one day, he insisted. "I won't leave your side until you accompany me," he said. "I'll be in your way all day."

I relented. I wiped my hands and hung my apron on its hook. But I walked at a remove, keeping my eyes on the ground, ostensibly in search of stones.

"Why are you punishing me, Marie?" Bérenger asked after we'd walked in silence for some time. "I've apologized, haven't I? What more must I do?"

I looked away, embarrassed. "I do not mean to punish you, Monsieur *le curé*."

"*Monsieur?*" he said, and laughed bitterly. "You haven't called me that for years."

I kept walking.

"Won't you even look at me, Marie? Marinette?" He stopped and took my arm, gently, in his. "Please."

I turned to face him. "I am only trying to avoid tempting you. You were right. I have been selfish."

"No, no, Marie," he said, pressing his thumb into my palm. "No, I was unfair. Please. I desire your friendship. I am not myself without it."

I nodded, unable to keep a tear of relief from sliding down my cheek.

He rubbed it away with his thumb. "How

I cherish you," he whispered.

I was glad for our reconciliation, glad to be relaxed and natural once again in his presence. But I remained cautious, and grew more judicious with my affection.

I was curious, too, about the old leather-bound book. When Bérenger was out, I took to snooping: I tunneled through his closet, rustling each of his shirts and pants and standing on a chair to look in the corners of the top shelf. I knocked along the length and breadth of each wall, searching for hollow spots. I wrested off the panel of the crawlspace, and sullied my skirt and hands feeling around in the dark. I even attempted to pry up one of the floorboards — but I was neither strong nor skilled enough to do it.

I was rewarded for my efforts one afternoon as I was replacing the freshly laundered linens in the sacristy chest. The drawer would not close properly, it felt as if something was blocking it, and so I opened the cabinet below and leaned into the dark chamber, feeling around for the obstacle that might have gotten lodged behind the drawer. My fingers found leather, gripped and pulled, and moving back into the room, I found myself holding the leather-bound book that had been buried beneath the church floor.

With no regard for the time of day or the chores I should have been attending to, I sat in a shaft of blue light — sunlight filtering through the stained-glass window — and began to read.

The pages were irregularly cut and brittle, their bottom edges broken and torn. I held the book between my knees, keeping it only partially open so as to preserve the binding, and handled the pages gingerly. It was just what Bérenger had said, an old church register, a record of the marriages, births, and deaths that had transpired in the parish between 1694 and 1726. Mercifully, the handwriting was legible, though the ink had partially faded, and despite the indirect lighting, I could decipher the text tolerably well. The first several pages held nothing of interest — names upon names, none of which were familiar. But when I arrived at the pages detailing the events of 1705, I stopped short.

In the year one thousand seven hundred five, the thirtieth day of March, died, in the castle of this place, Lady D—, about seventy-five years old, widow of Sir A. D—, lord of Pauligne, old treasurer of

France in the generality of Montpellier. She was buried the thirty-first of said month in the church of this place, in the tomb of the Lords that is beside the Balustrade.

I shut the book, then opened it again. *The tomb of the Lords that is beside the Balustrade.* I held the book on my lap, my pulse racing. There was a tomb, after all. Amazed, I walked into the sanctuary and knelt before the knight's stone, running my fingers along its surface as if the tiny dips and swells of the stone might provide a tactile code I could decipher. Was this the exact location? The balustrade that separated the choir from the nave was just here, two stair-steps removed from the stone. I gripped the edge of the stone with my fingers and gave it a perfunctory tug, but it did not budge. Absurdly, I put my ear to it, as if I might be able to hear the voices of the dead calling out to me, but I felt only the cold floor against my skin.

I sat in the front pew and opened the book once more, rereading the page where I'd found the entry. *The tomb of the Lords.* I knew it was customary, during the *ancien régime,* for aristocrats to be buried beneath the church. This entry seemed to be proof that there was a tomb — or had once been — in which the notable people of the community were buried. But this Lady D— had been buried there as late as 1705, a thousand years after the Merovingian presence on this land. So what of my imagined Merovingian tomb? Was that pure fantasy? Or had this tomb been remembered and used all those many years? The numbers of corpses, then, that might have been put to rest beneath this church . . . they would be incalculable. The church would be resting on foundations of human bone.

I read further in the register, searching for other mentions of the tomb, but found only one: a lieutenant colonel who had been buried there in 1724. The tomb was not mentioned again, and as the register only recorded events through the year 1726, I had no way of knowing whether the tomb had been used after that date.

I closed the book, smoothing the cover absentmindedly. Why hadn't Bérenger told me about the tomb? He knew of it — that much was certain. He said he'd read the book cover to cover. Did he not think it important? It was, admittedly, not unusual for old churches like ours to house the corpses of local dignitaries. Perhaps

Bérenger had thought it too mundane to mention. But why had he hidden the book so carefully? What was he afraid of?

Had he been at home, I would have gone to him at once and confronted him with my questions. But he was away yet again — in Montazels, helping his mother nurse a dislocated shoulder (inflicted by his father). How I wished Madame were there! I would have brought her the book that very moment, shown her the mentions of the tomb, asked her about the Templars, about Blanchefort, about the lords and ladies who were buried here, somewhere beneath my very own feet. I might even have brought her to the church and asked her to help me lift the stone and dig beneath the surface earth. But Madame had been gone a long time — I had begun to doubt whether she would ever return — and I was left only with my memory of our discussions, which had yielded little about Rennes-le-Château's recent history.

But though Madame was not available, her library might be. All I needed were the proper resources — records of Rennes during the *ancien régime* — and I might be able to find out more information about the tomb and who was buried there. If I could get permission from the mayor to peruse the library, I might find what I was looking for.

The mayor had become a different man since Madame had left. He spent most of his time in the tavern. When he wasn't drunk, he was asleep. He no longer stopped in for visits throughout the village, as he had been used to doing, often just on the cusp of mealtime. Some of the villagers assumed he had grown lazy without a wife to check his appetites. He had become the butt of jokes.

I was not surprised when, after going to the château in search of him, Mme Siau directed me to the tavern. I stood at the door, unsure whether I should knock. I had never set foot in the tavern. It was a place for men — except for Jeanne, the barmaid and wife of M. Chanson, the new owner. But it was a bright morning and the place would be at its most sedate. I hesitated outside the door, listening for any activity within, and then purposefully pressed the handle to lift the latch.

It was dark inside; only the smallest crack of daylight leaked in beneath the shutters, casting a thin line of light across several of the tables in the middle of the room. The room smelled of stale smoke, but it had been neatly arranged — chairs pushed beneath tables, glasses washed and arrayed on the shelves behind the bar, bottles lined up like obedient children. At first the place seemed empty, but a human rumbling awakened me to the presence of a man asleep on the floor beneath the bar.

It was the mayor. His vest was unbuttoned and his hat had fallen to the floor beside his head. Each reverberating inhalation sent his mustache vibrating, and when he exhaled, he emitted the scent of metabolized liquor.

I heard footsteps on the stairs, and straightened up to face M. Chanson, freshly shaven and cheerful. The Chansons were a young couple — relatives of the Ditandys, who had recently sold them the tavern. I did not know them well, though they seemed kind and well-meaning. "Oh, hello, Marie," he said, surprise in his voice. "What can I do for you?" He followed my gaze to the floor. "Is it the mayor you've come to see? Well, then." And, ignoring my protests, he straddled the mayor's broad chest and, grunting a little, lifted him to an upright sitting position and balanced him against the bar. "Come on now, monsieur," he said in a loud voice, gently slapping the mayor's face with the back of his hand. "It's morning and you've a lady to see you. Wake up now."

With a snort, the mayor awoke. His eyes

fell on me, as I was standing directly in his sight. He stood and nodded once to me, then turned his back to button his vest. M. Chanson handed him a glass of wine mixed with water.

"Pardon me, monsieur," I offered, for I was embarrassed and wished I had not come. "I don't mean to bother you."

"No, no," he said. "It's all right."

We sat at one of the tables near the door. "I've been missing my wife, you see," he said, laughing awkwardly, perhaps aware of my discomfort, perhaps ashamed of the looseness of his own tongue. "A man without a wife is a sad sight indeed. I've no one to live for, no one to care for me."

"You've the village," I offered.

He spluttered. "The village doesn't need me. Anyone can do what I do — sign a few papers, stamp a few letters. Chanson, you could," he shouted, scraping his chair against the floor. "You'd be a great mayor."

"Not like you," Chanson said, sorting through a stack of receipts.

"Or you, Marie." The mayor turned back to me, his chair tipping with his weight.

"No, monsieur."

"You must think me weak. Well, you're right. I am. I want my wife back. Why won't she come home to me?"

"Monsieur," I began, searching for some words of comfort.

"I'll tell you why. She doesn't care for people. She's always got her head mixed up in her books. I should have known she'd never change. But I thought once she had children, she'd become, you know, more like a woman. Instead, I've become the woman. Crying day after day for a lover who doesn't come." He laughed scornfully.

"Marie came here to ask you something," M. Chanson offered.

"It's all right," I said, standing up. "I can come back another time."

"No," said the mayor, grabbing my wrist and pulling me back down toward the table. "Sit down. Ask away. How can I be of service to you, mademoiselle?" His voice became obsequious, and he made a small bow with his head and a grand gesture with his arm, which again sent his chair off balance.

"Really," I said, standing. "I'll come back some other time." I looked toward M. Chanson for help.

"I've only myself to blame, of course," the mayor continued. "For following her here. I should have listened to my mother. Ha! Hear that?" He directed this last to the ceiling. "But I was young and arrogant, and she was so exotic, so beautiful — such a princess. You should have seen her in her youth, Marie." And he closed his eyes, as if transported.

What he said took me by surprise. "What do you mean, 'following her' here?" I asked. "I thought she came here to stay with you and your family when her father died."

He opened his eyes again, and studied me quizzically. "No," he said slowly, as if thinking it through. "My family is from Couiza."

"And isn't Mme Laporte your cousin?"

His eyes opened wider. "Who told you that?"

"She did."

He regarded me once more and then burst out laughing, slapping his hands on his thighs. "Ha! You're joking. I like a woman who can joke."

I glanced at M. Chanson, who raised his eyebrows at me and shrugged.

"Yes," I said, affecting a generous smile, and sat down again at the table. "I do like to joke."

Over the next hour, Mayor Laporte told me his version of the story of his marriage to Mme Laporte. Granted, he was still drunk and most likely prone to exaggeration, but the details he provided gave me much to wonder about. Madame, he told me — or Simone, as he called her — had come to Couiza all the way from Paris with no one but a maid when she was twenty-five. They arrived in a horse and carriage, stopping in the village square, and when Simone descended, she drew the eyes of every man in the square. Her height, her severe beauty, her evident wealth and air of calm intelligence fascinated everyone. He had been playing *boules* in the square with a bunch of friends, but they stopped their game and watched the coachman approach them. He asked if anyone might serve as a guide to take the lady and her maid up to Rennes-le-Château. Philippe won the small skirmish that broke out, and moments later found himself loading luggage onto a mule and leading the small procession toward the hill.

As they walked, Philippe managed to learn that Simone had come to inspect the château, which had just been put up for sale. Simone was a distant relative of the Berthelot family — the family that had owned and managed the affairs of Rennes-le-Château and the surrounding area for centuries until the death of the woman who was long thought to be the last in the line, Anne Marie de Berthelot. Upon her death, the castle was sold to a family from Toulouse who came only infrequently.

"That Anne Marie was crazy," said the mayor. "Just like her mother before her. Of course, there was reason for the mother to be mad, poor woman — she'd lost her son and heir when he was eight. She died just before the Revolution. They said she used to disappear for days at a time, and then reappear in the church graveyard with dirt in her hair and beneath her fingernails. You'll have heard of her, of course," he added. "Or seen her gravestone in the churchyard at any rate." I thought of the woman Bérenger had described — the lady of the village, sadly unhinged.

Simone's family, the mayor continued, had been estranged from the Berthelots since Simone's grandfather, the cousin of Anne Marie, had converted to Judaism. He had fallen in love with a peddler's daughter and, as she would not leave her family to marry him, he decided to leave his. His conversion — let alone his marriage — was unheard of at the time, and his family could not accept it. They had cut him off from his inheritance. He and his bride moved to Lyon. There he began experimenting with silkworm cultivation and eventually grew a prosperous business, which made him wealthy, independent of his aristocratic family. He and his wife had many children, including Simone's father. Simone, the sole descendant now of this branch of the Berthelots, had nursed a fascination with her Christian relatives, and when she read that the château at Rennes was again up for sale, she had been compelled to come and see it.

The residents of Rennes came out of doors to greet Philippe, Simone, and her maid as they walked the narrow footpaths through the town, leaving the mule to graze on the hillside. (So different from how we were greeted when we first arrived! I could not tell whether this was the truth or an embellishment of Philippe's.) Philippe felt like a lord as he escorted her through the village, showing her the castle and the grounds, the decaying church and cemetery, and the breathtaking views. He knew the village, having discovered it as a young boy exploring the hills, and felt possessive of its rare beauty and proud to share it with a woman as rare and beautiful as Simone.

Simone fell in love with the village and the castle, despite its decrepit state, and signed the papers then and there with a wild excitement in her eyes. Both Philippe and the villagers fell in love with her. The previous owners of the château had not been well-liked — they had let the castle fall into even greater disrepair — and the villagers looked forward to having a maiden of noble birth among them. Only a few whispered that welcoming a Jew to the castle was like giving the devil an open invitation.

Philippe asked her to marry him that night as they descended from the village, and Simone, perhaps intoxicated by the beauty of the place and the recklessness of the purchase she had made, perhaps truly in love, agreed. When they told their families, they were horrified, for the religious question could not be overlooked. But the couple would not be deterred, and so the marriage went forward, and Philippe and Simone moved into the château together, estranged from their families but giddy with the glory of their futures together. Philippe gained a wife richer and more beautiful than he could have imagined, and the village had a new lord and lady, their own royal family to celebrate and envy.

Over time, the enthusiasm waned — both Philippe's and the village's. Simone held herself aloof and provided no children, and her eccentricities — her excessive fondness for books and her refusal to believe in any kind of superstition, Jewish, Christian, or otherwise — only cemented the anti-Semitic views of some and the anti-aristocratic views of others. Philippe grew lonely without the company of his friends and family. Simone closed herself in her library for nights on end. Unlike the villagers, he knew the reason for their lack of children: his wife insisted on keeping her own bedroom, and slept there on certain days of the month, refusing to succumb to his entreaties. (He told me this shamelessly.) Over time, she slept there more and more, until what had been their shared bedroom became his alone.

His story finished, I thanked him and stood to take my leave, my nerves humming with excitement. I had much to think over.

But the mayor stopped me. "You came to ask me something?"

The prospect of riffling through a heap of dusty village records seemed beside the point now. "That's all right, monsieur. I just came to find out how Madame was faring. Please send her my regards."

"Better you send her mine, Marie. She always liked you."

I left, feeling sorry for the mayor's pain but also thrilled by what I'd learned. Were the two madwomen one and the same? Could I take the mayor's story as a cor- roboration of the one Bérenger had told me? Was the mayor telling the truth? Given some adjustments for exaggeration and self-pity — I was not, for example, willing to cast aspersions on Madame for refusing her husband children, nor could I think of her as cold — I was inclined to believe him. His story made greater sense than what Madame had told me. If, as she had said, she had moved to Rennes-le-Château to stay with Philippe's family, why was there no trace of them in the village? And what accounted for Madame's distinct air of aristocracy, if not that she had come from wealth?

The greater question, then, one that bewildered me for months afterward, was why she had lied.

BEIT ANIYAH

On the road they met a woman walking alone. When she saw Yeshua, she strode purposefully toward him. Kefa and Yochanan moved as if to protect him from an assault, but Yeshua touched their shoulders and they stood aside. "Marta," he said, bowing his head.

"Rabbi." Marta bowed her head as well, but when she lifted it, her eyes flared. "Why did you not come?"

"Here I am," Yeshua said.

"You knew he was sick, and you didn't come. Now he's dead. Elazar is dead. Our hearts are broken. We thought you would come."

Yehudah stepped forward. "How could he have known? We've been traveling since Shabbat."

"Shh, Yehudah," Yeshua said. "I knew."

Marta jerked her chin skyward. "How could you let him die?"

"And how many other people died on the same day as your Elazar?" retorted Yehudah. "How many others are suffering? Why should you receive special treatment?"

"Yehudah," said Yeshua, shaking his head. "You are too full of anger." Then, turning to Marta, he said, "Listen. Elazar will rise again."

Marta met Yeshua's eyes. "You'll bring him back to us?" she asked.

"Where is he buried?"

She pointed to a distant hill, its face spotted by several tomb-rocks, all shining a bright painted white against the tawny soil.

"Go get your sister and bring her here. We'll go see him together."

Marta left, walking briskly toward the village.

The men dispersed. Some gathered beneath a plane tree; others jogged downhill in search of a brook to quench their thirst. The women — Miryam, Shoshannah, Yochanah, and Shlomit — sat together a short distance from the plane tree. They were wary, perched on the grass like alert cats.

"Who was that?" asked Yochanah.

They turned to Shoshannah, their oracle. She memorized names and relationships, stored information like grain. "The sister of Yeshua's wife," she said, as she twisted a blade of grass around a fingertip. "She had two sisters — the other is also called Miryam." She smiled shyly at Miryam of Magdala. "Elazar was their brother. When Yeshua's wife died, everyone thought he would marry Miryam. She's younger and very beautiful."

Yochanah glanced at Miryam of Magdala, pity in her eyes. "Where do you hear these things?" she asked Shoshannah, trying on a bit of indignation for Miryam's sake.

"I spoke with Yeshua's mother." Shoshannah, too, eyed Miryam nervously, as if she was afraid she might burst into a jealous rage.

Anger and shame rushed through her. Their assumptions shrank her. She wanted to sling their pity into the dust like a soiled cloak from her back. Yet she could not deny her feelings; she felt envy overtaking her despite herself.

From the road they heard a woman crying. She wept in the same way, over and over: a sustained wail dissolving into descending sobs. They watched the road as the sound neared and saw Marta with her arms around the shoulders of a smaller woman whose face was hidden by her shawl. Yeshua moved quickly toward them. He knelt before the weeping woman and she fell into his arms. Her wails rose in pitch and intensity. "Where were you?" she screamed between her sobs. "Where were you?"

Yeshua held her to his chest, which she knocked at feebly with her palm. He grimaced and then began to weep, his sobs coming like bleats. Alarmed, the men by the plane tree began to walk toward the three mourners.

"I am here now," Yeshua said. "I am here."

It would be easy to be jealous. But how could she keep such a tight grip on her heart when daily she saw how vast an expanse his roamed? He suffered, always. Each death, each injury affected him as if it were his own. Even the trampled body of a baby starling inspired some small lament. It was as if the blood of all creatures, all living things, thrummed through his veins. It amazed her that he didn't weep incessantly, feeling all that he felt. It amazed her that he could teach and heal, that he could even walk, with all the grief he carried in his heart.

After a time, he stood, lifting Miryam of Beit Aniyah to stand with him. Followed by Marta, then by the disciples, and then the women, Yeshua led a procession up the road toward the hill where the tomb was. Miryam, having exorcised herself of jealousy, went prayerfully, filled with anticipation. She knew Yeshua was planning to raise a man from the dead, a thing that she had never seen with her own eyes. It was said that in Kfar Nahum, before she had been with him, Yeshua had revived a young girl a few moments after she had died. But this Elazar had been dead for days now. He had already been washed and oiled with nard and myrrh, had already been laid in his tomb.

Had it been a month earlier, she might have doubted Yeshua's ability to carry it off. But lately something had transpired in her, the orientation of her mind had somehow shifted. He could do it, she knew — but that was a minor fact now, of little importance. The miracles themselves were almost beside the point. Yes, they mattered, and mattered greatly to those who were healed, but the simple fact of this person's cure or that person's exorcism was less important than his presence, his example: the love he bore in his bones for every person, the poor and leprous alike, even the Shomronim. The same love that caused him to weep at the sight of a woman's grief was what gave him the power to bring back what that woman had lost.

The tomb was one of several on the hillside, and, like the others, it had been cut into the rock and covered with a large boulder, painted white. On top of the boulder towered a few cairns of small stones, left there by mourners. Elazar, it appeared, had been well loved, for the cairns were tall.

Yeshua knelt before the tomb for several minutes murmuring a prayer. Marta and her sister stood by and Miryam and the other women watched them. Some of the men ventured near the edge of the road to see if they could glimpse the towers of Yerushalayim. They were close to the city now, only two miles off.

Finally Yeshua stood and, brushing off his robes, asked for help in rolling the stone away from the tomb. Marta, afraid now, protested. "Rabbi, it's been four days. There will be an odor."

But Yeshua, with the help of Kefa and Toma, leaned into the boulder. All three of them pushed and heaved and finally, as the men roared, the heavy stone budged and lumbered aside, and the maw of the vault gaped before them.

The stench came like a sudden blow. Miryam gasped, then retched. Covering her mouth, she stumbled to the far side of the road and vomited. Kefa and Toma did the same. They all three returned to see Yeshua, his cloak pulled over his nose, ducking into the vault. Miryam stifled her urge to call out to him, to tell him not to go inside. Miryam of Beit Aniyah squatted by the entrance to the vault, peering after him.

"How can he stand it?" murmured Yochanah.

A few moments later, Yeshua emerged alone. "Kefa," he said, beckoning. "He can't yet walk."

Kefa, horror in his eyes, took a breath and followed. Another moment passed and then the two of them emerged once more, this time bearing a corpse between them — Yeshua at the feet and Kefa, the strongest among them, carrying the head and shoulders.

They laid the lifeless body on the ground before the tomb. The *soudarion* still swathed its head and face, and strips of linen bound the hands and feet. Miryam of Beit Aniyah knelt and touched the arm. She looked questioningly at Yeshua.

"Unwind the linens," he said.

Miryam of Beit Aniyah began with his hand. Her own trembled. Marta came forward and began to unwrap the other hand. The skin was dusted with white, like bread that had begun to mold. The sisters wiped the hands with the linen.

Next, they unwound the cloths from the feet and finally moved to the corpse's head. Marta lifted it off the ground while her sister took off the *soudarion*.

Elazar had been a young man. His skin, though gray, was unlined. The same dusting of white that had appeared on the hands and feet had formed here, too, on the nostrils and eyelids and, spottily, across the cheeks. Miryam willed back another wave of nausea.

"Elazar," said Yeshua, speaking as if to awaken a sleeping child. "Elazar. Your sisters have need of you."

The eyelids fluttered.

"Oh!" gasped Marta, jumping away.

The eyes opened and stared, gradually

quickening into alertness. They blinked and rolled, settling on Miryam of Beit Aniyah, who was kissing the hand she held again and again, little gurgles of laughter erupting from her throat.

Miryam stood closer. She had witnessed the births of her three sisters, so she knew something of the amazement and joy that accompany the entry of a soul into the world. This was not altogether different. Elazar blinked and stared, as a newborn did, and he seemed just as helpless and weak. He moved his mouth soundlessly. He seemed unable to lift his limbs or his head. All that indicated he was alive again were his moving eyes — a thinned blue, like lakewater.

Marta was kissing Yeshua's sandals. "Thank you," she wept. "Thank you." Kefa knelt first in awe, and seeing him, each member of their group followed his lead until they all knelt, their heads bowed, before the spectacle of this awakened corpse. Yeshua said a prayer of gratitude, as he did before and after every miracle he performed — and Miryam could hear the elation in his voice, and the pride.

It took some time before Elazar was able to talk, and even longer before he could stand, so they spent the afternoon there by the tomb, waiting until they could all descend the hill and enter the town once again. The men hummed with excitement. They spoke of the miracle as a victory and anticipated how triumphant they would appear, entering Beit Aniyah led by Yeshua and Elazar. "Everyone will come running to see!" shouted Andreas.

"Anyone who doubts the coming end now," roared Kefa, "will be powerless before this! Praise God!"

"And when we enter Yerushalayim," added Levi, "with Elazar at our side, who will be able to stop us? We'll part the crowds like Mosheh himself at the Red Sea!"

"Elazar will not be going to Yerushalayim!" snapped Miryam of Beit Aniyah. She had lifted Elazar's head and shoulders onto her lap and was cradling him there while Marta hummed a meandering melody and oiled his feet with the aloes that had been left in the tomb. "You can forget that idea. He'll be resting at home with us."

She was strikingly beautiful, it was true. Her dark eyes and wide cheekbones seemed animal in their wildness. How different she was from her sister! Marta was so measured, so reasonable, while Miryam of Beit Aniyah seemed to be all rapture and fire. What had their other sister been like? Had she been as beautiful as her sister Miryam or as passionate? Had she been as conscientious as Marta? Had Yeshua loved her?

Miryam looked away from the reunited family. Yeshua had gone off to pray. Yochanah and Shoshannah were in search of water. Shlomit was sitting alone, smiling bewilderedly, as she usually did, over the rumpled and scattered group. Miryam was filled inexplicably with sadness. She was tired now, thirsty and hungry.

She should have been glad: there was much to celebrate. Soon they would be in Yerushalayim. She hoped to find her family there. Yeshua was spreading his good news; people were receiving him with joy. The men were pulsing with anticipation, expecting the imminent arrival of the Kingdom, the restoration of justice and peace in the land. And, of course, this latest miracle. But she felt empty, full of gloom. Elazar's resurrection, the animation of a dead thing — it was unnatural, even horrible. He had been at peace and now he was awake again, and would once again be assailed by the battery of desires and aversions that made up a mind, a life. She could not celebrate it; she did not understand it. The expansiveness she'd felt only an hour before had left her. She was her small self again, her grasping, craving self — free of demons, perhaps, but just as defenseless. "All flesh is grass," she whispered. She walked uphill past the tomb, watching her feet cough dust into the air each time she set them down.

CHAPTER NINE

Despite my wariness with Bérenger, I might have shared with him the new information I'd learned from the mayor if Michelle had not arrived the next night from Carcassonne with a very real, pressing drama of her own.

Over the few years that Michelle had spent in Carcassonne, she had written regularly, telling us of the mundane details of her life: how content she and Joseph were, how Joseph was succeeding at his job, how she was happy to be keeping house, shopping in the fine shops there, working on her dolls, which she sold at market every week, and which modestly augmented their income. We were all satisfied to know Michelle was happy. So you may imagine our surprise at seeing her standing on our doorstep, her eyes red, her hair and dress wet from the rain, and a bulge at her belly. Mother exclaimed in horror and brought her directly to the fireplace, where she stripped off her wet clothes, wrapped her in a blanket, and brought her some hot brandy.

Michelle sipped the brandy and told us what had happened. Joseph worked so hard, but was plagued with a bitter and ungrateful boss who took pleasure in humiliating him and often did not pay him when his salary was due. Michelle, having already lost one baby, was ready to give up on Carcassonne and move back home, where they knew Joseph could at least find work at the factory. But Joseph had refused — he felt it would be a worse humiliation and he could not bear it. He believed things would improve. Finally, after months of arguing and suffering with the fear that this next baby would be lost as well, Michelle had left on her own — run away in the middle of the day while Joseph was at work. She had walked up the hill from Couiza in the rain.

My mother was furious with her —"If you were so worried about losing your child, you never would have climbed that hill!"— and setting up a cot by the fire, she ordered her to bed. She kept the fire going all night and all the next day, going from the kitchen to Michelle's side, bringing her tonics and brandy, oiling her belly, until she was convinced Michelle was well. And she was; Michelle had always been a healthy girl.

Joseph came the morning after Michelle, pounding on the door, and when he saw her lying on the cot by the fire, he fell on his knees beside her and wept. No measure of comfort from any of us would stop his crying. It was not until Michelle stood up and began to walk all around the house, lifting her arms and her knees in a series of calisthenics to demonstrate her health, that he stopped sobbing and stood, begging her to stop for she was endangering the baby's life. Then he embraced her and asked her forgiveness. They would move back to Rennes-le-Château, he agreed. It was madness, their life in Carcassonne. He would be glad to be away from his despotic boss, glad to be back among their families, glad to raise their child in such a beautiful place, among such kind and loving people. My mother wept to see them reconciled, and my father stood outside and shouted at the top of his lungs, "I'm going to be a grandfather!" while Claude shyly placed his hand on Michelle's belly to feel the baby kick.

Michelle and Joseph moved in with Joseph's family, and Joseph found a job as a supervisor at the factory. He left every morning with the rest of the men, making the trek downhill, their dinners wrapped in handkerchiefs.

Michelle's pregnancy affected me deeply. I had grown comfortable with the notion of chastity and its attendant state of childlessness. Or, perhaps more truthfully, I had never truly considered the prospect of bearing a child. Maternity did not tug at my apron, like it seemed to for so many girls.

Watching Michelle, however, as she grew bigger and more immobile, awakened me to a new sense of expectation, the anticipation of a sure and unprecedented joy. I felt, as I hadn't before, the close interweave of my family, our dependence on one another, not just for practicalities (meals, income, the innumerable chores) but for hope, for sustenance of the spirit. As I helped my mother and Michelle sew tiny dresses and knit booties for the layette, as I watched Claude carve from cast-off pieces of chestnut and oak little rattles, boats, and toy animals, and my father fashion a beautiful wickerwork cradle, I understood for the first time how basic and essential the birth of a child was. I felt my heart softening for this baby, even before I saw him, and as it softened, my increasingly solipsistic world enlarged. There was more, then: something beyond my own tortured faith, beyond the search after the Austrian's elusive and as yet mythical book, beyond even the fluctuating gradients of my intimacy with Bérenger and the moods they inspired. I was not born to be a mother. But an aunt: this title I could cherish.

The baby arrived on a hot day, made even hotter by the steam from the kettle that the Marcels kept boiling over the fire. Their front room smelled like a humid herb garden, for the midwife had hung sprigs of rosemary from each of the lintels to help along the early stages of labor. I stayed by Michelle's bed — a litter of linen strips covered with a sheet that Joseph's mother had set up by the hearth — holding her hand, rubbing her back where she felt the pain most, and praying despite myself, praying fervently for a healthy delivery. When the midwife finally pulled the baby from between Michelle's quivering legs, I reeled, sure it was a stillbirth, for his skin was the color of dust and his body was striped with blood. But within minutes, after the midwife had wiped him down with a warm cloth and rubbed lard into his puckered legs and arms, he grew rosy, and as he peered at his mother, I saw that he was alive, healthy, and perfect. He nuzzled Michelle's breast, and then opened his miniature mouth to suck himself to sleep, his tiny eyelids fluttering pleasurably. I felt as if I had witnessed the virgin birth itself.

Michelle named him Edouard, after Father, but we called him Pichon because he was so small. Michelle appointed me his godmother, and I accepted my role with all the pride and trepidation of a new mother. I clasped him to my chest as we walked to his christening, keeping my neck as rigid as a pole so as not to invite the evil eye. After the service, Bérenger kissed him and called him his little nephew while Father stood on the steps of the church and tossed figs and sugared almonds to the children. I stood aside, cooing worshipful phrases into Pichon's tiny curled ear.

Pichon, then, became my hope. I no longer languished with boredom in my free time, dreaming up fruitless fantasies, grieving myself over Bérenger's latest minor betrayal. I visited Michelle and rocked Pichon in my arms; I boiled his diapers and spit-soaked clothing, not minding the perspiration beading on my forehead from the fire; I prepared meals for the entire Marcel family and carried them over, one dish at a time. Bérenger spent many evening hours by Pichon's cradle, rocking it gently with his foot, humming tuneless lullabies. My father sang to him, too, beautiful melancholy melodies that reverberated through the small house. Father no longer frequented the tavern; when he returned from the factory, he went directly to Pichon, ludicrously contorting his face in his determination to elicit a smile. Claude, too, changed: he became newly histrionic, relating stories from the factory in broad caricature. Pichon's favorite — when he was old enough to sit up and watch — was Claude's imitation of the foreman, who wore his pants too tight and walked as if he was holding in a fart. Claude mimicked the gait for us, bringing my mother and I to giddy tears, and then my father, smiling behind his mustache, stood to offer his own impression, which sent us all rolling on the floor.

I had not forgotten about the Austrian and the mysterious book. The mayor's story had opened up a whole new set of questions, as well as given me exclusive knowledge that I savored by keeping it secret. For I was the only one who knew what I knew: that the madwoman who had had visions of Marie Madeleine was the mother of Anne Marie Berthelot and the relative of Madame. I had no proof of this, of course, but I felt it must be true. And for the time being, possessing that knowledge was enough. As far as I could tell, Bérenger had lost interest in the stone and the tomb — he continued to occupy himself with the deluge of Mass requests as well as some minor repairs in the church — and if he was not actively searching for the tomb, I felt no pressing need to pursue it either. I bided my time, busying myself with Pichon's infancy.

Then, some months after Pichon's birth, my father fell severely ill. He collapsed on the path one day as he and Claude were returning from the factory, and Claude had to carry him uphill on his shoulders. Claude arrived at the door of our house weeping, Father draped around his neck like a carcass. Mother loosened Father's vest and belt and patted his face down with a wet cloth. I ran to get Dr. Castanier. He came immediately, and by the time we had returned, Father had revived a bit, but was incoherent and feverish. The doctor declared him in danger and ordered him to bed.

We spent our days working quietly in the house, whispering if we spoke at all, so as not to disturb Father. Mother barely left his side; she sat by his bed, knitting and spinning, brushing his hair from his forehead, whispering in his ear. Claude and I tended to the needs of the household: he by working at the factory, me at home. I prepared snakeskin infusions for Father, and changed the compress on his forehead every hour.

Father drifted in and out of consciousness, sometimes strong enough to sit up in bed and smile weakly at the jokes we told to entertain him, other times unable to lift his head from the pillow, his strength depleted by fits of coughing. Bérenger came to sit with us by his bed and sometimes read the newspaper aloud — my father's republican newspaper — with commendable restraint.

Dr. Castanier visited once again, and declared Father pneumonic, and that the only remedy was rest, hot compresses applied to the chest, and regular applications of steam. "It's this damned house," he said. "The wind blows through here as if you were out on the bluff." We followed his advice diligently — every hour, I prepared a pot of steaming water suffused with garlic, and held Father's head, draped with a towel, over the pot — but we noticed no results. If anything, Father seemed to be getting worse, his coughs racking his body, his fatigue becoming more and more pronounced, until after one of his visits, Bérenger brought us downstairs and counseled that we must be prepared for his death.

My mother raged at Bérenger, calling him a liar and a fool, insisting that Father was looking better every day. Her voice grew louder and more desperate until Claude reminded her that Father needed quiet.

"There is hope, Isabelle," Bérenger offered. "My brother David keeps a bottle of water from Lourdes. He has been saving it for himself or someone close to him, should the need arise. With your permission, I could go to Narbonne tonight and bring back the bottle for Edouard."

My mother only stared at him.

"Would he give it to us?" I asked.

"I think he would."

"Well, Mother?" Claude prompted. "It seems worth a try."

She looked to me and I nodded, despite a sickness in my gut, for I knew that were Father alert, he would protest. It would seem an indignity to him: to subjugate his fate to the whims of a God he didn't believe in. I could almost hear him shout: "I won't be made to drink old water from some polluted stream!" But we were desperate enough to risk his disapproval.

Bérenger left that afternoon. We kept a vigil by Father's bedside while he was gone, only dozing for minutes at a time through the long night. My mother knelt in prayer by his bedside, her hands folded on the white coverlet like trembling pigeons. I tried to pray, but the reverent gloom distracted me, and I could only think of how Father would insist that there were no such things as miracles. *Wake up, Father,* I thought, *wake up.*

The wind whistled through the cracks in the stones like a gleeful ghost. Leaving my mother by Father's side and Claude snoring on his cot, I pulled on a cloak and left the house with a lantern, not knowing where I was headed. I wanted only to walk, to be away from the sounds of the wind in the house and the bubbling of my father's breath in his lungs. I held the lantern before me at first, but discovered that though it cast a circle of flickering light which allowed me to see within its compass, the darkness beyond the light was blacker and more virulent than if I carried no lantern at all. So I put it out, letting my eyes adjust to the darkness until it became benign and the shapes that had loomed or been fearsome assumed their customary proportions once again: the stone at the edge of the meadow, the border of the woodland just beyond.

I sat on that stone, near the place where Michelle and I used to spend afternoons so many years earlier, and listened to the wind riffling the leaves of the oaks and the pines. The grasses in the meadow bent and trembled, while just above them the *feux follets* — the will-o'-the-wisps — flared in momentary brilliance, extinguishing themselves in blackness. Each new snuffing of light seemed an omen, and I found myself growing more and more panicked, sure that as I sat ineffectually in the darkness, my father was dying, breath by breath, in his bed. It was too early for him. Pichon was only a baby, and it would not be fair to rob him of his grandfather. Was this God's plan, then? Having given us Pichon, had he decided to take Father? Unjust as ever.

As I sat on my stone, fuming at the sky, I saw a shape emerge from the tops of the trees and soar toward me. It was an owl, rushing silently, its wings spread wide. It flew over my head and off into the dark sky.

In our region, the call of an owl is said to announce impending death, though if you can shoot the owl and tack its feet to your door, death will pass you by. This owl, though silent, seemed to be a heavenly taunt, an apposite response to my supercilious prayer. Had I a rifle, I might have shot it and saved Father, but of course, I had none, as God well knew. Cold with the fear that my father's spirit had already left him, I sprinted home. When I reached Father's bed and saw his chest still rising and falling, I dropped to my knees beside him and wept.

The next afternoon, Bérenger returned, the flask of water tucked in his pocket. He came directly to Father's bedside and we all gathered about — Michelle, Pichon in her arms, Joseph, Claude, Mother, and I — while Bérenger lifted Father's head from the pillow.

"A little drink for you, Edouard," Bérenger said, and Father's eyes fluttered open. Bérenger held the flask to his lips and, blessedly, Father drank, offering us a weak smile before he sank into sleep once more.

"What now?" Claude said, as if he expected Father to rise immediately from his bed like Lazarus himself.

"Now we wait," replied Bérenger.

Wait we did, all of us, until, exhausted by the previous night's vigil and reassured by Father's continued breath, Mother and Claude fell asleep. I was resolved to stay awake. If the water worked miracles as it was supposed to, I wanted to see it. Strangely, my scolding of the heavens the previous night seemed to have given me some comfort. I picked up the little *santon* of Marie Madeleine that my mother kept by the bed, fingering the folds of her robe, and prayed — experimentally and humbly — for Father's immediate recovery.

I must have fallen asleep finally because I

woke the next morning, still gripping the little *santon,* to the warmth of my father's hand on the back of my neck.

"Your neck will be stiff," he whispered. He fingered my forehead, which had been pitted with the impression of the Madeleine's open hand. "You've been sleeping with a saint, Marie?" he asked.

He ate a good dinner that day, slurping the *aigo bouido* from his spoon. Over the next several days, he grew stronger, stayed awake for longer, and finally, after a week of steady recovery, rose from his bed to stretch and take a breath of fresh air.

Bérenger proclaimed Father's recovery a miracle, and attributed it to the extraordinary blessing of Our Lady of Lourdes, and publicly we all agreed. Privately, I wondered whether my own prayer had anything to do with it. I thought again of the owl, the wake of its flight-wind on my face, and wondered whether what I had interpreted as an omen was actually an apparition, a holy incarnation. I had grown so accustomed to doubting, had cowered within the shell of my unbelief like an embryo. My urgent communion with the awesome and mysterious night was the tapping that cracked the shell, and now I was shivering and blinking in the bright foyer of wonder.

It was a quiet wonder, a general sense of *maybe so, after all.* It was walking through the day, holding a spoon, stirring, tasting a dish, sneezing into a rag, always thinking, *what if?* and *perhaps.* It was a delicate transfer of feeling, from the heavy-handedness of doubt to the lightness of possibility. I still chafed at a Church that damned my father to hell simply because he would not submit to its doctrine, still despised the hypocrisy of an institution that could massacre thousands in the name of God — but I felt now that belief was something to consider. I wasn't sure what I believed. I had no name for it. If I believed in anything, I suppose, I believed in the unfathomable power of nature, in its potential to heal as well as destroy. Illogically, I made the little *santon* of the Madeleine my talisman, endowing her with the power I had witnessed that night on the meadow, with the silent rush of the owl's wings. I prayed to her, making small experiments: I asked her to make Claude less of a grouch in the mornings, and, miniature miracle, the next morning he kissed me cheerfully on his way out the door. I prayed to the *santon* that Pichon would love me better than any of his other relatives, and several days later, he spoke his first word: my name. She was not one hundred percent reliable, of course — I asked her again and again for insight into the workings of Bérenger's heart, or, if not that, at least for him to tell me his secrets — and this did not happen, or at least not right away. Nor did the *santon* bring Madame back when I asked her to, not for some time. But the *santon,* and, by extension, Marie Madeleine herself, had won my affection, not just because of the little wishes she granted but, more profoundly, because of the peace that burned like a candle within me as I held her figure in my two hands and pressed it to my forehead, or kneeled before the painting Bérenger had made of her on the altar. It was this feeling I clung to, wondered at, and longed for, this sense of communion with the larger mystery that encompassed and transcended everything I could perceive.

The village celebrated Father's health. People laid gifts of fresh vegetables, oil and honey, wine, and dishes of food on our kitchen table, and everyone stopped by to see the miraculous recovery for himself. My father loved the attention. Sitting up by the fire, a blanket over his knees, he held court in the living room, entertaining, listening to stories, tasting the gifts of food and wine, even singing a few bars upon request, to demonstrate the improving vigor of his lungs. My mother waited on him, anticipating his every desire. And Bérenger sat with him in the parlor, receiving guests as if he were another member of the family.

The doctor visited and pronounced Father's recovery an act of God. "And for such a sinner as you, Edouard!" he said, shaking his head.

"It's because I've a priest for a son-in-law," my father said.

"Shut your mouth, Edouard," said my mother. "Don't listen to him, Doctor. He's still delirious."

"I'll tell you something," the doctor said, licking bits of goat cheese from his fingers. "If you don't fix up this house, get some mortar into those cracks, miracle or no, that pneumonia will come back with a vengeance."

But we had no money to hire a mason, and it was not the sort of work that could be done easily by volunteer neighbors. The stones were irregularly sized. One or two had already come loose and had to be wedged back into their spots with the help of wet woolen scraps. Other stones threatened to do the same. The stones on the north side of the house were slick with slime and a thin coating of moss. A family of doves had nested in the eaves just above the door and used our doorstep as a chamber-pot. "It's not worth fixing," Claude said one winter evening. "You'd have to spend a year's worth of pay just to get the stones cleaned up, forget about the mortar. This place is as old as the castle."

"Why not move in with me?" Bérenger suggested. He was sipping some spiced wine that Mother had served, leaning back in his chair, expansive and merry.

My father did not shift his gaze from the fire.

"Consider it a kind of insurance," Bérenger said. "Just until Edouard recovers fully and you can afford to have a mason patch up the house."

My mother set the skein of wool she was winding on her lap. We all looked at Father. Taking his time, he rocked for a long moment. "It's a generous offer," he said.

"You think it odd, Edouard," said Bérenger, smiling apologetically.

"You know me," my father said. "Altruism makes me suspicious."

Bérenger shrugged. "I have the room. You have the need. It's very simple." When my father still did not respond, he said, "You're my family here."

My father beckoned for Bérenger to approach him and when Bérenger moved close enough, Father grabbed his face and planted a kiss on the top of his head.

We moved the next month, before winter set in. The presbytery was not much larger than our house, but it was much better insulated. There was an extra room upstairs, which my parents took as their bedroom, and a small chamber next to the kitchen, which I claimed. Claude slept on a cot by the hearth. He had taken to staying out late — he was old enough now to frequent the tavern — and he did not like to disturb us when he came in. It would not be too long until he found a bride, a girl he met at the factory, and moved to his own house, also in Rennes-le-Château. And as for my father, after several months of rest, he was able to return to work.

Meanwhile, I began to pray often, finding comfort and peace from my prayer. God expanded in my mind to fill the sky and the earth, the *feux follets* and the swift-winged owl; he was no longer limited to the dimensions assigned him by the Church: Father, Son, and Holy Ghost. Or, rather, the God I had only experienced as Father and Son I now grew to know more fully as Holy Ghost: immanent, omnipresent, accessible, close by.

The reawakening of my religious feeling did nothing to ease my physical longing for Bérenger, as one might expect. If anything, it intensified, for Bérenger, as my priest, was my mediator to the world of spirit. My new yearning for intimacy with God merged with my desire for physical intimacy with Bérenger — despite his secrets from me. To embrace him would be, somehow, to embrace the mystery that was belief, that was faith.

Now our constant proximity kept me in a state of perpetual want. I inhaled deeply in his presence. I stood closer to him, brushed my sleeve against his when I served him. It was not a calculation, I had no plan to seduce Bérenger, in fact, quite the opposite, for I wanted nothing but to keep things as they were, to maintain the affection we shared, the coziness — but the impulse toward touch was an instinct, irrepressible. I was a cat drawing toward warmth, a child clamoring to be held. It embarrassed me, my need. I wanted to box it up and tuck it away, but it would not be hidden. It painted itself across my face, emanated from me like a fragrance. Even through anger I felt it, tingling at the tips of my fingers, causing an excitement of sensation just beneath my skin.

I always knew his location in the house, for my body acted as my compass. If Bérenger walked above in his room as I worked in the kitchen, the hairs on my arms and my neck tugged me toward the ceiling; if he came in while I was upstairs making the beds, I felt the air between us funnel into a directional current — my mind, which might have been wandering peacefully, snapped back into my body, and, united, mind and body would converge on him. I listened for his movements, anticipated the first footfall on the stairs, his voice calling my name. I parsed his behavior in an effort to know his mood, to decipher his thoughts. Nor was I alone, for I could feel the same emanation from him, the want traversing plaster and wood, seeking me. He always looked for me upon entering the presbytery, and only when he'd found me and learned how I was occupied would he go about his own business.

Still, he managed to be restrained. I do not know from what reserve he drew his will. He returned my touches affectionately — if I leaned into his shoulder while serving his plate, he would pat my wrist; if I stood close to him, he might place a momentary hand on my waist — but with no impropriety. This is not to say that he was not moved: for I could see the skin at his nostrils whiten with the effort of his restraint, and I could sense the power of his own longing. But he was valiant, unwilling to renounce his priestly vow. I think he received consolation in the knowledge that his will was victor over his desire.

There was always this underlying inequality between us, this imbalance of powers. I reached up to love him, heavenward, while he had to slide down. Loving me kept him tethered to the earth. I tempted him, drew him away from his more perfect self, beckoned him from his spirit to his flesh. This was how I spoke to myself on bad days, when Bérenger was moody or unfriendly. I told myself I deserved his scorn, for if it weren't for me he would be free to float, spirit hovering in body, living in the world but not of it. This was pure fantasy, however, for Bérenger was not and never had been a spiritual person, despite his ambitions. He was squarely in and of the world. His love for me was simply a manifestation of his earthly orientation; his obsession with building was another. Still, he had made his vows, and that very fact made us both aware that his was the greater sacrifice. What did I have to sacrifice, after all, to love him? Children. Normalcy, perhaps. But these were things I had never really wanted; he was what I had wanted. Bérenger, on the other hand, longed to live in the sheltering shade of God's love. We both knew, then, the measure of self-hatred and guilt that colored our love, we both feared and regretted that he was choosing me, an earthly companion, over an eternal one.

Home, I am afraid, became somewhat hazardous for Bérenger. If he was not working to resist me, he could be found arguing with my mother, for they had lost some of the mutual respect that had once characterized their friendship. She sniped at him, making insinuations about his moral health, until he grew sullen. She would occasionally apologize when she saw that she'd wounded him, for she did love him and knew that we owed Father's health to his generosity. But she could never entirely forgive him for his imperfections — his weakness in the face of temptation, his this-worldly love of me.

It was partly for this reason, then, that Bérenger turned his attention once more to his construction projects. He spent the cold winter months drawing plans for a garden to be planted in the church courtyard, a half-acre of land in front of the cemetery, and when spring came, he set to his project with enthusiasm, laying paths, installing benches, planting hedges and dwarf trees as well as a variety of flowers. He ordered a statue commemorating Our Lady of Lourdes and erected it that June in an enclosure of the garden he had dedicated to the Virgin. People were so pleased with the garden — they strolled through it and lounged on the benches all that summer — that no one objected to Bérenger's next project: to dig a cistern adjacent to the cemetery entrance. He declared that he needed it to water the garden. But I was suspicious. I wondered whether his ulterior goal was to gain access to the tomb. I inspected the progress of the project during the day and listened for strange noises at night. If a branch rubbed another in the wind, or a dog scrabbled in the dirt, I would stand in the dark doorway in my nightdress, trying to discern Bérenger's shape in the vicinity of the garden.

The cistern was completed by summer's end. As far as I could tell, after peering into it several times, there was no secret doorway. Bérenger planned to build a chamber above the cistern to serve as a library, but he did not accomplish this project until the following year. He had become very busy with the temporary assignment of an extra parish in

Antugnac, some three miles distant. Every Sunday after our Mass, he would set out with his walking stick and would return after nightfall, bathed in sweat. I sat with him as he ate a late supper of fresh vegetables and *chèvre,* listening to him complain about the unfriendly treatment he was receiving at his new parish. Some nights we sat together in the garden, feeling the wind cool our skin, letting the roses and the lilacs overwhelm our senses. I could not help but feel on those evenings that the universe favored our intimacy. God had blessed us with a love. Why should we not revel in it?

Eventually, Bérenger turned his attention to the installation of the new pulpit — another ornate creation he had ordered from Toulouse. The work team arrived one morning in September to prepare the floor for the installation. By afternoon, they were gone: Bérenger had fired them.

"They were lollygaggers," he said. "We can find better men."

His decision was strange, for he had admitted the previous day how excited he was for the new pulpit's arrival. "It's beautiful, Marie," he had boasted. "Decorated with gilded plaster statuettes and all surrounded by pastel blue arches." He had seemed so impatient. Now he would have to wait longer while he looked for a new crew.

But I was beyond surprised — I was shocked — when I walked into the church later that day to find the Virgin's altar demolished and the knight's stone missing. In place of the stone lay three wooden planks side by side, surrounded by a flimsy wire fence. I ran to find Bérenger in the presbytery.

"Where's the stone?" I demanded.

He affected a confused expression.

"The knight's stone," I persisted. "Don't pretend you don't know what I'm talking about."

"Oh, the men took it out. The new pulpit will be put in its place."

"Why didn't you tell me?"

"It was routine work, Marie. I didn't think of it."

"You knew I was interested in it."

"I'm sorry." His tone was dismissive.

"What have you done with it?"

"It's in the cemetery, in perfect condition."

I found it there moments later, propped up against the outer wall of the church, its carved surface facing inward. I pulled at it, but it was too heavy to budge, so I knelt beside it and inspected it with my fingers. Satisfied that it had not been damaged, I returned to the sanctuary, where I intended to move aside one of the planks to see what was underneath, but when I got there, Mme Flèche was already in her pew, so all I could do was stand by the fence and peer over it futilely.

The new pulpit was not installed for more than a month. In the meantime, the planks and fence remained, taunting me. Once, when the church was empty, I went to pry up one of the planks and look beneath, but I found that the fence, though flimsy in appearance, was locked and would not be budged. When I asked Bérenger what was under the planks, he simply shrugged and said, "Dirt, Marie. What else?"

I was certain he had found the tomb. He grew more aloof, more evasive, and appeared to be losing sleep. He brooded continually, and if I asked what was bothering him, he became snappish. One evening, I heard the front door creak open after midnight. I listened, thinking it might be Claude returning from the tavern, but heard no further sounds. Quickly, I donned my robe and slipped out the front door. The night was chilly; I clasped my arms to my chest and ran to the church door.

It was locked. A dim glow lit the windows — lantern light. I rattled the door. "Bérenger!" I shouted. But he did not come. I waited until my skin was rigid with goose bumps and my teeth began to chatter.

At home, I sat on the settee, resolved to stay awake until he returned. Claude had come home and was snoring by the hearth. I watched the coals grow dull. The room was cold; I curled into a ball, my feet tucked into my gown, and rested my head on the cushion. Finally, I fell asleep.

I woke to the creak of the door. Bérenger was shutting it behind him, dressed in mud-smeared trousers and a work shirt. He started at the sight of me: my face undoubtedly haggard and drawn, my hair loose.

"Marie," he said.

"What have you found?" I asked.

"Marie, you're shivering." He stepped closer, touched my hand with a warm finger. "Your hands are ice. Get in bed this instant."

He was right: my body was tense with cold. I allowed him to walk me to my bed and tuck me beneath the bedclothes, then waited, still shivering, while he went to revive the fire. He heated the kettle, then brought me a cup of steaming coffee and a bottle of hot water, which he set at my feet.

"You're keeping things from me," I said. "What were you doing in the church all night?"

"Hush, Marie," he said, his brow creased with concern. "Drink your coffee."

I fell sick, then, with a brutal cough, and had to stay in bed for weeks. Mother nursed me and Bérenger visited me every afternoon and evening, ignoring my demands for him to tell me what he was up to. I found it difficult to maintain my self-righteous anger, for he was so faithful, so thoughtful, so concerned. He brought me beguiling colored stones, told me of Pichon's latest triumphs — his first two-word sentence (*Mama, no!*), his efforts at walking — and prayed for me, earnestly and with evident apprehension. "You must get better soon, Marie," he scolded me. "I'm in need of your fine cooking."

I did, finally, just before Christmas. I woke one morning feeling as though the weight that had been pressing on my chest had lifted, and I sat up in bed, calling for Mother. When she entered my room, she rushed to me and hugged me hard. "Your eyes are clear, sweet — are you better?" I nodded. She rocked me in her arms. "First Father and then you — it has been a trial.

But God has answered my prayers."

The next day, when I felt well enough to leave the house, I demanded Bérenger take me into the church. He had told me about the installation of the new pulpit, and I wanted to see it for myself. He escorted me; I leaned happily on his arm.

The new pulpit towered over the nave like a jeweled giant. It recalled the design of the tabernacle — the two pieces worked nicely together, in fact, bringing a coherence to the interior. It was so large, so striking, that I only belatedly noticed that the floor of the nave had been tiled in a bizarre black-and-white checkerboard pattern.

"It was the only tile they had available," Bérenger explained, "I didn't want to wait longer."

We approached the pulpit to get a closer view. At its foot were the same planks I'd seen a month earlier.

"Ah," I said accusingly. "That must be where you've been digging."

"It's a wonder to preach from way up there, Marie," he replied evasively. "You'll see, this Sunday. My sermons feel more forceful, anyway, even if they're the same old drones."

Then, five days before Christmas of that

year, 1891, the mayor shot himself in the
head with the pistol that Madame kept in
the top drawer of her desk. We all heard the
report, though most of us dismissed it as a
hunter's shot, and imagined we would hear
of the pheasant or the boar that one of the
boys had gotten later that evening. It was
Mme Siau who told us. "The mayor's shot
himself," she said at the presbytery door.
"I'll need some help mopping up."

He left no note, only a half-drunk bottle
of liquor on Madame's desk. I couldn't help
but think that he had chosen that spot as a
way of reprimanding Madame for her long
absence: blood splattered on the expensive
Oriental carpet, the window, the books.
With our hardest scrubbing, we could only
remove a portion of the stain.

It was a sad day when we buried him. As
his death was a suicide, he could not be
buried in consecrated ground, nor could
Bérenger say any blessing over his body. M.
Paul, M. Chanson, and M. Verdié dug a
grave in an unused corner of the castle
garden — which happened to abut the
cemetery, though it was separated from it
by a tall, vine-covered wall — and we
gathered there, the whole village.

Madame came — I had sent her a telegram. She wore a black widow's shawl and

stood at the edge of the crowd. Joseph, Gérard, and M. Verdié lowered his body, wrapped only in canvas, into the ground. Each of us threw a handkerchief, a coin, a twig of rosemary, or a handful of dirt on the grave. Many wept, for the village cared for him; he had been a good mayor and a good man.

Afterward, many of us adjourned to the château, where Mme Siau had prepared a pot of salted cod soup and M. Flèche supplied a torte. I say many but not all, because some refused to set foot in the château. They deemed the castle cursed and said that the mayor had gone crazy, just like the Berthelots before him. His suicide was a sign that the coming year would be doomed, and entering the castle would guarantee a failure of their crop, a bankruptcy, a death in their family. Others declared they would never again acknowledge Mme Laporte. An untimely death always invites blame, and who better to blame than the wife who had abandoned her husband, and a Jew besides? There was hateful talk. Madame cloistered herself in the château. A few of the teenage boys hung about outside, looking menacingly up toward the windows, stubbing out cigarettes against the front door. Mme Siau shooed them away, but they returned, their eyes alight with criminal fantasies.

The morning after the burial, which happened to be Christmas Eve, my mother and I went together to the château. We brought a black-and-white pudding. Mme Laporte answered the door in a high-collared nightgown, her hair lank, her face drawn and pale. "Please forgive my appearance," she whispered. "I am not feeling well." She accepted the pudding graciously, then moved back into the darkness of the house.

"We hoped you might join us for supper this evening, Madame. If you haven't other plans, that is."

"Thank you," she whispered, and shut the door.

She did not appear that evening. As we had an hour or two between supper and Mass, I walked over with a sampling of the foods we'd enjoyed: pigs' feet, bread, beans, potatoes, and salted cod. I knocked twice, three times. Just as I was turning to go, the door opened: Madame stood, barefoot and still in her nightgown, on the threshold.

Her face bore such an expression of misery — I am not sure how to describe it, for it was unique to her. It was not pure grief, though that was there, the heaviness in the skin and eyes, the searching gaze, the guilt, but there was also real fear, horror even, in the dilation of her pupils, the scattering glances she made at the darkness, the path behind me. She embraced me, which was startling, for she did not tend toward the demonstrative; then, perhaps sensing my surprise, she released me, smoothing my hair. "It's good to see you," she said.

"Are you ill?" I asked.

She did not answer, but led me to the parlor and sat down next to me on the settee, keeping my hand in her lap and stroking it like a cat. I was taken aback and fought the urge to tug my hand away. We sat like that for a time until she let out a little laugh, and placed my hand back in my own lap. "You'll think I've gone mad," she said.

I was thinking the very thing. I had been much affected by the mayor's death, and was inclined to believe in haunted houses, castles or otherwise.

"Are you well, Marie? You look well." There was an artificial brightness to her voice.

"Very well, thank you."

"And your family? You are living at the presbytery now, I understand?"

"Yes. We're all well. My father was ill, but he's recovered. Michelle and Joseph have moved back home. They have a baby now."

"So I saw. Delightful. And Monsieur *le curé?*"

"Fine, thank you."

We did not know where to go from there. I was concerned about Madame, but her uncharacteristic lack of composure and neediness disoriented me. I felt I did not know her as I once had. I wanted to ask why she had stayed away so long, why she had lied to me so many years ago. But she was changed, though whether it was due solely to her grief or to some other cause, I could not tell. I fiddled with the brocade of the settee, wondering whether I should leave her alone, whether my presence was too much of a strain. Then I wondered whether she truly grieved at all. Perhaps it was a show she put on for seemliness.

"Philippe cared for me quite a bit it seems," she offered, shyly. "I hadn't known."

"Hadn't you?"

She darted her eyes at me guiltily. "Marriage settles into its own rhythms, Marie," she said. "These become ruts, and then gullies, ravines. You can't get out easily." She lifted a hand to the collar of her nightgown and adjusted the cloth at her throat. "He was not the type to do such a thing," she said, and her eyes grew unfocused and once again full of fear. "He was so happy all the time, so glad to be in the company of other people. Of all of you."

"He fell into drinking after you left," I said.

She nodded absently, her finger dipping below her collar, moving back and forth against her neck. She would suffer always with this guilt, this final violence.

"I loved him once," she said. "He seemed to embody the France my father so loved — he was generously, profoundly democratic. Philippe never had a bad word to say about anyone."

I nodded; it was true.

"He sent me a letter," she said. "He told me I was like a star, distant and glittering. That was all the letter said. Two lines: Dear Simone, You are a star, distant and glittering. Philippe. I laughed when I got it. I thought it was a love letter."

"It was, I guess."

"It was his note." She brought her eyes into focus then and turned to me.

"Why did you tell me he was your cousin?" I asked.

Her eyes flickered in surprise. "An impulse, Marie. I'm sorry."

"It wasn't an impulse. You planned to tell me. You were the one who brought it up. You could have left all of it unsaid."

339

She nodded slowly.

"Monsieur Laporte told me the truth," I continued. "But I could easily have found out from anyone else in the village who had been here long enough. It wasn't even a good lie."

She laughed sadly. "You're right," she said. "It wasn't. I'm not accustomed to lying."

I waited.

"I was protecting myself. That's all. It was a fib, really. A way to avoid telling a much longer story that I wasn't quite ready to tell."

"So I imagine your father's alive and well?" I said cavalierly. She flinched, and I immediately regretted the question.

"No," she said. "That part was true. He died before I came to Rennes, before I bought the castle here."

"I'm sorry," I said.

"It's all right. You have a right to know."

"Why didn't you just tell me the truth, though? It's not so much longer. It's not even such a different story, after all."

"I suppose not," she said, though her tone was evasive.

"What about the caves?" I asked. "Was that an invention, too?"

She considered me for a long, serious moment. "No, Marie," she said. "That was no invention."

I breathed, relieved. But before I could press her further, she began to question me.

"I must know about the stone, Marie. Where in truth did you find it?"

I felt that if I was demanding her honesty, I had to give her the same. "Here," I said. "In the church."

She nodded, as if she'd expected the answer. "Is it still there?" she asked.

"Yes," I said. "Behind the church, anyway. In the cemetery. Monsieur *le curé* removed it to tile the floor."

She fell silent a moment, then asked, "Please tell me how you found it."

I told her the story of its unearthing, feeling my betrayal of Bérenger lodged like a bone in my throat. I left nothing out, however, from the Austrian's initial letter to my discovery of the flask, from the story of the madwoman and her visions to my latest recovery of the old register and the entries that mentioned the tomb.

"You haven't yet found the book?" she asked when I had finished.

"No. Monsieur *le curé* might have, though, for all I know. I'm sure he's found the tomb."

"And what will he do with it, do you

think, if he finds it?"

"I don't know," I said.

"How curious," she mused. Then she glanced at the grandfather clock, a queer light in her eye. "Do we have time, do you think, Marie, to look at the stone before midnight Mass begins?" It was eleven o'clock.

She buttoned an overcoat over her nightgown. The night was frigid, the wind stinging our cheeks. We carried a lantern but did not light it, for we wanted to remain inconspicuous. Luckily, most everyone was tucked up in his house, reveling in the holiday. We passed the tavern, where a few men hunched at the bar, and continued on toward the church, tiptoeing through the garden to reach the cemetery.

Once there, sheltered by the church walls, we lit our lantern. The light barely dispelled the darkness; we could see only the few closest graves, their stones tipped and half-sunk in the soil like a miniature ruin. Animal refuse and unearthed bones were strewn across the ground: the dogs and boars were not averse to digging.

Holding the lantern high, I led Madame along the church wall to the place where I knew the knight's stone to be. "We'll have to turn it over," I whispered, setting the

342

lantern on the ground. "It's very heavy." Together we pushed it away from the wall. It thumped against the hard earth. Madame dropped to her knees beside it and I held the lantern aloft once more, shining light over the stone's curvaceous surface.

"Oh," Madame gasped. She bent reverently over the stone, tracing the shapes with her fingers. "It's larger than I had thought. And much rougher than your sketch, Marie. Difficult to discern what the shapes are exactly."

"Yes," I admitted. "I drew from memory. I might have taken some liberties."

"It's centuries old."

We were silent a while longer as Madame examined the carving. I huddled in my shawl. The stone walls sheltered us from the worst of the wind, but the air was bitter cold.

"I will confess to you, Marie. When you brought me your sketch, I thought it depicted a particular story about the secret transport of a child. But the shapes are far less defined than I had imagined. It's impossible to tell whether a child is present at all. It could be almost anything: a statue, an urn, even. Still, one could imagine —" She broke off, tracing the stone once more with her fingertips.

"What was the story?" I prompted.

"I had two in mind, really. One I spoke to you about. I thought the stone might have depicted the flight of Sigebert IV, the son of the murdered King Dagobert II. It was unusual, a knight riding with a child. And the bears or creatures in the top panels seemed to imply that the horse and rider were moving below-ground, as if they were in hiding. But I had a second theory as well, one I did not share with you."

Madame inhaled deeply. Then she stood, brushing the dirt from her skirt, and gestured toward the lantern.

I followed as she picked her way through the graves until we came to a small upright stone. Squatting, I read the lettering in the lantern-light: LADY JEANNE CATHERINE BERTHELOT. DIED 1781. This must have been the woman the mayor had referred to, the woman who had gone mad at the death of her son.

"She was an ancestor of mine," Madame said. "My father's great-aunt. I never knew her."

Madame, I learned, came to Rennes not simply to buy a castle, but to find the answer to a question, to satisfy a matter of curiosity that had grown into an obsession after the death of her father. When she was a teenager and had begun to ask about the Christian branch of the family, her father had told her the tragic story of his great-aunt Jeanne Catherine de Berthelot, the onetime resident of the château, a woman of noble birth who harbored delusions that she and her children were descendants of Jesus, literal children of God.

She had held this belief long before her son was born, and though she had seen doctors and priests, no one could convince her of the impossibility of such a thing. According to her fervid imagination, her family had descended from the Merovingian kings, who had, in turn, descended from the man they eventually claimed as their messiah. And the female progenitor of this line, according to Jeanne Catherine, was Marie Madeleine, the bride of Christ.

"Apparently, the other members of her family found Jeanne Catherine's notions pleasantly ludicrous. They called her eccentric, imaginative. And the delusion might have remained a benign fantasy had she not given birth to a son."

When her son was born, Madame continued, Jeanne Catherine believed him to be the reincarnated Christ. She celebrated his birth as the Second Coming. Upon his death — he was thrown from a horse when

it reared and then trampled beneath its feet
— she lost all hope, all semblance of sanity.
She spent nights scrabbling at the graveyard
dirt, trying to unearth her son's body. "He's
suffocating!" she cried to the silent dark, for
she was certain he would be resurrected,
and would wake trapped in his coffin. She
broke fingers with her frantic digging,
disturbed the villagers with her wails, and
grew ill from so many nights without sleep.
Finally, hoping to cure his wife, her husband
reinterred the child in the tomb beneath the
church and then ordered it sealed.

Jeanne Catherine's condition only wors-
ened. She grew incoherent, sometimes
speaking in a babble that she claimed was
Aramaic. She began to confuse herself with
Marie Madeleine, insisting that she had to
get to the tomb, that the Lord was waiting
for her there. Her husband locked her in
the castle. He escaped to Toulouse, where
he had many business interests, but he left
his daughter, Anne Marie, with strict instructions not to allow her mother to leave
the castle. Anne Marie followed his instructions to an even greater degree than he had
intended, for she never left the castle either,
even after her mother's death. She died
unmarried, leaving behind a vast library.

I was quiet, my fingers pressing the cold

dirt of Jeanne Catherine's grave. The story, though outrageous, seemed to corroborate what I already knew. "So all those books?" I asked. "They weren't your father's?"

"Some were. But most were Anne Marie's," Madame admitted. "The previous owners kept the library intact, and passed it on to us."

"But how did he know all of this? Did he know Jeanne Catherine or Anne Marie?"

"He never met them, no. But he corresponded with Anne Marie. He was sorry for the division in our family, and wrote to her in an effort to heal it. Anne Marie wrote back, intrigued by the fact that he was a scholar."

I nodded, growing accustomed to the new information.

"My curiosity about Jeanne Catherine took on a new urgency after my father's death. The claims she made possessed me, the possibility of their truth. Understand, Marie, that in my mind Jesus was not God, but a man — a great man, a charismatic rabbi, but a man nonetheless. And why not a father? All the Jewish men I knew, including our own rabbi, were fathers, were even commanded to be fruitful by God. Why not Jesus? Of course the task of tracing his lineage, if it existed, through two thousand years was unwieldly to say the least, if not altogether impossible. But my grief blinded me to practicalities. I wanted revenge. If the bigots who killed my father could learn that they had killed a descendant of the very man they worshipped . . . I came to Rennes-le-Château with revenge on my mind."

She continued, faster now, apparently finding some relief in the telling of her story. "I learned all I could when I first arrived, diving into Anne Marie's library, reading histories and genealogies, listening to legends from the oldest residents of the village. They were the ones who told me about the Cathars, the Visigoths, the Merovingians, and the network of caves that I never succeeded in finding. I tried to convince the priest at the time to reopen the tomb, but he would have none of my stories. He was suspicious of me. Everyone was. Philippe humored me at first, but as I pressed on he grew more distant, more inclined toward the villagers' point of view. They all assumed I was following the same road to madness as my ancestors."

"But what did you think finding the tomb would prove?" I asked. "You didn't know about the book."

Madame nodded. "What, indeed? I might have found the casket of Jeanne Catherine's

348

son. But that would prove nothing. It *was* madness, Marie. I was descending into madness. I had begun to have recurring dreams of a child traveling through tunnels, transported on the back of a galloping horse. This child, I imagined, was my ancient ancestor, the ancestor of my father's great-aunt, the child of Jesus and Marie Madeleine."

A new light suddenly cast its brightness on us from above. We looked up: candles had been lit in the church. Madame looked frightened.

"Please," I whispered. "We still have time. It's just Monsieur *le curé,* preparing for the Mass."

She hesitated, listening for any threatening sounds. Then she went on. "My reasoning, you must understand, Marie, had become very confused. I was convinced that that child had traveled with her mother from the shores of ancient Israel to Gaul. And then, that she — for I imagined the child to be female — had been separated from her mother, taken away and given a new name, for her own safety. In my increasing delusion, I came to believe that the girl had been brought here, through the network of underground passageways, to Rennes-le-Château.

"If I could find the passageway, then I might find evidence of the child's existence, though what that evidence might be, I could not say. It was madness, all of it, and yet the images — the child on the back of that horse, the close grit of the tunnels — had so captured my imagination that I could not rid my mind of them."

How my sketch must have startled her! I felt a pang of guilt.

She went on. "My marriage began to deteriorate. Philippe wanted children but I was too frightened. I feared a child might cause me to lose my mind utterly. There were days, Marie, whole days that I spent as if I were Jeanne Catherine herself, living in the mental world I had imagined for her: trying to reshape the past through her eyes. I pored over my books, piecing together the information I found in the genealogies, histories, and legends, struggling to make her claim true, struggling for proof. But I came up with nothing, other than what I could imagine. Only a vast despair that seemed to swallow me up every time I took a breath."

"Oh, Madame," I began, wanting to say too much at once. I marveled at her strength, to have survived such an ordeal, and to be here, in this shit-strewn cemetery at midnight, telling it to me. And the story! How appealing, to imagine that our village might have been the haven for such a child — even to imagine that such a child might have lived! What a world might be born if such a thing were true! And yet how fanciful and unlikely, and how impossible to prove.

She continued. "I decided, once and for all, to reject it. To put it out of my mind. I read. I gardened, I traveled a bit — I did what I could to distract myself. When I met you, Marie, I was glad, for I saw in you a friend. Another curious mind."

"Me, too," I said. "I was glad, too."

"I think I even imagined I might someday be able to relate to you all of this — all that I am telling you now, and together we could put it aside, relegate it to where it belonged: to the realm of curiosity and imagination, perhaps, of things to wonder over, instead of where it had forced itself: into a position of charioteer, the rein-holder of my mind.

"But," she said, with a deep sigh, "when you came to me with your sketch, I became very afraid. I could not help but think of it as proof of Jeanne Catherine's tale. I felt myself spiraling once more into my terrifying obsession. So I fled — I went back to Paris, where my mother was. I begged her to take me in. She had never forgiven me for abandoning her and for marrying Philippe, but seeing my desperation, she relented. A blessing."

"Oh. Yes," I said. I was still too stunned to formulate a response. "And your aunt?" I asked tentatively.

"An excuse," she said. "She died many years ago."

She smiled graciously at me, but I was mortified. "Dear Madame, what pain I caused you. Forgive me."

"You couldn't have known, Marie. I don't blame you."

I managed a weak smile. Then in the same instant we both remembered what had brought her back to Rennes-le-Château.

"And then Philippe," she said miserably, and began to weep. "Oh, Marie. What a mess I've made. What a horrible, horrible mess."

"You haven't made it," I said, taking her hand. We stood and stumbled into an awkward embrace.

"We get so stuck, don't we? We think we're pioneering, blazing a trail, but in fact, we're just lurching down the path that's already been chosen for us. All we can do is put one foot in front of the other."

I did not know how to answer that, so

instead I let her weep in my arms, her thin frame shaking with each sob. I held her fast, as if I could tether her to the earth, keep her from floating upward into the ether of her grief.

The sound of voices startled us. Madame blew out the lantern and we stood listening, the cemetery illuminated only by the church candlelight. People were gathering for midnight Mass. We moved away from each other, embarrassed suddenly by the force of our emotions. I thought of my family and of Bérenger: they would be wondering where I was.

I moved toward the cemetery entrance. Madame did not follow. She was near the stone wall, fingering one of the woody vines.

"I don't want to be seen," she said.

The church bell tolled, making my heart leap.

As I watched, she hoisted herself up the wall, using the vine as her support. Arm over arm, lithe as a child she climbed, planting her feet against the stones, until, remarkably, she reached the top. She looked down at me from her height. Her face shone like a pale moon among the trees. "Good-bye, Marie," she said.

"Madame!" I called out, suddenly afraid

of losing her. "I'll come visit in the morning."

"No, Marie, thank you. It's Christmas. You'll have presents to open, your family to be with. Don't worry, please. It's done me a great deal of good, our conversation, seeing that stone. I'll be fine."

"Well — I'll find the book, then," I promised fiercely. "I'll find it and bring it to you."

But she gave no response, only slipped over the edge of the wall as quick as rainfall. I heard the thump when she reached the ground, a gentle rustle of leaves, and then silence.

YERUSHALAYIM

It was a place to sing about, a word that left the mouth humming. Its name was a paradise for the tongue and breath. *Yerushalayim. Peace be within your walls, and security within your towers!*

Miryam had visited every year at Pesach. They walked for a week, her father and uncles, her grandmother, mother and sisters, staying overnight in inns or the homes of welcoming strangers. The city's visage changed as they approached: from a small tawny settlement in the bowl made by the surrounding hills to a glowing fortress glittering with marble palaces and the glorious Temple itself, rising above them as they climbed out of the valley to its gates. The gates themselves seemed to soar above her, as if they truly opened onto holiness — if she only kept her eyes upward, on the stone. For once she let her gaze fall to their feet, she saw misery thronging: the lame and legless, sitting on woven reed mats caked with mud and waste, the blind with their groping hands, the emaciated women clutching cow-eyed babies, the swollen-bellied children who sat listless in the dust. Once, she had asked her mother for a dinar to give, but when she turned toward the group, the beggars came alive, howling, shuffling, writhing like a basket of snakes as they reached for the coin. She ran back and hid her face in her mother's legs, coin still in hand.

Above all, there were the smells. The acrid smoke from the perpetual fires of Ge Hinnom — where humans were said to have been sacrificed in ancient times — and which now were stoked with dog carcasses and the city's rubbish. The animal scents in the market squares, where goats, oxen, pigeons, and sheep bleated, lowed, and cooed imploringly, and at the Sheep Gate, where the people brought their lambs for the sacrifice. The grease from the ovens, and, on the Day of Preparation, the stink of the fresh blood and offal that ran from the Temple to redden the ravines bordering the city. On that day, the Temple sent forth the thick odors of burning entrails and incense, while every home in the city smelled sublimely of roasting lamb, seasoned with marjoram and thyme.

Yerushalayim was where she saw Roman legionaries mounted on horseback for the first time, wearing their formidable cuirasses and red cloaks, their absurdly plumed helmets. And it was in Yerushalayim where she had glimpsed a criminal dragging the heavy beams of a cross through the streets, being prodded forward by soldiers as he made his final march toward the terrible hill of Gulgulta, the place of the skull.

That was the place where men were put to death. Children in Yerushalayim spoke of it — they threatened to "nail each other up," or ordered their playtime enemies to spread their arms. Some bragged to have even seen the hill itself, the hanging bodies. Miryam had never seen it; her parents forbade her from venturing near that section of the city, which lay just outside the western gates. She had learned from the other children that the vultures pecked at the eyes of the dying men, and that dogs gathered at their feet to lick their blood as it dripped. Death came finally as a result of a protracted, agonizing suffocation.

But Yerushalayim was a place of extremes. Balanced against the horror of Gulgulta was the glorious splendor of the Temple. Soaring above the city on its hill, flanked by stone walls and terraces of olive and fig trees, its marble sparkled against the limestone like a diadem, and its cedar porticoes — where sacrificial animals could be bought and currency of all kinds could be exchanged — perched fastidiously above the thronging courts. Upon arriving in Yerushalayim, her family always went first to the Temple — not to enter the sanctuary, for to do that they first had to purify themselves, but just to see it. The fifteen speckled steps leading from the Court of the Gentiles to the sanctuary, the lofty colonnades that rose above the steps, enclosing first the women's court, then the men's court, and finally, beneath the tallest colonnade of all, the priest's court, where the sacrifices were performed. Then, above that, there was the holy of holies, God's dwelling place on earth, where only the high priest was allowed to set foot, and where he placed the daily incense offering. Moved to tears every year by the sight of it, her father prostrated himself, kissed the dusty ground before it, and sang the famous verses in his tremulous voice:

"How lovely is your dwelling place,
O Lord of hosts!
My soul longs, indeed it faints
    for the courts of the Lord;
my heart and my flesh sing for joy
    to the living God."

She longed now to see her father, longed to see his bright eyes. She longed to feel the soft enclosure of her mother's embrace. She was anxious to get to the holy city, to thread her way through the pressing crowds to the room that her family always rented, where she hoped to share the feast with them, if they would have her.

All of Yeshua's followers, men and women, were nervous, for they did not know what to expect when they arrived. They whispered among themselves. Yeshua's manner had lately seemed more intense, more fervent, especially when he spoke of the coming end of days.

"Is it now?" they wondered. "This Pesach? Will this bring on the Kingdom of God?" Many of them believed it was imminent.

"Didn't Daniel prophesy the resurrection of the dead at the time of the end?" they said. "And haven't we seen Elazar newly brought to life?"

Miryam asked Yeshua, "Is this the time, then, Rabbi? Should we prepare ourselves?"

But Yeshua would only say, "Always be prepared, Miryam, always keep your vigil. The Kingdom will come prowling, without fanfare."

They camped in and around Beit Aniyah. Yeshua stayed with Elazar's family; Miryam, in the women's tent near the house. She helped prepare the meals. Elazar lay on his mat and received visitors. Miryam brought him broth and wine, but always averted her eyes when she approached him. He sickened her; her skin seemed to callus against him. She — who had never given more thought than necessary to her own state of ritual purity — longed to be sprinkled with the purifying water, longed to feel the softening silt from the red heifer's ashes on her skin. She could not help but feel tainted in his presence.

Yeshua spent most of his time away from the group, praying. He seemed distant when he was with them. He no longer came to Miryam in the night; he drew into himself only and desired no company other than that of his Abba in heaven. The men observed this. Kefa smirked, triumphant. It was clear he imagined she'd served her purpose for Yeshua and could now be readily discarded.

Yehudah sought her out. "If he is the *mashiah*," he said, his voice agitated, "then why won't he say so? Why won't he announce it? We could enter Yerushalayim strongly then, as one voice. As it is, we're disorganized. He has to lead us."

"He's never said he was," Miryam said.

"But you believe he is, don't you?" Yehudah asked. "Don't you, Miryam?"

Miryam was silent. She was tired; she missed her family; she missed Yeshua. She was mistrustful of declarations.

They left for Yerushalayim early one morning, when the sun first pierced the metal of the night. Several of the men had not slept, so thirsty for the city they were, and these walked ahead of the rest. Miryam and Yeshua walked side by side. He seemed frightened yet resolute. He did not move his eyes from the road.

As they approached the city, the crowd of pilgrims grew. They came not only from Yehudah and the Galil, Canaan, and Peraea, but from the distant lands of Cyrenaica, Babylon, Cappadocia, Asia Minor, and even

Rome. They walked, leading their braying lambs beside them, so the crowds were thick not only with the heat of human bodies and the scent of sweat, but also the tang of the lambs' wool and the stink of their waste.

Though Elazar had remained at home with his sisters, word of his resurrection had spread through the crowds, and heads began to turn toward them as they walked, heads adorned by the simple hood of the Galilean peasant, the goats' hair cap of the Anatolian, the ornately embroidered hat of the Persian. The people wanted to see the man who had raised a corpse from his tomb. One man — a tall, turbaned Egyptian, gold in his ears and on his fingers, cloaked in purple — walked just in front of them, and when he heard that Yeshua was behind him, he turned and met his eyes, then knelt, bowing his head, and said, "Praise be to God, Blessed be he who comes in the name of the Lord."

Yeshua hesitated, standing over the kneeling man. The Egyptian's retinue knelt as well, and some in front of them turned to look. Someone yelled, "Make way, make way for the miracle worker, the one who raises the dead!"

Yehudah noticed a young donkey tied to a post, and he ran to untie it and brought it to Yeshua. Laying his cloak atop it, he said, "See how they long for you. Ride, Rabbi. *Mashiah.*" He regarded Yeshua with his darting eyes. They all knew that to ride into Yerushalayim on the colt would be to declare himself king, as Zechariah had foretold: "Lo, your king comes to you; triumphant and victorious is he, humble and riding on an ass, on a colt the foal of an ass."

Miryam glanced sharply at Yeshua. He was gazing at Yehudah, their eyes locked in a private, severe communication. But the word had already caught, as a flame touched to a branch in a dry wood. It was whispered first, person to person, wondered over, then declared, and then celebrated, shouted from treetops and shoulders, where some had climbed in order to see Yeshua better. "*Mashiah!*" they cried. "*Mashiah!*" Yeshua put his hand on the colt's cloaked back and looked to the crowds, and under his gaze they parted, creating a path that led directly to the city gates. Still, Yeshua did not move. One man laid his cloak on the ground, and he was followed by another, and then another, so that in a matter of minutes, the dusty ground was carpeted in colorful cloth. Those who didn't have cloaks to throw pulled branches and palm leaves from the trees and waved them madly, crying, "Hosanna! Blessed is he who enters in the name of the Lord!"

Miryam grabbed Yeshua's hands, terrified by the frenzy of the crowd. He took them and pressed them into his eyes, as if to blind himself, to blot out the mad scene. His brow was hot and damp. She wanted to embrace him, but feared the crowds.

Leaning in, she whispered, "Are you he, Rabbi, the one they long for?"

He raised his head and brought her hands to his mouth, kissing each palm at its center. His eyes, ringed with dark lashes, flashed uncertainty and fear. "You are a daughter of God, Miryam," he said. "Know yourself."

And he mounted the colt and rode it through the jubilant crowds to the gates of the city, where Miryam lost sight of him.

CHAPTER TEN

Madame had left her lantern with me, and I carried it to the church porch. As I entered the nave, heads turned and eyes traveled to my bodice and skirt. Graveyard mud was streaked across my clothing and likely my face. But most everyone was in too festive a mood to comment. Children whispered together, grandparents cooed and beamed, mothers fussed, and a few of the fathers were already snoring, even before the Mass began. I slid into my family's pew and sat rigidly beside my mother, who did not look up from her prayer. My father raised his eyebrows at me.

I only watched the Mass that night. I pronounced none of the responses nor the prayers, but kept my eyes fixed on Bérenger as he performed the dance of the office: raising and lowering his arms, turning toward and away from the altar, kneeling, bowing, letting his hands hover over the Eucharist in blessing. He knew nothing of Madame's grief, felt none of her pain. Yet for all I knew, he had found the tomb, the coffin of Jeanne Catherine's son, even the book, and was keeping it from me and in turn from Madame, who had more right to such knowledge than he did. His insistence on secrets galled me and, in my mind that night, became the cause of Madame's unhappiness. As the Mass progressed, I felt myself filling with anger and resolve.

When the Mass was over and the congregation had filed out, Bérenger retired to the sacristy. I swept the floor and tidied the pews while the altar boys — no longer the Baux brothers, for they'd grown too old, now the Fauré boy and the Verdiés' grandchild, Gérard's nephew — folded the linens and replaced the paten and chalice on the altar. I bade the boys goodnight when they had finished, and closed the church door tightly behind them, then proceeded to snuff the candles that hung in the mounted sconces along the length of the nave. Bérenger emerged, dressed in pants and a white shirt, wet circles beneath the arms. His collar was unfastened and stuck out from both sides of his neck like broken basketwork.

"Where is the tomb?" I demanded.

He stared at me fixedly, then shook his head, as if trying to clear it. He had drunk a good deal of wine at dinner, and I had no doubt that he wanted only to sleep now, for he had to say Mass again at dawn. He kept walking down the nave, toward me, toward the door. I grabbed his wrist. "Don't walk away from me," I said. "I asked you a question."

"A meaningless question," he said. He was not looking at me, but I could tell from the working of his temple that he was clenching his jaw, trying to control his temper.

"No," I said. I dropped his wrist; he did not yet move. "Not meaningless. Important. Imperative."

"What are you talking about?"

"You know very well. The tomb. The graves beneath our feet. Where is it? What have you found there, Bérenger?"

"Who put that idea into your head?"

"You can't keep secrets from me and expect me to love you," I said, my voice breaking.

"Marie —" he began in a conciliatory tone, but I would not let him continue.

"Where is it? Where is the book? Where is the tomb?!" I demanded, my voice increasing in volume.

Then, in a single motion, he grabbed both

366

of my wrists, straddled my legs, and pulled me backward, down the center aisle of the nave. I had to scrabble my feet on the newly tiled floor to keep up with him. He threw open the door of the confessional and tossed me on the bench inside. His face and chest loomed over me like a punishment. "You haven't yet made a confession to me, Marie, in all the years I've known you."

"I have nothing to confess," I protested tearily, stunned by the sudden assault. My head was full of the scent of varnish.

"That's a lie," he said.

"You're the one who should confess. All your secrets. What are you hiding?"

"Why is everything your business? I have my own private affairs that are no concern of yours."

"But my conscience is your concern? You're prepared to hear my confession and yet you won't give me yours?"

"I'm your priest, Marie. It's my job."

"You're not my priest."

He glowered. "Who am I then? Tell me who I am."

I stared at him, bewildered. "What do you mean?"

"Who am I to you, Marie?" His voice softened — almost into a supplication.

"For God's sake," I said. "I thought you

knew the answer to that."

He let the door to the compartment shut, trapping me inside. After a moment, I heard him step into the adjoining compartment and slide the window panel back. The scent of the sweet communion wine on his breath penetrated the screen.

"I've put you in an unfair position, becoming your friend," he said.

"My friend." I repeated the word with bitter irony. I was not his friend — I was his chaste consort, his unsullied mistress, not his friend.

"My companion. My confidante." Then, in a whisper, he added, "My heart, Marie. My very heart."

As an experiment, I spoke the first words of the act of contrition. "Bless me, Father, for I have sinned. It has been —" I paused, calculating. "Six years since my last confession." The number startled me. It seemed too large, and I calculated it once more to be sure.

"It's a long time, Marie."

"Since you came to Rennes."

We sat together in silence for a time, listening to the equilibrating rhythm of the other's breath, feeling our pulses slow.

"I've sinned too many times to remember," I began. It was awkward, confessing to

Bérenger as if he were an objective ear, as if he were not profoundly associated with my most personal thoughts and deepest feelings. I laughed self-consciously, wanting to continue — not to please him, for after overpowering me as he had, he did not deserve to be pleased — but because I wanted, suddenly, to feel cleansed. Cleansed as I had after making confession and doing my penance when I was a girl. Such enviable purity! It was unattainable now, I saw, and I grieved a little for it. But what could I say? Should I speak of my desire for him, describe my longing as a matter of fact, as if I were speaking to a wall?

"I can't do this," I said, pushing the confessional door open.

"Wait, Marie," he began.

"What?" I stopped, one hand on the door.

"I'm afraid I've hurt you, *mon ange*. I'm afraid I've done damage to you."

I sat back down. "By throwing me into the confessional?" I rubbed my wrist. "I'll be all right."

"No. Far worse than that. I'm afraid I've robbed you of your faith."

I paused, surprised. "Why? My doubts are not your fault."

"I haven't answered your questions well, Marie. If only I knew how to answer you better. I've prayed about it for years."

I was touched by his sincerity. "That's all right, *mon cher.* You've answered them as well as you could."

"I have not been a good priest to you, Marie."

"I have not wanted a priest," I said. "I've wanted you, a man."

He sighed heavily, as if facing his own doom.

"It's wrong of me, I know," I continued, relieved to finally be speaking the words. "I should have removed myself from you long ago. But I can't help but wonder whether our love is an intention of God's. He brought us together, after all, did he not?"

"I don't know anymore, Marie," he said. "I used to think he had done it as a test. A test of my fidelity to him."

"But now?"

"Now so much has happened. I'm not sure of anything anymore."

I leaned my head against the back wall of the confessional. I was sleepy, suddenly.

"I'm a coward, Marie," he whispered.

"Why, *mon cher?* Why say such a thing?"

"It's true. I have always been a coward. Unable to face my fears."

"What are you talking about? What fears?"

"My fears of oblivion, Marie. My fear, my

deepest fear, that all I do is in vain. That God does not hear me, that he has turned away from me. That I — we, all of us — are lost."

I waited, unsure how to respond. After a moment, I left my compartment and pulled the door of his open with a click. He sat on the narrow bench, his shoulders squeezed against either wall.

"You mustn't say that, Bérenger. You are not lost. God is with you."

"Ah, Marie. I am not so sure."

He squeezed out of the confessional, past me, and began to walk slowly, mechanically, up the length of the nave. When he reached the steps that led to the altar, he knelt there and bowed his head. The candlelight pooled around him and over him, lighting the back of his head and the narrow band of skin between his hairline and his collar. His hunching shoulders, the thickness of his waist, the small spot of baldness at his crown: he had aged since Michelle and I had spent our afternoons in the meadow rhapsodizing over him. He was so much of a man then, but temptation had weakened him. I had weakened him.

When he had finished his prayer, he came to stand in front of me. I could see the whiskers at his throat like a field of razed

wheat stubble. His smell rushed over me —
that delicious peppery scent, tinged with
incense — and I felt so tempted to cling to
him, to nestle my face in his chest and feel
him embrace me, that I had to step backward and fill my nostrils once more with
the stale air of the church.

"I don't know what God wants from me,
Marie," he said. His eyes darted from me to
the wall to the door, as if he was afraid
someone might be watching. "I pray to him
but he doesn't answer."

"What do you want from him?" I asked.

He barked a wounded laugh. "What do I
want from God? I want order. I want peace.
I want him to communicate with me, to let
me know that I'm doing his will, that I'm in
the right. Not once in my life, not once has
he deigned to grant me even a moment of
his presence. Me, a priest! Not once,
Marie." He kicked one of the pews, causing
it to scrape against the floor. "What have I
done?" he yelled to the ceiling. "How have I
offended you?"

His voice echoed against the sanctuary
walls. In the silence that followed, he slid
into the pew he had kicked, slumping
against it. He continued, his voice quieter,
resigned. "I entered the priesthood because
I thought it would guarantee me a place in

heaven. There would be rules to follow, a path to walk — and if I could only keep my feet on the path, I would come out all right. I have tried, Marie — God knows I have tried to honor him. There was a time when I thought I knew what he wanted. Church doctrine told me his mind. The words of the Bible informed me, indisputably, what he desired of me. The example of Jesus' life . . ." He trailed off.

I slid into the pew behind him.

He began again. "But I have become infected by doubt. What do I know of God? I read the scriptures indifferently. I mouth the Mass. My heart and mind are elsewhere — on banalities, Marie. Not on God, not on God. More and more it's the world of men I live in, Marie. I don't know how to rise from it."

He rested his head on the back of the pew, tipping his forehead toward me. If I had been more selfless, more ethical, I might have advised him to pray with renewed devotion, to seek counsel from the Holy Virgin Mother, to find inspiration in the saint he so loved, the Madeleine, whose passion for God had never abated, so it was said. I would have murmured some gentle words and then left him alone, to pray in peace. But I could not. His forehead — that

formidable brow, so stitched with pain —
rested inches from my lips. I laid my hand
across it. I rubbed his temples, drawing the
skin tight across his face; I dug my fingers
into his thick hair and rubbed his scalp. He
inhaled deeply. I leaned forward and kissed
his forehead. He laced his hands behind my
head and pressed me into him, then swiv-
eled and faced me, his forehead pressed
against mine. I closed my eyes. Our lips
met, then lingered.

"Perhaps God intends for you to live in
this world, *mon amour,*" I whispered finally,
my cheek to his. "Perhaps it is through this
world that God means for you to find him."

He released me and I lifted my head, feeling disoriented, flushed with pleasure,
ashamed. His eyes were still closed, his
hands gripping the pew between us. He
emanated such a brume of emotion that it
seemed he was considering whether to assault or embrace me.

"I'm sorry," I said. "I wanted to comfort
you."

He waited a moment, then covered my
hand with his. "Your suspicion was correct,
Marie," he said. "I've found the tomb."

This is what he told me:
This past fall, when the work crew had

lifted the knight's stone in preparation to install the new pulpit, Bérenger noticed that some of the dirt had fallen away. Looking more closely, he made out a single dusty step, partially occluded. Immediately, he dismissed the crew and locked the church. That night he entered alone, armed with a lantern and a shovel. It took him several grueling weeks of nightly digging — he had to fill a barrel many times a night and haul it out to the cemetery, where he emptied it — but eventually, step by step, he had uncovered an ancient stone staircase that led deep into the earth and ended facing a thick oaken door banded by iron, no higher than a child.

The door had not wanted to budge — he had used one of the smaller flagstones from the floor as a makeshift battering ram — and when finally it did open, it made such a scream he thought it would wake the entire village. He waited in anxious misery for several minutes, the circle of light from his lantern revealing nothing but a stone floor beneath the open door. Finally, after he was satisfied no one had heard, he ventured forward, stooping to fit beneath the lintel. Once inside the room, his lantern glowed more brightly, bouncing off the walls of hewn stone, and he saw that he was inside a crypt containing numerous coffins of differing shapes and sizes.

Here he paused.

"And so? What else?" I prompted.

"Nothing," he said. "I've found nothing more."

"Nothing? No evidence of the book?" I asked.

"I haven't gone any farther in," he said. "I can't bring myself to. I go down there nightly, ready to step inside, but I haven't the courage."

"But why didn't you tell me, *mon cher?* Why have you been so secretive?"

He sighed. "I have only been trying to protect you. I didn't trust that Austrian. I thought perhaps he'd gotten me mixed up in something larger and more sinister than I was aware of. I didn't want to involve you further."

I walked to the pulpit and fiddled with the fence surrounding it. We would need a lantern. I looked toward the pew I had been sitting in, realizing I'd lost track of mine. "Have we a light?" I asked.

Bérenger stood, taking a long moment to realign the pew he'd kicked before following me up the aisle of the nave. He walked just beyond the pulpit to the wall, where he removed a candle from the sconce, then handed it to me. "Marie," he began. Then, in a rush, he seized me by the waist and fastened his mouth on mine with such transcendental recklessness! I have heard it said that a kiss can take the breath away, but that is not precisely what I felt. It would be more accurate to say that it was as if I was momentarily freed from my breath, from its perpetual tidal impulse. My body was the breathing thing, the feeling thing, the thing that nuzzled and kissed and gazed and kissed again, seeking his lips like a newborn seeks the teat. And yes, I was my body, breathing, feeling pleasure, but I was simultaneously *not* it, outside sensation, soaring above it. I felt as if he had kissed away my self — all my eccentricities, anxieties, obsessions, all the patterns of mind that circumscribed my identity — so that I was free momentarily to join the larger Self that is existence, that is the breath that enlivens all the earth. An illusion, perhaps, and certainly fleeting, for I never again felt the same, even after years of kisses — but sweet, so very sweet.

We clung together by the pulpit for a long time, kissing, gazing, whispering endearments. Some time later — minutes, probably, though it might have been hours —

we parted, aware of the task that yet lay ahead.

Bérenger opened the fence with a key. The three planks beneath the pulpit were still there, startlingly vulnerable. Anyone who had the idea to lift one of them would see the staircase and naturally be curious as to what it led to. But the pulpit, large as it was, had the effect of overpowering the space around it so that the planks and the fence appeared inconsequential.

Guarding the flame with my hand, I watched Bérenger lift the planks and set them aside. There it was, just as he had said: a stone staircase, very steep and uneven. He took the candle from me, kissed me once more, and started down. I followed, wishing I had another light. The steps were narrow and my feet unsteady.

It grew colder as we descended. I was astonished at how deep we had to go before we reached the entrance. Bérenger had only dug a narrow passageway, just wide enough for himself, so his body blocked even the dim light of the candle. I balanced myself by holding on to the walls. The soil was cold, and clods of it came loose beneath my touch. I looked back from where we'd come and saw only darkness — the opening was no longer visible. Panic rose in my throat.

But Bérenger continued to descend and I made myself follow him, despite the frantic fluttering of my heart.

Once in the crypt, however, my fear gave way to fascination. The candle illuminated dozens of coffins of all different sizes, some stacked atop each other. Some were humble pine boxes, others were mahogany or chestnut and ornately carved with fleurs-de-lys, vines, crosses, or rose blossoms. One coffin was metal — lead, perhaps — while two others appeared to be more ancient, as they were made of stone and very large, perhaps meant to accommodate several bodies. I took the candle from Bérenger and, walking the length of the crypt, was astonished to find that it extended into another room, just as large, this one filled only with several of the larger stone sarcophagi. At the end of this room was an archway, beyond which descended yet another set of stairs just as steep as the first. "Have you been down here?" I asked. He stood a few feet behind me, in the dark center of the room.

"No," he said. "I hadn't gone beyond that first room."

I followed the steps carefully, though they were easier to pass than the first flight, being wider and uncovered by dirt. At their base was another archway, which opened into a third room with walls of packed dirt. This room appeared to be the more ancient. There was only one roughly cut stone casket, placed against the wall. Behind it, extending along the length of the wall, was an enormous pile of bones, neatly stacked. Skulls, forearms, thigh and shinbones, collarbones and broad-winged pelvises lay one atop the other, fitted together like a jigsaw puzzle. Some had spilled onto the floor; it was littered with finger bones and vertebrae as well as many unidentifiable chips and slivers that might just as well have been oddly shaped rocks. A fully intact skeleton still lay on a ledge in the far corner of the room, a corroded iron blade by its side.

"God save us," whispered Bérenger.

The room ended in a landslide of earth and rubble. I picked at the crusted hill, wondering if it might be blocking Madame's famous passageway.

"It's a catacomb, Marie," Bérenger said behind me. "A catacomb beneath our church."

"Incredible," I said.

We did not proceed any further that night. It was late — or early rather, almost dawn. We had only a few hours before Christmas morning Mass, before the church would once again be full of people. We needed time to think about what we might be entering into, for we were partners now.

Christmas day passed happily — Père Noël brought us each a few gifts, and we spent the day feasting on the leftovers from the previous night and playing with Pichon as he toddled about. My thoughts returned continually to the previous night, to the catacomb, the book of visions, and to the passageway that I thought might lie beyond that avalanche of dirt. Most of all to the pleasure of our kisses. In the daylight, it all seemed too fanciful to be real. I waited impatiently for the night.

I may have forgotten my anger at Bérenger, but Madame's agony still weighed on me. I itched to tell her about the catacomb, but I restrained myself, thinking of how my sketch of the knight's stone had so distressed her. I thought I should at least wait until I could explore the crypt more thoroughly, until I found the coffin of Jeanne Catherine's son and the book, until I could dig a short way through the wall of dirt and discern whether it did indeed obscure the tunnel Madame had long sought.

What a strange story it all was! I sympathized with Jeanne Catherine. I don't know whether it was my renewed belief in the miraculous or simply my longing for some experience beyond my own, but I was willing to accept the legitimacy of her visions even before I had set eyes on them. It was tempting, of course, to entertain such a thought — that a woman who lived in our village might have been an unrecognized saint. Why shouldn't Marie Madeleine have visited her? Hadn't Our Lady herself appeared to Sainte Bernadette at her grotto in Lourdes just a few decades earlier, calling herself the Immaculate Conception and directing Bernadette to the source of the healing spring beneath the earth? If the Church could approve of Sainte Bernadette and her visions of the Holy Virgin, why not Jeanne Catherine and her visions of the Madeleine?

The answer to that was simple, of course: Jeanne Catherine's visions would never be approved because they opposed Church doctrine. The notion of Jesus fathering a child, the idea that he might have loved a woman with spirit *and* body — these ideas were much too dangerous, much too blasphemous to be aired. But why? My own protests came one after the next. What was so unholy about the body? Didn't God create us this way, in his image, replete with desire and flaws? I thought of Pichon at his birth: the filmy fingernails, the tiny arcing lips. How could we call his genesis an evil act? Must holiness imply stoicism, the absence of pleasure? God, forming Adam: Mustn't he have enjoyed it, shaping his limbs from the wet clay?

My thoughts strayed again to Bérenger. His confession had not entirely surprised me. I had suspected that his virulent defense of Church doctrine stemmed not from true zeal but from fear. His words on doctrinal matters so often rang false, revealing a desperation only partially disguised by his bluster. He feared that any tug at the loose threads of belief would lead to a tangled, unsalvageable skein. His fear was not unfounded, of course: I knew that from the unraveling, and now the tentative rewinding, of my own faith. But I hadn't thought his faith to be so close to fraying. Nor had I guessed how deeply it, too, made him suffer.

It occurred to me then that perhaps the book of visions would help to jolt Bérenger from his habits of mind, like a stick of intellectual dynamite. Imagining another Marie Madeleine, one whose love for God could be both spiritual and physical, might help to soften his rigidity and strengthen his faith. The book became, in my mind, the panacea I sought for the ills my loved ones faced: it would restore Bérenger's faith, assuage Madame's anguish, and confirm my own fledgling belief in the integrity and holiness of the natural world and of ordinary human experience.

I tried to put myself in the mind of the priest as he was deciding where to hide the book for the second time. If he had claimed that Jeanne Catherine's body had withstood the ravages of worms, he must have wondered about her son's corpse, buried in the crypt. Would his body be free from the effects of decomposition as well, even years after his death? The priest must have opened the child's casket — how could he have left such a question unanswered? And regardless of the state of the boy's body, what better hiding place could be found than within one of the caskets in a secret tomb? Even savage revolutionists would not likely go to the extent of prying up the flagstones of the church floor to find the tomb. And even if they did, they would surely hesitate before lifting the lids of the coffins.

Still, he must not have felt that his hiding place was completely secure, for he had gone to the further trouble of asking the favor of his friend and hiding the flask in the baluster. I imagined the poor tortured man, bent over the baluster in the dead of night, cutting away the slab of wood from the capital, then meticulously drawing the map of the sanctuary, with the knight's stone clearly delineated. When did he scribble that verse from Job? As a last fevered thought before he rolled up the parchment like a cigarette and stuffed it inside the flask? And what was he thinking of as he did? The tomb itself? The terrifying madness of his patroness? The visions?

That night, when the house was quiet and everyone was asleep, Bérenger and I slipped out together, leaving the door ajar to avoid its creak, and walked to the door of the church. We each carried an unlit lantern. Bérenger handed me his when we arrived and told me to wait a moment, then disappeared into the darkness of the garden. When he returned, he was carrying a shovel, a hammer, and a pry bar.

Gently he pushed open the church door, then closed and locked it behind us.

"What are those for?" I asked in a whisper. A match flared in the darkness: Bérenger's face appeared, lengthened by shadows. He lit his lantern, then mine. I fought the urge to touch his cheek, suddenly shy. We had not touched all day.

"The book must be hidden somewhere in the tomb. Where else but in one of the caskets?"

It startled me that he had come to the same conclusion as I had, even with half the knowledge — for I had still not told him of Madame and her story. Reflexively I offered another idea. "It could be somewhere beneath that mound of dirt in the tunnel."

"Possibly. But the caskets are the more likely place, don't you think?"

I shrugged, affecting nonchalance. "Perhaps." I hesitated, considering whether or not to tell him what I knew.

"What are you going to do with it?" I asked. "If we find it?"

He gave me a surprised look, as if he had expected I already knew. "Why, I'll finish what the old priest started. What he didn't have the strength to do."

"Burn it, you mean?"

But Bérenger did not answer me: he was grunting beneath the weight of one of the planks of wood covering the hole.

I continued, my words gaining force as I spoke. "But you can't really believe that the Church would be threatened by such a thing. Even if the Austrian were to get his hands on it and publish it, what lasting effect could it possibly have?"

"It wouldn't topple the Church, of course. But it would be one more corrosive element, one more thing for the freethinkers to use to undermine the Church's authority, to cast her in the mud."

"But what about your own doubt? Your estrangement from God? Everything you said last night?"

"What about it?"

I was silent.

"Marie," he said softly. "It has occurred to me that perhaps God has set this task in front of me as a test. A chance to prove my loyalty. If I can find this heretical book and destroy it, then he'll come to me, he'll finally grace me with his presence."

"A test. Like you've thought of me. As a test."

He gave me no answer.

"Why would God concern himself with an old book full of a crazy woman's delusions?"

"Everything concerns God, Marie. Every last thing."

His resolution wounded me. It was clear that our passion last night was not likely to be repeated tonight, nor ever again, perhaps. Not only that: I saw how despite our most valiant efforts, we could never truly be intimates, not in the way I had envisioned for us, united in thought, married in mind. He clung to the rotting vine of the medieval Church; I stood before the same vine, pruning scythe in hand.

"Will you help me, Marie?" he asked.

"Of course," I lied.

We descended the steps once more, myself in front with the lanterns, while Bérenger staggered behind me under the burden of the tools. I managed to convince him that we should begin with the older rooms, reasoning that Jeanne Catherine's confessor would have wanted to hide the book as deeply below ground as possible. As we passed through the first room, I quickly surveyed its contents again, singling out the few smaller caskets, the ones that appeared to belong to children. One, stacked atop two other larger coffins, bore a tarnished brass plaque boasting the name of Berthelot, but I did not stop, for fear of drawing attention to it. I followed Bérenger through the second room, then down the steep stone staircase to the lowermost room of the crypt. Our lanterns cast a brighter light than the candle had, diminishing the room's ominous quality. The rust-colored walls, the stacked and scattered bones, the stone sarcophagus, and the mountain of earth were all illuminated. I wondered once again whether the earth had slid naturally by some disturbance, a mild earthquake perhaps, or whether the dirt had been piled there by human hands.

Bérenger set the shovel and hammer on the floor, keeping hold of the pry bar, and stood before the sepulcher. He muttered a few phrases in Latin and made the sign of the cross, then wedged the pry bar beneath the lid, knocked it in with the hammer, and leaned on the bar with all his weight. The lid did not budge. He repeated this several times, up and down the length of the casket and along both ends, until finally, his forehead glistening, his face red with effort, he broke the seal with a pop.

I rushed to him as he slid the lid aside. The must of centuries assaulted us; we both reeled. Bérenger covered his nose with his arm; I used my blouse. We stepped forward again. The lantern cast a warm light over the contents: a skeleton, with a few scraps of colorless cloth still draped over the ribs and pelvis. Just beneath the left hand was a simple gold band, presumably having dropped from the finger when the flesh fell away. Beside the right hand lay an ornamental dagger of intricately carved jet. At its feet was a collection of smaller bones, the skull elongated, the rib cage broad, the four legbones tiny: a lapdog, buried with its master. Next to the lapdog was a small effigy of a ram with garnets for eyes and nostrils, and rubies lining its golden horns like knots in the branches of a tree.

"Dear God," Bérenger whispered.

I thought of Childeric's tomb, the cloisonné bees, the gold and garnet bull's head. "How old do you think this is?" I asked.

"I couldn't say, truthfully," he replied. "Sixteenth century, perhaps?"

We stood together, both wanting to handle the treasures, neither of us daring.

"Such a piece of art, Marie, would be worth thousands of francs," whispered Bérenger. "At the very least. And the dagger —" He finished the thought with an awe-filled silence.

We opened several more caskets that night — I held the lantern as Bérenger pried open the lids — and found treasure after treasure: a golden bracelet studded with sapphires; rings of gold and silver, bearing jewels of varying weights and sizes — polished jet, luminous amber, a diamond cut in the shape of a star; a necklace of pearls the size of knuckle bones. And the weapons! Swords fashioned most commonly from iron but occasionally from silver or copper and set in hilts of arabesquing brass, shaped and hammered gold; daggers, the leather of some sheaths still partially intact; shields, emblazoned family crests; dirks with handles of engraved horn; sabers, cutlasses, rapiers — all manner of blades, lavishly and plainly decorated. Occasionally, a casket contained nothing other than bones, though almost always we found at least one artifact that had been buried with the owner: a ring or bracelet with the women, a sword or dagger with the men.

We touched nothing, not at first. We were too awed by the enormity of what we'd found, too cowed by the age and the contents of the coffins. My thoughts of the book of visions, of Jeanne Catherine and her unfortunate son, even of our kisses, were all but forgotten.

RESURRECTION

In the city, Miryam made her way to the rooms her family always rented. She stood before the entrance shyly, unsure how she would be received. Her father came to the door, embraced her, and ushered her in, praising God for returning her, and her whole family gathered around her — her mother, sisters, grandmothers and aunts, uncles and cousins. She wept with relief.

When she told them of the exorcism of her demons, her parents knelt in grateful prayer, her mother holding fast to Miryam's hand. They led a joyous feast that night.

But though Miryam rejoiced at the homecoming, she could not celebrate with a whole heart. She sang the songs absently, for her thoughts were with Yeshua. After the lamb was eaten and the bones burned in the fire, after the table had been cleared and the dishes all washed, after she had sat around the fire with her father and uncles, telling them of her travels and the miracles that Yeshua had worked, they had finally all fallen asleep, made drowsy by the four cups of wine and the festivities. She remained awake, looking out the window onto the empty street.

Was Yeshua that savior that the Lord had promised to his people Yisrael? Was it he whom the prophets — Mosheh, Daniel, Yeshayah — spoke of? It was written: a star would come forth out of Yakov, a new king to rule the world. Yerushalayim would be rebuilt in a troubled time and an anointed one would come, but would eventually be cut off, left with nothing. Was this, then, Yeshua?

Yeshua had prophesied, too, made puzzling, troublesome statements that Miryam could not pretend to understand. He had declared his coming would bring anguish, fire, dissension, and war — not the unity of nations, as Yeshayah had foretold. Sometimes he spoke as if he were the Lord himself, declaring himself to be present in the heartwood, in the soil beneath a stone. And his statements about the Kingdom, the coming end, were changeable and various: sometimes he spoke of an end like the one foretold by the prophets: the destruction of the Temple, war and calamity, and then the reigning of the Prince of Peace over the living and the resurrected dead. At other times, his vision of the kingdom was more ill-defined and yet more illuminated: a kind of inner dwelling, a place of peace that existed now, out of the sight of men, a place that demanded the renunciation of all else in order to be found. Away from him only hours, she was already losing sight of him. Who was he? What did he offer the world?

Finally, just before the cock crowed that dawn, she fell asleep on the floor next to the window. She did not wake until several hours later, when it was too late.

She hurried to Gulgulta, having heard on the street of Yeshua's capture. When she arrived, he was already close to death. She called to him, shrieked until her voice broke, but he remained motionless, pinned against the sky like a skinned calf. She wrapped herself around the cross and shimmied toward him, splinters gouging her thighs and hands. When she reached his feet, she clung there, nuzzling them, kissing away the blood that snaked from his wounds. Her arms trembled with the exertion, but she held on, praying for God to topple the cross, to restore him to life.

A pair of hands grabbed her hips and pulled her down. On the ground, she cursed at the soldier who had pried her off. "He's done nothing!" she screamed. "Take him down! Take him down!" He swatted her across the mouth with the back of his gloved hand. Her lip split. She broke for the cross once more, but the soldier knocked her to the ground. Pain shot through her wrist.

"Try that again and I'll beat you to death," the soldier growled. She spat in his face. He moved off.

She stared at Yeshua. He was so still, his belly flat and unmoving. Then, suddenly, he gasped, straining at his bindings. She cried out, looking around for someone to cut him down. He was dying. How could they let him die?

A short distance away, Yeshua's mother

knelt, staring mutely at her son. Miryam went to her, knelt beside her, took her hand.

A while later she saw Kefa peering in their direction from the city wall. "Coward," she murmured. He stayed several minutes, then disappeared.

Late that afternoon, Yeshua's spirit rattled through him one last time, then departed. His corpse slumped. Finally, the guards took it down. A council judge and another well-dressed man stepped forward, giving orders.

"Where will you take him?" Miryam asked.

"There is a new tomb in a small garden near here. We'll lay him there," one of the men said.

"Whose tomb is it?"

"His now," the well-dressed man said, and Miryam gathered that it had once belonged to the man himself.

They laid Yeshua's body on his mother's lap. That Miryam cradled it, letting her fingers travel over the wounds: the blood-encrusted holes in the wrists and at the ankles and the scabs at his forehead and temples where the thorny crown had been placed. Miryam of Magdala watched her, filled with sympathy. To be the mother of such a man.

Someone brought a bucket of water. Miryam of Magdala dipped the hem of her cloak in it and gingerly wiped Yeshua's wounds. When she was finished, the men lifted Yeshua and placed him in a cart. As they did, Miryam offered a ladleful of water to the other Miryam, saying "Drink, mother."

She took it, but did not bring it to her mouth. "He loved you," she said.

"Shh," Miryam said. Gently, she helped Yeshua's mother lift the ladle to her lips and said, "Drink."

At the tomb, the men anointed the body with myrrh and aloe, wrapped him with linens, and laid him down. When they rolled the stone over the opening of the tomb, Miryam felt as if it rolled across her own body, crushing bone and organ, preventing breath.

On the morning after Shabbat, Miryam of Magdala rose at dawn and went to the tomb. When she arrived, she saw that the rock had been rolled back. She thought first of Elazar and was immediately fearful, imagining Yeshua, skin a ghastly pallor, emerging weak and monstrous into the dawn. She approached the tomb with trepidation. But when she looked inside, she saw no body, only the strewn linens that had covered him. The tomb smelled still of myrrh and aloe.

Who has done this? she thought. *Who has taken him?* She rushed into the garden, thinking only of his missing body, her eyes senseless to the beauty of the dew that silvered the new flowers. But she was stopped in the garden by a voice that called her name with the passing breeze on her cheek. She breathed, listened, and then, with the fresh morning air, a rapture penetrated her heart and enlarged it beyond all containment. It seemed to fill the whole of her body and mind, making the blood beat at her fingertips and the inner drums of her ears. "Yeshua," she whispered, and heard, within that glorious expanse of her new heart, his response: "Miryam."

She saw him then, not with her eyes, but instead with this sudden great heart: Yeshua wholly transformed. He was not embodied — he was instead a radiance, a shifting emanation of light that took shape now as the glint of silver in a dewdrop perched on the lip of a petal, now as a flash of brilliance cast across the surface of a wet stone, now again as the shimmer on a moth's wing, glinting and fluttering with the speed of a thought, and now once more as an elliptical flame, bending and twisting as in a wind.

"Rabboni," she cried. "Wait. Wait!"

The patterned light dissipated into the bright morning. She cried out once more. "Where are you? Where have you gone? Don't go!" But she saw nothing more. The breeze caressed her cheek.

When the wind stopped, Miryam looked around, noting now the beauty of the garden: the orchids and the meadow-saffron, the cyclamen, the lilies and the irises, the milk-vetch and the rock rose, the panicles of henna, and the almond tree with its white blossoms, all jeweled with quivering drops of dew. She breathed deeply, catching the sweet scent of the wet narcissus petals and the heady urgency of the mandrake, and exhaled, letting the breath shudder from her lungs. She still felt her swollen heart, its pleasant pressure against her throat, her chest, her belly, even her thighs, the spreading peace that came with each pulsation. It was the peace she'd felt when he first healed her, that astonishing sense of newness, the unfamiliarity with herself. And she felt the knowledge, newly born within her, as evident as the empty tomb, that she was with child.

CHAPTER ELEVEN

We returned to the crypt night after night. Bérenger was careful not to touch me, not even casually, not even in the protective darkness of the church. I gathered he regretted our indiscretion, and though I was sorry, I did not blame him.

Our pace in opening the caskets was rapid. I feared we would reach the little Berthelot coffin and the book of visions I felt sure was hidden inside within the week, and that Bérenger might set fire to it there and then, without even allowing me to handle it, so convinced he was of its poisonous qualities. Once again, I considered telling him Madame's story in full, explaining her family history and her rightful claim to the book in the hopes that he might see reason. But he had never harbored kind feelings toward Madame. He suspected it was she who had reported him to the State so many years earlier. And, perhaps because of his suspicion, he tended to take the point of view that she had been at least partially responsible for the mayor's suicide. It was not likely he would soften his stance for her benefit.

So I had to find the book before he did. It would be difficult, for he seemed intent on opening every casket as quickly as possible. The sight of so much treasure energized him; he barely slept.

I thought, then, of involving Madame. If I could tell her where the coffin was located, and instruct her how to enter the tomb, she might be able to search for the book alone while I kept Bérenger occupied with some other task.

I went to Madame the following day, a few days after Christmas Eve. Mme Siau opened the door as usual, and asked me to wait while she called for Madame. Mme Laporte came to the door a moment later dressed in a black gown, her face washed and rested.

"Hello," I said. "You look well."

"Thank you, Marie. I feel better. You look a bit peaked, yourself."

"I haven't been sleeping."

"Come in, please."

I followed her inside. She guided me to the parlor. Stacked against the far wall were several large crates I had not seen before.

Madame had hardly sat down before I blurted out my news: "I've been exploring the tomb the past few nights. With Monsieur *le curé*."

"Have you?" Madame said. Her face betrayed no expectation. "And what have you found there?"

"It's incredible. The bones, all stacked as high as our heads. And the numbers of coffins. Dozens upon dozens! I've spotted the one I think belongs to Jeanne Catherine's son, but we haven't opened it yet —"

"Opened it?" Her gaze was uncharacteristically judgmental. "You're not opening them, are you?"

"Well, yes." My enthusiasm for our project withered.

"What for?"

"To find the book, of course," I said impatiently. "It must be in the little boy's coffin. It's the only place it could be."

"It seems dreadfully morbid."

My heart sank. I had never before felt her disapprobation, and it wounded me. I didn't dare tell her what we'd found in the coffins. "I thought you'd be glad, madame. You wanted to find the tomb. And I thought you hoped to see the book."

She took my hands in hers. "Marie. You

are kind to want to help me. But please, I do not want you to disturb the dead for my sake. The story you've told me is enough. Truly. It's given me a good deal of relief, knowing that my Jeanne Catherine's tale was honored enough to have been written down. I find I have little desire to read the visions myself. Even if they were to be found. I would rather leave the contents of that book to my imagination."

I nodded as though I understood. "I thought it might help you. To read what she'd written. It might be a kind of proof." Though as I spoke, I knew it wouldn't: a book like that, of one individual's visions, could never prove anything.

"You're very kind, Marie. But I don't require proof any longer, thank goodness. What I require is peace." We regarded each other for a long moment before she spoke again.

"And now I have something to tell you. I am going to be moving. For good this time. To Paris."

"No!" I shouted, surprising both of us with the force of the exclamation. Madame made a small leap backward in her seat. "Oh, no, madame," I said again, more quietly. "Excuse me. But I would miss you so."

"I will miss you, Marie. Very much. But it's time for me to go. There's little keeping me here now."

I swallowed, feeling the sadness collect in my throat.

"I would like to leave you with something, Marie. A gift to remember me by. I would like you to have my library."

I hesitated, amazed. "Madame," I whispered. "All those books?"

She nodded, delight in her eyes. "Paris has more books than I will ever be able to read. And it would please me so to know the books were in your care. Will you accept them?"

"I'm honored, Madame. I don't know what to say."

"Of course, I realize it may be hard for you to find the space for them. You won't need to move them from the castle for some time yet — I don't plan to sell it immediately. In the meantime, I thought Monsieur *le curé* might be able to build you a library of your own to house them, since he takes such pleasure in building."

"Yes," I answered gratefully. "Yes, I imagine he might do that."

I left the château that day in a pensive mood, saddened by the impending loss of Madame, humbled by her great gift as well

403

as by her wisdom. She was mistress of herself, more so than anyone I knew: she knew her own demons and dealt severely with them. Likewise, she understood the nature of pleasure: how the imagined, anticipated event was often far more rich and rewarding than the event itself. And she had suffered so. Perhaps it was true, then, that suffering was a necessary predecessor to wisdom.

Two nights later, Bérenger and I reached the little Berthelot coffin. I held my breath as Bérenger forced open the fluted lid, eager to snatch the book from the coffin before he could grab it and afraid, too, of what more we might find within. I had dreamed that afternoon, in an hour of stolen sleep, of a lifelike corpse with skin as smooth as Pichon's and eyelashes as long, darkening the full cheeks with a filigree of shadows. But there was no undecayed flesh here, no undefiled arm to reach out of the grave and circle its slender fingers around my wrist. Nor did I glimpse any book. There was only bone: a small skeleton draped with bands of tattered gray cloth. Emboldened by disappointment and relief, I picked up the skull. Its lightness was remarkable. On its left side, just above where the ear would have been, I noticed a slight indentation about the size of a horse's hoof. I laid it down again, and as I did, the knobs of vertebrae clacked delicately, one against the other.

In the end, we opened all the tombs, and even dug a few feet into the massive pile of dirt that blocked the bottommost room, but found no evidence of the book of visions nor of any ancient passageway. Only more earth, more rubble, more dirt — and more wealth. Bérenger worked with the same driven meticulousness that he used when planning and supervising the construction in the church. He steadily opened the tombs, and though he wrote nothing down, I could see him cataloguing each item in his mind as he saw it, making note of its relative worth, the quality of the material, the weight. He had begun to touch the jewelry — only to touch, and he replaced each item just as it was — but his wonder in the age and the fine crafting of some of the items became more and more proprietary. Little by little, these small treasures seemed to be supplanting his thirst for God's favor.

When we did not find the book in the crypt, we decided to turn to the cemetery, where we wielded our shovels and picks to exhume the graves of the more recent dead, including Jeanne Catherine Berthelot's.

(Inside it, we found a golden bracelet endowed with a large ruby and a skeleton — clean, like her son's.) We dug in the churchyard cemetery by night off and on over the course of the next year, trying to find an alternative entry into the crypt and hoping, despite all signs to the contrary, that we might still find the book of visions.

Throughout that year my dreams were filled with dirt. Dirt gritty against my palms, in my mouth, sifted into my clothes and hair, lodged beneath my fingernails, settling into the deepening lines of my face. When I woke, I found my sheets silted with dust; when I ate, I crunched grains of sand between my teeth. I drifted through those days — for I slept irregularly, catching a fitful hour or two some nights before going out to dig and then sinking into a deep sleep just before morning — with dirt and dust on my body and my mind. I felt it always on my skin, and despite my most vigorous efforts with a washcloth and basin in the silent predawn, I could not scrub it all off. I saw it everywhere: inside and out, beneath my feet on my way to the grocer's, clinging to the cloth I swiped over the shelves, in the air as motes turning in a sun ray. I felt it filtering into my lungs when I took a breath. Pulverized rock, bits of skin and bone, decayed flakes of flesh, minuscule pieces of waste, hair, fingernail, dirt, soil, earth, ground, clay, mud, land. I ingested it, I breathed it, I imagined it, I *was* it: I was the dust that would return to dust. Each moment of each day, I knew the eventual fate of my own flesh, my own bones: my eventual grinding down, my disintegration.

Disintegration. A funny word, for it appears to mean the opposite of mixing, of merging, and yet the disintegration of one thing must imply the integration of another. I saw, more clearly than ever, the disintegration of previous wholes: bones, stones, roots, tree trunks, teeth — all ground down and newly integrated into this one thing: the astonishing red-brown dirt.

It was this dirt, I saw, this pitiless, masticating earth, from which the Church strove to save us. Hell was not fire and brimstone — nor unending pain, for pain implied vitality. Hell was the apprehension of this nothingness, the unfeeling sleep of the dead, our own soulless decomposition. What a brutal, unjust end: to live for years, sensing, recoiling at pain and luxuriating in pleasure, dreaming futures, remembering pasts, constructing stories of ourselves that spoke of nobility, strength, hope, and unmet yearning, and finally to have it all cease, to have it come to nothing but dust. It was too cruel a fate to abide.

Yet the alternative seemed equally cruel. Could I really hope for my own soul to persist for eternity? This immaterial assortment of grasping desire, of need and disappointment, of pain, confusion, resentment, self-pity, and, yes, cruelty — could I justly pray for Christ to preserve such a soul? My soul was a burden, a thing just as mortal as my flesh. How could I faithfully ask for God to save such an evil thing, to gather up such a blighted harvest and accept it into his Kingdom? And if his Kingdom housed a store of souls like mine, what sort of a heaven would that be? I believed I should prefer the hell of nothingness to an eternity of human limitation.

But that is not heaven, Bérenger insisted when I confessed my worries to him. Heaven is bliss. Heaven is living in the presence and the sight of God himself. Heaven is to breathe, to drink, to soak, to swim in God's love for all eternity. There is no place for human failure in heaven.

But how can we deserve such a place? I would ask. How can we free ourselves of sin? We are flesh, God has made us so, and flesh knows only its own desires. Must we shun our own bodies, our own selves?

You have to want it, Marie, he would say. You have to long for salvation with all your heart, soul, and mind. You have to pray and yearn after God and strive to avoid sin. And repent. You have to hunger for it.

He pronounced the words, but it was a rote response. He no longer hungered for heaven — he had given up. The world had thoroughly seduced him.

Though he had initially balked at our first transgression, it was not long before we succumbed once more to the mounting pressure of our desires. We began to sneak kisses throughout the day — at his desk, over a bubbling soup pot, even out in the open air, if we felt sure no one else was about. Kisses grew into devastating embraces. Finally, one night after I had been asleep for a long while, I awoke to a knock at my door.

"Hello," I whispered, still half-asleep.

Bérenger entered, dressed in his nightshirt.

He lifted me from my bed by the elbows and held me aloft while he kissed me ravenously: lips, ear, throat. When he finally set me down, his hands were trembling too much to unbutton my nightdress. I slipped it over my head, then held the bedcovers open for him to climb in.

We shared a bed more often than not after

that. At night, we would dig in the graveyard, then stumble into bed together, our
dirty fingers fumbling at each others' clothing. On nights when we were too exhausted
to dig, I would tiptoe upstairs to Bérenger's
room and wake him with whispers. The days
were a haze of sensuous recollection, the
evenings a stretch of voluptuous anticipation.

Finally, done in by exhaustion and increasingly disturbed by Bérenger's fervent cataloguing of the treasures of the dead, I
declared I would help him no longer. He
continued to search the graveyard, albeit at
a slower pace. And he still came to me
nightly, smelling of soil and sweat. He
pretended that he still sought the book of
visions, but in truth he was tabulating a
grim inventory. He had to know what was
in each of the graves, what sort of wealth
we were sitting on. The discoveries continued: heirloom necklaces and earrings,
antique pistols, hand-crafted belt buckles,
engraved pewter mugs, silver letter openers,
even slugs of raw gold. He described each
discovery to me in loving detail. And along
with his descriptions came ruminations,
tentative forays into the blind logic of sin.

"It makes one wonder, Marie," he ventured, "why people insist on burying their

treasures with them. They've no use for them where they're going."

"It's to comfort the families of the deceased."

"Yes, true. Still, it's puzzling, don't you think? What good is gold to a corpse?"

I shrugged, unnerved. "It belongs to the earth, now," I countered. "It's gone back where it came from."

"Of course, Marie," he replied. And then added, defensively, "I'm merely raising a hypothetical question."

Finally, after a few years of Bérenger's nightly excavations, the villagers began to complain. What was M. *le curé* doing, digging in the graveyard after midnight? What sort of sordid activity was he up to? He met the first complaints with the excuse that he was removing the old bones to make room for the new. And he dug at night so as not to upset people. This excuse was, as always, half true. The graveyard was overcrowded and disorganized. His digging served a dual purpose, for as he disinterred the old bones, he piled them in an ossuary he had installed at the corner of the cemetery. This kept the criticism at bay for a time. Eventually, though, the municipal council issued an order prohibiting him from digging in the graveyard.

By that time, Bérenger had come to the conclusion that the Austrian's story must have been a distortion of some kind, that the old priest he had met in Vienna must have embellished the tale, and that the objects we'd found beneath the knight's stone were the only things his friend had hidden. That there was no book of visions.

I entertained a slightly different explanation, for I was too attached to the existence of the book to allow that it might have been an invention. I imagined that the priest must have changed his mind at the last minute and sneaked into the tomb one final time to retrieve the book and carry it with him over the mountains, to keep him company in his exile.

Whatever the truth may have been, the book was irretrievable. I believe Bérenger was, strangely, relieved. His mission had failed. And the failure of his mission allowed him to relax, to accept his position as an earth-bound priest, a man not of God, but of the world. He began to talk of the treasures as if they were gifts from God, meant expressly for his — our — use.

"What about the test?" I challenged him. "The way you would find your way back to God."

"I tried, Marie," Bérenger responded. "We

don't have the book."

"But don't you think this might qualify as a test as well? An even greater one? All this wealth at your disposal? Might not God be testing your loyalty?"

"Perhaps, Marie. Perhaps. But perhaps he is smiling on our church, on my plans for the renovation, on the future of our village. Perhaps he intends for us to take advantage of what we've found."

"That's a false argument, *mon cher.* You can't mean to imply that God intends for you to steal."

"Of course not," he replied. But his tone was not convincing. Nor could I pretend to speak to him from a position of moral authority, for I had expressly encouraged him along his path. Hadn't I been the one to suggest he find God in this world, not the next?

I never saw him steal, nor do I have any concrete evidence of it, other than the steady increase in his wealth and his multiple trips away from home, valise in hand. I have not even been down to the crypt since we last left it together, but I believe I would find the coffins empty now, no more than boxes of bones.

There is another possibility: that he did, in fact, find the book, tucked in a hidden corner. Rather than burn it, he might have brought it to one of his superiors in the Church. For such a book, Bérenger could have finessed a healthy sum.

And who am I to criticize or condemn? He hurt no one. Rather, he helped, for with the proceeds of his thievery, he was able to finish his work on the church: he installed a fountain in the garden, a stunning calvary, and a beautiful and serene grotto made from stones he gathered himself on his daily walks over the hillside and the nearby woods of Rennes-les-Bains. He ordered a new rendition of the stations of the cross, done in painted terra-cotta, and hung the fourteen pieces along the walls of the church, giving the nave some sorely needed life. From the same artist he bought several sculptures of saints, also in painted terra-cotta, including the Virgin Mother, Saint Roch, Sainte Germaine, Saint Joseph, Saint Antoine de Padua, and his beloved Marie Madeleine. The cemetery walls he repaired and he installed a tall iron gate at the entrance, to keep out the grazing animals. He also built a sturdy cobblestone path up the hill from Couiza to enable the myriad workers who came and went to drive their mules and carts up the steep hill with more ease.

All these improvements benefited the villagers. But it would be misleading to claim that he robbed those graves like a Robin Hood, as if his intentions were pure.

Between 1898 and 1899, seven years after he first opened the tomb, Bérenger bought several parcels of land adjacent to the presbytery. He bought them in my name, I should add, for he was still concerned that the republican government might someday decide to confiscate any property belonging to the Church. In the years that followed, he razed the few abandoned hovels that were left on that land and built his dream, his fantastic playground, where he could pretend to lead the life he might have led had he never been ordained, never promised his life to God: the Villa Bethania and its grounds, with their pebbled pathways and meticulously trimmed lawns, the Tour Magdala, where he housed my library and his office, the promenade, from which the view of the valley and the distant Pyrenees could be seen in all its spectacular beauty, and the conservatory, where he planted several orange trees and kept his monkeys, who swung happily from the branches.

And he was proud of it — how proud he

was! It was, admittedly, a remarkable achievement. The villa, designed by an architect from Limoux, towered over the valley like a modern-day manor. It held two kitchens, one in the basement to be used in the summer, for it was always cool, and the other just above it for the winter. Bérenger kept the cellar full of fine wines and liquors, delivered from two different suppliers in Carcassonne. There were four bedrooms in the house on two upper floors, which were only used by visiting guests (I never slept in the villa, despite Bérenger's urgings), one of which held an impressive canopied bed. For the dining room, fitted out with Louis XV furniture, he purchased Limoges china — as well as flowerpots and vases — and pottery from Toulouse. The living room he furnished in the style of Napoleon III: red-and-pink-banded sofa and armchairs, a black wood table inlaid with brass, and a marble fireplace and mantelpiece, on which stood a statue of the baby Jesus on a pedestal of gilded wood, robed in velvet and wearing a crown of jeweled gold.

He also paid to have a Parisian photographer come to take our portraits, his and mine, and hung the larger-than-life photographs on the wall of the living room, the gold frames nearly touching. Over the entryway to the villa he installed two stained-glass windows with the image of the pierced and bleeding Sacred Heart of Christ, as if to quell the doubts of anyone who should think the enterprise was anything less than holy.

Once the villa and grounds were built, and the construction of the tower was well under way, he entertained visitors from all over France. He had cultivated relationships with the notable figures he'd known in Narbonne and people he'd met during his travels, and he invited them all to Rennes-le-Château to dine at the villa and enjoy the grounds. He welcomed dignitaries of all stripes: army officers, parliamentarians, moneyed aristocracy, anyone curious to see the extravagant estate built by the eccentric priest. He even welcomed some of his brother David's friends — artists and musicians, freethinkers — for he grew less stubborn in his politics as the years passed. He was an impeccable host. He loved showing off his property, discussing his future plans for improvements on his land and in the village: he intended to bring running water to every house, and wanted to build a road for automobiles. For my part, I enjoyed the praise I unfailingly received for the elaborate meals I cooked: terrines of pork, confits of turkey and pigeon, dozens of cassoulets, pastries stuffed with goat cheese, and of course, my house specialty, rabbit stew.

Despite Bérenger's ready excuses — that he had received many generous donations from anonymous donors — the villagers still tossed about the rumor of treasure. But the unwritten village contract, the cardinal rule of minding one's own business, saved Bérenger from facing any direct confrontations. I escaped out-and-out accusations as well, though I will admit to being generally friendless, with the exception of my family, who remained loyal. I — shamefully — was not above flaunting the gifts Bérenger showered me with, despite my suspicion and my disapproval of the source of his wealth. Bérenger stocked my wardrobe with dresses of the finest Parisian design, and the deliveries came to our door with astonishing frequency, the boxes smelling of perfume, the clothing wrapped in meters of tissue paper. He did not skimp on his own wardrobe, either, ordering suits, shirts, hats, scarves, belts, a dashing woolen cape for winter travel, all straight from Paris. The villagers took to calling me the priest's Madonna, for they said that Bérenger worshipped me more devoutly than the Holy Virgin, bestowing gifts upon me that should have been offered to her.

As for my parents, they continued to live with us in the presbytery and hardly batted an eye at the minor kingdom Bérenger constructed. Father's health had become a burden to him — he was often bedridden and his eyesight had already begun to fail. Mother disapproved of the ostentation, but she, too, was growing old, and was too concerned with Father's health to worry much over the impropriety of Bérenger's conduct. They were both grateful to him for his continued generous support, for Father's medical bills had increased substantially and he was no longer able to work in the factory. Bérenger supported us all; Mother could not complain.

Bérenger said that he had built his estate for the eventual use of the Church, that after his death and mine, the villa, the tower, and the grounds would be given to the bishopric for the housing of retired and infirm priests. It was a legitimate wish, and I believe one he would have carried out had his eventual trial not been so protracted and his disillusionment with the Church so thoroughly effected. But despite his stated intentions, the immediate goal was clear: while we lived, the estate was to be used for his —

and my — own enjoyment.

And we did enjoy it, all of it, for a time. In spring, when the early blossoms were out, we walked the grounds together, smelling the wet soil, breathing thirstily the warming air. We strolled on the promenade and leaned against the railing, letting our vision apprehend the spreading landscape — the mountains, the fields, the vast overarching sky. "This is why God made us, Marie," Bérenger would say. "To revel in his glorious creation." He seemed, in the days just after the estate was completed, joyous, even at peace. His happiness pleased me, as did his seemingly opening mind, his admission that to take pleasure in this world might not necessarily be the damned activity he had previously considered it to be. It was during that time that we approached my early fantasies of what our joined lives might resemble: comfortable connubial peace.

But like all worldly things, our pleasure was ephemeral. It soured as fast as a bucket of forgotten milk. I could not escape my own remorse; it rose like bile in my throat, lending a perpetual taste of bitterness to the sweet luxuries of the new life I led. I can't identify the specific transgression that toppled our momentary bliss, whether it was the thievery, the wealth, or our unchastity. By the time the estate was completed, four years after construction had begun, Bérenger began to retreat more frequently into stoic silences. He sought out the comfort — or perhaps the torture — of solitude, closing himself in his garden office for hours at a time, tending to his monkeys and birds, a peacock and a cockatoo, or pacing the length of the promenade with his dogs, Faust and Pomponnet.

We began to argue. I stopped accepting his gifts, insisting they were too extravagant, that he should be spending his money more wisely.

"What is the difference," Bérenger would ask, insulted, "between enjoying the gifts of the flesh and enjoying wealth?"

"It *is* different," I maintained. "Wealth harms. It takes from the poor, implicitly. I don't need any more jewels. But the poor need food, shelter. Basic comforts."

He fumed, peevish at my sermon.

"But sensual pleasure takes from no one. It is an expression of love, a basic human joy: to adore a loved one with one's whole self, body and heart and mind."

"It is God who should be loved that way, Marie. Jesus tells us so."

"God, yes, but not God alone. Jesus does not prohibit us from loving one another. He

421

commands it, in fact, does he not? To love one another as we love ourselves?"

"Yes, Marie," he responded, his face red with aggravation. "Of course. But not carnally. Please, don't belittle the gospel with your absurd contortionist readings."

"That's not what I meant. Not everyone. But surely one person, one beloved — God would not deprive us of the love, the full physical love, of that one beloved person? Why else has he made us this way? So susceptible, so needy? Why, Bérenger?"

"It's different for me, Marie!" he would shout. "For God's sake, I'm a priest! I took an oath. And I've broken it. How can he trust me any longer?"

Then later, when we had quieted, I offered: "But God forgives, *mon cher,* does he not? He understands."

"Not me, Marie. He will never forgive me."

It is this confession, this terrible confession, that I hear now, his voice waking me in the night. *He will never forgive me.* That was his conviction, that he had strayed so far as to be unforgivable, that having turned away from God, God had turned away from him. This knowledge of his suffering is my roving nightmare, my cross. For I am sure of my guilt now. I strove to reason it away then, to hide behind the arrogance of my relative youth, my secular mind. But I am older now, and wiser, and I know the truth: I am as much of a thief as he was. Worse, even. For while he stole petty treasures from the dead, who had no use for them, I stole his one treasure: his righteousness, his reliance on his all-powerful God. And in its place, I offered him only the paltry comfort of my own flawed love.

Is it a characteristic of human love that we must strive to remake our beloved in our own image? Must we always destroy the one we love? For such a remaking necessarily involves destruction, just as the restoration of a building demands a partial demolition, just as the rebirth of a nation requires the violence of war. Must we lose our lives to love each other, then, just as Christ declares we must do to live in his favor? I am afraid I required from Bérenger too great a loss — in my zeal to love him I destroyed him irremediably. I recognize that such a claim is a proud one, as it assumes I held his fate in my hands. Yet I do not think it far wrong, for where else can we find the shape of our fate but in the hands of those we love?

A few years after the final work on the estate

was completed, Bérenger received the first blow from the Church. It came in the form of a letter from the new bishop — Monseigneur Rouby, a cruel and officious man. It stated, in brief, that Bérenger was to be reassigned to the parish of Coustouges within the month. He would have to leave behind his beloved Rennes-le-Château.

Bérenger was distraught, as was I. We had not anticipated such an eventuality, though why not, I cannot guess. A priest is a soldier in the army of God, after all, and obligated to follow orders. After a flurry of letter-writing to friends asking for advice, a great deal of agonizing, and no small measure of private raging at the new bishop, Bérenger submitted his resignation. The bishop accepted it at a meeting in Carcassonne a few months later. He declared that a new priest would be installed at Rennes-le-Château that summer. He also made the official demand that Bérenger stop soliciting Masses, or risk being charged with simony.

The accusation both surprised and relieved me, for it meant that the episcopate only suspected Bérenger of criminal behavior but had not discovered his true offense. But the charge was valid. Bérenger had not fulfilled the voluminous Mass requests honorably; he had fallen behind, and had eventually given up even the pretense of fulfilling them. One day, as I was sorting through his accounts, I saw the proof of his guilt: a line drawn in September of 1893 across the log of Mass intentions I'd scrupulously kept. "Stopped here," he had written, and beneath that he had crossed out the requests I'd entered by date, amount, and name. Yet he had continued to accept the honoraria for Mass intentions that he knew he would not fulfill.

Bérenger did stop soliciting requests when commanded to by the bishop. But one or two of his advertisements, by some oversight, continued to run in the Catholic papers, and they quickly came to the attention of the bishop. He submitted his charge and the ordeal began.

The villagers, bless them, were loyal to Bérenger despite everything. The municipal council — headed now by Joseph, who had become mayor — wrote a letter to the bishop declaring that no one but Bérenger himself would be allowed to live in the presbytery. When the new priest arrived, he stayed with a family in Espéraza, and hiked up the hill every morning for Mass. Most of the villagers boycotted his Masses, going instead to Bérenger's unofficial ones, which he conducted on the veranda of the villa.

(One notable exception was Mme Flèche, who was so old by that time that she may not even have noticed the change.) Bérenger was touched and surprised by their loyalty, for there had been not a few among them who had grown angry at his decadence.

But as the trial stretched out over years, Bérenger grew unwell and seemed unable to offer any evidence to defend himself against the Church's accusations. The villagers grew less forgiving, less loyal. Some began attending Mass in Couiza; others stopped attending altogether.

Bérenger declared the Church's accusation ludicrous. He claimed that the amount of Mass requests he would have had to receive in order to fund his building projects would have been outrageously high. Pressed to provide an accounting of the origin of his wealth, he used his old excuse: gifts given by anonymous donors, names he could not reveal without compromising their trust in him or even, in some cases, their well-being. This, needless to say, did not satisfy the diocese.

Bérenger hired a lawyer, a M. Baguet, whose overconfident manner indicated to me his probable incompetence from the first. But Bérenger insisted on his trustworthiness. M. Baguet was a former priest himself; Bérenger had known him in seminary. M. Baguet claimed to have important connections in Rome, and he advised Bérenger to ignore the summonses of the episcopate while he himself traveled — racking up astounding expenses — to appeal directly to the Vatican. Summons after summons appeared, and as Bérenger ignored every one, the bishop finally suspended him indefinitely, until he could repay the money he had supposedly embezzled. As far as I know, M. Baguet enjoyed an extended Roman holiday before disappearing altogether.

It was not long before the debts Bérenger had accrued began to increase, and the money that had once been so abundant grew scarce. When he finally died, some eight years after he was first accused, he was broken both in bank and in spirit, for he had long since given up any attempt to be in communion with the God he had once been so intent on loving. He continued to follow the forms of his faith: saying his rosary, occasionally even performing the entire Mass, and though he could not legally administer communion once suspended, he took it daily (as did my mother and I). But his heart had grown hard, and his faith perfunctory.

He grew weak and fell ill, hounded by a

persistent cough, and we could find no relief for him. Dr. Castanier diagnosed exhaustion. I tried to reenact the miraculous cure that saved my father so many years earlier — I prayed to my *santon* regularly and visited the meadow at night, watching for that silently soaring owl. The year before his death, when he was sixty-four years old, I took Bérenger on the train to Lourdes, a two-day journey. I held him by the arm as he bathed in the healing waters. But his health only continued to decline.

On the evening of January 21, 1917, after he had been in bed for a solid month, Bérenger told me to send for Abbé Combes, his friend from Rennes-les-Bains. A few hours later, the curé took Bérenger's final confession while Mother, Father, and I waited in the kitchen. When the priest came downstairs, he fixed a condemning stare on me and said portentously, "God save the poor soul." Bérenger died at dawn.

HOME

Inside, there is half-darkness, like the gray pallor of early dawn. She sits just beyond the mouth of the cave, on the mediating moment between light and dark, between the grotto's mouth, where the midmorning sunlight reaches and illuminates the glinting mica in the walls and the small mineral iridescences, and the dark, narrowing tunnel. Here, in her place, this pallor is perpetual, as if the walls collect daylight and radiate it once the sun goes down. It is damp where she is — the clay floor, the silty walls, the toothed ceiling: wet earth hardening into hanging spears. The smell in the cave is wet and green, the smell of new life converging on death, for as soon as the moss grows, it rots. The wind speaks at the mouth of the cave: moaning, whistling, gusting. There is a constant dripping. She knows its rhythm, has memorized it like Torah, its steady incantation, its half-dashed hope and dogged persistence. The water is like her: it longs to be delivered up, at peace and still, instead of caught in the perpetual cycle of union and dispersal, of motion, continual motion. Sometimes she hears or sees animals at the entrance to the cave: squirrels and birds, most often; foxes and bears on occasion. Once, a wild boar snuffled in and fixed its eyes on hers. The hairs on his snout twitched. She was glad and tried to discern what sort of creature it was that had come to give her the gift of death, but the boar turned and snuffled away.

Noises, voices resound within her, chasing away silence. The thuds of the stones against the disciple Stephen's skull, and the sickening slump of his body when he fell. Miryam of Beit Aniyah's wails when Elazar died a second time, and no Yeshua there to revive him. Her daughter's cries at birth — rapid and shuddering — and then Miryam's own cries when they were parted in this new land, when she doubled over with grief, unable to watch her child being carried off on the back of a donkey, despite her knowledge that it was for the girl's safety. She hears the brusque and brutish voices of the Roman agents who pursued them from their arrival in Gaul and the rapid muffled beating of her daughter's heart as they hid in caves, in bread ovens, beneath floorboards, all to avoid the terrible clutch of the Gallic governor, a bloodthirsty man who had imperial orders to exile or kill any Christians he found. She hears her daughter's mature voice, imagined, perhaps, but joyful and at peace, calling to her from that distant haven on a remote hillside, singing her name like a blessing. She sings back, a returned prayer for her continued peace and happiness. She hears, too, the voices of the people she met in this new land: the wonder of those who heard her stories and her proclamation of the peace of God's kingdom without scorn, and the scorn of those who listened without wonder. Always, she hears Yeshua's voice, variously exultant or angry, as before the crowds, joyful, as at a shared meal, fatigued and gentle and full of grief, as when alone with her.

She forgets what time is. She is skinny, and recognizes in herself, as she did in Yeshua, a body given up to spirit, for she cares now only about prayer, about communion with the divine. Eating, drinking, urinating, defecating, sleeping — these are all vulgar necessities, pleasurable in their own way, but ultimately elements of death. She eats berries and chews on leaves or sticks; she drinks from the stream that runs downhill a few paces from the grotto. Sometimes, she imagines she is once again in Palestine — that arid, tawny land, that place of sun-baked rock and unexpected lakes. She sees once more the blinding beauty of the Temple — now, she understands, razed to the ground. She remembers the droop of the branches of the fig trees, the luxuriant fruit. The golden hills, spotted with the whitewashed tomb-rocks. The thick forests on the way to Yerushalayim. And Magdala in the Galil, with its moody sea: its blue serenity and its thunderous, ship-devouring waves.

Mostly, though, she is within the tunnel of earth that has become her home, this dripping grotto, this half-lighted dwelling.

His name pools like oil on her tongue, and she pours it from her lips like oil. She envisions him, skybound and bound within her, his great heart united now with hers, beating within the shell of her body. Repeating his name, she knows how her body falls away each moment, flaking like stone from a mountainside. Repeating his name, she feels how her skin encloses a tunnel to her heart, where he is, where he beats. She repeats his name and feels her body flake like rock in wind and rain and feels her heart beating steadily and greatly as his did when he lived and does now, in hers. She repeats his name and knows how her heart also is a tunnel, a thing enclosing space, a space as vast as heaven and as tiny as the seed of a pomegranate, a space that admits nothing but his name, which she repeats, as a beating of a heart in her mouth, as oil pouring out: Yeshua, Yeshua, Yeshua.

EPILOGUE

It has been eight years since Bérenger's death. My mother and father and I still live in the presbytery. My father is blind now; my mother spends her days tending to him, shuffling downstairs to assemble his lunch on a tray, climbing up to read to him while he eats, napping beside him in bed in the afternoon. I tend to the both of them. I rise early with the cock to feed the chickens and the rabbits and milk the goat. I knead the dough for the bread, and while it rises I make the coffee and serve the breakfast. We eat upstairs together, in the bedroom. When we finish, I wash up and put the beans on to boil. In summer, I weed and water the garden, harvest my vegetables, launder the linens and hang them out to dry; in winter, I kill a rabbit, drain it over the basin in the kitchen, scrub the washroom floor, make an errand to the grocer's or the tailor's. I still dust and sweep the church, polish the candlesticks, the paten and the chalice, and refresh the holy water stoup, though no one will come to bless it. I work in silence, my companions my animals — the rabbits, chickens, and goat.

Claude visits when he can. Michelle is gone — she moved back to Carcassonne with Pichon and his new wife after the war. Pichon came through all right, minus one arm. Joseph we lost on the battlefield.

I kept up a correspondence with Madame for a time, but stopped a few years before Bérenger's death. I wrote once more to inform her of his passing, hoping she might respond. But the letter was returned unopened, with a note declaring the address to be invalid. That night, I dreamt of her, lithe and ethereal, skimming through a dark and sinuous tunnel, her feet hovering just above the ground.

I have, finally, I believe, forgiven the Church its trespasses. Its offerings are too rich — its stories of sacrifice and renewal, its profound and transformative prayers, its rituals that lend meaning to mundanity — to reject out of hand. But I insist, still, on praying to *my* God, the God I have come to know through the world, through his glorious creation, the God I can apprehend through the sensors of my heart, God the

Father, yes, God the Son, and God the Holy Ghost, but God also of rock and wrist, water and throat, of the bloody pulsing heart and the exalted desire that we know as love.

I visit Bérenger's grave nightly, to kneel and talk with him. The *feux follets* follow me there. They bob beside me like restless children, but they know I am intent on my purpose and not inclined to be distracted or dismayed by their presence. They do not venture beyond the graveyard gate. The graveyard is not their domain, for the air there is hushed and heavy with the slow activity of decay. It is the home of darkness and earth and does not countenance their frivolous mischief. It is peaceful there at night, sheltered from the winds by the church. How different a place it seems to me now than it did those many years ago, when Bérenger and I came there together in the black nights, armed with shovel and lantern. We were like the *feux follets* ourselves then, our spirits restless and flitting from hope to desire to disappointment; only we were not so wise, for we did not stop at the gate, but continued on into forbidden territory, turning earth that should have remained undisturbed.

I loved you, I tell him as I pick the light

green weed shoots by his gravestone. *I loved you as well as I knew how. But it was not enough, was it?*

It was, Marie, he answers. It was everything.

It was not God.

My choices were my own, Marie. It was my life. I am responsible.

What is it like? I ask. *Where are you now? And how do you exist? In what state? Where is God? Do you see him?* I bombard him with questions, and I can almost see him shake his head in amusement, but he gives no answer. It is just as well, for I know I won't be satisfied with a mere description. He knows, too, I expect. I try to imagine him as he might be, beyond death, in heaven: his face a beacon, his body insubstantial, a shifting specter clothed in white light. I pray that he is with the God he so loved in life, the God he doubted and betrayed, the God whose capacity for forgiveness he failed to comprehend.

What a choice you made, I say. *To be a priest.*

Be quiet, he says. What did I know?

You should have been an architect. In Paris. The gorgeous structures you would have built.

I would not have met you, then, Marie.

Better yet, for you.

Not so, he assures me. Not at all.

Have you forgiven yourself? Has enough time passed?

I am no longer myself, he answers. I am forgiven.

Who are you, then? I ask. *Will I recognize you?*

But he does not need to answer, for I know what he will say.

ACKNOWLEDGMENTS

Pride of place goes to James McPherson, my professor at the Iowa Writers' Workshop, who introduced me to the notion of a bloodline descended from Jesus and Mary Magdalene and loaned me the book *Holy Blood, Holy Grail* (1983) by Michael Baigent, Richard Leigh, and Henry Lincoln. Someone should write a novel about this, he said.

My agent, Stéphanie Abou, gave me unfailing support, advice, translation help, and friendship throughout the research, writing, and publication of this book. I could not have done any of it without her. I was lucky enough to work with two wonderful editors. Jennifer Hershey read the book again and again with a keen eye for both structure and language, bringing the book along much further than I would have been able to do on my own. Aimee Taub's fresh eyes caught many lingering flaws, and her enthusiasm helped usher the book through to publication. Other indispensable readers at every level of the process were LeeAnn McCoy, Sarah Marx McGill, Allen Gee, Jennifer Whitten, Megan Pillow Davis, Sara Bellini, Judy and Bill Davis, Kathy Hassinger, Rich Hassinger (who also answered lots of prying questions about what it was like to grow up Catholic pre–Vatican II), Nate Lesser, Chani Bloom, Emily Laugesen, and Adam Davis, who wins the prize for reading the most drafts when it was not his job to do so.

During my trip to France, Anne Petit-Lagrange was not only a kind and welcoming host, she was tour guide, research assistant, and translator, arranging interviews for me and coming along so I could understand what my interviewees were saying. She cooked delicious meals, introduced me to the gorgeous countryside, and treated me not just as a guest in her B&B, but as a friend. Antoine Captier and Claire Corbu were also generous with their information and time, agreeing to meet with Anne and me at the last minute in their home and serving us cookies and tea. René Pech shared his knowledge of the local history of Couiza. Philippe Laurent was kind enough to invite me into his cozy forest shack as I was hiking by and to tolerate my abysmal

French as we chatted about Rennes-le-Château. The staff at the Atelier Empreinte in Rennes-le-Château run a fine bookshop and helped me find many a book.

My office became an annex of the Michigan State University library during the writing of this book, and I am grateful to the staff there for enabling my periodic plundering of their collection. Bob Anderson, religious scholar and provocative preacher, gave me a video of a colleague's presentation on Mary Magdalene. Rabbi Larry Milder answered my questions knowledgeably and with a sense of humor. I have mentioned my primary research sources in the Author's Note; I'll thank those authors here once more for lending their expansive and steady shoulders for me to stand on.

Finally, I want to thank my husband, Adam, and my daughter, Hannah, for their constant love and support throughout the writing of this book and always.

AUTHOR'S NOTE

Bérenger Saunière was parish priest in the small village of Rennes-le-Château, where he lived from 1885 until his death in 1917. During the course of his restoration of the village church, he became mysteriously wealthy, eventually building a villa, tower, and promenade, as well as a garden and grounds adjacent to the villa, all of which can still be seen today. His longtime servant, companion, and, as it was rumored, lover, was Marie Dénarnaud, who was known in the village as the priest's Madonna.

There have been numerous theories about where and how Saunière found his wealth, ranging from plausible to sensational. They include, among others, the discovery of treasure — deriving from numerous sources, from the gold mines in the area to the lost treasure of Jerusalem — the illegal solicitation of Masses, and blackmail of the Catholic Church.

This last theory was put forth in a book called *Holy Blood, Holy Grail* by Michael Baigent, Richard Leigh, and Henry Lincoln, first published in the 1980s but newly popular in the States thanks to the success of Dan Brown's *The Da Vinci Code,* which relies on it as a source. I first learned the story of Rennes-le-Château and Bérenger Saunière from *Holy Blood, Holy Grail.* The book poses the theory that the Holy Grail was not a cup, as Western culture has so long imagined it to be, but was instead a secret bloodline, passed down through the centuries and originating in the child of Jesus and Mary Magdalene. *Holy Blood, Holy Grail,* while unreliable as a historical source, tells a wildly compelling story, one that promises to inspire countless future creative projects. I've retold some of the stories from that book, including the legend of Dagobert II, his marriage to the Visigothic princess, and the escape of his heir, Sigebert IV. Let me emphasize the word *legend.* The account of King Childéric's tomb also came from that book, though the discovery of that tomb has been well documented elsewhere.

I have also relied heavily on *L'Héritage de l'Abbé Saunière,* by Antoine Captier and Claire Corbu, and am grateful to them for their thoughtful and well-documented work.

I've drawn on their thorough descriptions of the Villa Bethania and the rest of Saunière's estate. The anonymous letter Bérenger receives (pp. 230–231) is my translation from the French of an actual letter that they have in their collection, as is the passage Marie reads from the old church register (pp. 278–279), which mentions the "tomb of the Lords." I was lucky enough to meet with Antoine Captier and Claire Corbu in their home in Carcassonne — they are delightful and generous people.

I have made ample use of several of the Rennes-le-Château websites (of which there are many), two of the most useful being priory-of-sion.com and www.renneslechateau.com. The latter website includes some wonderful drawings by Paul Saussez of the church's interior and the hypothetical shape of the crypt beneath. Saussez's research also helped me to imagine the role that the mysterious Austrian visitor may have played in the story. For innumerable questions on Catholic doctrine and practice at the turn of the century, I turned to www.NewAdvent.com. Malcolm Barber (*The Cathars*) deserves praise for his excellent research on the Cathars. I have referred to many sources on French history and culture, one of the more valuable being *La Vie Quotidienne des*

Paysans du Languedoc au XIXe Siècle by Daniel Fabre and Jacques Lacroix.

I tried to be true to the basic facts of the story, while admittedly taking a few liberties. The presbytery, for example, was not restored by the villagers but by workers that Saunière hired, and it was not completed until 1897, when the Dénarnauds actually moved in. As far as I know, there is no proof that Rennes-le-Château ever harbored Cathars. While there may have been a flask hidden in an old baluster, the anecdotal evidence says it was found not by Marie, but by the bell ringer at the time. The Dénarnauds' hat shop and the fire that destroyed it are inventions, as are all of the characters in the village, including Madame Laporte. Marie did have a foster sister and a younger brother, but I have changed the names of her relatives to emphasize the complete invention of their characters on my part. And, of course, I do not pretend to represent the characters of Bérenger and Marie as they were in reality: they are also my creations.

In writing the sections of this book that tell Miryam of Magdala's story, I have drawn on the Hebrew Bible and the gospels, as well as on recent historical research into the life of Jesus. My sources include works by Susan Haskins, John Dominic Crossan, Paula Fredriksen, and Elaine Pagels, as well as James Carroll's impressive and soulful book, *Constantine's Sword,* and Willis Barnstone's translation of the gospels and commentary, *The New Covenant.* I must credit Fredriksen for her incisive reasoning in *Jesus of Nazareth: King of the Jews* and her compelling thesis that Jesus was killed as a way to halt the burgeoning rebellion in Jerusalem. I also made use of the website from the PBS *Frontline* program, "From Jesus to Christ" (www.pbs.org/wgbh/pages/frontline/ shows/religion).

I've made some unconventional choices. I have been primarily concerned with faithfully representing the ancient Jewish world in which Jesus was entrenched. Thus I've used the Hebrew names, where possible (Yeshua and Miryam for Jesus and Mary; please see the glossary for a translation of unfamiliar names). One of the best sources I found for details on daily life in ancient Israel was *Daily Life in Palestine at the Time of Jesus* by Henri Daniel-Rops.

The traditional image of Mary Magdalene as a penitent prostitute was made Church doctrine at the end of the sixth century, when Pope Gregory the Great declared that three women mentioned in the New Testa-

447

ment gospels — the women from whom Jesus cast out seven devils, identified as Mary Magdalene; Mary of Bethany, the sister of Martha and Lazarus; and the woman known as the "sinner" who anoints Jesus' feet as he dines at Simon the Pharisee's table — were one. This conflated Mary Magdalene has been passed down in the Western Catholic tradition — she, as three in one, is celebrated on her feast day, July 22. Alternatively, the Eastern Orthodox Church honors each of the three women separately, on different feast days. Representations of the Magdalene in art, literature, and folklore perpetuate the notion of her as the "beautiful penitent," the woman who gave up her sinful ways to follow Christ, and who is redeemed for her past through her devotion to him.*

But the gospels provide no evidence that she was a prostitute or even a great sinner. The synoptic gospels — Matthew, Mark, and Luke — agree on four facts: Miryam of Magdala was a follower of Jesus, was present at his crucifixion, witnessed the resurrection, and was the first to be charged with

---

* Susan Haskins, *Mary Magdalen: Myth and Metaphor* (New York: Harcourt, Brace, & Company, 1993).

spreading the Christian message. John states that not only did she witness the resurrection, but that she was *the* witness, the only person who saw the risen Christ and spoke with him.

Gnosticism — a collection of eclectic ancient sects that promulgated the belief in salvation through *gnosis,* or secret knowledge — considered Mary Magdalene to be even more important than she appears in traditional Christian teachings. Gnostic writings dating from the first and second centuries refer to her as a disciple of Christ, "the woman who knew the All," and the chief link between Jesus and the rest of the apostles. The Gospel of Philip names her as Jesus' companion, or *koinonōs* in the Greek, a word that is more accurately translated as partner or consort, which connoted physical as well as spiritual togetherness.★

As for any anachronisms, maddening historical inaccuracies, or otherwise bizarre notions you may come across herein, I am fully to blame.

★ Susan Haskins, *Mary Magdalen: Myth and Metaphor* (New York: Harcourt, Brace, & Company, 1993), pp. 33–40.

GLOSSARY
HEBREW/GREEK/ARAMAIC

Andreas (Greek)	Andrew
Beit Aniyah (Hebrew)	Bethany
bima (Hebrew)	"high place," from where the Torah is read
chazzan (Hebrew)	leader of prayer services, cantor
denarii	currency of the Roman Empire used in ancient Israel
Elazar (Hebrew)	Lazarus
Eliyahu (Hebrew)	Elijah
the Galil (Hebrew)	Galilee
Ge Hinnom (Hebrew)	Gehenna
Gulgulta (Aramaic)	Golgotha
Kefa (Hebrew)	Peter

Kfar Nahum (Hebrew)	Capernaum
Marta (Aramaic)	Martha
mashiah (Hebrew)	messiah
Miryam of Magdala (Hebrew)	Mary Magdalene
Mosheh (Hebrew)	Moses
musht	fish native to the Sea of Galilee, also known as "Saint Peter's fish"
Natzaret (Hebrew)	Nazareth
Parush scholar (Hebrew)	Pharisee
Pesach (Hebrew)	Passover
Rabboni (Hebrew)	exalted form of the word *rabbi*
Shimon (Hebrew)	Simon
Shlomit (Hebrew)	Salome
Shomronim (Hebrew)	Samaritans
Shoshannah (Hebrew)	Susanna
Toma (Hebrew)	Thomas
Yakov (Hebrew)	Jacob
Yehudah (Hebrew)	Judas Iscariot; also Judea
Yerushalayim (Hebrew)	Jerusalem

Yeshayah (Hebrew)	Isaiah
Yeshua (Hebrew)	Jesus
Yisrael (Hebrew)	Israel
Yochanah (Hebrew)	Johanna
Yochanan (Hebrew)	Jonathan (John)
Yosef (Hebrew)	Joseph

GLOSSARY:
FRENCH/OCCITAN

aigo bouido (Occitan) garlic soup, made with herbs, bread, and eggs

cassoulet (French) traditional Languedoc dish, a slow-cooking bean and pork stew

cousinat (French) creamy chestnut stew, often with fruits

estofinado (Occitan) dried cod with potatoes, eggs, nut oil, and milk

feux follets (French) will-o'-the-wisps

garrigues (French) dry hilly terrain, full of scrub brush: holm oak, broom, rosemary, thyme

Marie Madeleine (French)	Mary Magdalene
sabots (French)	wooden clogs
tabac (French)	tobacco shop, often a gathering place
terradorenc (Occitan)	landsman, compatriot, *paysan*
tramontane (French)	strong wind that blows through the Languedoc

ABOUT THE AUTHOR

Amy Hassinger is a graduate of Barnard College and the Iowa Writers' Workshop. She is the author of *Nina: Adolescence,* and teaches in the University of Nebraska's MFA Program in Creative Writing. She lives in Illinois with her husband and daughter.